THE DOCTOR IS IN.
SO IS HER DOG . . .

"I'm here to give them their annual physicals," Shona said. "Didn't anyone from the Corporation notify you I was coming?"

The woman waved a hand. "They told me, but it ain't gonna make a toot's worth of difference in an airlock to them. When they come here, they want a drink and a little company, not a poke and a prod."

Saffie, disliking the woman's tone of voice, barked warningly. Girelda peered over the bar.

"Dog, eh? You'll get patients quicker if you advertise you've got a pet. These folks like animals, but no one can keep 'em on a mining scout."

"That's a good idea," Shona said. "I have a lot of pets."

When miners began to return to Glory II in the next few days, there was a sign in the bar directing them down the corridor to "Dr. Shona's Traveling Menagerie and Medical Clinic."

TAYLOR'S ARK

JODY LYNN NYE

ACE BOOKS, NEW YORK

This book is an Ace original edition,
and has never been previously published.

TAYLOR'S ARK

An Ace Book / published by arrangement with
the author

PRINTING HISTORY
Ace edition / February 1993

The Putnam Berkley World Wide Web site address is
http://www.berkley.com

Make sure to check out *PB Plug,*
the science fiction/fantasy newsletter, at
http://www.pbplug.com

ISBN: 0-441-79974-4

ACE®
Ace Books are published by
The Berkley Publishing Group, a member of Penguin Putnam Inc.,
200 Madison Avenue, New York, New York 10016.
ACE and the "A" design are trademarks belonging to
Charter Communications, Inc.

PRINTED IN THE UNITED STATES OF AMERICA

10 9 8 7 6 5 4 3

For Sibeol
and synchronicity

Acknowledgments

The author would like to thank Dr. Jeffrey Scott Nye, neurobiologist, and Dr. Elizabeth Nye, OB-GYN, for their research and input, and acknowledge that any errors made in the use of their data are her own. The author sincerely thanks Beth Fleisher for lending her countenance to this project. She is also grateful to Sue Stone for her experience, and to Peter Heck and Laura Anne Gilman for patience and advice and more patience.

CHAPTER

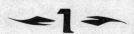

~1~

THE GREAT COLONY ship stood on the launch pad, looming uncon-
cerned above the whirl of preparation which went on around its
base as its crew made ready to board. The shimmering vessel was
one of the vast fleet used by the government of the United Galaxy
to convey pioneer settlers from Marsbase, in the Sol system, to
their designated planets. Its cluster of cylinders joined by buttresses
and braces looked gothic and ornate, but were actually functional
conduit and passageway. Through the smoke-tinted atmosphere
dome above it, the two small moons of Mars, Deimos and Phobos,
were visible, racing one another across the sky. The ship's current
complement of colonists were bound for the outer reaches of
Twelfth Sector, beyond the current perimeter of U.G. space.
Because half of the ship's yearlong trip would carry it away
from the last available repair facility, it needed to be as self-reliant
and as immune to incapacity as human technicians could make it.
Rigorous inspections had been carried out and double-checked.
Most of the loading was complete. The last items to go on were
the small containers of personal possessions, intended to make the
long journey more comfortable and lend a touch of civilization to
the colonists' new home.

The colony leader, a tall, rawboned woman clad in the thin
metallic weave of a pressure suit, watched the wheeled loaders
with a careful eye. She winced as one of the polygonal boxes
missed the hatch and slammed against the side of the vessel.
"Clumsy louts. It's enough to make my blood pressure skyrocket."
She glanced at the medical technician who was examining her.
"Off the record of course."

"Of course! Raise your arms, please." Dr. Shona Taylor, a cheerful young woman of twenty-six, prodded the captain's elbow with
a small piece of medical apparatus, urging her to raise her arms
above her head. She was the physician assigned to the colony until
it lifted off. Her job was to make certain the crew was as ready as

1

the ship for its long and rigorous journey. Shona held the device a few inches from the woman's rib-cage and walked around her.

"Good thing we're getting out of here today," the captain said. "If anyone pokes any more holes in me, I'll leak."

"This is the last, I promise you. I'm just getting one final check in before you seal the hatch." Electrocardiogram normal, electroencephalogram within normal range, resting pulse low, Shona noted, and check, check, check on the rest of the captain's metabolism.

"I'm curious," Shona said, glancing at the businesslike crew around her. She was interested in what made people tick. "Your settlement party is composed entirely of women. That's an unusual choice."

"It's our contention that an all-woman colony gets along better than one that's co-ed or all male," the captain said firmly. "Because of the climate and wildlife on the planet we're taking, we need to stay a sisterhood as tightly knit as we can make it. Each of us must be prepared to take charge if necessary. If we don't, we won't survive. I don't want to have a dominance battle with a man who attempts to take over the whole settlement and run things his way. Our shrink interviewed a lot of people. A lot of good technicians and admin people didn't make the cut because they couldn't function under the circumstances we'll be facing. We managed to convince the government that the colony would function better for us this way. One little thing could undo all our careful work. Someone who complains too much, one with pernicious body odor, one with annoying nervous habits—that could kick us all over the edge if we're forced to hole up and hibernate together over the winter season. I can't afford to take that risk."

It was true. The makeup of a colony was a very personal and particular thing. It took the vision of an individual, who usually became colony leader, to design a world view that would hold together for the initial months of settlement, the most difficult phase to survive. Once the colony was well-established, things might change, but for the early stages it was vital that it follow one plan, one direction. Once the delivery vehicle left atmosphere, the group was on its own. Shona remembered that on her second mission, the group was a patriarchy. The colonists were all related to one another, and led by an irascible old man who was the descendant of a hundred generations of cotton farmers on Earth. The government had assigned them a planet to raise cotton and silk, lucrative cash crops. The Cotton Consortium had even legally adopted enough babies of both sexes to grow up to be spouses to

2

the current infants in the family. That was carrying unity pretty far, Shona had thought but that settlement had been as closely woven as a piece of its own fine percale cloth. The mission specialists were the only outsiders in the group, and treated as such. Shona was sure if it had been her first mission, she might have taken such destructive treatment personally. As it was, the botanist with them nearly went crazy. Shona and one of the others had to be with the woman at all times, fearing a suicide attempt. They had been grateful and relieved when the retrieval ship came for them at the end of six months. Some of the colonists they left behind were also showing signs of strain under the autocratic rule of their leader, but the ones who survived would prosper and do well. Shona expected to hear about the richness of that settlement for generations to come, and of this one.

"Naturally that brings me to the next question," Shona asked. "How do you plan to . . ."

One corner of the captain's mouth went up. Shona guessed she had answered the same query a hundred times over the last months. "Propagate the species? Well, you might have noticed that about half my settlers are already carrying. Then there's that." She gestured toward one of the vast modules with a "Science" designation being loaded into the rear cargo bay. "Zygotes, to be implanted *in utero*. Very safe, relatively foolproof. As we come to need greater population growth, some of us can carry a few at a time, instead of one. After that, it's cell-implantation in egg nuclei. Healthy, and always XX. I might carry another or so myself, if all goes well."

"But what about the male zygotes?" Shona said, a horrible thought suddenly striking her.

It must have shown in her face. "Oh, we just don't use them," the captain said, shrugging. "Analysis of one cell tells you what you've got before you'd do anything irrevocable with it. We'd never destroy them. We just don't use them. Want a few XY zygotes? Guaranteed healthy genes. No charge."

"No, thanks," Shona laughed, pointing to her midsection, which bulged against the fabric of her environment suit. "My husband and I prefer to start them the old-fashioned way."

"Boy or girl?" the captain asked, with friendly curiosity.

"Don't know. I'm letting it be a mystery," Shona said, her eyes alight. "I've delivered a lot of babies, but I've never had one before. I want this to develop slowly, so I can enjoy it."

"No morning sickness," the other woman deduced sagely. "Well, I've had five girls, and been sick as heck every time."

Shona made some notes on her clipboard. "I saw your girls. They're adorable." Satisfied by the readings on the whirring device, Shona nodded to the captain to lower her arms. "Good."

"How am I, Doctor?"

"You're in fine shape," Shona said, her wide mouth stretching into a smile. "Same as always. Your circulatory system is strong. That's important when you're going to spend a lot of time in zero gee. Don't forget to keep taking your calcium and magnesium."

"I already take so many tablets I rattle!" The captain's retort was followed unexpectedly by a loud vibration and a bang that made both women look around in surprise. Beside the ship, the skid loader had turned over on its side, spraying packages and boxes halfway across the loading dock. A carton slid to a halt at their feet. The captain's face flushed angrily. "Burning stars, I told you idiots to watch it!"

"Someone's hurt," Shona said, seeing an outstretched hand behind the upturned fins of the loader and the heap of containers. She gathered her medical gear up and hurried over. The captain followed, loping in her heavy boots.

Shona ignored the argument starting behind her back between the captain and the loader operator, and pushed through the crowd that was gathering around them. There was a woman on the floor half-buried by the boxes. The doctor dropped to her knees and helped the crew uncover her. Shona could tell immediately by the angle of the woman's leg that it was broken. Gently, she probed through the soft metallic fabric of the suit leg and found the place where the bone had snapped. The flesh around it was already beginning to swell. Her patient sat up, her brown-skinned face hollow with shock.

"Is it broken?" she asked.

Shona nodded. "Clean snap, I think. Do you want a pain-killer?"

"No—no," the woman said. "Clouds the mind. I'll be all right. I'd rather know what's going on. I'm the colony doctor."

"Were, I'm afraid," Shona said, unsealing the suit seams and pushing the folds of silver-white cloth aside to examine the woman's thigh. The deep blue-blackness of edema had begun to color the flesh. "I can't let you go like this. I need to image this, set it, and get you into a cast pronto. You'll be on your back for weeks."

"Please, Doctor," the captain said, hearing Shona's reply. She turned away from her argument and dropped down beside them. "You can't take her off assignment. Muñoz is our G.P. We can't leave her behind. Without her, we're below the minimum med staff level."

Shona considered, drumming her fingers on her own leg. "When do you lift off?"

"About an hour. There was a delay in getting supplies from one of the private companies. That's not much of a window, but there's a Corporation colony leaving an hour behind us. If we miss the slot, it may be weeks before we leave, and we could arrive too late to put in a first crop. That could convince the bureaucrats to turn the whole place over to the G.L.C." Without that crop it was likely a new colony would be unable to afford the things it would need to thrive later, or maybe survive at all. If this was to be the case, the colony could lose its charter before they had even left.

A small silence fell between them as each assessed the other's possible reaction. Where the government ships carried the bare necessities for the comfort and entertainment of its employees for the long hauls, the G.L.C. ships were lushly outfitted, featuring game rooms, fresh-food storage, and other enviable amenities. The Galactic Laboratory Corporation supplied through itself or its many subsidiaries nearly every commodity or service money could buy. The G.L.C. was the government's partner and rival in the space race, often claiming systems right under the government's nose, and occasionally settling personnel on the same planet. Rumor was that armed skirmishes had broken out on some of those invaded worlds, but no reports had ever come back to substantiate it. Because of the Corporation's careful demonstration of propriety in matters of charity and endowments, the public tolerated its bendings of the system, but in private some citizens felt that it was high-handed and abusive, writing its own versions of the law. Though almost half the population owned a few shares of the giant corporation's stock, few people felt comfortable voicing that sentiment aloud. The Corporation seemed to have ears everywhere, and its influence was powerful. Its all-round utility gave it leverage.

Their colonies were not intended, as government settlements were, to operate independently as sovereign worlds each with its own economy. Each had umbilical supports from the home system of the Corporation, never entirely being free until, if they could, they bought themselves out. The lawsuits to attain self-direction had been making the news lately, Shona recalled. No one had signed on deliberately to make themselves and their children virtual indentured servants, but that was what the suits alleged. Appeals were in and out of court nearly every month. Shona acknowledged that competition did promote more development of the outer worlds by both parties than might have been accomplished by either working alone. Technology had improved geometrically, even exponentially, since the Corporation won permission to compete in the space race. Private industry provided money for research that the government, with more duties to fulfill, could never afford.

Forty minutes might be enough time. Shona had to make a quick decision. "I want an MR image. If it's not too bad, I'll let her go. I can get her leg set and put her on painkillers. Your flight is long enough for her to recover full mobility before you set down, if all goes well. You have another medtech in the crew?" Dr. Muñoz, grimacing, nodded. "She'll have to monitor you, but it *should* be all right."

The captain let out a whistle of relief. "I was afraid you were one of those port doctors who never saw a real patient."

"I served as a colonial doctor before rotating back here," Shona assured the worried officer as she continued to probe the break.

"Thanks," Dr. Muñoz added weakly, but sincerely, pulling her gaze away from the swelling leg. "I don't want to pass up this mission."

"Even in a body cast?" Shona asked.

"Even that," Muñoz said passionately.

Shona grinned, in spite of herself. "All right. I know how you feel. I'll do what I can."

With the help of the emergency medics, Shona rushed her patient on a gurney to the Space Center's clinic. A magnoscan proved that the fracture was a clean break, as Shona had predicted. In no time, she set the leg, bound her patient to the hips in a quickset cast, and dialed up an oral pain medicine. She wheeled Muñoz back on the gurney, the colony doctor flat on her back, but grinning. The other physician and two more settlers who identified themselves as nurses took the wheeled cart from Shona and pushed it up the tilted gantryway. They still had almost fifteen minutes to spare.

"Good luck!" Shona called after them.

"Thank yooo-oooo," Muñoz's voice echoed from the metal-walled lift. Shona smiled to herself. If it had been her with a broken leg, she'd have begged just as hard for the same chance to go.

"Many thanks, Doc. That was quick, clean work," the captain said, joining Shona beside the ramp's foot. "You sure you wouldn't like to come with us? You're capable, and you're friendly. Do you have a specialty?"

"Environmental illness."

The captain nodded slowly. "I could sure use you."

"Sorry," Shona said, grinning. "I'm bound for temporary reassignment on Earth in a few weeks. I wish I'd met you all six months ago, before this"—she patted her belly—"got started. I'm hoping to get assigned to another mission as soon as the baby's old enough for a nanny. I'm getting antsy already, and there's four months to go before this little one arrives."

"Hope it's a girl," the captain said, tipping a finger toward Shona's bulge.

Shona laughed. "Good luck and happy landing," she told the captain. It was the traditional farewell. They clasped arms, and Shona left the landing bay. The thin Martian sunlight brightened the stark shapes of rocks and lichen on either side of the semitubular walkway leading back toward the main domes. A Klaxon began to sound, indicating the approach of a ship. She started to make her way out of the bay and back toward the medical center. A crewman in coverall and protective helmet stopped her and read her I.D. card.

"Oh, it's you, Dr. Taylor. Not going on this one?"

"Nope," Shona said with satisfaction. "Got another mission." The man inadvertently looked down at her tummy, and she winked at him.

"We're going to miss you down there on Earth," he said, grinning. "Soft life you'll have, inoculating cruise patients with mal-de-space. Well, you'd better get going. There's a transport ship landing on Pad Three, and we've got to spray it."

"An empty coming back? I'd better move it. Those bus drivers get impatient at the end of the run."

Shona hustled toward the shielded dome as fast as she could. Her center of gravity had shifted a lot since her pregnancy began, and she wasn't used to it yet. The heavy swaying slowed her down. Behind her, the vacuum-sealed blast doors began sliding shut one at a time. The approaching ship must have been coming in pretty fast. She forced herself to an uncomfortable run. The environment suit's helmet, which she had taken off after leaving the colony group, bounced annoyingly against her back. The last set of blast doors was so close she could almost feel it nip her in the tail as it boomed shut. Panting, she leaned against the transparent side of the tube to watch the landing.

The ship must already have been cleaving atmosphere when she met the crewman in the tunnel, indicating that air-traffic control had waited a little longer than usual to sound the alarm. Just as she slid inside the door, the sirens went off, and the dome across the field, reduced to ambient atmosphere, slid gracefully open. The great ship appeared in the sky. It was just a dot of light at first; then the dot grew to a flame, and the flame became larger and larger as it descended majestically onto the scorched pad. The

7

white tubes and arches flushed with red, reflecting Mars's rusty landscape, until they were swallowed up in a rush of flame and flying dust that battered against the transparent walls of Shona's refuge.

There was a stirring of action at its base, as tiny figures, technicians, ran around it, taking readings and checking fittings. The gigantic dome rose out of the floor on either side of the pad. The two pieces slid ponderously together, then closed and locked with a boom that echoed all the way through the miles of corridor. White steam from the decontamination process surrounded the vessel momentarily, hiding it from sight. Spaceborne parasites and particles which clung to the vessel from its latest drop point would be destroyed by the hot vapor. When the halves of the dome parted, the ship looked clean and shiny. Another host of technicians sent out the gantry to the hatch from another quadrant while the halves of the dome withdrew and sank out of sight. The workers started attaching hoses to the various orifices of the ship. The schedule on transport ships was tight. Refitting was supposed to be accomplished as soon as possible. There was another colony group waiting here on Mars for the use of this one. If any lengthy repairs had to be made, it further pushed back scheduled departures. Watching the frenetic activity with a touch of envy, Shona felt the tension of activity, and loved it, as she had from the day she decided to join the space service. She wished that she could get on another mission right away, but she was simply going to have to wait. She patted her belly.

"Baby, one day you and me're going to get on one of those ships and take off for the stars. Won't you like that?"

Returning from her musings with a sigh, she recalled other beings to whom she was responsible. Clapping herself on the head for her inconsideration, Shona hurried through the dressing rooms and shed her protective suit. The secretary of the Health Department wouldn't keep an eye on her dog forever.

Saffie leaped on her with a joyful bark as soon as she appeared. She was a big animal, with a shaggy black coat and huge paws into which she'd never seemed to have grown. Shona backed against a wall to keep from being toppled over by her pet's enthusiasm. Her balance wasn't as good as it used to be. The dog licked her face.

"Sorry, May," Shona apologized to the secretary, calming Saffie, and hooking a hand through the dog's collar. "I had a medical emergency to take care of."

The older woman clicked her tongue. "It's all right I don't mind keeping her so long as she's quiet. She never barked until just now, when you came in. I just don't know why you don't have a cat, like everyone else. They're smaller," May said pointedly, looking at Saffie, who looked back curiously, knowing she was being discussed.

Shona laughed as she wound the dog's leash around her hand. "Oh, I do have a cat. But he thinks it's every cat for himself if trouble comes along. I can count on Saffie. Come on, sweetheart. Let's go home." At the sound of the word 'home,' the dog dragged her eagerly out of the chamber.

There was some measure of envy she met in the eyes of people she passed on the street for having such a large and obviously valuable pet, and a little sympathetic worry in the faces of people who recognized that sometimes on Mars these days, a bodyguard of some kind was necessary, even for a small, pregnant woman. But Saffie was more than a mere companion or theft deterrent. She was part of what Shona liked to think of as her team. Before she came back to Mars to start a family, Shona was a specialist in environmental illness, and Saffie, like the rest of her pets, served a special purpose.

Environmental illness was new, an Industrial Age phenomenon and problem. When apparently unrelated groups of people began to suffer symptoms of fatal diseases, sometimes years after exposure, an EIS was enlisted to trace back the common cause. In a way, the EIS was a doctor, a detective, and mother-confessor rolled into one. In colony work, not only did a doctor have to beware of toxic chemicals or radiation, but also new allergens, histamines, or bacteria. It was Shona's job to locate those stimuli, and try to determine whether the irritant could be moved, vaccinated against, or whether it required the removal of that member of the colony from the source of distress. The government put an EIS envirotech on assignment to a colony where there might be hidden threats to the health of the settlers. Particularly which a number of those on the mission were related to one another such things threatened the survival of the mission. What affected one might affect them all. The Cotton Consortium had been just such a case. Shona had found a tendency in the family members for a kind of anemia which could lead to leukemia, and had persuaded the patriarch, with considerable difficulty, not to build their colony center on a site which, though otherwise suitable, stood over a natural source of mild radioactivity, a condition which practically guaranteed trouble somewhere up the time-line.

Saffie was a vaccine-dog. Her breed had been created from a standard Earth strain which had an unusually efficient immune system. A vaccine-dog, when injected with an infector, generated antibodies to combat it faster than any comparable mechanical unit ever invented. The dog's handlers had to move quickly to extract a sample of the antibodies to synthesize before the dog's very healthy system cleared out all trace of the test. It meant Saffie had never had a sick day in her life. She even seemed to repel parasites and vermin. Shona was envious, considering how many organisms on new worlds seemed to like to taste human flesh.

The mice were a new strain of Harvard mine-canary mice first bred in the late twentieth century, similar to humans in their sensitivities to carcinogens, but multiplied several hundred or thousand times. It was a nuisance to notify the Health Department every time there was a new litter of mice, but it kept her from being raided by the exterminators. Martian law made very little differentiation between mice used in scientific experiments and wild rodents.

Cancer had been licked about a century past, on Earth, but it was still one of the most prevalent ailments to trouble humans wherever they went. Shona was too attached to her brood of mice to sacrifice one whenever it caught the local strain of cancer or pneumonia, so she did her best to cure them, using genetic vaccine strains available commercially, or employing Saffie's talents. Shona never named the mice. As a hybrid bred particularly for their susceptibility to disease, they didn't live long, and she hated to get as attached to them as she did to her other animals.

Besides Saffie and the mice, there was a pair of dwarf, lop-eared rabbits, fancifully named Moonbeam and Marigold, whose job was mostly to test native food for its side effects. If the lops refused to touch a comestible, Shona recommended against its use by beings of Terran origin. Of course, the colonists didn't have to pay any attention to what she said. That was their choice. But her rabbits were seldom wrong.

Shona's cat, an Abyssinian, was named after her uncle Harry. When he deigned to do his job, Harry the cat's sensitive nose was better than any bloodhound's in locating the source of escaping gases or finding faint traces of chemicals. Normally, cats were sight hunters, but Harry's line had been bred to take advantage of the sophisticated feline sense of smell, and he was raised among dogs. Shona had an array of instruments to determine what the gases were once the cat had pinpointed them, but she didn't need the devices if the mix included sulphur, because Harry would pointedly throw up as close to the source as he could. It was one of Harry's less endearing traits. He was also good at hunting down small animals and larger insects that had been in the colony camp. Specimens, sometimes alive but just as often dead and in one or more pieces, often ended up in her slippers. She appreciated the gesture. It meant the family feeling between them was mutual.

"You just like animals," her husband Gershom had once accused her, with a twinkle. "Your job is a good excuse to have your own zoo."

Strictly speaking, the ottle wasn't part of her menagerie at all. He, she, or it was an intelligent, sentient visitor, more or less permanently adopted by Shona from his home world. "Ottle" was the human name for the species, because it resembled a combination between Terran turtles and otters. The flat, disklike body's shape was similar to that of a Terran turtle, but it was as flexible as an otter's, and it was covered with smooth, shiny fur, for the ottle was a littoral creature. The species had been discovered by an exploration team evaluating the ottle world for potential use as a pastoral colony planet. The humans and the indigenous species were surprised to see one another.

Once communication had been established, the exploration team discovered that the population of the new find was remarkably intelligent, and most interested in learning more about its new friends. Though they had no mechanical devices of their own, they had a highly developed language and culture, which had not heretofore accepted the existence of other intelligent species in the universe. Whether or not any of the newly named 'ottles' should accompany the human team offworld was the subject of hot debate in the ottles' loose form of parliament, but it was eventually resolved in favor. A number of the aliens, Chirwl among them, rode back to Mars in the exploration vessel, which they found as inexplicable as the humans themselves. Some of them, like Chirwl, were trying to find a way to explain the existence of machines, and humans, in terms congruent with ottle philosophy. Chirwl spent most of his time researching his own thesis to see whether machines were natural offshoots of humankind or not.

The laws regarding the hosting of an ottle were very strict. The government had made it clear to the aliens that if ever one expressed a wish to leave, it was the responsibility and the expense of the host family to have it transported back to its native system, a pair of large binary worlds circling a small yellow sun not unlike Sol about twelve light-years away. Shona's guest wanted to travel and see the galaxy. He didn't seem unhappy to be temporarily relegated to a ground post while Shona ca[r]ried her baby to term. In fact he was as much interested in the p[rocess] of human gestation as he had been in her travels on missio[n for the] government. The relationship would terminate only w[hen he] decided he wanted to go home. At regular intervals,

11

representative from Alien Relations visited them to make certain Chirwl was happy and healthy.

He was very intelligent and keen to learn all about his host species. Sometimes Shona felt it was like talking to a rocket scientist only imperfectly acquainted with the English language but light-years beyond her in terms of knowledge. At other times, she found herself explaining the most basic things carefully in words of one syllable, as if the ottle were a small child. That was just one of the natural incongruities of their relationship. He knew nothing of human interaction, and didn't understand why humans, so much greater in size than he, tended to be afraid of him, nor why it was safe to walk some places in Mars Dome #4, and not in others.

It had been easy to afford her menagerie on wages paid for space service, even for a physician as inexperienced as she was. The much smaller stipend, stripped of the bonuses and hazard pay she got for grounder work while on family leave, didn't make a patch on her previous income. It was Shona's only regret for taking three or four years out of the middle of her career that she would have to learn to economize. Gershom sent home money occasionally, but his trading ship, the *Sibyl,* was always eating up extra income for repairs and licenses bought in each new system the *Sibyl* opened trade in. Shona felt herself fortunate that the government gave her a partial subsidy for the care of her animals as being part of a very effective though expensive medical evaluation team.

Most of the time, she was simply glad of their company. She and Gershom had been trying for some time to start a family. It wasn't until, during a physical examination, the unexplained tenderness in her breasts and belly led to a test that showed there was a baby on the way. Instantly, she'd messaged the good news to Gershom via tachyon squirt, and started looking around for a place for them to live. She had intended to spend the rest of the pregnancy and the first couple of years enjoying her child's infancy here on Mars. Her pay was pulled back to match her temporary assignment as ground staff, but that concerned her less. The one thing her salary couldn't buy her was preferred living space.

Housing Authority had been sympathetic but unable to help ng from its perpetual housing shortage, and ted. Her application for living quarters for nals went on a waiting list. She needed a e of the menagerie, and was grateful that it here had been more than one neighbor of the to move to a remote dome because he owned ad the additional excuse not only of additional

12

room, but for remaining in the main domes, that her animals were part of her work. They couldn't promise her anything sooner than the date of the baby's arrival, and possibly not even that.

During her visit to Mars, she had been staying with her Uncle Harry and Aunt Lal, in the vacant room which belonged to their eldest daughter, currently away at University. It was the same chamber that had been Shona's while she was growing up in their care. She appealed to her aunt and uncle to let her live in it until she could find a place of her own. A good deal of her impedimenta had been placed hastily in storage.

There were some times Shona was grateful that her relatives welcomed her back. She loved her four young cousins like brothers and sisters. Angie and Stevie, in particular, were her devoted followers. At others, she wished she could be living anywhere else, even in those frightening abandoned buildings near the Space Center. The crowding in the small dome was nearly as bad as it would have been on shipboard, a similarity which her aunt, an unabashed groundhog, wouldn't have appreciated. Aunt Lal was scared stiff of anything which smacked of going outside of the domes, let alone blasting off into space.

Since she wouldn't be able to get back to her real work for many months yet to come, Shona was assigned to give the final physicals and examinations to teams about to depart and filled the rest of her days studying the latest digests on her speciality. It was almost as good as going, though not quite. She'd get a small taste of space travel in a few weeks, when she took ship for Earth. There was a law under discussion in the legislature that would ban space travel from Mars for pregnant women and minor children, and Shona had no intention of getting caught by any rule that would ground her for good. She had already made her plans to evade entrapment.

A painful twinge erupted in the small of her back, and Shona stopped walking to massage it. The way her back and feet felt today, she was going to have to cut back on the hours she spent on her feet doing examinations. Saffie, throwing an occasional concerned glance over her shoulder at her mistress, trotted more sedately toward the transport stop. Shona smiled and patted the dog's head.

Behind her, a slight sound disturbed the silence—a hiss, the sound a shoe might make brushing against the pavement. Shona glanced around casually, then warily. There was no one there.

"Hello?" she said. The street was empty. Her voice echoed against the derelict storefronts. She clasped Saffie's leash tighter and wished the transport would hurry.

• • •

Everything in the office suggested power. It did not shout or intrude its message directly on the consciousness, but it implied subtly to an observer that at this desk sat a most important man, with important choices to make that could affect thousands or millions of lives. The desk alone, custom-styled and handmade of the most expensive and rare materials available anywhere in the galaxy, spoke quietly of money and influence.

"Report," said the man seated behind it addressing the screen of a private communications unit. It was set into a pull-out panel at the rear of the expensive Earth-wood desk so that no one walking into the office could see to whom the executive was speaking. "This is a secure frequency."

"Yes, sir." The man on the screen was named Wrenn. His police file described him as an amoral sociopath, brilliant and dangerous. Five years ago an extended sentence for assault he was serving in the Martian Detention Center had been cut short by the intervention of the Corporation executive. He had used his considerable influence to urge members of the parole board to be lenient at Wrenn's last parole hearing. Wrenn felt only minimal gratitude for his benefactor's aid, but he enjoyed the assignments he was given. Wrenn knew that if he tried to betray his employer, there were probably other people like him on the payroll who were as tough as he was. His employer paid him enough so that he could trust Wrenn to keep confidences. The relationship suited both of them. "I finished sorting through the personnel files. There's four candidates whose profiles fit what you wanted. I don't see how a single person's going to help you keep better control of the colonies."

"Judiciously utilized," the man behind the desk said, "one person will be more than enough, providing that it is the right person. The situation is getting out of hand. I am extremely troubled by the tendency of the Galactic courts to prematurely sever Corporate contracts between this office and colonial worlds. After the last outrage, awarding damages to Iomar IV against their claims that the Corporation didn't live up to the clauses in its contract, I can tell that it is time to take a more direct hand. Hence my need for a specialist. Let me see the files."

Wrenn nodded, and leaned toward the video pickup as he located the datacube recess in the public comm-unit and inserted a cube. The executive's screen blanked out and filled with a four-way view, each quadrant displaying the moving image of a man or a woman. The first person was a man in his fifties, mustachioed, respectable in appearance. The second was a young woman, fresh-faced, with freckles and thick brown hair. The third was a thin, black-haired woman in her thirties. The last was a man of forty, round-faced and cheerful. "I think you'll like number two, sir," Wrenn's voice continued over the recorded images. "I followed her home today. She's everything you specified when you gave me this assignment. Like you always said, you want the best tool for the job."

The executive touched a control, and the image in the upper right-hand corner enlarged, filling the screen. He scrolled upward to read her psychological profile. "Very good. *Very* good. All I desired for this job. Excellent. She would be just right. I do like the policy of establishing psych profiles. Takes a great deal of the guesswork out of finding the ideal person to fit the job. I see this candidate is employed by the government. She *was* out in space, and now I see she is in a ground-service position."

"Yes, sir. She's pregnant. But she's expressed an interest in returning to active colonial service."

"Hmm," the executive mused, tapping his lip with a forefinger. "I need her available to travel *now*. The new legislation the Pro-Child League has just intimidated the Martian Council into passing will preclude that." He touched a control which saved the personnel data into a private storage area, and the holotank cleared, showing Wrenn's face. "See to it. Then steer her this way. I want her to join the Corporation, and not the government, once she resumes active service."

Wrenn remained expressionless. "Yes, sir."

His employer cut the connection. Wrenn waited until there was no one passing by before he left the public booth.

CHAPTER

~ 2 ~

"HEL-LO?" SHONA CALLED, from the front door of the Elliott house. The mushroom-domed house was quiet but she could hear a voice speaking somewhere. "Auntie?"

"Shh!" her aunt hissed from the family room. Shona and Saffie hurried in to see what was going on. "Quiet. The news is on."

"Anything good?" Shona asked.

"They've got footage of a landing. Be quiet!"

"Oh!" Excitedly, Shona dragged Saffie through the house to her room and thrust the dog hastily inside. Shutting the door on Saffie's whined protests, she hurried back to watch the report.

She settled down beside her aunt, who shushed her again and pointed at the glowing images. Uncle Harry, her late father's brother, on his exercise machine in front of the screen, glanced over to beam at her. "Look at that, baby," he said, puffing as he paced up and down on the hydraulic steps. "We're getting further out there!"

"Shh!" commanded his wife.

The announcer's face disappeared, replaced by the Corporation logo. It dissolved into a puff of smoke, which Shona recognized not as a display of special-effect pyrotechnics, but as the explosive charge of the camera module detaching from the side of the colony vessel on which it had been riding piggyback all the way from Mars. A long black line eddied between the module and its parent ship, which gradually shrank as the camera moved backward until the viewers could see its entire outline. Its surface, brilliant with a sheen of ice crystals, reflected the light of the system's sun. A tiny shadow consisting of a polygonal box and a thread outlined sharply on the bulkhead had to be the camera and its umbilical. Above it, on the side of the great ship facing the camera was the Corporation logo and the vessel's name, *Geneva*.

Off-camera, the announcer's voice said, "The *Geneva* carries a complement of two hundred and fifty men, women, and children to their new home. With the establishment of their settlement on Zizzobar III, the Corporation is proud to announce that new sources of rare commodities will soon become available, for industry, science, and space exploration. Captain Schönbern, colonists, welcome to Zizzobar."

"What a funny name," commented Stevie, Shona's youngest cousin. He was ten.

"Shh!" his mother hissed.

The ship's retros fired, the glare obscuring the lower half of the screen until it and the camera module had touched down. As the flames and smoke from burning vegetation underfoot died away, Shona glanced eagerly past the outline of the ship at the new world. In the far background, tree-tall plants of a dark blue-green corkscrewed toward the sky. Some sort of small creature, possibly avian but featureless in the distance, soared above them.

A hatch opened near the base of the ship, revealing an array of glass tubes and other testing apparatus. Lights flashed as the unit performed each test: oxygen quality, bacteria, temperature, and so on. Then the hatch slid shut.

The family held its breath until the gantry was lowered, and the first colonists, wearing protective environment suits, stepped down onto the ground. The leader unfastened his helmet and lifted it off his head. He leaned back as if he were sucking in a great, deep breath of air. He smiled, his thin-jawed face creasing from ear to ear, and signaled to his companions to follow suit. Shona found she was holding her breath, and let it out with a sigh.

"What's this one going to do?" Shona whispered curiously.

"Shh!" her aunt said again. "They're digging for precious metals. The place is full of them."

"Zizzobar," the off-camera voice continued, "will be supported by the Corporation during its years of development, but will eventually earn independent-world status by establishing its own economy. In the meantime, the people there will work off their debt by setting up a processing plant to mine the planet's mineral wealth."

It was no secret that they'd work for less wages than they would if they were contract employees just doing a job, because they were paying off transportation to the planet, food, raw materials, medical care, an expert sociologist, exobiologists, and anything else they needed. Under the narrator's lugubrious voice Shona and her family could hear loud cheering from the growing party of settlers. A safe, satisfactory, happy landing had been achieved.

Shona watched with pride. She had been on two such missions for the government before coming back to Mars Dome #4, and her memories were vivid ones.

"You wish you were still out there, don't you?" her young cousin Angie asked, watching her face change. Angie was fourteen, the third of Aunt Lal's four children, a slim girl already growing tall. Shona smiled sadly at her.

"I do. I envy them being out there. A new world to explore . . ."

Her aunt shivered. "Ugh! You'd never catch me hiking around in an unsettled wilderness. Who knows what horrors are out there? Give me a nice safe dome any time. Only *crazy people* would leave a controlled environment for the jungle."

"Now, Laurel," Harry began, leaning over the handles of his treadmill. She rounded on him next.

"And you! You're no better, spending all your time at your bank on loan papers for the Corporation, so they can buy more equipment and send more of our resources out of system. You should be ashamed of yourself."

"Lal, they're our biggest loan client. They do more business with us than all of our other customers combined."

"Well, they should stop. Pretty soon there'll be nothing left here for the rest of us."

Shona stopped herself from correcting her aunt or trying to defend the theories of space exploration, and its benefits for the home systems. This was an argument that Shona had learned long ago that she couldn't win, and if she was smart, wouldn't continue. Aunt Lal had an unreasoning fear of anything beyond the edges of the domes. Uncle Harry tipped her a wink behind his wife's back.

"Laurel, why are you so interested in the landings, if you don't like to think about space travel?" her husband demanded as the lights came up. He got off his exercise mill, puffing. Uncle Harry was plump. His eternal fitness quest seemed to do nothing more than keep his physique in the state it was. He bore little resemblance to his younger brother, Shona's late father, except for the freckles and brown hair that she, too, had inherited.

"I just like to see that they got there safely, that's all." The older woman waved a dismissive hand, pushing away the uncomfortable topic of space exploration, and gave Shona a squeeze. With her small, delicate features and long lashes, Aunt Lal had been considered beautiful when she was young. She hid her good looks by wearing an unattractive hairstyle, and clothes that were almost purposefully dowdy. Shona loved her but she didn't understand her. "Hurry up, then, and get washed. Supper in ten minutes."

Thankfully, Shona excused herself and went back to her chamber to feed her menagerie.

18

It was hard to believe, looking around at all the laboratory paraphernalia, books and assorted junk that filled her room to the roof, that it would all fit into one modular cargo container, and still leave room for her furniture and wardrobe. The ultrasound unit should have been reclaimed months ago by the Health Department and reassigned to another physician, but the government moved slowly. The unit was too delicate to put in unheated storage, so it stood at one side of her room, taking up precious space. Shona didn't mind if they waited a while longer to take the machine back. She did periodic low-power ultrasounds on herself to check on the progress of her baby.

The cat and the dog were at her feet at once, demanding attention and their dinners. Saffie leaped up, seeking to plant her big paws on Shona's shoulders and lick her face. Shona fended her off, and led the way to the cupboard where the food was kept. Harry wound his way around her feet, his narrow tail an erect curve.

"Chow time!" she called, looking around for the ottle. It was simple to feed. The alien liked the same kind of food the cat did: heavy on protein and oils, and the stronger smelling the better. Once the brand she used had been tested by Alien Relations, Shona was given permission to let him eat it if he wanted to.

The alien slept papoose-style in a dark brown pouch on the wall, which had been specially textured so he could climb up and down it unassisted. The floor underneath it was littered with small round disks of wood which were the ottles' system for recording data. Chirwl wasn't very tidy. It must be from living in a jungle; when one dropped something from a high tree limb, one didn't have to worry about it anymore. The highest he could get in Shona's quarters was four meters, which meant the detritus was always well in evidence. She went over and prodded the soft bag. "Hey! Dinnertime. Are you hungry?"

She peeped inside. There was no one in it, but among the chips on the floor below was a clue.

The alien had discovered he was fond of Crunchynut bars, an Earth candy that Shona loved. Now and again, Shona bought a bag of them to share with Chirwl. She'd had them tested at her own expense to be certain they wouldn't play havoc with his digestive system. His greed for sweets surpassed hers. He would eat them to capacity if he had had the opportunity, but since they were imported from Earth and were priced accordingly, Shona's thrift alarm went off whenever she reached for a bag in the store. The last package had been purchased two days before, and she hadn't opened it yet. And she thought she had concealed it cleverly enough. The trouble was that the little alien was too intelligent not

19

to have figured out where his treat must be. Shona picked up the cellulose candy wrapper and looked around for more.

"I'm going to have to start storing them in my locker at work," she said to herself peevishly, "and bring them home one at a time."

There was another wrapper just behind the door. She bent, her belly making the motion ungainly, to pick it up. Just outside the door, almost invisible against the hall carpet was another. And another.

She followed the trail of wrappers into the bathroom. Except for Shona's office, the bath was Chirwl's favorite place in the house. His arboreal world was filled with pools of clear water, and the swirling bath was the closest he could come on Mars to such a feature.

"Aha!" she said, pointing from the doorway. Grimacing guiltily, the small sable creature dropped what was left of the Crunchynut bag, and dove fluidly into the water. Shona examined the remains of the package with despair. It was nearly empty. She glared at her charge, who gazed up at her through the water with big, innocent brown eyes. Shona was not amused.

"If you're not too full," she announced to the round shape at the bottom of the bathtub, "dinner is served." From experience, she knew he could read her lips perfectly well. She turned on her heel and marched out.

While she was dishing out the animal chow, her cousin Angie came in to watch.

"You had some mail today," Angie said, leaning against the door frame.

Shona plumped the heavy bag of rabbit chow to the ground and dusted her hands together. "I did! Great. Where from?"

"Oh, you don't want to know," said the girl coyly. "So I had your messages transferred to my room. Want to give me the communication code so I can read them? I'll let you know if there's anything good in them."

"Oh, you!" Shona leaped for the girl. Angie bounded over the bed, and Shona hurried around it to grab her. Saffie barked, forelegs flat on the floor, trying to decide which one to chase.

A tickling match ensued. The girl was agile, but, Shona was faster, in spite of her unwieldly belly, and she used her extra bulk to block the door, cutting off Angie's escape from the room.

"Uncle!" Angie cried, trying to stop her cousin's tickling fingers from getting to sensitive spots like her ribs and upper arms. "They're already on your terminal, really! Gershom and Susan!"

"Thanks, pip," Shona said, pulling her fingers away.

"It's not fair, you know," Angie panted, eyes brimming with laughter. "Two against one."

Shona let her go with a quick hug, and punched in her comm code. Still excited, Saffie licked at Shona's hand and worked her bony head under the young woman's fingers for a scratch. Angie picked up Harry, and carried him out of the room, chattering baby talk to him. Harry assumed a long-suffering expression, and hung limp in the girl's arms. Shona shut the door on them so she could hear the audio better.

She signaled the console to play the messages, and waited impatiently through the leader which showed the tachyon beacon data, tracing the path the message had taken from its source to the Mars receptor end. By the succession of jumps listed, Gershom was a long way away.

The holotank screen bleeped and went black, and then Gershom's face was looking out at her, his warm brown eyes crinkled at the corners with his smile. "Hi, sweetie," he said.

"Hi, love," Shona whispered. The three-dimensional image made it look as if she could reach out and touch his face. It couldn't just be the separation from him that engendered poignant longing. He'd been out in space six to ten months of every year almost since they'd met. Hormones must have something to do with it. To her, his sweet tenor had all the music of violins. For a moment she just closed her eyes and let the message play.

"If this reaches you, thank modern technology," Gershom said in an amused tone that belied the plaintiveness of his words. "How are things with you? Is your back still giving you trouble?

"Ivo, Eblich, Kai, and I are sitting out the worst ion storm we've ever seen in the shelter of an asteroid belt. It was lively getting out here to Damson, but it was worth it, sweetie! These folks were so glad to see new faces that they practically signed a permanent contract with us. We were the first to make it here after they declared stability. I've seen that kind of isolation fever before, so I wouldn't take their mark, but it was a temptation. Merson and Company were only two days behind us, and the Corporation a day behind them. We're on our way back, with only four stops scheduled in between jumps." Shona's eyes widened incredulously, Gershom grinned, as if he could see her surprise. "I'll be back with you in time for the baby's birth, or as close as time and warp allow. I miss you, sweetie. Hope you're well. The others send their best. We're all looking forward to seeing you, but me most of all. I love you, sweetie. See you soon." Gershom's image blew her a kiss, and the screen went black.

21

"Oh! Darling," Shona breathed, glad tears stinging her eyes. "I can't wait." She felt a warm glow of love for him. She missed him. They didn't get to spend much time together—less than she liked—because of their respective careers.

After a few years of scouting and carrying out small errands for both the United Galaxy government and the Corporation, as well as the government of individual systems, Gershom had negotiated a loan for his own scout ship, and began trading. Now, after eight years of boomtime (even Gershom had to admit that the time had been just right for him to have prospered so well), the big trading ship he flew belonged mostly to him. He had three permanent employees aboard who also shared in the net profits. As soon as he'd taken possession of the *Sibyl,* Gershom asked Shona if she wanted to join the crew. She'd always intended to, but at the time, the government had offered her too good a job at too tempting a salary. Later on, she promised him, the Taylor Traveling Medicine Show would take to the skies. They wanted to raise their family on board the ship, but Shona had wanted to get in an honest apprenticeship under senior physicians before she set up shop on her own. Once she'd worked out her blind spots and inexperience, she wanted to set up practice on her own.

Gershom's work meant that they seldom met, but the separations lent delightful spice to the times they were together. The last time she had seen him, five months ago, he was on his way out to Alpha, no more than a milk run for a swift, long-range trader like his, because he didn't want to be caught out on a longer trip on which he might get delayed coming back. He wanted to be there for the baby's birth.

She played the message again, this time for the animals. Saffie came over and dropped her head on Shona's knee, and whacked her tail against the console joyfully. Harry had appeared immediately when he heard Gershom's voice, and hunched up into a neat bundle on the bed. The alien jumped up beside him, and assumed the same position. Chirwl loved to tease the cat by imitating what he did. The cat pretended there was no one there but him. Harry showed a feline's approval for the message from Gershom, slitting his eyes with pleasure, and hunching his paws further underneath his chest.

Shona watched the message over again, feeling a rush of warmth and love for her husband. His large dark eyes looked out at her ardently from the screen. It was hard being without him so long. She put a hand on her belly, which was the perfect calendar of their separation. They hadn't been together in five months. The tachyon squirt she'd sent to inform him of her pregnancy had been directed to follow the beacons along his registered flight path to tell him that there was a baby on the way. That kind of message was expensive, requiring as it did the redirection of a LaserCom dish, but she'd felt it was worth it. Since then, Gershom had sent a message every week full of love and curiosity, demanding news, asking how she was and what it was like with the baby developing inside her. He had a knack for making her feel that he was close when he was light-years away from her. The screen faded again, and the image was gone.

Shona cleared the thickness from her throat. "Well, moving from soap operas to News of the Galaxy . . ."

"Hi, twin!" her best friend's message began. Susan still lived on Shona's home world of Dremel, making her living as a professional videographer. Her usual work was documentary video films made on a zero-budget basis, which she financed by signing broadcast contracts with the public beacon companies. Her videos didn't make her rich, but they gave her a measure of critical public acclaim. Aunt Lal's children loved it that someone they knew made videos. They were favored viewing in the Elliott household. "I have got some *great* news. Not as earthshaking as yours but not bad for me." The government had announced that a new trading hub would open in their old system thereby making the real estate more valuable, and creating thousands, if not millions, of jobs. The developers had hired her to make disk records of the sites, and to follow the phases of the construction for the home office. "They hired me over a bunch of others all equally qualified because I said I had my own jets. Can you imagine that old clunker of mine being the deciding factor for anything? When it's all over, I'll probably have enough footage to produce a small documentary, and the developers said they'd give me all the help I need. Shona, it is a dream job."

Shona rejoiced, clapping her hands together. "Oh, it sounds great! I wish I could be there, too." She pictured the two of them bouncing around the system in the ancient little scout craft Susan maintained. It was a rickety old beast that had been bequeathed to Susan by an older cousin when he left for University in another system, safe as a rocking horse and nearly as underpowered. Secrets told in the absolute security of that old jalopy were securely kept between the three of them. Shona missed that intimacy.

She and Susan had kept in touch since Shona had left in the company of a government caretaker when her parents had been caught in the fatal dome collapse. Though her uncle's family had been kind to her, she missed Susan terribly. Both eldest children, they had been like Siamese twins ever since infancy. Where Shona was freckled with brown hair, Susan was fair and blue-eyed, but they felt as if they were truly sisters. Their separation had torn away a part of Shona's soul.

She'd gone through school on Mars, doing well academically, and made other friends, though Susan would never be supplanted as first and best. Susan had been the first one Shona had told about choosing the health profession narrowly over pilot training, and her overwhelming infatuation with Gershom Taylor, whom Shona had met in the lower forms. He was a few years older than she was, and graduated. She'd sent Susan a detailed description of their courtship and romance, and was bolstered by her best friend's sympathy and advice while she fought through her insecurities. Susan had managed to come out standby and skin of her teeth to Alpha Centauri to stand up beside Shona when they got married. Shona was shocked when she realized she hadn't seen Susan in person since. It had been a good six years.

"As soon as finances allow, I'll come and see you and little Whatsisname," Susan offered gleefully. "Or maybe the two of you can come out and stay with me for a while. It'd be good to have you back home. I know what it's like staying with relatives—no fun at all." Susan paused, eyes wide with mischief, her hand over her mouth. "Boy, I hope you're alone when you hear this."

Shona laughed.

"Dinner's ready," her aunt's voice announced over the com. Hastily, Shona switched off the console and flung off her work tunic. Aunt Lal liked her family to wear something nice to dinner. Hastily, Shona chose something out of her closet that would go over her belly. She put it on, fastening the back as she hurried out to the dining room. She made herself a mental note to answer the transmissions later, when everyone else had gone to bed.

Her younger cousins were already seated. Stevie pushed out her chair for her with his foot.

"Pee-yew!" Dale said, holding his nose. He was Aunt Lal's second, aged sixteen. His older sister was away at University in Mars Dome #8, making him the senior child at home. "You stink."

Shona took a cautionary sniff, and sensed nothing unusual. "What do I smell of?"

"Money!" Dale crowed, pointing at her dress. Shona made a face at him. He'd learned that phrase from his parents, and she hated it. He was at the age when he made a point of saying and doing things on purpose that annoyed people.

"Gershom got that for me in a trade, so knock it off," she warned him. The dress *was* expensive, made of a dove-gray fabric so light it floated, and embroidered with jewel-like bands and threads of cobalt blue and crimson. Shona admitted to herself that she loved

24

pretty clothes, and Gershom liked to indulge her tastes. It would be a long time before they could afford similar indulgences until Shona started getting space pay again, and without Gershom at home, no place to wear the pretty frocks she had.

"There's yours," Aunt Lal said deprecatingly, pointing to a dish. It contained a colorless mash that steamed faintly in the light shining on the table. Shona felt the desperate urge of pregnancy cravings. "I feel like the evil stepmother, feeding you that stuff. There's nothing to it. Are you sure you won't have some of the stew? Vegetables? Fruit?"

At the very thought of solid food, Shona's stomach did barrel rolls. She slid hastily into her chair. "No, thank you, Auntie. Nutri contains everything I need: vitamins, minerals, protein, carbohydrates . . ."

"Hah! Everything but flavor. It looks like such a nasty mess. And it doesn't taste like anything at all!"

"Auntie, spacers eat this every day, for every meal, spiced or unspiced. It'll be fine. I'm used to it."

"You remember what it was like to want weird things to eat when you were carrying, Lal," Uncle Harry reminded her gently.

"Well, all right. I suppose I do; I had four healthy babies. There's second helpings in the pot," her aunt admitted grudgingly.

"It's so weird of you to want to eat that stuff now," her cousin Dale said disapprovingly. He was scornful of everything adult. "You said when you came back from your last mission that you never wanted to look at nutri again."

"Tell it to my baby," Shona shot back. Barely waiting for the others to be served their dinner, she started spooning it up, at the same time annoyed with herself that she wanted it so badly. Nutri was the blandest substance that had ever been invented, she was sure of that. The impression she always got eating it was that it was just barely more solid than milk, and, in its unaltered state, of a less interesting texture than mashed potatoes. Yet it could be frozen, fried, or baked, chopped, sliced, or ground into interesting and varied textures, and spiced to taste like any food in the known galaxy. The great Spice War of the twenty-second century was over sources for exotics to give taste to nutri for the masses of astronauts exploring and expanding the frontiers of space for human expansion. Shona could easily understand the need.

Her craving abated about three spoonfuls from the bottom of the bowl, and her distaste for the substance returned. She started to push the bowl away, and noticed her aunt's watchful eye on her. Reluctantly, she ate the remainder, stifling the gag reflex as her throat remembered the six weeks she and the rest of the specialty team had gone without flavor extracts on the way back from the Cotton Consortium. It was like sensory deprivation. Some of the crew had been near suicide by the time they made Marsport. As soon as they cleared Fumigation, Taji Chandler, her friend the biologist, a man who loved spicy food with about the same ardor as he loved breathing, had walked into the nearest quartermaster's office, and drunk a pint bottle of curry-flavor extract straight.

Her aunt waited until she put her spoon down. "More, honey?"

"No, thank you," Shona assured her, hoping she wouldn't insist. "That was enough."

"Take your vitamins," Lal reminded her, pointing to the colorful heap of pills next to the empty bowl.

"Yes, Auntie." Shona obediently gulped them down. As soon as her aunt was satisfied that she really had swallowed them, she nodded. Shona pushed back from the table and went back to her room.

Nutri! It was one of the necessary evils of her job. Why did she feel compelled, in the midst of variety, to eat the one thing that had been her sole item of diet for two six-month missions planetside, and two extended round trips through space on either side. It was humiliating not to be able to control the cravings and other impulses that hit her. Shona felt a yearning for the excitement of space travel, of being on a colony mission, and a strong restlessness with being groundbound for a whole four years to come. It was as though she were no longer making things happen; they were happening to her instead. She would change that as soon as possible. There was a lot to be done, even before the baby arrived. Until its birth, it was an unknown quantity in her life. But it wasn't too late to make plans to follow its birth. She and it, and a suitable child-care provider, could continue to go on missions from Earth. It would be an exciting way for a child to grow up, constantly surrounded by new things. One day, they'd join Gershom aboard the *Sibyl* for good.

The morning message dump had brought five letters and resumes in answer to her advertisement in the child-care bulletin board for a nanny. She was too excited to concentrate on them properly, so she posted them to her personal memory space, and went into the government database to read Help Wanted ads.

The posting board on the Galactic Government computer net had job listings, updated every few hours, for medical technicians, doctors, nurses, and pharmochemists. Instead of searching only for her speciality, Shona let the long list scroll up, scanning individual ads. Who knew? Something different might strike her fancy. If she was near enough to qualify for a job she liked the sound of, she still had years to close any gaps in her education.

Harry settled in her lap as she read them. It wasn't too early to start checking the colony openings for three years hence; project coordinators liked to fill the rosters as early as possible so they could begin briefings, study the material known about the planet they intended to settle, and introduce the settlers and specialists to one another.

" 'Wanted: general practitioner for a petroleum/radioactives mining colony,' " Shona read, scratching the cat between the ears. "No way. Can you just imagine the crop of industrial accidents when that gets going? They want an E.R. surgeon, not a G.P. Here's another: 'G.P./OB-GYN wanted for incipient settlement—' Incipient population explosion, sounds like! Wait, here's a good one."

As Shona started to read it, she stopped scratching. A slim, fox-colored paw stole lazily, almost self-motivated, up toward the Delete key at the base of the keyboard. His mistress caught the small pad just before it pressed down, and set it down on her lap with a pat. "Hold on right there, Charley. I might be interested in this one." Harry, affronted, curled once more into an inscrutable ball and shut his eyes. Shona leaned forward over him to read the entry on the screen, with growing excitement.

" 'Project to revive rare fruit tree varieties on pastoral planet seeks general practitioner, departure date 2240. Don't let an apple a day keep best candidate away.' These sound like my kind of people." She gathered up Harry and dropped a kiss on top of his head. "Don't you think so? They've got the same bad sense of humor as I do. And it's a perfect time frame for me: three years from now. Baby will be just big enough to eat unripe apples. What do you think?" Harry purred and bumped his head under her chin.

There were a few more ads that interested her in the file. She typed in the command for a printout, and went over to the board for news headlines.

On the news menu, the landing on Zizzobar rated News Flash status. She selected the story, and waited through the flashy Martian News logo—a planet with two moons—that showed the source of the news item. The holo which followed was the same footage of the ship descending and the captain emerging and taking off his helmet, with the tedious details of soil and atmosphere tests cut out for brevity.

"Mmm," Shona said. "Makes it look like you can just unload and go. So why do they need me?" she asked the cat. Harry murmured something, and curled into her lap.

27

"Is that the news?" Chirwl asked, climbing down the wall from his pouch. He scurried across the floor to join her.

"Yes, it is," Shona said, patting the bed behind her. "Come on up." She scrolled through the headlines, passing up uninteresting headlines for stories she wanted to see. "Sports scores, no; trade meetings on Alpha, no. What's this? New child-care restrictions? Not yet!"

"They will restrict who can take care of children?" Chirwl inquired, rolling over to sit on his tail with his hands clasped over his belly.

"Not exactly." Shona said grimly. She chose the headline, and waited.

The screen changed to a Martian News logo over footage of a protest march before a large, official-looking dome building. As the logo disappeared, Shona could read the signs the protesters carried "Space is No Place For Our Youth"; "Restrict Export of Our Most Precious Commodity."

Off-camera the news reader said, "The Child Protection League, shown here at a rally in Dome Number One, saw its demands answered in this morning's session of the Martian Congress when a bill, sponsored by Senator Bryan Culsen, was passed into law prohibiting pregnant mothers or the parent in custody of children under age eighteen from leaving Mars. It is said to be in the best interests of children to have a stable environment while growing up."

"This will keep innocent youth from being galloped around the galaxy without any sense of home or permanence," a man's voice said.

"Senator Culsen was quoted as saying," the news presenter continued, over the video, which changed to a scene of a chamber with crowds packing semicircular tiers of seats listening to a man standing at the podium in the center of the arena. "An exception will be made for families departing on permanent colony assignments. The law is expected to take effect within the next month." The scene changed once again to the protest marchers.

"What?" Shona demanded, leaning in toward the tank. "I'm glad I've already got passage off-planet. I'd better see if I can get my departure date moved up so we can get out of here soonest."

"Do they not think you will care for your own young correctly wherever you are?" Chirwl asked, screwing up his muzzle as Shona reached over to the console to replay the news announcement.

Shona listened to the report twice through, and shook her head. "I'm going to do something about this. No one is going to keep me and my baby out of space."

28

CHAPTER

SHONA'S NOTION WAS not an isolated phenomenon. The shipping office at the far west edge of the city dome was noisy, crowded, and hot. Workers in uniform shifted from one foot to the other and looked unhappily at the clock, which showed time moving at a far faster rate than the queue. Many of the women waiting in line were pregnant as Shona herself. One tired mother had an irritable toddler by the hand. Grown impatient with the long wait, he was sniveling and whining for attention, enraging the already-tense adults cooped up with him. The mother breathed her gratitude when Shona knelt beside the boy to amuse him as the long queue wound its way toward the desk.

"Earthbound?" asked the clerk, reading the disk-ticket Shona handed her.

"As soon as possible, please," Shona said. She peered over the hood of the console to watch the clerk's swift fingers tapping away at the plastic-covered solenoids.

"Things are getting pretty crowded after last night's broadcast," the clerk said, scanning a list, "but you've got priority status. Your disket is full fare. I'll see what I can do. Your live baggage might be a problem. Hmmm."

Shortly, Shona boarded public transport to take her home, clutching the precious disket that allowed her passage on a ship two weeks sooner than her original flight. The Medical Center already knew she was leaving. She wouldn't be causing any real hardship by taking off a little sooner. Two days seemed so short a time to wrap up all her business on Mars and say goodbye, but it was the best thing she could do for herself and her child. No planetbound bureaucrat could possibly know how it felt to be grounded. For now at least the Earth laws were more lenient concerning individual rights.

The railbus ride to the terminus was a slow one. Soothed by the hum of the vehicle's impulsors, Shona started to drift off, then sat upright as she sensed again the intrusive presence of eyes staring at her, watching her. She looked around. Everyone in the open-topped conveyance stared straight ahead or perused personal readers. No one was looking her way. Settling down again, she wished she'd brought Saffie with her. This part of the dome was unfamiliar to her. Most of the structures here were offices for off-planet industry. It had a bad reputation, though everyone she had met seemed friendly enough. Still, there was that feeling between her shoulder blades. Had one of the local street thugs picked her out as a potential target? At the next stop she moved close to the security alarm button in the center of the car.

Wrenn kept his eye on Shona throughout the ride, and at her northside stop, he too left the railbus, in back of several other passengers. Maintaining a safe distance behind her, he followed Shona all the way to her aunt's home. When he saw the door close behind her he slipped into the nearest communication booth.

"Sir, she's trying to leave Mars," Wrenn reported as soon as the secured channel was confirmed. He explained the details he had elicited from an illegal tap of the shipping company's computer through his personal reader.

"That cannot be tolerated," the executive said, turning his handsome head to peer obliquely at Wrenn's image. "I want her to remain on Mars until I need her. Stop her from going. Any way you need to."

The following afternoon, the doorbell sounded at the Elliott house. Impatiently putting aside her housework, Laurel Elliott swiped her hair into order at the hall mirror and answered the door. She smiled at the young uniformed man standing outside on the step.

"I'm with Alien Relations, ma'am," he said, touching the brim of his cap politely. "Is Dr. Shona Taylor at home?"

"I'm sorry," Aunt Lal said, brushing wisps of hair out of her face. "She's at work for another three hours. Is there any way I can help you?"

"Quarterly interviews, that's all," the young man said, with an aggrieved sigh. He looked like a chauffeur. There was a fancy personal transport on the pavement behind him with its parking lights on. "The brass wants to talk to her and her guest alien. Standard procedure. Is the, er, ottle at home?"

"He certainly is." Laurel beamed. She turned and bellowed down the hallway. "Chirwl!"

30

"Is it me who is summoning?" Chirwl asked, loping into the foyer.

"Don't talk gibberish," Shona's aunt scolded down at the innocent black eyes. "You know perfectly good Standard English. This man is here to take you for a talk with Alien Relations."

"Got the transport out front," the young man said, pointing over his shoulder.

"I do not enjoy care for machines," Chirwl said cautiously. "Awaiting Shona should be the correct procedure."

"There isn't time, friend. I'm a good driver. I'll see you there and home again before you know it."

"How would it be I do not know it?" the ottle asked, puzzled.

"Oh, go," Laurel said, impatiently. "You can be home before Shona is. She'll be pleased she didn't have to make an extra trip out in her condition. Go on."

"As you pleased," Chirwl said. Refusing help from the chauffeur, he rolled on his spine down the stoop and came up on all fours before the door of the transport. The man stood by politely and closed the door after him.

Chirwl nestled uneasily into the dished, padded seat. He missed Shona's company. Traveling in one of the human-made machines was profoundly unsettling for one of his species. It was not uncommon for visitors from his world to become disoriented in this land without wind or natural smells.

The ride seemed to take a long time. He looked out the windows of the closed car, but the sights whizzing by left him no more enlightened than he had been. Most of the views he had had of the dome had been on foot in Shona's company, from a level below the knees of most humans. A neatly kept area of plants went by. He thought he recalled that park, but was not certain. Shona had told him there were over twenty such oases within an hour's walk from their home. His friend Saffie's clever nose would have helped him to discover if he was at all close to familiar ground.

Chirwl was flung over backwards into the bowl-like depression in the seat when the machine hunched swiftly to a halt to make way for other, obviously superior machines. When those had crossed their path, they were permitted to continue. It was curious how such matters of dominance were settled.

The car lurched once again, thrusting him forward. Chirwl dug his sharp claws into the upholstery as the vehicle came to a final halt and stopped humming. The driver appeared at the newly opened door, and stood by as the ottle clambered out onto the pavement. Before him loomed a gray plastone dome with broad, steel doors, unlike any through which he had previously entered.

Nor were there any familiar scents. He twitched his whiskers, perplexed.

"I do not recognize this as Alien Relations," Chirwl said, looking up to the human for clarification.

"Regular doorway to the dome is under construction," the chauffeur explained stiffly. "Service entrance. Come on, will you?"

The hallway was as soulless as the exterior of the dome had been. Chirwl smelled only concrete dust and the tang of metalwork. His fur was becoming dirty. A long swim would be welcome when he returned home. He could smell water somewhere within this unhappy place, but he mistrusted the probable level of cleanliness.

His escort stopped beside a lighted doorway. "In there."

Chirwl loped past him and stopped foursquare two paces over the threshold. The room had not been used for anything in many months, to judge by the deadness of all scents. "There is emptiness here," he said. He turned, but the door was already closing. The human's bland face, just visible through the narrowing gap, had changed to a contorted sneer.

"More than you deserve," the man hissed. "Aliens, go home!" The door snicked shut.

Chirwl was already at the panel with his sharp claws. One of his fingerclaws became trapped between the door and the wall. He smacked the door with a palmpad and pleaded with it to release him.

"For when I have done you no harm," he begged. "Let me go, let me out!" The door did not answer, but it sagged back on its spring a minuscule amount as the pressure that closed it relaxed. Chirwl was able to pull his nail free.

Licking his talon for apology, Chirwl explored the bounds of his prison. The metal walls were too slick to allow him purchase to climb, as he might have in a room in Shona's dome to make the lights go on or a door open. The humans created the machines to their own heights. He disliked trying to use machines, for fear he was interfering in the relationship between a device and the human that built it. Humans could be very possessive of their machines, and did not appreciate outsiders molesting them. Witness Shona's young male cousins and their noisemaking gear. One of the square black boxes shouted at him once when he touched it and brought the boy running and scolding. Since then, he had passed by the box at a distance.

He worked up his courage to try to make this device understand him. The signal that doors understood was pressure on the square plate on the wall. Gathering his rear legs for a great leap, he jumped up and struck the door panel with his paws. Nothing happened. The machine ignored him. The ottle skittered backward into the center of the room and tucked his feet under his body to think. These mechanical devices did not listen to reason from one such as he, nor was he strong enough to force his way out. There was no food or water in the room. Unless he was allowed out—and he did not trust the angry human to free him—he would starve, and die alone.

Shona came home from work feeling distracted. Everyone at the Space Center had been sympathetic and kind, and very sorry to see her go. May hinted strongly that although Shona wasn't required to come in on her last day of work, she had better show up around midshift at the hastily moved-up going-away party they were having for her. Shona was grateful to her co-workers, and wished she didn't have to leave them behind. Many of them had become friends of hers in the last months. They'd elicted promises from her to send messages as soon as she was settled on Earth. In the meantime, there was plenty to do.

Saffie dragged her immediately over to the food storage and waited while she dished up dinner for her entire menagerie. While they ate, she went over packing lists, numbers to call, and messages to be left on computer boards. The Martian Postal Service had given her a form to fill out to have messages addressed to her personal number forwarded to the Earth beacon four days from now. Borrowed equipment had to be labeled for pickup. She wished there was time for a quick checkup by another doctor to make sure everything was all right. Never mind. The ship's doctor would be briefed that she was aboard.

It was going to be an endless night She looked around at her room, and felt dismay. All that needed to be packed demanded her attention at once. Her cousins had offered to pack things and send them after her, but it was hard to know what would be needed immediately and what could wait. If she only had enough time to deal with all of her possessions, she'd be much more relaxed. Shona wondered if she would simply not end up at the launch gate with the animals, Chirwl, her medical bag, three maternity dresses, and a case of pet food.

She glanced over at the cat and dog, who were lingering over the bowls even though theirs were empty. One meal, Chirwl's, remained untouched. Saffie and Harry were eyeing one another and her, deciding whether to take advantage of the ottle's absence to filch the choicest nuggets. Shaking her head, Shona put the bowl out of reach and went looking for him.

He was not in his usual spot at the bottom of the bathtub, nor in his pouch. Shona went through the dome, calling for him.

"Where's Chirwl?" she asked her aunt, who was standing in the kitchen, stirring nutri.

Laurel's hand flew to her cheek. "Oh, I'm so sorry, sweetie. I forgot to mention it when you came in. Alien Relations picked him up for an interview."

"Oh," Shona replied, mentally cursing all bureaucrats. "I didn't know he was due for one. I'll put his dinner away."

"He should be back any time," her aunt assured her. "Come and eat."

After supper, Shona continued her task of cramming two weeks of preparation into two nights. Much of what she had done the night before was to set aside things she was giving away or putting into storage for retrieval much later on. Her problem was to handle what was coming with her. The cat and dog fled under the bed to be out of her way, fearing they too would be stuffed into suitcases by their suddenly cyclonic mistress.

By the early hours of the morning, Shona was exhausted. A quick glance in the mirror showed her a face as pale as a sea of milk, with her freckles floating islandlike on its surface. The baby was kicking at her belly in protest at all the unusual agitation. She dropped onto the bed for a rest and mentally willed the fetus to calm down, and realized with a start that Chirwl had not yet returned home.

Sitting up uncomfortably, she tried to think of good reasons why Alien Relations would keep him overnight without contacting her. None of them seemed logical. Only one idea struck her, and it was a frightening one: that Alien Relations had decided to remove Chirwl from her care. She called the switchboard and asked to talk to him.

"No alien visitor of that name is here," the male operator replied mechanically. It was the heart of third shift, and he sounded bored.

"Did they let him leave earlier?" Shona asked. "Didn't someone escort him back here? He gets disoriented by himself in the dome."

The operator stared at her dully through the screen. "No alien visitor of that name has been here in the last day. I have all the records right here. The previous appointment with Ottle Visitor Chirwl was thirty-four days ago."

Shona gawked at him. "Get me a supervisor on line, quickly!"

The screen went blank for a long time while the night operator connected her with an officer of Alien Relations, probably one in another dome on Mars where the sun had already risen. She found herself drumming on the console with nervous fingers. Saffie, at her feet gave a sympathetic whine. Chirwl couldn't be out wandering alone. Surely someone would have brought him back.

When the screen cleared at last she explained about the missing Chirwl to the harried woman in the government uniform tunic.

"You must be mistaken, Dr. Taylor," the woman said impatiently. "No transport, personal or otherwise, called for the visitor today. His file, at your request, I note, is being transferred to Earth. He is still your guest, so far as we are concerned. Your fears are groundless."

"Please," Shona said, feeling desperate and drained from lack of sleep. "My aunt said the driver who picked him up identified himself as Alien Relations. Is it possible that it was a random inspection interview?"

The woman pursed her lips, halfway between amusement and annoyance. "I don't know what you've heard about us, Doctor, but we don't operate that way. It sounds as though you were the victim of a prank. I suggest you file a missing persons report with the Martian police. Keep us informed."

Shona disconnected and called the police. Her hands were shaking.

The officer on duty was sympathetic but unable to help. "The inside limit on filing a missing persons report is two days, Dr. Taylor," he said. "We can't respond until that time has passed."

"But he must have been kidnapped. A driver came to my door and took him away under false pretenses. You've got to find him. I leave tomorrow for Earth. He's coming with me."

"I'm very sorry, but we're constrained by the rules. Unless he's under the age of consent we have to assume he's missing because he wants to be."

Shona was definite. "That's not possible! He hates riding in cars. He'll be frightened. He could be lost, or in great danger. Ottles become disoriented in city locations. They're jungle creatures."

The officer was patient. "Doctor, he's an adult being. You of all people should understand that. He might come home on his own. If he hasn't and the time limit passes, call us again."

Shona looked at the clock as she severed the connection. Only twenty hours until takeoff. If she didn't find Chirwl before then, the ship for Earth would depart without her.

Chirwl spent a lonely, cold night in the disused office. The building breathed and hummed to itself strangely. Every time it shifted or settled, the metal-paneled walls of the room crackled or squeaked. The faint ceiling light continued to shine, but was so weak it barely illuminated the corners. Chirwl was terrified to be in the midst of all that technology without anyone to translate its intentions for him. No one in his experience with Shona or the discovery team that brought him to her had ever forced him to be alone with their machines. The ottle hoped the human would return to let him out so he could apologize for whatever offense he had committed against him. He had not an idea in the world why the human would hate him so much, nor, if he saw Chirwl as an enemy, why he would seek to imprison rather than kill.

The door was tightly shut. Was there another route of escape? Chirwl investigated once again the small square grate in the wall perpendicular to the door panel. It was fastened in place by those twisted pegs Shona called 'screws' that bored into the metal the way woodworms did into the trees on his native world. He had no metal claw to remove them as he had seen her do, but he had his own. He hoped he would not be hurting the wall. Rolling onto his spine, he braced his back feet against the metal grate. Carefully, he inserted the points of two talons around the top of one screw and began to pull.

The metal worms held fast. After a long time, all Chirwl had to show for his efforts were broken claws and worn-out patience. His belly told him how long it had been since he had eaten. He knew he was not thinking his clearest under the circumstances.

Footsteps sounded in the hall outside. Chirwl abandoned the grate and flew to the wall beside the door where he would be the least visible in the empty room, and waited for the door to open. It was possible that if he was quick, he could scoot out between the feet of whoever came in. The walker did not stop at Chirwl's prison, but kept on walking. It was unlikely to have been his jailor. Chirwl regretted not calling out. He could have been free.

"Help me!" he cried, banging on the door. His pads made little noise. The footsteps did not return. Dismayed, Chirwl went back to work on the grille.

The metal worms refused to yield to him. It was useless to scrabble at the wall around them; the panels were stained already with his blood after many hours of effort. He gave up pleading with the unseen machinery to let him out, and worked silently, keeping from whimpering like a cub at his plight. The scent of water drifted to him again through the grate. There must be a well or a pond along the passage it was guarding.

In irritation, he grasped the metalwork in his claws and shook it. "You have no right reason for imprisoning me!" he cried. His voice boomed hollowly in the square lungs of the building.

The grille shifted.

Chirwl backpedaled, and threw himself over backwards in a loop to land on his feet in the center of the room. Cautiously, he approached the ventilator duct and sniffed. Nothing had changed, but perhaps the machines in the wall had taken pity on him. He put out one gentle finger and touched the panel. No response. He drew it toward him.

Creaking like an old ottle's bones, the whole duct face rose up on two spindly arms. They were secured fast to the metal worms that he had been scrabbling at so diligently. Chirwl noted this fact in a moment as he realized that he was on his way to freedom. He whirled around the room in a mad, happy dash, then stopped short. The sound he had feared was in the hallway, coming toward the room: the boots of the human who had locked him in. As the door slid open, Chirwl dove for the open duct and wriggled quickly into the building's ventilation system. A hand reached up behind him, followed by the man's curses, nearly clutching the ottle's tail. Chirwl didn't stop. Four meters into the duct, it became a T-intersection. Chirwl raised his nose and sniffed. The junction to the right led to water.

Wrenn was just in time to see the ottle vanish into the ductwork. The conduit was too small to admit a full-grown human being, but Wrenn knew where the pipes led. One way was a dead end at the air-recirculation machinery, but the other led to a series of air intakes set at intervals on the outside perimeter of the building. He had only one chance to guess which one the ottle would choose. Otherwise, the alien would slip right by him.

The assassin's face went blank as his mind worked, reviewing what he knew of the species. They were tree-dwelling, water loving creatures who hunted by scent and hearing more than sight. The ottle had been without food or water for more than a full day. The water storage tank!

Leaving the room and hurrying along disused passages and abandoned transit shafts, Wrenn drew his slugthrower pistol and checked the loads. It would cause more trouble than the job was worth to kill the animal, but if he needed to wound it to recapture it, he wouldn't hesitate.

The water tank stood inside an enclosure on the northeast side of the dome. If the ottle made it across the mesh top of the tank and over the wall, he was free. Wrenn dashed down disintegrating concrete steps and up the next set, mentally pacing the alien. The ottle had a more direct route through the ductwork but moved more slowly than he did.

He banged the panel to open the door to the tank head. The door slid creaking into its niche, and stuck partway open. Wrenn struggled through the gap while the servos whined inside the walls. Lack of maintenance cost him precious seconds.

Wrenn pounded open the door to the tank room, and ran onto the catwalk, searching for the ventilation ducts. Illuminated by a few, weak fluorescents, the hulking storage tank under its mesh cover filled most of the room. Its lip protruded sullenly a third of a meter above the floor. Nothing alive had been in here for months. Halfway around the tank's perimeter, an air vent cover was moving. A small dark shape slipped out of it to the floor, its head turning this way and that seeking direction, its features indistinct in the poor light.

Wrenn leveled the gun. "Stay right where you're standing," he said, in a low, dangerous voice intended to get the ottle's attention. It unsettled the dust, sent vibrations through the water-filled tank at his feet.

Chirwl's head sprang up, seeing the human for the first time. Without a doubt, it was the man who had brought him here. He looked angry, and sounded ready to kill. Chirwl froze in place, his button-shiny eyes fixed on the man, like prey judging what move the hunter will make.

"Don't move, and you won't get hurt," Wrenn said. He walked around the tank in a bent-knee stride that kept his upper body dead-still, the gun arm steady on Chirwl.

"For why are you capturing me?" Chirwl asked, remaining motionless. The human did not reply. As soon as the man was halfway around the tank to him, Chirwl ducked down flat against the catwalk and scurried in the opposite direction. Something went *ping!* against the gray panel over his head. Chirwl ran.

Chirwl led Wrenn around and around the reservoir. After the first shot, the assassin realized that though the neighborhood was abandoned, gunplay couldn't go unnoticed for long. He could risk one more shot, but his best bet for remaining undetected was to achieve a physical capture. The ottle faced him across the expanse of mesh. Wrenn faked twice to the right, then dashed a few meters to the left. Breathless with fear, Chirwl ducked down and fled in the opposite direction. Wrenn turned around and dashed the other way, intending to meet the alien head on.

Chirwl, realizing his danger, scrabbled at the tank's rusting mesh with his claws, took a deep breath, and dove into the water. His nostrils rebelled at the stale taste, and he spat out in a stream of bubbles the small mouthful he had taken in by accident. From the bottom of the tank, he could see the human running around and around, attempting to find a ladder.

The respite gave him a chance to calm down and consider his next move. His lungs were good, but he couldn't stay where he was indefinitely. The human knew that when Chirwl surfaced he would make for the side nearest the fence to make his escape. Best to attempt now while he was strongest. As time passed, he would begin to suffer from anoxia, and his many hours without food would tell against his stamina.

Exploding to the surface in a rush of bubbles, Chirwl swam in circles for a while pursued by the hunter who was always steps behind him, then shot straight upward for the mesh. The ottle hauled himself hand-under-hand to the edge of the pool. The man hurried around to catch him. Now Chirwl had to hope that the man's eagerness would betray him. It happened in a series of moves so swift that the ottle's survival reflexes carried his body beyond his consciousness. The hunter lifted the mesh cover, ottle and all. Chirwl swung up and propelled his body over the edge of the pool. The man dove for him. Chirwl felt for a horrible moment the grasp of muscular arms around his body; then the water soaking his sleek fur provided him with the lubrication to slip free.

Wrenn fell flat on his face as the ottle wrested out of his arms. He flung himself forward on his knees, trying for a fresh handhold. The ottle whisked his tail out of the way, and scrambled up and over the fence of the enclosure. Wrenn rose to one knee and fired off a shot. The slug ricocheted a centimeter from the ottle's head; then it was gone.

Crying in fear, Chirwl dropped heavily, taking the brunt of the fall on bended limbs and shoulder joints. A chip sprang out of the pavement beside him, cutting his forelimb. Ignoring the pain, he fled into the night, the man's cursing chasing him up the street.

The day for Shona's departure passed swiftly. Shona was worried half to death over Chirwl, wondering what his absence signified. Alien Relations cautiously suggested that there was an extremist element in Martian society that hated aliens. They had offered a reward for information leading to the visitor's recovery.

In a large ad in the personal advertising section of the computer net, Shona listed Chirwl's description with an offer of her own reward for his safe return. She didn't dare to be too obvious in her plea in case whoever had taken him would be angry or offended. The important thing was that Chirwl come back to her well and in one piece.

She hoped also that she'd get a quick response. The ship for Earth would depart, with or without her, at 2100 hours. A frantic communication she made to the shipping office had served to assure her she'd be able to get aboard with all the animals and her luggage if she arrived by 2030. That deadline crept closer and closer. She had finished packing everything she was taking. Once Chirwl appeared, they'd be ready to go.

To keep from going mad with worry, she took Saffie out for long walks searching for the ottle. They avoided the usual routes to the transport station or to the shopping precinct. Chirwl knew the way home from there. Shona tried to think what the world looked like from knee-level, how he might have become confused. Her heavy belly wouldn't allow her much physical exertion. She was forced at last to go home and wait for word to come to her. Her cousins took the family transport and made the rounds, calling the ottle's name and asking the neighbors if they'd seen him.

Twenty hundred hours passed. Worry made her snappish and incoherent. Wisely, her aunt served her meals of nutri in her room, and left her alone with the communicator. One tiny, selfish twinge told Shona that if she left for the Space Center now, leaving the investigation in the hands of the police and Alien Relations, she could still make her ship. She quashed it angrily, refusing to abandon Chirwl. She was responsible to him; he trusted her. It was two weeks until the deadline. There were other flights they could make—would make.

At three o'clock in the morning, the Elliotts' doorbell rang. The entire household sprang up and rushed to answer the door. Shona waddled heavily into the foyer in time to see an officer of the Martian police force. The man, grinning, indicated the strange brown bundle riding astride his tech-belt over his right hip.

"This belong to you?" he asked. It was Chirwl. The ottle twitched his whiskers at the family.

"I belong to these, certainly," he said with joy.

"Oh!" Shona rushed forward and seized the ottle in a tremendous hug. He wrapped his limbs around her body and nuzzled her face affectionately. "You're all right! Where have you been?"

"A building of dust and metal tunnels and water stale in taste," Chirwl replied. "It was among other empty places."

"I found him wandering around in the warehouse district," the officer explained. "I guess he was lost."

"My aunt said he was taken by a man in a limousine," Shona said, making way for the officer to come inside. "Chirwl, can you describe the man who drove you to that building?"

40

"I cannot know," Chirwl said, apologetically. "He had one chin over his other."

"What's that mean?" the officer said, amused by Chirwl's manner of speech. He pulled his recorder out of a tunic pouch. "A disguise?"

"Ss-sso you might say," Chirwl confirmed, his sibilants whistling through his front teeth. "If you take me through the dome, I will essay try to identifying him."

"No!" Shona threw up her hands. "I am not letting you out of this house until we leave for Earth. I've got to go back to the shipping office and see if I can get another reservation."

Chirwl told his story for the officer's recorder. Shona was horrified at the deliberate coldness of the abduction, and Chirwl's escape from death. She treated his torn paws with antiseptic, which he tasted curiously while talking. Shona was almost in tears at how normal he seemed after such a dangerous adventure.

Aunt Lal kept ducking out of the room, embarrassed, bringing coffee for the visitor and snacks for Chirwl, or tidying up almost obsessively. Shona followed her out of the room and took the stack of cups away from her.

"Auntie, come and sit down. They need to get your testimony, too. What's wrong?"

"Oh, honey," Laurel said, stopping. Her eyes were woeful. "Your little friend could have been killed! I feel responsible."

"You're not," Shona assured her grimly. "The man who took Chirwl would have gotten at him one way or the other. Please, come and help us find out who he is. I don't want him trying again."

Alarmed at the idea of a second attempt, Laurel hurried into the lounge and sat down beside Chirwl. The officer ran a computerized identification program. Together, Laurel Elliott and Chirwl constructed a face as close as they could recall. The policeman shook his head over the resultant portrait.

"Not much to hang an I.D. on," he said. "Even if he wasn't disguised, he seems to have an average face. A thousand people in this dome alone match this description. We'll run an investigation of that area, see if we can find out what warehouse he was in. There are a lot of empty ones in that zone. Don't hold your breath waiting for results. Without witnesses, or prints, or securcam videos, we'll probably never find who he was or why he kidnapped the alien visitor. Until then, take precautions."

Rattled, Shona made sure nothing more would happen to any of them. She arranged with the police for a security watch on the dome, and made certain none of her family was alone when they went out. She took Saffie along with her on the long, uncomfortable ride to the shipping office.

Halfway through the second railbus trip, she felt the sensation again of being stared at. She glanced at her fellow passengers in the worn plastic seats. None of them looked sinister enough to be generating the acute discomfiture she was suffering. She glanced down at the great black dog to see if Saffie had sensed anything. Saffie returned her gaze blandly and went back to studying ankles.

As soon as the bus stopped, Shona attached herself to a group of travelers and followed them into the main terminus. The feeling of being stared at didn't go away. She was being followed.

Glancing into any shiny surface she passed, Shona tried to spot her pursuer. No face stood out in the crowd. Who was there? Male or female? What was that person after? Robbery? Rape? She changed direction suddenly, pulling the protesting dog after her into the ladies' room.

As soon as she dropped into a chair in that sanctuary, she realized she couldn't stay there forever. It made her angry to be frightened into acting like a hunted creature. She got her breath, then marched purposefully out of the ladies' room, Saffie at her side.

The uneasy feeling returned as soon as she was out the door. Shona plunged into the thickest part of the crowd, aiming for a tall security agent she could see standing beside an escalator in the heart of the building.

"Officer?" Shona said, tapping the tall woman on the arm. "Can you help me? I'm trying to get back to the reservations office, and I'm disoriented in this mob."

The agent glanced down at Shona and her dog, and smiled. "Sure. It's through that hall, and down the corridor on the right."

Shona peered between seething shoulders and saw nothing but more moving bodies. "That hall? Which corridor?"

The woman realized the great difference in their heights; neither did she miss the furtive glances Shona was sending around as she spoke. The small woman was afraid of something. "Never mind. I'll take you over there. I'm due for a break." She spoke to the radio on her shoulder and beckoned Shona beside her into the crowd. In the company of armed security, Shona felt the unwanted presence depart, passing by her unseen.

While the guard bought herself a coffee, Shona messaged home from a public booth to have one of her cousins waiting for her when she arrived back. She was determined not to let the unseen pursuer get her alone for a moment. Perhaps it was connected

42

with Chirwl's abduction, that the man who took him was angry he had been rescued. Shona refused to be his second victim.

The security agent escorted her all the way to the reservations hall and gestured her forward. "There you go. Even someone as short as you could find it from here."

Grinning, Shona thanked her, and joined the queue.

The reservations clerks looked more harassed than ever. Shona explained her situation to the thin man at the desk, who kept shaking his head.

"There has to be another seat on one of these flights out," Shona pleaded. "Three days ago you had plenty of seats."

"Not one. That was three days ago, Doctor. We're going crazy here trying to accommodate all the people who want to leave before the law takes effect," the reservations clerk said. His thinning brown hair was mussed, reflecting his distraction. "I don't think there's anything, including unheated steerage. I don't think I could get you off here if you flapped your arms and—Wait you *have* a reservation." He glared at her accusingly. "Why didn't you say something about it? You leave ten days from today."

"I do?"

"You're Taylor, Dr. Shona, aren't you?"

Shona's mouth dropped open. "My original reservation! They didn't cancel it."

"No, ma'am. There's a surcharge payable on the balance because you didn't pay your fare by the deadline, but it's still good."

"Oh, I'll pay it," Shona said happily. "I don't care, so long as I get to Earth." She gave him her credit number, and watched as he tapped it in. He nodded sharply, handing her the replacement disk ticket.

"Have a nice trip," he said, harried but sincere. Shona smiled at him, and retreated.

The nice security officer was still waiting by the door. She walked Shona and Saffie to the railbus stop and waited, chatting with them until the transport arrived. She responded to Shona grateful wave with a nod, and disappeared into the mass of arriving passengers. Shona stayed close to police officers or transport security personnel until she arrived at her stop.

Wrenn was impressed by the woman's cleverness in keeping out of his grasp, making sure she had protectors or witnesses all the way home. Well, she couldn't evade him later. He had plenty of time to prepare for his next attempt.

CHAPTER

SHONA REARRANGED THE safety straps one more time to keep them from cutting into her belly and shoulders. The manufacturers were *not* thinking of pregnant women when they designed safety harness for space travel. That might make a good topic for the computer bulletin board she subscribed to, or perhaps a subject for a short documentary Susan could make. It was the perfect low-budget idea. She thought of using the seat's communications/entertainment ensemble to send a message to Susan, then remembered she hadn't yet applied for beacon privileges. That would have to wait until they were spaceborne.

The spaceliner was waiting for a few more shipments to be taken aboard before it lifted. Shona wondered for the tenth time, looking around at her irritated fellow passengers, why the spacelines always demanded that passengers show up hours before takeoff, then subjected them to delay after delay.

Chirwl, rejoicing in the first freedom he'd enjoyed since the kidnap attempt, was playing peekaboo with the small child in the seat behind him. The little girl seemed delighted with the animate stuffed animal chittering at her and twitching its whiskers.

Harry, Saffie, and the other animals were in live storage in a compartment down the corridor from Shona's sleeping compartment. She would have preferred to spend takeoff in the cabin with them, reassuring them that all was well, but regulations demanded all passengers remain in the launch lounge and all nonsentient animals remain in crash cages until the vessel had left Martian gravity. Making it easier for the staff, Shona fumed quietly, not the paying customers' comfort. Well, the ship was packed. As the clerk in the shipping office had promised, there was not a single empty seat.

The faint hum of servomotors vibrated through her feet, which were planted against the fixed metal leg of the table before her. More loading. They had to carry a lot of cargo to Earth; it helped offset passenger fees. It was one reason Shona chose this shipping line in the first place: it was the cheapest line that still had a decent reputation for safety.

Far away, she heard a tiny boom of metal striking hollow metal, and felt the vibrations as the entire ship shook gently. Something heavy was being set down inside the hold. The male passenger across from her met her eye and gave a wry smile.

"Citizens and guests," said a lugubrious voice over the public address system, "you are most welcome on the M.S. *Cloverleaf*. Please make certain your harnesses are securely fastened. We will be underway in a matter of moments. Cabin stewards, prepare the cabins for departure."

An attractive older woman in a pale green uniform, the steward for Cabin D, walked forward with the deliberately exaggerated pace that revealed she was wearing magnetic-soled boots. With a smile at the passengers, she opened a beige plastic hatch at the front of the cabin, and twisted a control. Shona wiggled to equalize the pressure of the straps as the seats all rotated to face upward toward the ceiling for liftoff. The steward smiled down at Shona as she passed by, making her way back to her own seat.

"I'll get you something to drink as soon as we're moving," she said, kindly. "Do you need a pillow for your back?"

"No, thank you," Shona smiled back. "I'll try not to be too much trouble."

"It's a pleasure to help," the attendant said. She gave Shona a thirty-second lesson on how to operate the hydraulic cushion system in her chair, which inflated or deflated pads. Then she clumped back to her seat and strapped herself in.

Shona glanced over Chirwl's head at one of the four great ports that served their cabin. The dome halves surrounding the ship were moving back, parting like transparent curtains to reveal the stony surface of Mars and the dark sky that surrounded it.

"It is most astonishing, is it not?" Chirwl said, awed.

Shona nodded appreciatively, catching glimpses of stars in the blackness. "Most astonishing. Looking out at space makes me feel so small."

She braced herself for takeoff, a sensation of anticipation and pressure she enjoyed.

The great engines fired, making the whole ship vibrate subtly. Chirwl looked to her for reassurance. She reached out to touch his forelimb.

"This is very loud," he said. "The engines are preparing for their great effort. They are complaining. Listen."

There was another boom deep inside the ship, an off-tone. Before Shona had a chance to think what that meant, the vessel slewed impossibly sideways and tipped, slowly, majestically, over until it struck the dome wall. It leaned there, twitching like a drunk, as the engines were abruptly cut. The passengers screamed.

"Passengers," the loudspeaker trumpeted, the announcer's voice still calm. "We are having technical difficulties. Please, remain in your seats."

"That's more than technical difficulties," the man in front of Shona shouted, struggling to get out of his prone chair. "Let me out of here. I've got to get to Earth. I'll find a ship that doesn't fall over."

"Sir." The steward clumped over to him in her heavy boots and took the panic-stricken man firmly by the shoulder. She eased him back into the couch. "Please stay here. You'll be safe and comfortable. I'll try to find out what's happening."

Shona was impressed by the woman's command. The trouble-maker grumbled, but he relaxed and sat back. Shona herself was shaking. What had happened? It was no more conceivable that a spaceliner would fall over than a building would. Outside the port, she could see reflections on the translucent walls of revolving red and yellow lights heralding the arrival of emergency vehicles. Whatever had happened was serious. She wanted to get out. Chirwl craned to see around him, frightened by the peculiar behavior of the machine. She tried to reassure him, but her voice kept cracking.

A hand touched her on the shoulder. She looked up into the face of the steward.

"Dr. Taylor, can you come with me, please?"

Shona struggled to sit upright as the steward operated the controls on the side of her seat. "Certainly. What can I do?"

"There have been some injuries," the woman said, assisting her to her feet. "Please follow me. You're needed."

"Shall I go along?" Chirwl asked.

"No," the steward said with a kind smile. "You won't be needed just now. Please stay here where you'll be safe."

Her fellow passengers watched curiously as Shona was led away. She could see the shock she felt reflected on every face.

They stopped in an alcove to put on pressure suits before descending in the crazily slanted elevator to the aft section of the ship. Shona realized the steward's calm demeanor was a firmly held mask. Inside, she was more terrified than her passengers, because she knew what had really happened.

'Some injuries' was a pathetic understatement. Shona felt her heart twist at the burned and torn bodies set out in rows along the edge of a sloping corridor whose far end was simply not there. Kneeling beside them was a plump man in a medical tunic and two younger men in nurse's uniforms under their transparent pressure suits.

With difficulty, the dome, easily seen through the torn and seared wall of the ship, had been levered closed again. Many of those hurt were also suffering from cold and lack of oxygen from exposure to the Martian landscape. Martian police were already all over the scene, investigating the explosion. Through echoes of sirens and the grinding of machinery, Shona heard speculations from those around her ranging from sabotage to poor maintenance to pilot error.

"The ship just imploded," said an officer wearing lieutenant's stripes. He grasped her arm and helped her safely down to the groaning wounded. "One moment all the engines were firing normally, the next *whomph*! Part of the ship just seemed to disintegrate. It was quiet—you could hardly hear it in the control room. Five of my crew are missing," he finished bitterly. "Vanished like boojums."

"A quiet explosion?" Shona repeated, disbelievingly.

She had no more time to work out what that meant. As soon as someone gave her a medical kit, she was hurrying from one victim to the next, stanching bleeding and assessing burns, broken bones, and slashed flesh. One poor female crew member had lost her arm to the shoulder in the explosion. It was cleanly severed, and the woman was talking very calmly to the attending nurse as if nothing extraordinary had happened. Shona could tell she was deeply in shock.

A man on a makeshift stretcher beside the amputation case had burns all over the left side of his body.

"I was facing that way when the bulkhead blew. There was no warning," he said, eyes wide with disbelief. "No warning at all."

Together she and the *Cloverleaf*'s medical staff worked to stabilize those who were most severely injured, awaiting ambulances from the Space Center facility. Four crewmen were dead, pitiful burned bundles hastily covered by firecloths. Others began to scream as their numbed nerve-endings came once again to life. Shona tried to ignore the wails and moans around her, and concentrate on saving lives.

"I have never seen a burndown like that in my life," a firefighter said, kneeling across from her to help strip away melted pressure-suit plastic from a woman's ribs. The patient was contorted in a fetal knot muttering to herself, refusing to acknowledge anything but her agony. "The whole lower fin and engine section melted, right into the pad."

By then, the crew was evacuating passengers and luggage to the terminal building. Rumor had fled up the levels of the ship, and everyone was talking at once, nearly drowning out the insistent public-address system.

"Passengers will return to the waiting lounge. Another ship will be arriving in six hours to accommodate passengers in need of immediate transport to Earth. Others who can wait will be put up at the Martian Dome Hotel until we can take you to your final destination."

Hearing that, Shona stood up with difficulty on the sloping floor, and turned to find the lieutenant to inform him that she needed to be carried on the substitute ship to Earth. The woman with the severed arm clasped her pants leg and hung on.

"Please, don't go," she begged Shona. "Help me. What happened to me?"

"I've got a bleeder here!" the other male nurse shouted. A spray of blood appeared suddenly over his head—a ruptured artery on the patient he was assisting. Shona turned the anguished woman over to the attending nurse and hurried over to help with the bleeder.

"Dr. Taylor?" It was her cabin steward. "They're beginning to board the substitute ship. I've seen to it that the ottle, your luggage, and your animals have been taken off the *Cloverleaf*. Do you want them put on the *Brigane?* It's in Bay Eighteen."

Shona looked around at the chamber, which had become a makeshift infirmary. She had been doing everything from triage to minor surgery for hours. Even with the influx of doctors and medical technicians from the Center, she still had her hands full. "I hadn't realized I'd been here so long. When is liftoff?"

"As soon as everyone's on. Perhaps twenty minutes."

The young doctor stood up, peeling off the disposable gloves. The wounded were still coming in. Many of them had been waiting for hours for care. Torn between the reflex that told her to go, and the need to help here, where there was a genuine emergency, Shona made her choice. There had been extensive casualties outside the ship as well. There were never enough doctors; it was unlikely anyone would arrive to replace her for hours. She couldn't let people die for something that was her personal need. Shona shook her head.

"No. Would you phase see to it that the ottle and my animals are taken to the Medical Center office? The receptionist's name is May. She'll look after them until I can get free. Explain to Chirwl where I am and what I'm doing. I'm still needed here,"

48

Shona said regretfully. The steward's face showed surprise, and admiration. "I'll take the next flight out."

"All right, Doctor. I'd be happy to do as you wish. And . . . thank you," she said, touching Shona gratefully on the arm.

Wrenching on a fresh pair of sterile gloves, Shona went back to her patients, conscious only that the sirens had stopped at last.

Many hours later the exhausted medical staff made their way down to the Medical Center's showers to clean off the blood and dust. Shona had spent the last hours of surgery sitting down. Her back and legs already under strain from the extra weight she was carrying, had gradually become numb. The *Cloverleaf*'s physician had departed with the transferees aboard the *Brigane*, apologizing for not being able to stay on.

Sixty-eight people had been seriously wounded or killed in the explosion. The police and fire department were still unable to put a finger on exactly what had caused the explosion, but they had agreed it was deliberate sabotage. The spaceline's representatives were running all over the Space Center wringing their hands, but fortunately had stayed out of the way of the doctors.

The moment she was free Shona put in a call to the line's office, requesting a seat on the next transport to Earth, scheduled for two days from then. It would give her time to recover a little from the heavy day's work.

The return message was waiting for her when she stopped at May's desk to reclaim the menagerie.

"What do you mean you can't find a seat for me?" Shona demanded angrily of the company representative. Even though he was safely miles away from her at the other end of the transmission circuit, the clerk shrank visibly from her wrath. "I gave up my place on this ship to help your crew in an emergency," she went on. "It's not a lot to ask to make my ticket good on another flight within the next two days."

"No question about it," the man said. "In fact, we're comping your ticket, Doctor. You'll be getting a full refund on your credit account. We're very grateful for your help. It isn't a question of whether we will honor your ticket, but when. All seats for the next flight are full. We have a waiting list, but I can almost promise you that under the circumstances there will be no cancellations. Circumstances similar to yours," he finished delicately.

"No good deed goes unpunished," May said behind her, with a sigh.

"I could go as a medical assistant," Shona suggested, starting to feel desperate. "Consider my situation. If I don't leave in the

49

next two days, I can't go at all. I'm being penalized because I considered it more important to stay with my patients than to take a cushy flight to Earth."

The clerk looked truly sorry. "I wish I could help you. There are no spaces left or you'd have one. All four of our medical crew on that flight are emigrating to Earth, too. All I can do is put you at the head of the waiting list. It is the only thing we can do. The line is grateful, I promise you. I simply can't create a space out of thin air. I've been turning away passengers for days now."

"I'll offer a reward," Shona said, thinking quickly. "Will you do that for me? Contact the passengers. I'll pay the entire fare plus a reward for anyone willing to exchange their reservation on that flight for one immediately after."

The clerk nodded. "That's a good idea. It might work. I'll be in touch, Doctor. I'm instructed by our management to give you our sincere thanks."

"They could show their thanks a little more substantively," May said cynically as Shona rang off. "Well, now all you have left to do is wait."

Two days passed with no communication from the spaceline except for an apology. The second flight departed as scheduled. The clerk had found no takers for Shona's exchange scheme, no matter how much of a financial sweetener he offered. Shona felt despair, but she was determined not to give up. In defiance, she sat up past midnight making plans as the deadline passed and the Child Protection Act went into effect.

Senator Chara Ulsuekke had a reputation for straight-speaking, which made Shona pleased to be in her constituency. A clear-eyed woman in her early fifties, Ulsuekke stood several inches taller than Shona, and had long hands with square palms, whose strong grip was intended to give one confidence in her character. "When you called my aide for an appointment, I reviewed the text of the new child protection law. I have no quick solution to offer you. I'm afraid that in the short term there's nothing I can do to help."

"Senator, there must be something," Shona said, trying to keep the agitation she felt from strangling her. "My baby is due in four months. As soon as it's old enough, I want to go back to the job I was trained for. This law—I can't understand how it got passed at all—makes it impossible for me to do my work. My baby will have to stay on Mars until it reaches its majority, and I'll have to stay here with it. The law interferes significantly with what I want to do with the rest of my life, how I

50

support myself. I would be grateful for any suggestions you have."

Ulsuekke clasped her hands on the desktop. "I'm very sorry. The law was designed only with well-being for all children in mind."

"I can't stay here on Mars forever," Shona countered unhappily. "My job is out there, with the colonies."

The senator brightened. "I must have misunderstood your concerns, Dr. Taylor. Are you asking if you can go out with your settlement group? The exception is written into the bill. You can depart as scheduled. When do you leave?"

"No, no, I'm only with one group for about six months at a time, depending on the situation," Shona explained. "I'm a medical consultant, sent in to help establish a colony on a healthy footing."

"That is just the kind of chopping and changing that the bill was designed to prevent," the senator replied, and smiled apologetically at Shona. "I'm sorry to word it like that but it's exactly what my learned colleague, Senator Culsen, would say."

"You're forcing other people like me to choose between family and career. That's not fair. This is government interference at its worst!"

The official sighed. "You are absolutely correct, Dr. Taylor, but I don't see at present that being right will help you at all. I voted against this bill, but we were defeated, albeit narrowly. The council is very heavily conservative this session."

"Should I get a lawyer and try to get the legislation overturned by the Judiciary?"

Ulsuekke shook her head. "I'm afraid it wouldn't be a speedy process. You'd have to start the challenge as a test case at the local court levels and move up. It might almost be faster to wait until the child is born and grows up."

Shona groaned as the thought of remaining planetbound for nineteen years hit her; she was equally distressed by the concept of being a test case. "Haven't other professionals and colony technicians complained to you?" she asked. "Some of us might have delayed starting families, or ruled them out altogether, if we can't never leave Mars at all while our children are growing up."

"That's not strictly true," Ulsuekke pointed out. "You can share custodial duties with your husband. While he cares for your family, you are free to go where you please."

"That's impossible in my case," Shona said, shaking her head. "Gershom's an independent trader. He can't take long periods of time out of the middle of his trade runs. He'd lose all his business.

That's the reason we've both got to work. We're still paying off the mortgage on the ship."

"Then I see no alternatives open to you," Ulsuekke said, spreading her hands with an apologetic shrug. "We'll have to wait for a genuine challenge to the law's constitutionality."

Shona stood up, a resolution forming in her mind. "I'll get in touch with legal counsel anyway. There must be something I can do. Maybe I'll start a movement to get it overturned."

The senator stood up, too. She took Shona's outstretched hand in both of hers and shook it warmly. "Good luck to you. If there is any way I *can* help, please let me know."

Later that day, Shona sat in the kitchen of her aunt's dome, fiddling with a stylus and pad while Aunt Lal fussed over the hot element, making a pot of tea for the two of them. On the top of the pad's screen was the text of the Child Protection Law. Underneath it, she noted everything she thought was a weakness she might be able to attack. Reading legalese was more difficult than reading a medical text—at least there one knew that the vocabulary was the problem, full of archaic or artificial words. Here the very structure of the sentences twisted and turned like snakes that threatened to rear up and strangle her understanding.

"It must be possible to get this monster overturned," Shona said. She accepted the cup of tea with a self-deprecating chuckle. "It's funny, I was looking forward to the next two years here, and now that I know I can't leave, I've got to get away."

"Your father was like that." Aunt Lal put a small vial of pills on the table and sat down opposite Shona. "He could never stay in one place for long. That's what took him out to the end of nowhere, where he met your mother."

"Dremel's not the end of nowhere," Shona said, then sighed heavily. Saffie matched her with a noisy exhalation of breath, and sank to her belly under the table. "Right now, I'll admit, it feels incredibly far away." Shona reached down to scratch the dog's head.

"Good day," Chirwl said, waddling into the room and leaping fluidly onto an empty chair. "Did you suffer any luck?"

"No," Shona replied sadly. "I'm thinking of suing to become an exception to the law based on a prior contractual commitment and cite hardship, or restraint of trade. *Something*."

"I don't think you have a chance," Aunt Lal said with a firm shake of her head. "You know how it is with new laws. They like to enforce them to the letter for a while."

"I'll wait," Shona said. "I'm not going to let them ground me forever. Earth citizens can still travel with their children. Alpha parents aren't under any restraints like this one. I'm sure it's unconstitutional." Shona drummed impatiently on the pad with her fingertips. She'd been at the Space Center when luxury liners plying the solar system had called in at Marsport. Those ships were full of children. But it was no good appealing to the Martian legislature by arguing that it was done differently elsewhere. By the time any change came, if it did, she'd probably be a grandmother. The feeling of the dome walls looming around her was more sinister than ever, and it was still nearly four months before the baby was due. She shivered, then burst out in frustration, "How does the government know what would be best for my child? He'll have a nanny, and I'll be right there to nurture and love him, every day of his life. The only difference is *where* he'll be growing up."

"I do not understand how why they stop you from working with your children," Chirwl agreed. "You must feed them, so you must go with your job where it takes you to other stars."

Laurel glanced with alarm at the ottle, then said to Shona, "What's wrong with staying here? Here, you're drinking something. Take your vitamins." She pushed the small vial of pills toward Shona.

"I don't want my vitamins," Shona snapped, and abruptly mitigated her tone when she saw her aunt's shocked face. "I want to take my baby *with* me, Auntie. I've got a job to do. I want to do my job so I can support the baby, give it the things it will need." She thought desperately of all the things she wanted to show the baby while it was growing up, the joy and the freedom of traveling with Gershom on his ship, visiting strange colony worlds and learning about them as she worked, seeing Susan, and it came to her finally, with the full weight of unexpected self-pity, that neither she nor they would be able to do any of those things. She realized her aunt was still staring down at her. "I'm sorry," she said. Her voice graveled and caught.

Her aunt moved closer to her. "I know you're disappointed, but why not make the best of it? There's no job more important than the one you're doing now." She touched Shona's belly gently in emphasis. "Everything else is ephemeral, but what you do for your child lasts forever."

Shona considered the truth of that when she went to bed that night. She felt the small weight roll around in her increasingly large belly and poke her experimentally here and there with tiny extremities or a small but amazingly hard head. She felt petty, mean, and selfish. But when she thought of the great expanses of space, and the thrill of new worlds, she was torn. Above her, she could watch the stars through her skylight. Deimos paused in the gap, its reflected radiance lighting her room in a cold, white gleam, robbing it of all color. Shona shivered.

She could hear the alien chuckling to himself in the pouch on the wall of the lab, probably writing another of his dissertations about humanity on a chip of wood. He didn't understand her problem in being confined to Mars during her child's upbringing; to suggest to one of his kind that one couldn't go about business as usual with a litter clinging inside its marsupial-like pouch was to be met with incredulous surprise. Shona wished that human beings were as advanced in their thinking as the ottles were.

Little life, she thought as the baby shifted its weight across her body, *I don't hate you for stranding me here. It's not your fault. I know it would be perfectly natural for you to be raised in space. After all, both your parents have zero-gee feet. It's just those damned bureaucrats make me angry.* She sighed. *I'll be happier when you finally get here, and I can hold you in my arms. Less lonely, too.*

Without knowing when or if the odious ruling would ever be overturned, Shona's plans were scrap. The next morning she turned on her comm-unit and recorded an angry note to Gershom, telling him all about it.

" . . . I don't expect you to come and take custody from me so I can go off on missions, but I'm so angry being trapped by this miserable law that if I ever met this Senator Culsen I'd give him a booster shot he'd never forget. I think he's from the South Pole dome, and you know what they're like: frost for brains." With a wry smile, she realized she was raving, and hit the Erase button. *Well, now that I have that out of my system,* she thought, *I'd better start over, and try to tell him what's really wrong. Maybe he'll have some ideas.* She pictured Gershom's face, his eyes full of sweet sympathy. It was easier to frame her words with an image to focus upon.

"Hi, love," she began "I miss you dreadfully. The baby's fine. I've been feeling him or her doing aerobics against my diaphragm and spine, not to mention my bladder. Perry, my supervisor, is starting to kid me about all the time I spend in the lavatory. He asked me if I wanted to see patients in there, and spare myself the trip."

She took a deep breath, and plunged forward onto the difficult subject. "Gershom, I'm stuck. Due to circumstances beyond my control—what a cliché—I missed my flight off-planet before the Child Protection Act went into effect. No one seems to know what I can do to circumvent it. If you have any ideas, phase send them soonest. Housing's short, so I may be stuck here indefinitely. Aunt Lal's being very sympathetic, but I think the idea of having me *and* the animals *and* Chirwl, who's always made her nervous, and a new baby in this tiny room forever would drive her crazy. She'll never say so, but I can see how the concept horrifies her. In fact, it's not doing much for me. I'm used to more space than this. Yesterday I actually started to feel the walls closing in on me like the traps in the old two-dee thrillers. I'm starting a letter campaign to get the legislation cancelled." She typed in a command copying the text of the law into the body of her message. "You read it. I think you'll agree that it's unenforceable as it stands. I don't want to stay here forever, and right now, I feel trapped. I wish I could see you. I can't wait until you get back. All my love, always."

She sent the message off, and exited the electronic mail menu. Changing over to the bulletin boards, she canceled all the advertisements for traveling nannies, writing an apology to all the applicants, then concentrated on rewriting her ad for live-in child care. "When I get somewhere to live, that is," she said to the animals. "It's going to be cozy in here until then."

She scrolled to the housing-request bulletin board, and searched for her own ad among the throng. With a feeling of hopelessness, she read all the pleading ads for small domiciles, and realized that it would be a long time before anything became available at the size she needed. Multiple-children families would get easy priority over a woman with one child and a lot of pets. Reading the entry dates on some of these ads, Shona knew it could be years. Even with the exodus of families fleeing before the odious law went into effect, there were not enough homes to go around.

"Are there any advertisements of note?" Chirwl asked, popping his head out of his pouch. He had remained discreetly out of sight while she dictated her message. Shona was grateful for his tact.

"Just sour notes," she said. "Nothing."

All the plans she made had to be altered, at least for the short term. She had intended to settle down for a couple of years and be the perfect mother with minimal professional duties, then take jobs while the baby was growing to an age at which she could begin to take it with her. There was an undeniable risk in exposing a child to colony life, but she felt she would have been equal to the dual responsibilities of motherhood and work, and the child would have found it an interesting way to grow up. For survival's sake she had to get used to the idea that she and it would spend the next eighteen-plus years right here on mundane Mars. She determined to do what her aunt had suggested: make the best of it, and enjoy doing the most important job in the galaxy. In the meantime, she would continue to plan for her escape.

"Good morning to you," Jachin Verdadero greeted his staff of secretaries and his personal aide jovially on his way through the office suite to his private chambers. The chief executive officer of the Corporation liked to maintain amiable personal contact with his employees. He was a stickler for performance but let it be known that he was not without heart. He was famous not for dismissals of non-performing employees, but reassignment. "The right cog in the right wheel," Verdadero was fond of saying. "The right person for the right job." His aide smugly took that to mean that since he had lasted five years in the job he now held, Verdadero felt he was the correct man for a most prestigious and well-compensated position. Not that his boss didn't make uncomfortable demands on him from time to time, such as now.

"Sir," the aide called, as Verdadero was opening up his office. "The chief comptroller asked if he could see you today. It's about notes from First Mars Bank."

"I'm not in to him," Verdadero said. He added a wink and a nod, but his smile had faded. "Field him if he comes back, son. I haven't got time for that muddle today."

The aide groaned inwardly. Lately, when rumors were flying about the Corporation's possible insolvency, he was more in the firing line as Verdadero remained concealed behind his beloved trappings of power. The boss's justification was that he never dealt with rumor, only fact. His aide knew *he* had to handle the comptroller brilliantly, and divert him from bothering the boss again. Secret dealings, the existence of which Verdadero had hinted at, would come through before there was any real trouble with the Corporation's financing, not that the aide could see any downtown forecast in the ledger sheets. Even on its marginal investments the Corp always made money.

"Can you believe it?" Shona said, chatting with May and one of the other ground staff the next day at work. "I knew politicians could be manipulated, but this is the worst I've ever seen."

"We heard," said her supervisor, Dr. Perry Helsper. "So you're going to be with us for good?"

"No offense, Perry, but no," Shona said firmly. "It's an unfair law. I am determined to get it overturned, or at least have a big enough hole torn in it to let me squeeze through. There's nothing wrong with raising children in space! Some of the old colonies had babies conceived, born, and learning to read by the time their ships landed."

"Uh-huh," May agreed. "The original colony flight to Alpha saw the babies of those babies born out there."

"See what I mean?" Shona exclaimed. "I don't necessarily demand that I give birth in space, but I don't understand why it would be harmful for my baby to travel. I was a child when I came to Mars, and I didn't arrive by railbus."

Perry raised his hands helplessly. "You've got my vote, Shona. I already agree with you."

"And I bet they don't impound the parents with kids who visit Mars on Earthliners," May put in.

"Uh-uh, never," Perry agreed with a grin. "The cruise lines would take us right off the itinerary if we practiced ritual kidnapping. Tourist money's too important to the economy. Let me warn you not to use Earth as an example to the legislature, Shona. They hate having someone tell 'em that they do it a different way somewhere else. *Especially* not Earth."

"Oh, I know. Martian pride. Even my aunt bristles if I compare Mars to anyplace else in the galaxy." Shona gave them each a small data disk. "If you're really willing to help, I need you to send a voice-mail message to each of these legislators. The last two addresses are the Martian Medical Association, and the Association of Space Health Practitioners. I called both of them yesterday. It seems I'm not the only one complaining."

"Sure, honey. It must drive you crazy, getting stuck like this," May said sympathetically as Shona put her hand on the door of the changing room.

"I'm not stuck," Shona said cheerfully. "Just temporarily delayed, that's all." She pushed the door.

May smacked her own forehead with her palm. "Wait a second, don't go in the changing room yet. There's a maintenance worker cleaning up. Chemicals! Bad for the baby. Come and have a mineral water." Shona shrugged, and came back to sit beside Saffie, who watched the dressing-room door alertly.

In the uniform locker beyond the decontamination chamber, Wrenn heard the chatter of voices in the outer office. It sounded as if they would be a while working over the day's gossip. That gave him plenty of time to do his job. He enjoyed his work, and liked to do it well. Clad as he was in the coverall, boots, and gloves of a maintenance employee, he was as good as invisible. It wouldn't occur to them to be suspicious if they didn't recognize him. The support staff here was enormous and was shifted around almost daily. He'd watched the place for over a week before he decided the time was right to infiltrate. Suddenly, he heard the connecting door swing open. He turned away from the racks of clean environment suits toward the small hatch underneath the dressing-room disposer. He yanked it open and replaced the transparent red catchbox that was half-full of ashy debris with an empty container from his cart. No sound of footsteps approaching. They were all waiting politely out there for him to finish. He grinned.

Swiftly, he pulled a vial from an inside pocket of his coverall. No crude poisons or obvious toxins for him. It contained a bacterial culture that an old friend in the government Disease Control office guaranteed would do what he wanted. He couldn't afford to miss the right bird, so if a few more people got sick, he didn't care. His employer wouldn't mind, so long as his objective was achieved—same rule that had applied when he fuse-bombed the spaceliner only days before.

Wrenn smoothed dabs of the culture on the inside of the neckpiece, the helmet lip, the glove wrists, and the crotch of every suit on the rack. There was plenty left in the finger-long bottle when he had finished. If she didn't catch it this time, he'd just come back and start all over again. He put away the vial carefully. Wouldn't want to get sick himself. He nudged a hidden communication unit in the sleeve of his uniform, and spoke quietly.

A pleasant chime sounded over the intercom, followed by the voice of a young man. "Dr. Taylor, Dr. Taylor, report to Bay Three, please. Dr. Taylor."

"That's it," Shona said, putting down her untouched glass. "Never mind modesty. Duty calls." She scratched Saffie under the chin. "Be good, all right? I'll come and walk you at lunchtime." Saffie whined.

"Some emergency?" Perry said, standing up. "Why didn't they call me? May, call Bay Three and find out what's going on."

May put on her earpiece and manipulated the controls on her console. "No emergency, Doctor. The team in there was just wondering where she was. They're only two hours from liftoff."

"Cry Pete, is it that late?" Perry exclaimed, looking at his chronometer.

"Oh, never mind, Perry," Shona said. "The maintenance man has to be done by now." She pushed open the door of the changing room and brushed past a burly man with a cart just coming the other way.

"Oh, excuse me," she said. She hurried through the outer chamber of the locker room, put away her jacket and handbag, and headed for the decontamination booth. The white steam rose around her, and she shut her eyes. She felt a breath of air from the fans lift her thick hair and tickle the back of her neck.

The intercom chime sounded again. "Dr. Taylor, please report . . ." the announcer repeated.

"All right!" Shona shouted. "I'm coming!" She ran her hands through her hair and flapped the edge of her tunic to release some of the fumes, then headed for the rack of clean environment suits. She pulled down the first one that looked small enough for her not to swim in it. The page came once more while she was sealing up the suit's seams over her rounded midsection. She stamped into one of the shoe-covers, tugging upward on the heel to get it over her boot, at the same time pulling on one of her gloves with her teeth. As she ran for the sliding doors she fastened the other glove, and got the helmet on just before they opened.

Her equipment was waiting for her on a gurney inside Bay Three. She grabbed the cart with one hand and dragged it behind her toward the small crowd that was gathered in one corner of the huge chamber. Overhead, the ship loomed like an intelligent building, seemingly alive with all its lights blinking and engines rumbling as the last-minute checks were carried out.

"Dr. Taylor," the tannoy began.

"All right!" she shouted back. "I'm here!"

At the end of the day Shona picked up Saffie in the office and made her way toward the transport stop. Her back hurt. She'd been on her feet more than usual all day long, and she was looking forward to a quiet evening at home. Saffie slowed her trot to compensate for Shona's uncomfortable gait.

Aunt Lal opened the door before Shona had finished putting in the lock's code. She ushered the young woman through the hall and into the dining room, shushing her when she protested.

"There's a man here from the local government office to see you," Aunt Lal said in an undertone. "He's in the family room."

"What's he want?" Shona whispered.

"Something about the animals," her aunt hissed back. "He wouldn't tell me. I don't like to have anyone from Dome Hall bothering us. It makes me nervous. Has there been some trouble?"

"Not that I know of. I'd better find out," Shona replied. She patted her aunt's hand and walked through to the family lounge. There was a plump man in an official tunic sitting on the couch, watching tri-dee in a desultory fashion. Uncle Harry, mounted on his exerciser, ignored the visitor.

"Can I help you?" Shona asked in a friendly voice. The man glanced up at her. Underneath a balding pate with a few strands of black hair plastered across it, he had small but bright black eyes, a nondescript knob of a nose, and a clean-shaven, egg-shaped face with a short neck so completely encased by his tunic collar that his head looked like an old fashioned light bulb.

"Dr. Taylor?" Shona nodded. He eyed Uncle Harry, and Aunt Lal, who was hovering in the doorway. "Can I speak to you privately?"

"Why don't we move into my quarters?" Shona suggested. She led the way to her room, followed by Aunt Lal, who stopped at the head of the hall and watched anxiously after them.

In Shona's room, the man glanced at the cages, the cat's and dog's beds, and the ottle's pouch on the wall. Shona gestured to the desk chair, and sat down on her bed. Harry immediately jumped up beside her and climbed into her lap.

"Doctor, my name is Cole. I'm from Animal Control," the man began. "We've had a complaint from one of your neighbors about your pets. Hi ya, visitor," he said to Chirwl, who appeared from his pouch at the sound of a strange voice. "How ya doing?"

"Very well, I gratefully thank you," Chirwl said. He joined Shona on the bed. Cole watched the ottle curiously as Chirwl flipped over and rolled into his favorite position for watching, on the base of his curved spine. Shona cleared her throat to regain the official's attention.

"What *about* my animals?" Shona asked, suppressing the suspicion in her voice.

"Your neighbor complained about having animals living right here in the center of the main dome. Um, how many animals are there?"

"Ten right now," Shona said, enjoying the look of shock on the man's face. "But six of them are mice. They don't really take up much room, which is good, because I haven't any to spare, as you can see." She swept a hand around. "Who's the complaint from? I'd like to go and talk with him. After all, until I get a permanent housing assignment, we're going to be neighbors for the foreseeable future. I want to be friendly."

"The complaint was anonymous," the man said, with some embarrassment. "Voice-mail only, sent from a public booth."

"That's childish," Shona said, aghast. "It doesn't give me any way to find out what the real problem is. Or solve it."

"The problem," Cole stated heavily, "is that he feels these animals are using up valuable resources that might better be used by humans or other intelligent beings."

"Mr. Cole, these animals are not primarily pets. They're a part of my work, a team. I'm an environmental physician. I've already hashed this out with the Martian government. I will take them away from this neighborhood as soon as I have my own home."

"I know, Dr. Taylor," Cole said, drumming his fingertips nervously on the desktop. "I looked up your dossier. Please don't consider this harassment. I'm just letting you know about the complaint. Could you consider farming out your . . . er, team to a less central dome? They might be happier where they had more room."

"No, I *couldn't* consider it," Shona said patiently but definitely. "I'm as responsible to these animals as I am to Chirwl. They depend on me for protection. And they will have more room as soon as I get a housing assignment of my own. I won't just send them away because you've had an anonymous complaint. Especially since it was anonymous."

"I understand, citizen, but people are concerned about their quality of life."

"And they see my animals as interfering with that? Don't people have better things to do?"

Cole shrugged sheepishly. "I guess not, Dr. Taylor. It's my duty to report these complaints, and follow up alleged violations to see if they exist. You're a little cozy here," he said, looking around again at the room, and all the containers and boxes heaped up between the furniture. Shona hadn't bothered to unpack after her last attempt to fly out and now was a little embarrassed at the clutter. Harry chose this moment to leap off the bed and start a close examination of Cole's shoes. The official paid no attention. "Fitted together like a jigsaw puzzle in here, aren't you? I could tell without your records you've been in space. But I see nothing actually wrong. It's not like it was a signed complaint. We get these anonymous calls all the time, but we have learned to look into them."

"Shona has always been most kind and careful of our well-being," Chirwl interjected, "as well as the care of what the neighbors need."

"I'm sure she is," Cole said. "Sorry to trouble you all."

Shona saw him to the door, and out into the street. Aunt Lal pounced on her when she returned. "Was there any trouble?"

"No," Shona sighed. "They had an anonymous call about the menagerie. He was nice about it. He won't be back."

Aunt Lal let out an exaggerated breath of relief. "Thank goodness for that. Now come along, dinner's about ready."

"In a minute, Auntie. I've got to feed everyone."

She hurried back into her room, and slid the door shut behind her. Here was one more reason why she wished she could get off planet. Sooner or later someone was going to ask why she had such a large diagnostic team when she no longer had a job in which they might be employed. She picked up Harry and hugged him so hard he let out a squeak. She felt hemmed in by these regulations, and by small-minded people so afraid of being honest that they left unsigned messages.

She put Harry down, who washed his fur to show his affront. The corner of Shona's mouth lifted in a half-smile. "C'mon, kitty. Dinner." He brightened up, tail erect, and dove between her feet to be first at the food cabinet. She filled his bowl and Saffie's, and poured a little extra ration of chopped fruit into the feeding dishes of the rabbits and the mice. Marigold and Moonbeam hopped over and hunched over the dishes, chewing busily. Shona watched their twitching noses. Without a space job, they *were* no more than glorified pets. Numerous, superfluous, glorified pets. She longed to get out into space, and stop taking the temperatures of miners and farmers about to leave for points unknown. Suddenly, the baby kicked at her left side, and Shona smiled, looking down.

"Hello, there, you," she said, patting her belly.

At least one thing in her life was going all right.

CHAPTER

5

"THREE LAUNCHES TODAY, Perry?" Shona asked, inspecting the duty roster in the office a few days later. "What are we trying to do, corner the market out there?"

Her supervisor shrugged and lifted a sardonic eyebrow. "The ships are available, baby—er, present company excepted." He sketched a bow to her protruberant tummy. "That's all I know. When the bird is ready to lift, she's ready. It's the last part of the season. Things'll slow down dead pretty soon."

Shona sighed, back into the rhythm of her job once again. She had never lacked for application to do a job well once she set her mind to it. Her primary concern now was making things comfortable for the baby when it arrived. She still felt a little envious whenever a ship lifted without her, but now she looked at each mission from the point of view of her role as the last doctor to see them, resolving any medical emergencies and questions before they left, not as it would be with her along. She kept in close touch with her government and professional contacts in hopes that one day she would be able to join a mission again as she had originally trained to do, but in the meantime life had to go on.

She suited up and made her way, to Bay Five. The first colony group of the day was all men, going out to do the initial terraforming on an uncompromisingly unlovable landscape before their families could join them. It was strictly a volunteer station, and all the men were nervous. Most of them were young, on their first mission anywhere. That meant higher blood pressure and increased respiration and heart rate. Shona had to prescribe relaxation exercises for at least a dozen crewmen before she could get readings she found acceptable.

Maybe all the tension in the air was catching. Shona began to feel a little lightheaded. Suddenly, she felt as if she might faint. She broke away from examining the First Officer to go and sit

63

down on a bench at the side of the hangar. The baby felt heavy and strange in her womb. She put a hand to her side.

Abruptly, there was an audible *Pop!* and Shona felt a rush of warmth down her legs under her suit. It shouldn't be, but it was: her bag of waters had broken. She was beginning labor. "No," she whispered. "It's too soon."

As if to contradict her, all the muscles in her abdomen tightened, pressing at the weight in her belly. The shock on her face attracted the attention of the men. They gathered around her. "What's wrong?" the First Officer asked. "Is there anything we can do for you?"

Shona couldn't answer him right away. She felt weak and sick, and scared. Her voice, when she forced it out sounded as though it belonged to someone else. It was reedy and distant, not connected to her at all.

"Get another doctor," she said. A contraction hit her, and she whimpered.

"Is your baby coming, ma'am?" one young man asked her, kneeling at her side and taking her hand. He was no more than eighteen, with centimeter-long blond hair and earnest blue eyes. Another contraction hit and she squeezed his hand involuntarily.

"It's too soon," Shona repeated, almost to herself.

Perry and an emergency team appeared on the double. The crash cart, which was always on standby, was right behind them. Something was very wrong with the way her abdomen felt. Usually, the swollen uterus was a comfortable round whole that sat under her skin and pressed against her bladder. Now there was heat, and the sensation of illness.

Shona went through the next twelve hours in a daze. The contractions, coming faster and faster, curled her into a ball of pain on the gurney. When they rolled her onto a table in surgery, there was one more sharp pain low on her back, and then the tightness receded. She felt woozy and disoriented. Bright lights glared in her face until a voice, the speaker unseen, barked to shift them. Her skin was hot, too hot. Sweat dripped into her eyes, and she reached up to wipe it away. A cloth came from the shadows at the side of the table to clean her face. She tried to speak, and another contraction came, squeezing all the breath out of her.

There were more voices, all ordering her to do things at once. "Push!" "Open your mouth, please." "Tell me if this hurts." "Push again! Harder! Now, relax." Shona ordered herself to follow instructions, but her strength was going. She had a fever; she knew all the indications. Her mouth was dry, and no one would listen when she asked for something to drink. Her back hurt. More voices plagued her with questions.

"How many weeks along are you?"

"Twenty-two," Shona responded. The total didn't sound right to her, but she couldn't concentrate well enough to add up the weeks correctly.

"Could you have been exposed to radiation anywhere?"

"No! I've always been careful."

"Or a chemical?"

"No, that's my speciality. I haven't even taken analgesics."

"How long have you had this fever?"

"Fever? I—I don't know."

In between, there were the contractions, which interrupted all her thoughts.

And then, after a long time, a female voice asked, "Would you like to hold your baby?"

Though Shona's mind was spinning from the medication and fever, the question got her attention. Her baby was born! Through a haze, Shona tried to sit up. "Oh, yes." A figure stepped forward and steadied her shoulders. Something soft was placed behind her, bracing her back. She held out her arms eagerly.

Instead of a warm, plump, red-faced armful, the masked doctor held out to her a fold of cloth on both hands. On it was a tiny form, like a doll. It was perfect in every detail, but so small and so still. It was a cruel joke. Shona looked up in shock at the masked face. The eyes regarded her sadly. "I'm sorry, dear. It was a boy. We did everything we could to save him."

"What happened?" Shona whispered, feeling all the blood drain from her face. She knew it was normal procedure to let a mother see the remains of the fetus. It made it easier for her to accept the loss. She was suddenly chilled. There were too many people standing over her, all strangers.

"Your child was stillborn. There was nothing we could do," the obstetrician said gently.

Another masked face, a man, spoke. "You were ill, Doctor. An oldie but a goodie: listeriosis. We got a positive culture from the lab. It's almost always fatal when transmitted across the placenta to a fetus from the mother."

"How?"

"Unpasteurized milk is usually the worst culprit," the masked man stated. "Have you had any suspect dairy products in the last few days? Most likely the exposure was very recent." Shona shook her head.

"I haven't been able to eat anything but unspiced nutri for months," she said with a bitter laugh.

"A dirty isolation suit?" the obstetrician suggested. "Inhalation of dust from a contaminated source?"

Shona shook her head disbelievingly. "I wear a fresh, filtered helmet and sterilized suit at work every day. There have been no cases that I know of there or anywhere else. I don't understand how I could have contracted it." Shona looked at the tiny figure on the cloth in her hands, willing it to move, breathe, do anything. The others stared down at her in silence. She began to cry, sobs knotting the place just under her heart.

"I sent a message to Gershom," Aunt Lal said, sitting at Shona's bedside the next day. She held Shona's hand, squeezing it now and again. Shona was grateful for the human contact. It anchored her from drifting away in a sea of misery and sedatives. Her whole body was numb. "He ought to know as soon as possible."

"Thank you," Shona said quietly. She still felt exhausted from the birth and the curettage which followed to free the placenta from her uterus wall. Laurel went on, talking almost to hear herself. Shona didn't protest. Anything that took her thoughts away from her tragedy was welcome.

"There's a message on your unit from him, and a couple from Susan. I sent her a quick burst too. I hope that was all right?" Shona nodded, staring at the wall. "Do you want them transferred to your reader here?" her aunt asked, gesturing to the unit that sat beside the bed on a high table which could be swung across over Shona's lap. "Your doctor wants you to stay here a few days until you're better."

"No, don't send them," Shona said. "I'll be home soon."

"Good. I've been feeding the animals. They miss you. Your cat's been underfoot all day long. I know when I get home he'll smell your scent on me, with his keen nose, and then he'll drive me wild all day long. We're all concerned about you."

"I did everything I could to have a healthy baby. I took my vitamins," Shona said weakly, almost talking to herself—but there had been that one day when she had refused. That one dose of vitamins! Had that weakened her resistance enough to bring on listeria? She panicked, wondering if she was guilty.

Another squeeze brought her back to the present. "I know you did, sweetheart," her aunt assured her. "You were taking good care of yourself. This is one thing you could not possibly have foreseen. No one is blaming you." Laurel was positive that the only way to rejoin life was to turn away from the past and go on. She picked

66

up the life-sized hospital hologram sitting on the bedside table. "Look at this. It's disgusting. They holographed that poor little baby, as if you wanted to be reminded of what he looked like. I cleared up all the new mothers' magazines you've been bringing home and gave them away, and I packed up the baby clothes for you. They're in a storage box." Laurel could see the tears starting under the girl's eyelids, and reached forward to kiss her on the cheek. "You're welcome to go on living with us."

"Thank you," the listless voice said carefully.

"I'd better let you rest now. I'll come by again tomorrow. Is that all right? Good. I'll see you. You get some sleep."

After her aunt left, Shona lay on her back and stared at the ceiling, ignoring the tears that leaked out of the corners of her eyes and ran into her hairline. Laurel was wrong. Shona did want to remember what the baby had looked like, and what had happened to him. She *needed* to. If she didn't know, if the hospital had swept the still form away before she had seen it, she might wake one night wondering where he was, flailing around for him in a panic. It was better, if more painful, this way. She glanced at the holo. The little face was still, serene, the hairless head bent over a tiny fist. There was no way to tell yet if it would have resembled her or Gershom.

If she had even suspected what would befall her if she got pregnant here, she'd have kept her knees together until Gershom made space again. First had come the hateful legislation which trapped her planetbound, then Chirwl's disappearance, followed by the endless disasters with her attempts to fly out, and ending with the horror of losing her child whom she and Gershom had wanted with all their souls. She was free once again, but she hardly had the heart to do anything with her renewed liberty.

"Sss-Shona?"

She opened her eyes to a dark brown mass, an inch or two away from her nose. Two bright orbs opened and shut, and that gave it enough definition for her to recognize Chirwl. "You're too close," she said peevishly.

The ottle backed away a little. He was sitting on her bedside table. "I asked to see you. There was the question if I would be safe until you were free of the disease, but Alien Relations came to meet with your doctors and now all seems to be well. We miss you," he said, cocking his head at her. "My friends Saffie and Harry especially. They seek you every day. Angie who brought me here said the cub died. Is this him?" He picked up the holo in his pawlike hands and turned it over. "Very fine specimen. You have my most sincere sorrinesses."

"Thank you," Shona said politely. "Would you mind if we didn't talk about it?"

"As you wish, as you wiss-sh!" the ottle assured her, whistling slightly. Recognizing a taboo subject, he tactfully put the small image behind him. "What would you like to discuss? You have viewscreen. News of the world?"

"No. Please." There was no escape from killing and death out there. Shona wanted to be insulated from the galaxy for just a little while longer.

"Then, shall I tell you of my latest research?" Chirwl asked eagerly. "I have been making many inquiries, none of which answer my question. When machinery becomes human's whole way of existence, does human cease to have reality of its own, or does it instill in machinery its own existence?"

Intrigued in spite of herself, Shona pondered. "I don't know. I've never thought about it before."

Chirwl pointed a foreclaw at her and shook it. "And well you might should have. There are many of your fellow beings, landing and living on places where no beings exist, and relying all on machines. Is this right?"

"That's right."

"No, you mean by right, *correct*. I mean *appropriate*. In our language," Chirwl said severely, "words mean what we say. This business of synonyms is as dangerous as your reliance on machinery."

Shona chuckled. Chirwl was terrified of using machines, and would wait for hours for her to operate one rather than touch it himself. "That's pretty deep thinking from someone who eats cat chow." The ottle and his firm contention of how the universe should work was better medicine than ten thousand pills and potions. It was the first time she had laughed since the tragedy of the delivery.

Within eight days after the delivery the infection had cleared up, and Shona was told she was discharged. The doctors at the Medical Center assured her that she would recover completely. "You should start exercising. That will help put you to rights more swiftly," said Dr. Robin, the woman obstetrician. Without her mask, she was young, not more than five or six years older than Shona, but the no-nonsense expression she wore and the firm wave of her blond hair bespoke a dedicated professional. "Begin slowly, with low-impact aerobics or just brisk walking. Don't tire yourself out, and you'll be back to normal before long."

"What about babies?" Shona asked, starting to put her clothes on. "Will I be able to have more children?"

Dr. Robin was kind but firm. "I'll have to be frank about the possibility you can't. There was a lot of damage to the endometrium and copious bleeding when we removed the placenta. That can happen during curettage, as I'm sure you know. There may be no place large enough for a new placenta to adhere. When you come in for your next examination in six weeks, we'll know more." She pulled her computer pad to her and wrote on it with her stylus. "I'm prescribing therapy for you rather than antidepressants. You can have them if you need them, but I'd prefer you tried on your own without chemical help. You're going to feel isolated and alone. I want you to know that there are people here to support you. Not just the father and your family and friends, but myself and the medical staff. Don't turn away help. You need to mourn, and then you need to get on with your life. I would suggest that you go back to work immediately. Having something to do will help you to adjust."

"Take my mind off it?" Shona threw back bitterly.

Dr. Robin stopped, and held the stylus balanced between her forefingers. "No, we'd never suggest that. But you have to keep going, live your own life. It hasn't ended."

Even if your baby's has . . . The phrase hovered unspoken in the air between them. Shona felt the stab of guilt and pain, but she nodded. Intellectually, she knew that the doctor was right. Emotionally, it was hard to make herself believe it.

"Be good to yourself. You are not evil. Nothing that you did caused your fetus to die. Listeria is notorious for causing premature labor and miscarriage, without other damage to the mother. You probably didn't experience any symptoms at all until the delivery started."

Shona shook her head, ghost-eyed. "No, I didn't."

"You see?" the doctor said. "That's typical. I'll see you in six weeks. Take care."

Shona was not reassured. What she had done wrong was to come back here, to Mars. Mars killed her baby. There was nothing she could have done to save it. She blamed the repressive planet that held her hostage. She hated the place now, and couldn't wait to leave. She didn't want to stay, and there was nothing to keep her here any longer. She felt horribly alone. Gershom wasn't due back for more than two months.

But that was destructive thinking, and her doctor had forbidden it. Instead, Shona made a positive affirmation. Her voice was soft

69

at first, but it became stronger as she remembered the oath she had taken when she first passed the boards. It was no longer required, but Shona loved the ringing words of it, and had recited it at the ceremony with the like-minded half of her graduating class. "I swear by Apollo the healer, and Asclepius, and All-Heal . . ."

Speaking the firm phrases of the ancient oath actually made her feel better. Keeping it in her mind to lock out the depression and self-pity, she packed up her small bag and the hologram of her dead son, and went home to her animals.

CHAPTER

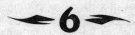

AS SOON AS she was up to it, she looked over her message file on her personal console. She erased without reading or answering all the replies in her file from nannies and child-care centers. She couldn't face them without tears. All at once, she felt as if her future had vanished, leaving her adrift with duties and responsibilities, but no reason for performing them. To Susan's anxious message of love and concern she replied briefly, promising more news later on.

To reply to Gershom was much more difficult. She tried to begin her message several times, and ended up staring into the screen blankly and bursting into tears whenever she attempted to speak. Instead of suppressing her grief, she switched off the unit and allowed herself a good cry. The words came more easily thereafter.

"I keep looking around because I feel like I've dropped something. It's a shock to have the bulge and the weight suddenly vanish from my abdomen, as if I was never pregnant at all. I wake up sometimes wondering if the whole thing wasn't a long dream that ended with a nightmare. He was company for me, you know, since you couldn't be here," Shona confided sadly, thinking of the tiny, still figure she had held only once in her hands. "I talked to him. He was excited when I was excited, playful and active when sometimes I wished he would calm down and go to sleep so I could sleep. The therapist is a nice, sympathetic woman. She encourages me to talk, just talk. I think it's helping. I feel like I'm running in place here. I wish you were closer to home. I haven't thanked you yet for your sweet message while I was in the hospital. It was so good to hear your voice, just when I needed it. I'm sorry I sound so low. I'll get over it soon." Shona found that her words sounded irresolute, even to her. She forced some gaiety into her voice, and closed the message. "All my love to you. Fly safely. I'll be waiting to hear from you next. Give my best to the others."

• • •

Senator Ulsuekke paid her a personal visit expressing her sympathy for Shona's loss.

"It is no consolation, but you'll be pleased to know that I and a number of my colleagues are proposing an amendment to the Child Protection Law. With your permission, we'd like to add your name to the list of citizens supporting our effort. I'm very grateful you brought your concerns to my attention. With luck, we may be able to get our bill into committee next session." The tall woman held out her hands apologetically. "Not that it means the bill will pass with any speed, but we are trying. If you let me have your communication number, I will make sure my secretary informs you whenever there's movement."

Shona thanked her, but she had little energy to rejoice at having gotten some action going against the unfair law. What she wouldn't have given to be still safely carrying her child, even if it meant remaining on Mars for years!

At work, Perry and the others treated her with kindness, providing a comforting shoulder or a sympathetic ear when she needed one.

"If you prefer to do only lab work for a while until you get your strength back, I can arrange it," Perry offered on her first morning back.

"No, thank you," Shona said. "I want to keep busy. I need to."

"Well, there aren't many ships in the schedule," the supervisor pointed out frankly. "Fiscal-year-ending is always the slow season. In fact, I'm overstaffed for the next several weeks. You weren't here last year, but I had eight doctors playing bridge in the locker room for two weeks at the height of the slump. If you wanted to take some time off, you could have it."

"No!" Shona exclaimed. "That's the last thing I want. Anything, Perry."

"If the government program can't use you, the G.L.C. always can," offered a burly man who'd been listening quietly to their exchange. The badge on his tunic identified him as a Corporation doctor. He tipped up his bottle of mineral water to drink the last ounce, and put the empty in the case on the floor. "We don't waste proven talent."

"We don't give our employees busy work when there's nothing legitimate to occupy them," Perry retorted good-naturedly. "Corporation short of money to claim jump? You have as few transports going out this season as we have, Dr.—er—Crane," he said, leaning close to read the man's I.D. card.

72

"I know." The man called Crane shrugged his massive shoulders and allowed a slight smile to crease a face that might otherwise be characterized as humorless. "Who knows what's going on in the finance department. Can't blame me for trying to recruit, Dr. Helsper. I hate to see talent go to waste." He stood up. "Got to go crank the perpetual motion machine. Morning, citizens."

Perry gave Shona the pick of the assignments that were available, but each lasted only hours over a few days, until the ships lifted. She threw herself into each job with energy, experiencing dread as each came to its inevitable end which would leave her with nothing else to occupy her. She transferred to the chem lab, running tests on biosamples submitted by prospective colonists and doing double-checks on research sent back to Mars by labs on other worlds.

It was horrible, prolonging her tenure here, since there was nothing now to keep her. None of the work she was doing would tax the abilities of a first-year medical student. Only a couple hours after the beginning of her shifts, she was back in the waiting room, passing time with May, Perry, and Dr. Crane. She didn't really feel needed, and she had too much time to think. Except to await Gershom, who expected to land close to the baby's original due date, still weeks off, Shona wondered why she was still on Mars at all. She had no need to stay.

Her aunt had called at lunchtime to say that Cole from Animal Control had returned, with another anonymous complaint, this time about Saffie.

"He claimed that neighbor said she was barking all night. I told him I never hear a thing from her," Aunt Lal said loyally. "She's a quiet dog. He went away again. I just thought you should know."

Shona thanked her and hung up. *I have* got *to get off this planet,* she thought, feeling threatened by the unknown people who could interfere with her life at their pleasure. It seemed an eternity before Gershom would arrive home. The wait was making her twitch with impatience. Impulsively, she stopped in at the Galactic government personnel office the next day after work, and requested immediate assignment to a colony project.

"Anything," she said, "so long as it leaves soon."

The personnel officer called up her file and reviewed it with a swift glance. "I've got one which would be most suited to your skills, Dr. Taylor. The assignment once you make landfall would be one to two years, depending on the colonists' need. You'd be working with the regularly assigned physician, exobiologist, and botanists. We'll give you the planetary data from the initial exploration, and you'll submit a budget for any extra equipment you think you'll need for the job."

"That sounds wonderful," Shona said, eagerly. "When do we lift?"

"Ah," the officer said, running his finger down the length of the file on his screen. "Ten months from tomorrow. Give you plenty of time to arrange things."

Shona barely kept herself from breaking in and interrupting him. "But I don't want plenty of time. I want to leave right away."

The man looked at her suspiciously. Shona hastened to reassure him. "I've been planetbound for so long, I'm almost itchy to get out on assignment again."

The officer squirmed just a little bit against his seat back, and Shona felt sheepish. 'Itchy' was probably not the best choice of words, but it passed. He nodded.

"You'd be a good choice for that colony assignment," he insisted, encouraging her. "The planned site is in heavy jungle. There might be numerous hidden risks you could uncover for them. It's a tough assignment, but your record shows you've done well before under hard circumstances."

"I'm sorry," Shona said, cutting him off. "I really want to leave as soon as possible. There's nothing that's leaving within three months?"

He eyed her curiously. "No, Doctor. Sometimes we get a spate of departures, and sometimes the Colony Center is completely empty, with no one at all organizing missions. This is just one of those times. Everything that's going has been filled up for a good while. I don't show any last-minute needs for re-staffing cancellations. Thought I'd get some after that child-care bill was passed, but no one on staff seemed to be affected. Did you hear about it?"

It was the last thing she wanted to be reminded of. Shona felt as if she had been struck a blow square in the solar plexus. Hastily, she stood up and offered the man her hand. "I'll think about the jungle assignment. Thank you." She hurried out of the building, trying to hold back tears.

The government was only one of the two powers placing colonies in space, as she'd been reminded by the ubiquitous Dr. Crane only that morning. He had said, "We don't waste proven talent." Without hesitation, she hailed a transport, bundled Saffie into it, and directed it to take them to the Corporation headquarters.

Behind her, a husky man dressed in the tunic of a Corporation doctor stepped out of the shadow of the entryway to the Government Employment building. With a smile, he opened the portable comm-unit he kept in his pocket and pressed a key. A humming note indicated that he had made his connection.

"She's coming," Wrenn said. He heard a double click, meaning that the message was acknowledged, and to say nothing more. Swiftly, he flicked the unit closed, tucked it into an inner pocket, and joined the throng of pedestrians hurrying down the busy main street.

"Excuse me," Shona said to the woman seated behind the huge marble desk in the center of an equally huge and impressive marble reception hall. "I'd like to ask about a job."

The young woman met her eyes with a pleasant, practiced smile. "What field are you in, please?"

"I'm a doctor," Shona said, presenting her resume cube. "I'm interested in a colony post of some kind. My specialty is environmental medicine, but I'll take any off-planet assignment."

The receptionist gestured her toward a row of chairs against the curved wall, chairs that Shona hadn't noticed, so well did they blend with the streaked stone paneling. "Please have a seat, and someone from Personnel will see you shortly."

Shona thanked hen and pulled Saffie over to sit down beside her. She was nervous. As a career employee of the government, she never dreamed she'd be sitting here in the offices of the G.L.C. But it was her last chance—unless she wanted to wait ten more months, and the way things were, she'd go mad first. Three was bearable, until Gershom returned.

"Doctor Taylor?" a man's voice inquired.

Shona glanced up. A man was standing over her with her resume cube in his hand. He extended the other hand and shook hers warmly. "How do you do? I'm Manfred Mitchell. I'm the chief for this Corporate sector."

"Oh! How do you do?" Shona responded. "I'm, er, waiting for someone in Personnel . . ."

"I'll be talking to you instead," the man said, assisting her to her feet. He stood very close to her, looking down into her eyes with friendly warmth. "If you please?"

"Yes, of course." Under other circumstances, Shona would have been pretty sure he was making a pass at her. Under other circumstances, if she wasn't happily married, she might have taken him up on it. The man was very handsome. He had wavy black hair swept back over a high forehead with sharply defined temple bones, and deep-set light eyes of an indeterminate shade—were they hazel?—that Shona found intriguing and attractive in a tanned face. She reached down surreptitiously to twitch a wrinkle out of her tunic.

He swept a hand toward a suite of posh executive offices Shona could glimpse through the open door.

"May we leave your friend out here?" He smiled at Saffie, who met his eyes curiously.

"She'll be good," Shona promised. "Saffie! Stay!" The dog grumbled a little, but settled down with her head on her outstretched forelegs.

"I had a quick look at your record just now, Dr. Taylor. You might be the solution to an emergency situation that has arisen," Mitchell said. "Call me Manny. May I call you Shona?" His hand cupped the back of her arm as he escorted her in.

"Yes please! What emergency is that?"

"In a moment, Shona. May I offer you something to drink?"

Shona sank into the plump cushions of the armchair he placed before the broad wooden desk, and her feet quickly buried themselves in the thick silky carpeting. Swiftly, she wriggled forward to the front edge of the seat; if she relaxed, she thought she might sink without trace into the furniture and never be seen again. But it seemed a wonderful place to disappear.

The office's appointments were mostly black basalt and genuine wood. The glorious, golden desk behind which Mitchell seated himself was made of more wood than Shona had seen in any one place on Mars outside of the Arboretum Dome where schoolchildren were taken on field trips. The rest of the decor was done in Earth style, all subtle blues and pine-greens, without a touch of Mars' iron or rusty red. Imported goods from all over the galaxy ranging from knicknacks to a hefty, patterned enamel vase were placed artfully around the office to draw the eye. There was a strange creature, a flat, furless being with green skin, about a handspan in length, living in a terrarium between the curved windows at Mitchell's back. Shona stroked the desktop. Its surface was polished to enhance the texture of the close grain. It felt no rougher than the skin of her fingertips.

"What kind of wood is it?" Shona asked, in a hushed voice.

"It's maple. Earth maple."

"Oh." The desk and everything else in the office was incredibly expensive and rare. Mitchell, in his elegant outfit and stylish haircut, fit in well with his surroundings.

"I'm curious as to why a sector chief would want to interview me," Shona said. "You must have hundreds of people coming by to apply for work every day."

An efficient young man in a plain uniform tunic came in and dispensed hot drinks from the wood-edged hatch at the rear of the office. Shona glanced up at him and smiled her thanks. The executive continued as if they were alone.

"Ah, but rarely does someone who fits a crucial need turn up at such an appropriate time," Mitchell said. "We've been advertising desperately for a specialist in epidemic control, without success. A transport vessel from our colony of Karela is on its way here to Mars. We were afraid we'd have to let it go off empty. And here you turn up on our doorstep, so to speak," he said with a charming air of self-deprecation, as if the vast marble foyer were a mere plasteel lintel.

"Well, I'm really in environmental medicine," Shona admitted truthfully. She had a strong desire to please this man, to be accepted by him. Manfred Mitchell, eh? Charisma must be his middle name. Manfred Charisma Mitchell. If he had a job to offer, on top of his charm, she was all aural receptors.

Mitchell had established control of the interview already. Good, he thought. It was what he was known for, why he had become sector chief of Sol Sector itself in his early forties, much younger than most of his counterparts in the other, newer sectors. And he was good at spotting talent. This woman's resume was impressive for all that it was limited by her youth. She seemed eager for a chance, even pathetically so. He found her artless energy refreshing, and kept watching with appreciation the way her smile enhanced her pretty mouth, not the tight-lipped rosebud of a professional executive but a wide symbol of joy. He wondered what she would say if he told her so, but no, her file said that she was married. If he'd met her socially, that was different. Mitchell was a careful man. The reputation of the Corporation was his first loyalty.

"The Corporation offers a wide range of benefits and the chance for advancement to its employees," Mitchell began. "Based as we are on a commercial form, our colonies, and hence, our reach out toward the stars, grows faster than the Galactic government's. We have automatic built-in prosperity, since we're backed by shareholders"—Mitchell allowed a small smile to wreath his lips—"not taxpayers. When problems arise that our colonists' own staff can't handle, such as certain medical emergencies, the benefits clause in their contract entitles them to help from the central office. It is this benefits package that compelled us to advertise for someone in your field. One of our colonies, Karela, has invoked the clause in its contract requesting a specialist. They're suffering from a fever epidemic. Our specialists tend to be given roving assignments, and there are none close enough to be sent to Karela in time. Mars is, oddly enough, closer than any of their present locations."

"I'm um, not sure I am what you're looking for, Mr. Mitchell," Shona said timidly.

He put her resume cube into his reader and perused the screen. "Manny. Please. I believe your qualifications dovetail nicely with our requirements, Shona. Although you are a trifle light on practical experience."

"I'm not actually an epidemic specialist," she repeated, a little louder. He seemed annoyed at being interrupted, and she blanched at his scowl, but kept talking. "I'm an environmental illness specialist." When Mitchell looked at her blankly, she tried to explain the difference. "If an outbreak of some symptom occurs, I study the local stimuli, take case histories to see if the sufferers have any potentially harmful experiences in common, any common allergies—"

He interrupted her. "So you *are* a plague doctor?"

"No, sir. Mostly, I do rashes."

He nodded, thinking deeply. "You've never been the sole or senior physician on any mission, have you?"

"No, sir." Shona held her breath. That was almost certain to be the fact that got her dropped from consideration. Curiously, he seemed pleased.

"You've had no professional experience of this kind?"

Shona hesitated. She had other experience in the field of infectious disease, culled during medical school and internship, not to mention having been her doctor father's daughter, though that kind of experience didn't show up on a resume, but it was Mitchell's word, 'professional,' which stopped her from mentioning it. It would sound lame to claim she worked in her father's office for six years as an unpaid apprentice, all of it before the age of fourteen. She bit her tongue, because she really wanted the job. If she was impertinent to this masterful man, the sector chief of the whole shebang, she'd never get it or any other job the Corporation had to offer. She might as well go home and wait for the government colony assignment ten months away. She waited.

"May I ask why you're so eager to leave Mars?" Mitchell asked blandly. "No legal entanglements, I hope?"

"Er, no," Shona said. "A personal tragedy." She left it at that.

Mitchell accepted her silence. He gave her the brilliant smile again, and a tingle swept from the nape of Shona's neck all the way to her toes. "Good. Not that we don't have the finest legal firm on Mars on retainer, but we hate to have to use them unless we absolutely need to."

It was a polite joke, and Shona chuckled appreciatively.

"Our philosophy is simple, Shona. We give the colonists anything they need." Noticing her skeptical expression, he exclaimed sincerely, "We do, honestly. I know what you've heard about us in the news reports, but the reporters are looking at it in the wrong way. They don't understand the way our business works. We're not making slaves out of these people. It's exactly the opposite." He thumped the desk with his fingertips for emphasis. "Our employees can call upon us for anything in their contracts they want. Each planet has a medical staff; that's a normal requirement. But they can request financial advisors, even well, interior decorators, *whatever* becomes necessary to promote the independence of their colony once the contracts have run their course. After that time they are truly their own men, if you'll excuse the expression, no matter what you've heard in the gossip columns. In this case, Karela is reporting sporadic outbreaks of fever. It doesn't sound that serious, but they want a specialist. That's where you come in." He leaned over his desk conspiratorially. "We're sending you to help them."

That was the first intimation that Shona had won the job, and she was thrilled. She tried to contain her excitement but the man watched her with a twinkle in his eyes. "Yes, Doctor. You're working for me now. I think we'll get along very well. Welcome to the Corporation. We're proud to have you." He reached out for her hand and squeezed it warmly.

Shona's eyes shone, but practical matters forced her to speak up, too. "Thank you, sir. I'll need to know what I'll be earning on this job, and what other benefits the Corporation offers."

"The receptionist will give you a disk listing all the standard benefits, and I'll be happy to answer any questions you might have about them. What are you making on your present job?" Shona told him, and he nodded. "What if we started you at thirty per cent above your current base rate, with bonuses and hazard pay, for a three-year contract, to be renewed at the consent of both parties?"

"It sounds wonderful," Shona said, delighted. "When does the ship leave?"

"It's on its way to Mars now. You'll be traveling on one of our supply transports that'll stop at Karela. It'll land here between a month and two months from now, and lift as soon as we've got you aboard."

Shona stopped, uncertain. "Sir, my husband is coming here to Mars to see me. He lands in eight weeks. I don't want to leave before he comes."

"We'll do what we can," Mitchell replied, his face bland but his eyes watchful. "Please keep in mind that this is an emergency. The ship can't wait."

Shona bit her lip. The longer the transport ship was delayed, the better the chances of Gershom's reaching Mars before she had to leave. She wondered if she ought to turn down the assignment and paused, torn. As much as she missed Gershom, there was still the huge debt remaining on the *Sibyl* to consider. Gershom would understand, but he'd be as disappointed as she was. She cringed mentally at the thought of another six months without seeing him. She *needed* him. "All right," she said.

A small grin lifted one side of Mitchell's mouth. "We won't forget about you in the interim, I assure you. We'll be keeping you very busy. Let Ms. Tagerdin give you the schedule for interviews and tests." He stood up, a cue for Shona to do the same.

"One more thing, sir," Shona said, rising with some difficulty from the deep, soft chair. "Perhaps I should have mentioned this before. I have a team of animals I brought with me on my assignments as a government physician. They're bred for certain tasks to assist me in my work. Saffie, out there in the foyer, is a vaccine dog. The others are similarly specialized. I want to take them with me when I go to Karela. They could be of great use to me."

"Mmm-hmm," Mitchell acknowledged noncommittally. "You shouldn't really need them for this assignment, Shona. I don't know if that's possible."

She felt her face go red, and made her voice a touch more adamant. "I'm afraid I'll have to insist. I can't go if I have to leave them behind. I can't leave them with my family; there isn't room. I'm the one who's responsible for them. Saffie alone can help me pin down the cure for an illness almost faster than a computer."

Mitchell raised his eyebrows in surprise at the young woman's defense of her 'team,' and considered the matter. "Very well, then, Shona. You win. They can accompany you. The Corporation is getting a bargain, a team for the price of one employee."

"Thank you," Shona almost crowed.

The executive held out a hand and clasped hers warmly. "Very nice to meet you, Shona. Please keep in touch and tell me how you get on. I'll see you out."

Jubilant, Shona sailed out of the office just ahead of Mitchell. She felt as if she could dance upside down on the roof of the dome. An older man strode toward them. His hair and his eyebrows were crisp silver, and his face showed deep lines running between nose and jaw, but his eyes were sharp. He was dressed no differently

80

than Mitchell, but an air of command and world-weariness set him on a higher level than the sector chief. It was hard to guess how high. Shona was impressed when the younger executive stopped beside her and looked expectantly at the senior.

"Good afternoon, sir," Mitchell said respectfully.

Verdadero glanced up as if he had only just noticed them. "Ah, Manfred. I was looking for you. And who is this charming lady?"

"May I introduce Mr. Verdadero, Shona. He is the Global Management Coordinator. *My* boss. Sir, this is Dr. Shona Taylor, who has joined us today."

"Ah!" The older man took her hand briefly and squeezed it. His hand was dry but very strong. "A pleasure. Happy to have you with us, Doctor."

"Thank you, sir," Shona said.

"You'll enjoy working with Manfred here. He's the best man I've got, my good right hand. It's good to have an employee so loyal to the company that I can count on him to accomplish *any* task. Well, then," Verdadero went on, smiling paternally at Shona, and then returning to Mitchell. "Well, well. Who do you like in the Solar Series, Manfred?"

"Oh, the Sox, sir."

"The Sox!" Verdadero scoffed. "Not before the domes open, boy. The Lasers, I'm certain. Betty Polowski in Research is giving me even odds on them."

"I'll give you three to two on the Sox, sir," Mitchell offered.

"It'd be taking your money, Manfred."

"It would be my pleasure to cover your wager, sir," Mitchell assured him, then turned to the woman at his side. "Shona, it's been wonderful meeting you. Welcome aboard."

"Thank you, Mr. Mitchell," she began, then amended as he shook a playfully warning finger at her, "—er, Manny. And goodbye, sir," she said to the senior executive, who glanced up at her briefly from the betting slip he was writing out, and nodded to her. Exuberant, Shona slipped out the door and went home to dictate a cheerful letter to Gershom, with all the details.

Perry and the others were sorry to hear that Shona had given notice, but pleased that she had found a job more to her liking.

"We're going to miss you in a few months when things pick up," Perry said.

"With any luck," Shona said, "the next time you see me, I'll be back for a visit from a new assignment."

True to Mitchell's word, the Corporation kept her busy. When Shona left work at the Government Health Center every day, she went straight to the Corporation Building. The Corporation required a physical examination, which the staff graciously delayed so she could heal further from her miscarriage, but there was a barrage of interviews and tests with psychologists she had to take. The personality profile was the same one she had filled out for her current position, nothing new there, but she found it curious that her answers had altered somewhat over four years. She was a little warier and more experienced, unwilling to make a judgment without sufficient data.

She was grateful for the distractions. Her six-week checkup with Dr. Robin was a depressing experience, leaving her disheartened. The obstetrician completed her examination with gentle efficiency, and waited until Shona was dressed and seated in her consulting office before discussing her findings.

"Do you want the good news first or the bad news?" Dr. Robin asked, and continued without waiting for an answer. "You've recovered well from the fever and the delivery. Your muscle tone is excellent. I'm glad to see you have been exercising. I've been in touch with your therapist. She's delighted with your progress. In her opinion, you're adjusting well."

Shona turned up her hands. "It's not so much me. I feel as if I'm being carried along by the activities from my new job. I'm off the treadmill and onto something at which I'm really needed again. I haven't worked so many hours since I got out of medical school, but I have all this energy coming from somewhere. It's wonderful."

"I'm proud of you." Dr. Robin smiled. "You're really rejoining life. Good for you. You're healing."

"I still think about my baby every night," Shona said softly.

"There's nothing wrong with that. Do you cry?"

Shona nodded, and felt tears starting in the corners of her eyes. She sniffed and blinked her lashes to dispel them. "My family has been so sympathetic, and Gershom has been more than supportive. He keeps telling me in his messages not to blame myself, but I can't stop thinking, wondering if there was something I could have done to save him. I think this feeling will follow me around all of my life. Even if I have other children, they won't heal that place inside me." Shona frowned as Robin dipped her head and broke eye contact with her. "The bad news?" she asked.

"I don't think you will be able to carry any more children," the obstetrician said sadly. She turned her desk screen toward Shona and called up her file. "I warned you about the possibility of endometrial scarring. It is more extensive than I thought. I don't think it's possible for you to complete a pregnancy."

It was a blow for which Shona had been bracing herself, but no preparation could be adequate. She began to cry in earnest. "We wanted to have a big family. If I'd been more careful, none of this would have happened."

Robin handed her a clean handkerchief across the desktop. Shona shook her head and closed her eyes to be alone with her grief, shutting out the office, and the sight of the scope which displayed corroborating evidence she wished for a moment she was too ignorant to understand. The doctor allowed her a few moments without interrupting her thoughts, then spoke again.

"You can mourn so long as you don't allow it to hold you back with false guilt. You didn't infect yourself with listeriosis, did you?"

"No, of course not!" Shona exclaimed, shocked out of self-pity.

Dr. Robin nodded. "Then you aren't responsible for your infant's death. Hold onto that. You will continue to heal. You're already functioning well. This new job of yours sounds terrific. Keep me posted on how you're doing."

Shona acknowledged that the thought of a new mission gave her the impetus to pull herself together and move forward. She studied the extracts on Karela, a jungle planet at the extreme vector of this section of the galaxy on which the Corporation had their plantations of a native vine called trelasi, from which was extracted trelastadin, a drug which swept the body clean of accumulated toxins, allowing it to sustain activity for extended periods. Shona had had personal experience with trelastadin. It was intended mainly for use by long-haul pilots, but college students, particularly those in medical school, frequently made use of it to stay awake for days-long shifts during internship and while cramming for exams.

She might have resorted to it in the following week. Beside her regular job and twice-weekly therapy sessions, she attended a daily exercise session, as well as having to fit in the Corporation's schedule of orientation meetings.

Shona joined a few dozen other new employees one evening in a brightly lit room that resembled a small lecture hall. The 'instructor,' a tall young man with classic good looks and brilliantly white teeth, met each of them at the door with an enthusiastic handshake. He asked Shona's name as she came in, and called it out to the others.

"Everyone, this is Shona!"

"Hi, Shona!" the others chorused.

"Hi," she responded pleasantly, wondering what exactly was going on. She found an empty chair on one of the tiers, and sat down to look over the portable pamphlet reader which the young instructor had handed her. The opening graphic on its tiny screen read "Welcome to the Galactic Laboratory Corporation!" It swirled around to form the logo she was used to seeing: the initials G.L.C. in the center of a stylized comet. The recording continued, presenting a history of the Corporation, from its humble beginnings as a chemical company, to its present preeminence spacewide.

The young man greeted the last arrivals, then strode to the stage facing the lowest her of seats and held up his hands.

"Everyone! Everyone, if you'll put away your booklets, we can get started. Now, some of you were only hired today, and some of you have been with us for a few weeks. We're going to get acquainted, and tell you a little bit about ourselves, and learn a little about you. As we go around the room, will you give your name and the department you'll be working in?"

Shona watched with amusement while the young man, whose name was Dale Wichowicz, urged all the new employees to join him in a cheer for the Corporation.

"Come on. You've just joined the best company in the entire *universe,* not just the galaxy. You'll have more than co-workers here, you'll have friends. How about it? G.L.C.! G.L.C.!" he cried, clapping his hands together on the beat.

Only a few half hearted, half-audible voices joined his happy yell at first but he finally managed to persuade nearly the whole crowd into a frenzy of cheering and shouting. She could tell that he really adored his job. He'd be a hell of a rabble-rouser.

"Shona!" he called suddenly, as if he was able to hear her thoughts. "Come on! I haven't heard you yet. Give us a cheer."

She grinned self-consciously and shook her head, unwilling to make a fool of herself before strangers.

"Oh, come on," he pleaded. "I'll cheer with you. You won't have to do it alone. It'll give us something in common, hollering dumb jingles. If we're all silly at once, it'll be okay. All right?"

Shona nodded, giggling. She knew her cheeks had reddened, but so had everyone else's. "Oh, okay."

"Good!" Dale said, happily. "Everyone! Help Shona! We're all one happy family now. You support your co-workers, and they'll support you. Ready? All together now—G.L.C.! G.L.C.!"

Shona started clapping along, and soon her voice was as loud as the others. She shared a glance of suffering amusement with the woman next to her. *I can't believe I'm doing this,* she thought "G.L.C.!"

In a more sedate manner, she went through several interviews with the administration of the medical department, so they could find out what she knew. To her delight, one of her examiners at the final interview was the biologist she had worked with on the Cotton Consortium.

"Taji Chandler! How wonderful to see you!"

"Shona!" He rose and took her hand. "You haven't changed, my dear."

"Neither have you, Taji," she said happily He was a short, slender man, no taller than Shona herself, with tan skin and liquid black eyes. The childhood acne scars that riddled his handsome face in no way detracted from the long, serious lines of cheekbone and jaw. Chandler turned to the rest of the panel. "No need for me to question his professional history, friends," he said in the clipped, precise tones that Shona remembered so well. "When Shona and I shipped out together, she was a punk kid with only one field operation under her belt, but she held her own. It was a rough assignment. Other, more senior personnel would have cracked up. What have you been doing, pet?" He gave her a quick peck on the cheek and led her to a seat facing the half-circle of examiners.

She tilted her chin toward the datacard clipped to the board one of the members was holding. "You've got it all there, Taji. I don't think there's anything left to know about me. But ask away. I'll tell you anything you want to hear."

The interview went on for hours. The examiners turned her memory inside out, exploring her life, her education, and her aspirations with equal thoroughness. By the end of it she was exhausted. When the others pronounced themselves satisfied and had no more questions to ask her, Chandler carried her off to the building commissary for a cup of tea.

"Or something stronger, if you want it," Chandler said as soon as the door dosed between them and the rest of the panel. "I'd also be delighted to take you to dinner—tomorrow, if you're free. You deserve a reward for living through that interrogation. You must have answered ten thousand questions."

"Twenty thousand," Shona corrected him, blowing out of the corner of her mouth at a few hairs that had escaped from her barrette and drifted across the side of her face. She batted at them uselessly, and wished for a mirror. "But I've got a question for you, Taji if you don't mind. Why did you quit the Health Department?" Shona asked.

"Money, girl," Taji said, with only a touch of shame, as he ordered their drinks. "Among other things, of course. They needed an exobiologist with my experience for lab work and teaching right here on Mars. I said they couldn't buy me away from my job. But they did." He sighed. "They did. It wasn't just money they offered me," he assured her. "I've got my own lab, and I can use it for my own projects when I'm not working on an assignment, without anyone breathing down my neck. And I've got a ten-year contract. Benefits. Good bonuses. And six weeks' holiday a year."

"Sounds wonderful. What's the catch?"

Chandler shook his head. "No catch, except there's no 'iron rice bowl' in this job. The Corp is swift to throw away anything it doesn't want or need anymore. They can be pretty ruthless. If your position becomes redundant, when your contract's up— pfft!" He swept a hand, palm down, across the table. "Out you go. You'd better have something else lined up, because they'll escort you to the door and take your keys away. I've seen it happen a few times."

Shona laughed. "I'll keep that in mind."

"But that's just at the end," Chandler said hastily. "You'll like working for the Corp, Shona."

"I'm sure I will," Shona said, putting her glass down and giving his arm a friendly squeeze. "See you tomorrow."

She passed her usual shuttle stop, and kept walking. The high spirits bubbling through her blood were too active to let her sit still on the long ride home.

Saffie met her at the door of her room with an excited bark and an eagerly waving tail, curious for a dog that didn't make a lot of noise. Shona dropped to her knees beside Saffie and scratched at her neck and ears. "What is it, sweetie? What are you so excited about?"

An amused voice said, "Isn't that funny? She was quiet all afternoon until just now."

Shona looked up, with a startled intake of breath. "Gershom! You're home!"

He rose from a chair under the window, smiling a little, his quiet brown eyes watchful. Gershom was a tall man, looming head and shoulders above his wife's meter and three fifths. The top of her head only came up to the middle of his chest. Gershom was slender and broad-shouldered in the way of any long-time spacer who was used to pulling himself around in zero-gee with his hands, but most of his length was in his legs. Shona had seen him so often in her dreams over the last few months, she hardly believed he could be real now. The soft, straight, dark brown hair, which fell over his eyes if he didn't brush it away, drifted around the corners of his jaw.

"Hello, love," he said, grinning. "I landed about two hours ago. Angie told me where you were. She didn't think you'd be back too late, so I waited in here for you. When they heard about your new job, everyone on the *Sibyl* decided it was better to skip the last stops and get straight back here to you." He bent to take her hand, and she went into his arms, clutching him to her like a life preserver. "I didn't mention it because I wanted to surprise you. I guess I succeeded. Are you all right?"

"Oh, love, I'm fine. I'm so happy you're here," she murmured into his shoulder. "It's the best surprise I could ever have. I'm so glad to see you!" She rested her head against his chest and listened to his heart. His hand came up to cradle her head and play with the hair over her ear, a familiar gesture. She squeezed him closer, and closed her eyes. The *thump-thump* of his heart was strong and reassuring, like the endless pace of a cardiac pump. That made her think about the emergency-room doctors' desperate struggle to find a heartbeat in her stillborn child, and then the tears started again. She tried to stifle them, but a sob broke free and everything poured out after it. All the grief she thought she had dealt with came back in a rush. She was still too vulnerable to the memory. "I couldn't do anything to save him."

"I know," Gershom said awkwardly. He patted her but did not let her go, for which Shona was grateful. She kept on talking, telling him everything that had happened to her in a low, rapid voice, and weeping softly until he shifted to press something into her hand. It was a handkerchief. "Here," he said. "My tunic's getting wet."

She chuckled, and dabbed at her face with the cloth.

Chirwl chittered at her from his pouch. "You are all right?"

"I'm fine," Shona assured him. "I'm happy."

"Then why do you cry?" he asked. She and Gershom laughed.

"Tell me about the job," Gershom said, when she had dried her tears.

"All right," Shona said, all at once eager to talk about it. "The people at the Corp have been wonderful. They're all so enthusiastic. Especially one gung-ho type who made us sing silly songs and chant out loud. Did I tell you about that?"

Gershom shook his head. "Not a word."

"I was probably too embarrassed to open my mouth again that night," Shona admitted. "It was an exercise in bonding, but I think it was more traumatic than it needed to be. There's still no data from Karela on the fever that's going around. I've asked every day. It's difficult to prepare when I don't know for what. Strange that they haven't sent an image of a culture yet. I'd know then what I'd be dealing with. Mr. Mitchell—I mean, Manny—

said it doesn't sound too serious, but he's fulfilling the Corp's contractual obligation to them by sending me. This is really out of my field, as I said in my messages, but I've been reading journals frantically. That is, between tests. The Corporation panels have been turning me inside out. I didn't answer so many questions or take so many tests in all of medical school." Then she paused. "I worried that the transport ship would arrive before you got home. They wouldn't have allowed me to wait. I thought I might have to refuse to get aboard if you hadn't landed yet."

"Why would you do that?" he asked cheerfully. "It's your career. You couldn't just sit here and wait for me. I'm a trader. I would have understood if the ship lifted before I got back. There could have been unavoidable delays in our passage. I might have been months getting back here instead of sailing in early. We just skirted a black dwarf Eblich didn't have on the charts, and the grav pull played hell with the ship's shields. I'm glad you *weren't* already gone, but I wouldn't have been upset."

Shona felt a wave of shame. "All I could think of was getting off Mars as soon as possible."

"Now, *that* I understand," Gershom said, cheerfully.

"And now that you're home," Shona continued, "I don't want to go at all, and the transport could be here as soon as next week."

"Don't take it," Gershom advised, and she glanced up, startled. "*I'll* take you out to your assignment. We'll get the Corporation to hire us to transport you. I looked up Karela in the charts. I can get you there in a few months, certainly faster than an aged colony transport ship. It'll give us some time together, and besides, I might sell your new employers something."

Shona's spirits lifted to a height they hadn't been since she found out she was pregnant. She clapped her hands with glee. "Wonderful! What a wonderful idea! I'll call Mr. Mitchell in the morning," she added with mischief in her eyes, "and tell him I can save the company a few credits."

Gershom struck himself in the forehead histrionically in mock dismay. "Is that all my offer means to you? To put myself and my crew out, at our own expense and out of the way of our trade routes, to take you to the other end of the galaxy? Saving your employer some money?"

"Certainly not," Shona said, turning her face up to his with impish pleasure. Her eyes sparkled and she tightened her arms around Gershom's waist. "The *Sibyl* has a few other amenities that no Corporate ship could match. It'll give us months together, absolutely uninterrupted."

He leaned down to kiss her, and she responded joyfully. All that time to be alone, roaming through space, away from places that reminded her day after day of the loss of her baby, on her way to a new and exciting assignment. It sounded like paradise, but to be with Gershom was the best part. How she had missed him! Gershom was her anchor, her sounding board, and her playmate. They found joy in other things as much as they did in making love. It was wonderful for her to listen to the soft murmur of his voice, and realize it was right here, not on a tachyon message coming from light-years away; to feel his touch and know it wasn't a dream.

At the back of her mind, a harsh, guilty feeling began to grate against the warmth she felt, and memories poked and taunted her. *This is how you got into trouble in the first place,* an inner voice cackled. *This is how all your troubles began.* The pictures under her eyelids changed quickly: the bright lights in the delivery room, the sea of masked faces, and lastly the cruel, sharp-etched memory of the masked doctor holding out to her the tiny body of her dead son. Before she knew what she was doing, Shona shouted, "No!"

Her cry distracted her husband. "What?" Gershom demanded, almost angry until he saw the fear in her face. "What's the matter, Shona?"

"If it started again, if I got pregnant . . ." She looked up into his face, her eyes wide with fear. "If I lost another one, what would I do?"

"The doctor didn't think you could have any more," Gershom reminded her with infinite tenderness. "Remember? That's what you told me."

"I know it's ridiculous. It's probably wishful thinking," Shona said. "I always pictured us with a lot of children, traveling around between the stars. It's so hard to get used to the idea that it can't happen now."

"I cried, too," Gershom admitted, and pain crossed his face. "Not just for the baby, but for us. I felt helpless being light-years away from you when we needed each other. I've had a lot of time to deal with losing him, and it hurts; it will for a long time. We'll just have to be satisfied with each other."

"I never meant it to sound as if you and I weren't enough of a family," Shona put in quickly.

"Neither did I." Gershom smiled down at her, his dark eyes focused on hers. "This is just for us, now and forever. Just the two of us."

Shona's eyes fell, and she nodded. The memories faded, and she refused to listen to the cruel inner voice. Gershom walked her toward the bed, his hands stroking her hair, her shoulders, her body. Shona, relaxing, surrendered herself to the soothing, erotic touch, concentrating on how happy he made her feel after so very long a separation. She closed her eyes, and let her head droop against Gershom's arm as her hands played over the muscles under the thin fabric of his tunic.

"I said just the two of us," Gershom stated sharply. Startled, Shona's eyes flew open. "Out!" She looked up in time to see Saffie and Chirwl hastily clambering off the bed, where they'd been watching the loving reunion. "There. That's better," he said, sweeping Shona off the floor into his arms. "I'm not making love for an audience."

CHAPTER

7

MITCHELL APPROVED OF Shona's initiative in finding a more efficient transport out to Karela, and negotiated a fee with the captain of the *Sibyl*. Moreover, he made a further offer to use the *Sibyl* in conveying Shona to future assignments. Shona and Gershom were overjoyed.

A few days later, with a distinct sense of satisfaction, Shona oversaw the loading of her laboratory module into the cargo hold of the *Sybil*. In shape, the trader scout was a cross between an arrowhead and a loaf of bread. Its living quarters were minuscule compared with the cargo holds: twinned, rough semicylinders seated side by side horizontally at the rear of the ship. The starboard cargo bay doors slid open as the crane bearing the module approached and slid its burden forward on the slick tracks in the bay floor.

The original lab units had actually been made using the shell of cargo containers. Logic dictated that there would be less breakage, and less time wasted setting up a laboratory if it was never broken down and packed in the first place. Over time, the module containers came to be custom-designed, using the original shape to ensure that they could fit into a standard hold, but now they were made of a durable ceramic over a titanium frame that was lightweight, radiation-resistant, shockproof, and heatproof. The units could even be offloaded from low orbit to surface without damaging the delicate equipment inside, though Shona doubted she'd enjoy the sensation of dropping hundreds of kilometers and crash-landing on a difficult site just to prove it could be done.

The Corporation and the Galactic government shared the available laboratory modules between them, allowing each group to have access to a greater number than either would have alone. Normally, Shona would have been assigned her old module container, a unit with a leaky water-recycling system and a noisy air-recirculation intake like an asthma sufferer, in which she had lived through two long missions under sometimes unbearable conditions. By a stroke of good luck, it was not available, and she wondered sympathetically which innocent scientist was stuck with it out in the void. Instead, she was assigned a brand new unit that was so fresh off the line, the plastic coats over the applied metal trims hadn't been peeled off yet. The maintenance record showed it had even been modifed by GLC to add some new goodies.

Half the module was designed as living quarters. Shona's room was quite small compared with the chamber set aside for her menagerie. The bed was crowded by her entertainment center, reading shelf, and the console for the personal communicator, which, when activated, automatically established a digital link with the nearest beacon. In between was a bathroom that contained a bathing pool almost large enough to satisfy the ottle's yen for water sports. It was purely a luxury. Shona filled the pool for bathing only while the container was planetside; the rest of the time, she used the sonic shower. The small clothes cleaner, which fit in a corner of the room, was an efficient one, using little power, water, or cleaning solution.

The module was designed to be occupied on a full-time basis. She would eat and drink, wash, sleep, and work within its confines. The water, air, and waste-recycling units were under the floor, next to the storage tank for the food supply. Nutri. Shona sighed. Well, nothing was perfect. Government and Corporation policy both dictated that a medic on assignment must not eat any of the indigenous food supply, to avoid becoming one of her own patients. At least she could eat normal ship's food in transit. She would just make certain that there was plenty of salt, spice, and flavoring on board before she made planetfall on Karela. And under a floor panel with a custom lock that responded only to her fingerprints at normal body temperature, was a case of Crunchynut candy bars. Chirwl watched woefully as she shut the treats away.

There was a protest from the Galactic Government Import/Export Service when Shona declared she was taking her menagerie off-planet with her within a couple of days. GG took a minimum of ten days to process a license for each animal before they would be allowed to leave Mars, but the Corporation exercised its massive pull, cutting through the red tape so that she and they could leave immediately, citing an emergency case. There was another small protest when she applied for a short-term license to carry seeds for restricted plants, most especially cannabis, used to treat glaucoma, a typical ailment in mining colonies. That was another good reason for having Saffie around, Shona thought. The odd thrill-seeker who broke into her lab looking for dope would face squarely 100 pounds of highly trained guard dog. The module featured small hydroponic tanks for forcing medical plants while she traveled, easily large enough to grow fresh herbs to spark up the endless meals of nutri. The plant waiver was also granted without delay. Shona, who had decried the Corporation's vast powers, was now grateful for its influence. She wanted to lift ship as soon as possible.

"All safe and locked down," Ivo called down to her, waving. The *Sibyl*'s engineer and shuttle pilot was a large, dark-skinned man with incongruously meaty arms to go with the rest of his spacer's physique. Shona beamed at him.

"Can we go, then?" she called back.

"They're still talking," Ivo said scornfully, jerking his head in the direction of the bridge, where Gershom and Kai sat over the navicomp examining planetary location maps for the colony, messaged to them by the Corporation, and deciding whether to take on cargo and what items they might take to offer the Karelans. "As soon as we know where we're going, we go!"

Liftoff was Shona's favorite part of any spacebound trip, but this time her enjoyment was diminished because of her desperation to get offworld. With the moment imminent, she could hardly wait for the ship to close and be on its way. She'd said her goodbyes to her friends and co-workers twice now, and she and her aunt had each shed tears, Shona because she'd miss the kindness Laurel had shown to her over the last, trying months, and Laurel, because she was partly convinced that Shona was putting herself unnecessarily into danger.

All the visitors had left the bay when the first siren sounded. Shona climbed aboard the *Sibyl* and signaled Gershom to shut the hatch. She felt more alive just knowing she was once again launched on a job she enjoyed doing, one on which she was really needed. The last information the Corporation had released to her on Karela said that there had been five fatalities from the fever, but that empirical treatment was proving successful. She was eager to go out to the colony and help, but not too eager that she wasn't going to enjoy the time with Gershom.

The animals were unhappily confined in their impact cages. Harry complained when she went aft to see how they were doing. He had not yet reaccustomed himself to the ship's scent, and was probably suspicious that this was a disguised, long way to go to the veterinarian. Saffie, who had been on more flights than the cat, merely huddled down and looked miserable in her small bed.

"Come on, guys," Shona coaxed them, putting her fingers through the thickly padded mesh. "It'll be all right. You'll be out of there in no time."

Chirwl's pouch had straps across it, holding it in place. The ottle hung partway out, facing the viewscreens which displayed the same view the pilots had. It was the least they could do, letting him see what was happening to him. Only his faith in his human friends kept him from protesting what the unpredictable machines would do.

"This will be some interesting, yes?" he inquired, cocking his head at her when she checked his safety harness.

"Oh, yes, Chirwl," Shona assured him.

"You have become happy, I observe," the ottle said. "I am pleased. The time for mourning has passed, and now you exist, am I right?"

"I'm *more* than existing, thank you," Shona replied, patting the pouch where the ottle's tummy was. "I'll come and get you out of there when we've taken off."

The *Sibyl*'s bridge had eight impact couches, two for the pilot and co-pilot before the main control boards, and the others in two tiers of three against the bulkheads, like triple bunk beds. Shona was cradled in her couch, staring intently at the screen at the end of the bunk over her feet, all her muscles tense as the trading ship tilted back on its tail for the launch. *Sibyl* lifted with a slow majesty, and the rusty disk began to recede behind them. Shona willed herself to relax, so she could feel the powerful kick of the engines resisting Mars's gravity. Swiftly, the red planet shrank into a crescent and then disappeared as they circled around to its nightside. Saturn and Uranus appeared in quick succession, growing to broad, ringed disks, then vanishing, as the *Sibyl* swept toward the radiopause, beyond which the ship could make her first warp jump. She was spaceborne once again. Inside Shona's head, a tiny voice sang a song of triumph, ignoring the sad and guilty voice of grief that still haunted her.

The living quarters of the *Sibyl* were small by any standards except those of dome-living, but Shona had no trouble adjusting again to the narrow metal corridors and pressure doors, and the light-gee which was most commonly used aboard ship.

She fell in quickly with the crew's well-practiced routine. Ship-time was based on Earth's rotation, rather than Mars's or Alpha's, giving the crew three shifts of eight standard hours. Her animals were given the run of the ship, except for the bridge, to which only Chirwl was granted access. The animals found the lighter gravity disorienting at first, but became acclimated before the end of the first jump. Shona ordered a full-gee exercise period every day so her menagerie wouldn't be too weak to support their own weight on Karela when they got there. She worked out too, getting her body back into shape. Exertion improved her mood.

Shona hadn't spent much time on the ship of which she was a part owner. She was already in medical school and then engaged on her long residency when Gershom had purchased it. Most of their income was still tied up in quarterly payments, and the *Sibyl* was always in need of some kind of refitting or repair. Shona knew nothing about ship mechanics. The bills for replacement modules always shocked her until she compared them with the cost of similar pieces of medical equipment. Precision was required in the manufacture of both, because lives were dependent upon them, and skilled labor cost money. Over time, the trading business had improved so that most of the day-to-day bills were covered by profits. Shona was proud of her husband's acumen, and, personally, could see no flaw in the ship he flew.

At first, she spent a lot of time at the viewports and screens, renewing her love affair with space. In time, since the view of the constellations didn't change very quickly when they were in 'real' space, and there was nothing to see during a jump, she turned her attention inward, to her shipmates.

Ivo and Gershom's teammates, Eblich and Kai, welcomed her heartily on board. Eblich was a small-boned man whom she knew was rather shy. He didn't speak much, but he smiled warmly at her whenever he saw her. Eblich acted as navigator and co-pilot, and also as bookkeeper—an equally necessary function. Somewhere back on one of the colony worlds, he had a wife and five children. They ran the general store in the capital city, aided greatly by Eblich's connections with goods suppliers.

Kai was the stores-master. He was from Alpha, and was the first of the permanent crew Gershom had signed aboard. He had a faultless system for organization in the *Sibyl*'s hold, from which he could call forth any item, no matter how small, on demand, and keep anyone else from finding anything he didn't want them to. He had reacted to the introduction of Shona's lab module with a noncommittal shrug, and rearranged their trade goods to make it fit.

"When you gonna give up working for other people and stay with us?" Kai asked.

"Soon, Kai," Shona promised him. "Gershom and I have been talking about it. I think this contract will probably be my last working for someone else, no matter how good the money is. We'll get by, somehow." She grinned. "Three years, and I'm all

95

yours." The other crewmembers cheered, and Shona sighed with joy. She was beginning a new life, with a clearer idea of what she wanted out of it than she had before.

"What about you, Chirwl?" Gershom asked the ottle, who was seated atop the back of the co-pilot's couch. "Are you going to sign on and join the Taylor Traveling Medicine Show?"

"My time with you, though long, shall be finite," Chirwl replied. "So soon as my thesis is complete on the properly interaction of machines to humanity, I will wish to return my planet home. There is much rivalry among we ottles-ss-s in the pursuit of probable theories. I may resume my place there when I may acquire a higher standing."

"Oh-ho," chortled Ivo. "So its not that you can't go back for love of a lady ottle, eh?"

"In this case you are correct and not incorrect," Chirwl said. "For my lady-ottle-love-would-be-co-mate is in factly my chief rival of theories. It is my hope that we shall be equal in integrity. To that end, I strive to work at practicality in my seek of knowledge."

Ivo knocked himself in the head once or twice over the ear with the heel of his hand. "D'you know, I think I understood all of that. You'll be welcome among us until you finish your 'seek,' then."

"For that I gratefully thank you," Chirwl said, with a solemn twitch of his whiskers.

"Eblich, can you send a message for me?" Shona asked. "I'm introducing myself to the doctor on Karela. I haven't heard a word directly from him yet, and I still don't have direct data on their fever epidemic."

"Sure," Eblich beamed at her, accepting the small disk.

With that done, Shona had little left to do aboard the *Sibyl* but watch the entertainment beams. When the *Sibyl* was in warp, no new signals could reach the ship's antenna array, but when she was out, the crew uploaded anything from the digital system beacons within line-of-sight all the way back to Sol. Her favorite program was a science-fiction show that had been aired since video was in 2-D. She loved the oldest episodes, especially the one that featured Mars as the primogenitor of ancient Egyptian culture. Gershom and Ivo followed sports, especially the Interplanetary Football League. Chirwl was more interested in the news reports.

"Do you own Corporation stock, S-sshona?" he asked, while waiting for her to finish cooking the evening meal. The five humans took turns a day at a time preparing meals. Shona cheerfully accepted a shift It was no more difficult to cook for five adults and an ottle here than it would be for her aunt's family and an ottle back on Mars. The galley area was about the same size as Laurel's kitchen.

Shona tasted a simmering vegetable puree. "Mmm. That's just about ready. Nope. I didn't buy any before I left. Should I have?"

"I own some," Kai said, pouring himself a drink from the cold cabinet. "You've got to diversify against inflation. Good news or bad news?"

"Good news for some, bad for others," Chirwl said, clambering up onto a chair. "Corporation scientists have succeeded in artificially producing a chemically pure form of trelastidin."

"That's great," Shona exclaimed, setting down her spoon. "It's a valuable drug."

"Spacers on difficult runs use it to keep from oxidizing in their own juices when they have to stay awake for several days on end," Kai added. "The real drug is expensive. It's good to hear they've come up with a sub."

"Not good for the growers of the root in which it appears naturally," Chirwl said severely. "They have lost their livelihood."

"Win some, lose some," the stores-master said, cheerfully, patting the ottle's back.

"Isn't Karela where they grow trelasi root?" Shona asked, remembering her briefing.

"That's right," Kai said. "If they're grateful for your services, I hope we can bargain for a load of raw root. It'd bring a good price on the market from people who prefer organics."

"They're so far away," Shona mused, bringing up the star chart of Karela on the computer screen. "Do they know that their crop has been made obsolete by a new chemical compound?"

"It won't matter," Kai said, with a shake of his head. "The Corporation guarantees purchase of their product in ten-year exclusive contracts. Gives them time to shift, find another crop to raise."

"How long until we get to Karela?" she asked.

"Oh, two months, at this rate. Karela is a long way out."

"That's the worst of these assignments," Shona said with a sigh. "Space travel takes time."

"Oh, I don't mind," Gershom said, coming into the galley and catching her eye with a wicked wink. She grinned broadly, and winked back.

Eblich signaled to Shona in her lab eleven days later. "Your message from Karela just came off the beacon. From a Dr. Dai Minaukan."

"How bad's he sound?"

"Not bad," Eblich replied with his usual economy of words. His image in the screen tank wrinkled its nose. "Sounds more perturbed."

"Pipe it back here, will you? Thanks." Shona waited for the colored light to come on, indicating that the message was cued up for her to see.

A man's face appeared in the screen tank. He was thin and sallow-skinned, with dark hair and a tired-looking mustache sagging around the corners of his mouth.

"Dr. Taylor, I am Dai Minaukan, of Karela. I have already sent the corporation full details of the epidemic from which some of our people have suffered. Luckily, we have had no further fatalities, because it has been fruitless waiting for a reply from you or any other specialist as we requested some time ago. The five who died lived in a remote reach of the colony, and the bodies, after autopsy, were burned. Complete data has been in your hands for some time. It distresses me that you are approaching us unprepared to deal with our situation."

"Well," said Shona aloud, "that's a stinker of a message." The data must have gotten lost in transmission. Mitchell had told her nothing came, even though she'd asked him to retransmit the query once a week. "We must have sounded like idiots to him, asking again and again for something he'd already sent."

Minaukan went on. "We cannot identify the strange bacteria that seems to have caused the deaths some weeks ago, but since there has been no repetition of the ailment so far, it is less of a concern to us. The site has been quarantined against possible reinfection among those here."

Shona let out a sigh of relief. The recording bore out Mitchell's contention that didn't sound like much of an epidemic. She recorded a message informing Minaukan that no data had been received, and suggested very politely that he check his transmission equipment for glitches. "You know how the message systems can be. I am on my way to you, within forty days of making planetfall. May I ask for details of the disease, even if it has passed? Since you haven't identified the infector, I offer the use of my database for you to cross-match the bacteria. I would also be grateful for the autopsy reports so that I may be up to date when I arrive."

She and Gershom had more time to talk and simply be together than they had since they were in school. Shona was discovering all over again how comfortable he was to be with, and reaffirmed her decision that this contract with the Corporation would be the last.

98

"I don't want to be separated from you again for any reason after that," she said. Twined together with Gershom on his bunk, she enjoyed the closeness, where every movement was a caress.

She felt guilty. In a way she felt as though she was running away from her husband, but when she pinned down the sensation and analyzed it, she saw that she really needed a little time away from everyone she knew to heal. On the other hand, it wasn't his fault that their child had died, so it was unfair to be leaving him behind again. Her dream of being the best doctor in the galaxy could be accomplished right here, as a freelance traveling physician. Still, she had signed a contract, and she was held by that promise.

Gershom broke the silence, voicing exactly what she had been thinking. "You don't have to go off on this mission," he said. "You can stay right here on the *Sibyl*."

"I do have to go," Shona said, and sighed thoughtfully. "They need me, and we really do need the money. I signed a contract that binds me for three years. It isn't forever. I'll be seeing you more often, since Manny agreed to let you carry me from assignment to assignment. But I want to prove to myself that I can do something right."

"You do plenty of things right," Gershom said, running a finger down her bare ribs. He leaned over to smile at her, and his long hair drifted down across the side of his face.

"Besides that," Shona said, returning with a glance through her eyelashes the suggestion implicit in his words. "This is a great opportunity for me. I've never been on assignment by myself. We always said that I ought to get in some more experience before we took the show on the road. I . . . it's what I would have done if I hadn't stayed on Mars all those months." She closed her eyes as she felt a pang in her heart.

"Shona?" Gershom turned her chin so that her face was toward his. She kept her eyes down, and there were tears under the lashes. "Shona, you have talk about it. He was our child. He existed. He did! By not talking, you keep it bottled up. Learn to let go of your feelings. We'll always love him, and remember him. And I'll always love you."

For answer, Shona squeezed Gershom's ribs with all her strength, and relaxed against him. "I still feel as if I did something wrong. What did I miss?"

"You did nothing wrong. It wasn't your fault. Know that."

Shona sniffled, but she raked her gaze to meet his. "I do know it. I can't help it. I feel guilty anyway." She blinked at the haze of tears.

The corner of Gershom's mouth lifted. "So you'd rather be back on Mars living with Aunt Lal under the Child Protection Act?"

Shona's eyes flew wide open, and she sputtered. "Not that!"

"I didn't think so. Well, it wasn't time yet. He wasn't meant to stay with us. The child we're meant to keep will come along in a better time, and a more appropriate place. You'll see."

Shona didn't mention again what Dr. Robin had said about the high odds against her conceiving, but she nodded. "I'll try. I've got some hard thinking to do first, but I'll try."

"That's all I ask," Gershom said, pulling her close. "Then I can wait three years to have you all to myself."

Shona checked the beacons for messages coded under her personal number whenever the *Sibyl* dropped out of warp. It was almost twenty days later when she received a second message from Dai Minaukan. The Karelan looked more tired than he had been in the previous transmission.

"I was too harsh in the previous message, Dr. Taylor," the man began. "I apologize for my fit of temper. I would appreciate your assistance. The fever has returned and become widespread. Many of our elderly are dying of it. Children, too, are dying. It is confusing. I have been unable to identify a vector by which the infectious bacteria was spread, and there is little time to halt the disease once it has taken hold. Quarantining seems to do little good. In two to five days those who have become infected are dead. The situation has become extreme. We beg help, but it may be too late. Please review the following data which I have compiled. This is Dai Minaukan on Karela, out."

Shona was shocked at the change in the Karelan's appearance. His cheekbones stood out sharply in his thin face, and there were shadows under his eyes and around his mouth. His droopy moustache looked like melted wax. "How old is this message?" she asked Eblich.

He ran the log back and checked the tach encoding on the previous transmission. "Ten days, maybe twelve," he said.

"Those poor people!" Shona exclaimed, running the message a second time. "We have to get there as soon as possible."

"We can't get there any faster than we're going," Gershom reminded her. "There's nothing you can do for them yet. It's going to take time to get to Karela." He patted Shona's shoulder. "You're on your way. They can't ask better than that. Take it easy."

But Shona couldn't take it easy, and the review of the files that Minaukan had appended to his message worried her more.

The victims suffered from high fever, chills, headaches, and rapid heartbeat. Within a day or two, the patients exhibited delirium. There was no clue as to the source of the malady, except possibly the small, raised punctures on shoulders, arms, or necks, which suggested an insect bite was to blame for the spread of disease.

Shona bit her lip as she considered the possibility. She had studied the environmental data on Karela, and while the life forms there were carbon-based, the odds were against the existence of an alien insect whose bite was capable of making a human being ill. Such a bite should have caused a toxic reaction, irritation or poisoning, or have no effect at all. Contrariwise, a native insect carrying an alien Earth-type organism should have been killed by it.

The answer might lie in the bacteria itself. Shona examined the image of the invading organism found in the victims. It was a bacillus bacteria, stained blue to indicate that it was gram positive. Shona called up her cross-reference program, and ordered it to identify the image. The computer flashed its "Working" graphic. At last, the words "No Match" replaced the graphic. Shona groaned. Perhaps there was an alien organism which could affect human beings. If a fever epidemic with a high mortality rate had been discovered here, it could mean Karela becoming quarantined forever. What was left of its population would have to be evacuated.

She ran the autopsy tape, and studied the images of pale bodies with horrible black swellings under the arms and at other points she knew to be lymph nodes. Minaukan's voice narrated the findings as the bodies were examined. The swellings in the nodes varied from mere lumps under the skin to matted hemmorhages, followed by necrosis, as the blood clotted within blood vessels, starving vital organs. Something swam up from the depths of her memory of medical school. She called back the slide of the organism. It was familiar, but with one important difference. Telling the computer to ignore the blue gram stain, she ran the cross-reference program again. A screen popped up immediately. The images were identical, except that the bacillus pictured was stained gram negative, or red, not blue. It confirmed her guess. She sat back, puzzled. Where did Karelan mosquitoes or fleas, or whatever the vector of infection could have been, get *yersinia pestis?* It was impossible to mistake the appearance of buboes, hemorrhaged and distended black clusters of lymph nodes, for anything else. These people had died of black plague. It had been virtually unknown for centuries. No wonder Minaukan couldn't recognize it. The organism had mutated slightly, enough to throw off her computer program and probably enough to negate whatever treatment the Karelan doctor had tried to use to save his patients.

Alarmed, Shona recorded a message to Minaukan, giving him her findings, and including a complete history of the ancient disease.

"Are there fleas in Karela, or any other biting insect parasite?" Shona added. "If it is spreading through infected carriers, rats or other small creatures used by the insects as a reservoir, you might be able to halt further infections by wiping out the vermin. Burn any clothing or porous hangings that have been in contact with the patients. Take all precautions to avoid the spread of the disease. It's vital to begin treatment as soon as symptoms arise. If it follows the classic pattern as you describe, the patient undergoes systemic sepsis within three days . . ."

Shona stopped the recording, and realized the horror of what she had just recited so calmly. The Karelan doctor could not possibly receive her message for another four to six days. How many more would die in that time?

"Gershom!" Shona dashed out of her laboratory toward the bridge. "How long until we reach Karela?"

"At least seventeen or eighteen days," he said, twirling his couch around to face her. When he saw her face, he stood up and held out his hands to her. "What's wrong?"

Shona held fast to his hands as if to a lifeline. "Those people have plague," Shona said. "The old one, the *original* plague. They're dying. They need help. I've got to get to them."

"You are getting to them, as quickly as you can," Gershom assured her. "No one could be with them faster than you will. That's why the Corporation is sending you. You were the closest, remember?"

"Gershom, it may be too late," Shona exclaimed. She tried to find a way to make him understand the desperation she felt, remembering the history lesson that went along with the instruction in infectious diseases. Bubonic plague had wiped out most of the population of a continent, millions of lives lost. Karela had only thousands.

"Shona, stay calm," Gershom said. "Worrying won't get us there any faster."

Shona nodded. She had to do something else with her agitation. Hurrying back to her lab, she completed her message to Dai Minaukan and sent it off. After a moment's thought, she copied the information, and included it in a message to Manfred Mitchell, with a repeat of the Karelan transmission.

The Corporation needs to be informed what's happening on its colony in case anyone else has been exposed, she reasoned. *Once I get there, I won't have time to send any reports.*

102

Each time she looked out of the ports and saw how little changed the pattern of stars around them was from the last time, she felt frustrated and helpless. She was still so far away. With every hour that passed, more Karelans could be dying of a disease so ancient that it was believed to have been wiped out.

After only a few days, Shona felt nearly worn out from worrying. With commendable patience, Gershom persuaded her to calm down. "It'll be another twelve days, even if we strike it lucky on the warp jumps."

The next four days, while the *Sibyl* was traveling in real space to the point where it could make the next jump, were almost intolerable for Shona.

Another message came two hours after they emerged from their third jump. It was much more recent, and the news it contained was much worse.

"I speak for Dau Minaukan, who died three days ago," the young man on the viewscreen said. "Everyone has the fever now. Robust adults are dying, and even those with milder symptoms are weakening. Only a few of us remain alive, and probably not for long."

Shona's agitation nearly tore her apart. "I should be there," she wailed.

"We're close," Ivo assured her. He was piloting the second shift. He ran up the star map on the viewtank. "Do you see that?" he asked, poking a forefinger right into the heart of the projection at a bright, yellow-white spot. "That's Karela's primary. You see that?" He pointed to a place just beyond the star. "That's us. An hour or two in warp will bring us within the system. We're nearly right on target."

CHAPTER

IVO PUSHED THE *Sibyl*'s engines mercilessly to squeeze out one tiny jump to get them the rest of the way there. Shona fidgeted while they were in warp. By the time they were ready to make orbit, she was so impatient and concerned, she was ready to parachute down. In the last few days, she had scrubbed the lab until it was glowingly clean, and prepared change after change of disposable environment suits.

"May I not come and see the colony when we land?" Chirwl asked. "It is a new planet. I am interested in visiting."

"Impossible," Shona said. "I don't know if you can catch what these people have, but I refuse to put you at risk. If you'd do an important job for me, I'd appreciate it."

"If I may help, I seek to," Chirwl assured her.

"Keep track of the menagerie. I don't dare risk exposing them, either, and they won't understand why I have to move them out of the lab and into the other cargo bay. If this mutation behaves like bubonic plague, they could become carriers."

"I will look after my friends Saffie and Harry," Chirwl promised. "The others pay little attention to their surroundings. They will not mind."

With her pets and the ottle out of the way, Shona sealed off the living quarters of the module. She put together a portable case with her monitoring equipment and a supply of antibiotics and other medicines that she could carry off the ship. Trying to quell his own fears for her safety, Gershom warned her to be careful before putting her into Ivo's care for the shuttle ride down to Karela's surface.

Even though the computer had precise coordinates, Shona could hardly find the colony when the shuttle with her capsule aboard was landed there. Karela was a planet of wild growth, based on a rich soil ground by the tough roots and tougher pollinators out of the lava spewed up by its many volcanoes. The green jungle that had grown up around the habitations was as thick as the thornbushes around Sleeping Beauty's castle. What met Shona's concerned gaze when she and the shuttle pushed through the underbrush was like a scene from the fairy tale, but much more unpleasant. People had fallen where they stood when the plague hit them. Hardly waiting for Ivo to drop the ladder, she sealed her suit jumped out of the cockpit with her medical equipment, and ran.

The last message must have been several days old. These men and women were all dead, some of them for some time. From the look of them, they had lain where they were for days before expiring. Shona closed the eyes of a woman lying under a tree, curled around her own belly as if its pain was the last thing she had responded to. Beside her, almost overgrown by the tough, fast-moving trelasi creepers, was a bundle of tools, tied together with a once-colorful scarf. It wasn't clear on first examination if the woman had died of the fever or thirst and exposure.

The vines had crept across the pathway to the village and were working their way vigorously under and between the stones that marked it, but the way was still easy to find. Fighting down panic, Shona ignored the corpses on either side of her, hoping that in the population center she would find someone who still survived. She heard a weird cry behind her and jumped. Probably a bird, she chided herself as she hurried on. A rustling in the brush on either side of the path matched her pace. Something was alive here, something sinister.

It was the first time she had been on an atmosphered planet since she had left her last government post. The sensation of a non-controlled environment was strange and distracting, and not a little frightening. It was hot and very still under the giant trees, with a heavy green scent that penetrated even her suit's air filters. Shona dialed up the cooling system in her suit to a more comfortable temperature, which dehumidified the steam inside her plastic faceplate. Strange shadows followed her everywhere, and moved suddenly in an unfelt breeze, making her jump. Small shapes, all but unseen in the bush, rustled and vanished. Shona wished she had a team with her, just so she wouldn't feel so alone and vulnerable. She crossed a well-marked burn line two meters in width surrounding a high-walled compound, which the fast-growing vines were already beginning to cover over. Every building in the small village was festooned with a shaggy mass of creepers. It astonished Shona how fast the native vegetation grew. The single-story houses appeared to have been made from the native wood but thatched with tiles of dense plastic brought

105

with the colonists from their home world. Either seemed to provide a suitable foothold for the trelasi. The green vines rustled in the wind with a sinister muttering.

Shona went from house to house, calling. Everywhere she found more dead settlers. There were no domestic animals to be seen anywhere in the compound. They must have run off seeking food when their owners fell ill. She found one young man pathetically clutching a squeaky toy which could have belonged to a child or a beloved dog. Hastily, Shona turned away from that door and moved on to the next.

A faint rustle attracted her attention from the biggest building in the compound. All at once, she thought of poisonous reptiles, and wondered if they were attracted to Terran-based life. Carefully, she picked up her feet so as not to make any noise, and peered through the corner of the window.

The doors of the big building stood ajar at the opposite end from where she stood. Several dozen small woven mats were laid out on the tiled floor, and the people on them were moving weakly, but they were moving. She had found her survivors. They were trying to take care of each other.

One of them, a young woman with a long braid of black hair down her back, knelt beside the mat of an old man who lay with his hands crossed over his thin belly. She was trying to feed him with a spoon, but the food dribbled from his mouth. Patiently, she scooped the food up with the side of the spoon and tried again, speaking in a low and coaxing tone as if the old man was an infant. She looked so exhausted that Shona's heart turned over. The woman noticed the shadow as Shona moved to get a better look at the rest of the room, and glanced up. A look of hope almost like a planetary beacon crossed her face, and she raised a hand to beckon to her. Breakneck, Shona dashed around the angle of the building and in at the door.

"Thank goodness you are here," the woman said, settling back on her heels. "At least there will be someone to bury us. I am Altuine."

The room stank. Even through the filters in her suit, Shona could sense the appalling odors of hot human waste. She saw the covered pots—an attempt to provide for sanitary facilities—but at some point they had overflowed, and clearly no one had had the strength to empty them. Containers of colorless nutri were scattered and spilled at the opposite side of the room, and flies buzzed and mumbled in the puddles. Shona counted only sixteen people, mostly women, old men, and children, still among the living. They were covered with piles of scarves and blankets that had more life in their brightly-woven stripes than any of the faces they framed. There were two dead men just under the window from which she had been watching. Their bodies were beginning to decompose in the hot weather.

Shona shook her head. "I'm a doctor. My name is Shona. Tell me everything you can about the epidemic. Is there anyone else besides the people in this room?"

Altuine shook her head. Shona realized that she was very young, no more than twenty, but she was so worn out that she looked twice that age. Her eyes were sunken, and her skin had a chalky pallor that worried Shona. There was color only in her dark irises and hair, and in the yellow- and red-striped shawl across her shoulders. Even her lips were pale and sallow. "Anyone who could make it here when the fever struck came. The weakness came on suddenly. There was no strength in most even to eat. The strong ones died first, leaving us alone." She sagged, and Shona rushed to support her. The young woman's skin was dry, burning with fever. She had the disease, probably as badly as the others, but was fighting it. "We have tried to get along, but it has been hard. It is nearly over."

"Don't believe that," Shona said desperately, though privately she was certain Altuine was right. She helped the woman over to an empty mat and made her lie down. "You should rest."

"I can't," Altuine said, trying to sit up. "I must help my people."

"You get a little rest, and then you can help more," Shona said, pushing the young woman's shoulders to the mat and pulling one of the discarded shawls over her. "There's not much you can do if you're all but falling down yourself. You've done a hero's job already." Reluctantly, Altuine stayed where she was. Shona pinched up a fold of her patient's arm and observed that it did not smooth out immediately, a sign that she was severely dehydrated. Shona opened her case and started running an IV to get fluids and nutrients into her system.

The others looked up at Shona with an almost disinterested air, as she went from one patient to another. She smiled at them, chatting in a low, comforting voice as she took their vital signs. Respiration in all was shallow and quick. One of the old women was wheezing, fetching each labored breath with conscious effort. Two small girls were tucked up together on a simple mat bed, their cheeks rosy with fever, but the rest of their skin devoid of healthy color.

"You've come," an old woman said, her voice thin and so faint Shona had to stoop beside her and beg her to repeat her words.

"Help the children. There's nothing you can do for us."

"I'll try to help you all," Shona promised, heartsick.

The old woman coughed and shook her head. "Don't waste effort on us." Shona squeezed her hand and set it down with a pat.

She gave everyone a quick examination, and took blood and tissue samples. She wished that Ivo would get through with her lab. An antibiotic was indicated here, but she was reluctant to administer any medication that would further irritate their already overtaxed immune systems. Like Altuine, most of the patients were malnourished and suffering from dehydration. She didn't want to load them down with drugs when what they needed was food and water. Once they were stable, their own immune systems might help in the fight, if it wasn't already too late.

There were two IV kits in her bag. She started glucose drips on a couple of the worst cases, an old man and woman who lay together in the middle of the room, undoubtedly husband and wife. There was almost too much for a single physician to do. Shona cleaned up the mess of nutri on the one side of the room, and checked on how many unopened tins still remained. She was hesitant about giving them food from open containers in the climate. While nutri couldn't go bad, it was the perfect breeding medium for bacteria.

With professional briskness, she removed the two corpses from the sickroom, and laid them down one at a time in the building next door. The bodies were distressingly light, as if the disease had ravaged away much of their substance. Shona attacked the mess in the sickroom. She hauled out the slop urns and emptied them as far from the door as she could, and washed out their stink under a pump in the middle of the street. She was grateful for the helmet air filters that kept most of the stench out of her nostrils. With the waste-pots out of the sickroom, the atmosphere lightened up considerably. A couple of the patients stirred a little in the fresh air.

She opened a new can of nutri, and poured some into a small bowl. She brought the first serving to Altuine, who ate gratefully from the spoon Shona offered. As soon as she had eaten, the young woman fell into an exhausted sleep. Shona patted her hand and tucked it under the edge of the coverlet. Altuine looked as if she hadn't slept in many days. The effort to save others might have cost her her own chance at survival.

Shona was torn between taking the time to research the virus in her lab, and nursing her patients. She feared that if she left them for long, she might have no one left to cure. It was up to the

108

computer to analyze the samples and give her what data it had. She took nutri to each patient who could swallow, hoping she could help them build enough strength to survive. Ten of them were still able to eat, but three barely raised their eyelids when Shona approached them. She let them alone, marking them for intravenous drips as soon as her equipment arrived, and moved on to the next patient.

"Anything I can do?"

Shona glanced up suddenly from the child she was feeding to the E-suited figure in the doorway. "Ivo! I didn't hear you come in. I've got to run some blood samples. Where's my lab?"

"Out there." The spacer jerked his head toward the way Shona had come into the village. "Can I help?"

Shona persuaded the limp child in her arms to take one more sip of the liquid nutrient before setting her down on her mat. She looked up at the shuttle pilot "No. Thank you for bringing me here. I've got to work fast to save these people. It's going to be a long fight, and they don't have much strength. Your schedule's tight. You'd better go. I'll help you unload the module, and you can take off."

Ivo took one look around and said, "I'll go get Gershom and the others. You'll need a lot of help."

"You can't. This is serious, probably still contagious. What if you were accidentally exposed? It's my job, not yours."

The spacer shook his head, and pulled Shona out of the others' range of hearing "Shona, Doctor, ma'am, you're a realist, I'm going to tell you something real. We're going to have to take you away with us soon. There's going to be no one left alive here in a few days except you and us."

He was just about right. In spite of an infusion of broad-spectrum antibiotics and food, the people of Karela were too weak to fight off the advance of the disease. Shona's computer obediently spat out an image of the bacterium, which agreed with her earlier assessment that it was a reverse image of the Terran plague organism. Since she had never heard of a gram-negative mutation, she was reluctantly forced to conclude that the bacterium was a native one which no one had heretofore documented, leaving her to treat the symptoms empirically, as if it was actually plague. It was heartwrenching, exhausting work. She was grateful for the help of the other crew members, and especially for Gershom, whose presence gave her strength.

By the evening of the next day, everyone had died except Altuine and one of the children, a girl of about ten. Gershom helped Altuine, staying by her throughout the night.

"I'm used to late nights," Gershom said gently, when Shona protested that he looked too tired to stay. "I use trelastadin myself. If it will do any good for the people who grow it, I'll stay and help them."

Altuine woke up now and again for sips of water to soothe her dry mouth. Shona had put her on a fast-drip IV to replace the liquid in her tissues, but she still seemed to burn as if her substance were tinder. The young woman's heroic strength had at last given way, and the fever consumed her as it had done with all of her people. Shona feared that her treatment was too little, too late.

The antibiotics appeared to have done some good for the child, who became more active rather than less. She had probably caught the disease in the final wave. Shona stayed by the little girl all day long, keeping her cool, forcing liquids, and starting a glucose IV when the child was too weak to swallow. Ignoring the claims of her own body for rest and food, she threw all the energy she would have devoted to saving the entire colony into seeing that this one child survived. She took only moments to go back to her module to make sure her menagerie was comfortable and fed before returning to the child's sickbed.

It was difficult. The little girl was weak and frequently delirious, batting at Shona with frightened grunts and eyes that were open on unseen terrors.

"Come on baby," Shona said, coaxing her to take a mouthful of nutri. "Let's get that GI tract back in operation, can we?" She had sweetened the dull gray mess as much as she dared to get the child's taste buds into the act without sending her into insulin shock. The girl's tongue pushed the food out, spilling it down her chin. Shona scooped it up and tried again. "Come on, sweetie. Say 'ah' for the nice food. What's your name, honey?"

"She is Leilani," Altuine whispered from her mat. "She hasn't spoken since her parents died, ten days ago."

It was the last thing Altuine said. While Shona struggled to make Leilani drink a few sips of water, Gershom came to tap her gently on the shoulder. Shona looked up, and he tilted her head toward the other mat. He had covered the dead woman's face with the red- and yellow-striped shawl.

"She just went very quietly." Gershom's face was expressionless, and his voice was very low, almost hoarse. Shona nodded sympathetically. There was nothing she could say to ease the shock of having someone die at one's feet. It had happened to her before, but probably never to him. Gershom swung a fist impotently through the air, then turned and strode swiftly out of the building. Shona let him go. After he got the frustration out of his system, he'd be all right. The young trader had probably seen violent death among the asteroids, but there accidents were a matter of having put oneself in their path. These people were helpless to get themselves out of the way of disaster. It was hard to accept fate's whim. Shona, too, was depressed by the deaths she couldn't stop. She had learned to detach herself somewhat from her patients to continue to function as an effective physician, though as a human being she still cared and ached on their behalf.

A cough from Leilani attracted Shona's attention. Shona picked her up and cuddled her against her shoulder. The girl was very light. Shona felt her bones right through her spare flesh. In Leilani's small face, her big, dark eyes stared dully, and her pointed chin seemed unnaturally sharp.

"There, there, sweetheart. Shona's here. You're not alone. I promise, you won't be alone." She rocked her, humming a little tune. Leilani snuggled into her arms like a baby, bending her long, thin legs to fit close. Shona's heart contracted with longing, and she pressed the girl close to her, hoping to infuse her with her own strength.

"Come on, baby," she repeated. At last she was able to get the small mouth to accept a spoonful of nutri. She worked to compound her success. Even an ounce of the unappetizing substance would give the child sufficient protein and carbohydrates to fight another day. She left the girl only when the creepers, unchecked by the colonists constant chopping to keep them back, grew up against the side of the little hut and threatened to block out all rays of the strong, yellow-white primary rising in the east.

She missed her baby. Although she'd never been able to hold him in her arms, he had been a perceptible presence inside her, a sentient companion for the last three months of the six she had carried him. For a little while, this helpless, sick girl was taking his place. Shona needed her as much she needed Shona. Fearing reinfection, the crew moved the child out of the main building and into a small house nearby. Shona burned the girl's clothes and wrapped her in disposable gowns from her lab supply.

She and Gershom decided to cremate the bodies of the colonists, as much not to leave them to the rigors of the jungle as to destroy a possible breeding ground for the bacterium. It was no more than a decent gesture on behalf of fellow humans. Once Shona felt she could leave Leilani for short intervals, she and the crewmen gathered together all of Karela's dead.

All that they could find they hauled inside the main building and laid out in rows. With her monitor, Shona took images of each one for identification by the Corporation office. There were only a few hundred. Shona knew they had missed many in the surrounding land, but the jungle must already have claimed those bodies. No more were found, not even bones. The unseen shapes amid the thick growth had undoubtedly taken care of any others. Shona was exhausted by the time they were finished with the grisly job.

She sent the images with her report to the Corporation, telling what she had found on Karela, and requesting instructions on what to do next. In the meantime, she would stay by Leilani, and help her to recover. But before she could turn her attention wholly to the child, she had to see to the rest of Karela's people. The bodies of Dau Minaukan and his assistant were in a small office of a warehouse on the edge of the compound. The warehouse was full of processed trelasi roots. Now no one would ever come to pick up that shipment, and no one would be around to harvest more. Shona felt horror at handling the bodies of people she had seen alive, but never met.

From a distance away, Ivo set the building on fire with the asteroid laser in the nose of the shuttle. Shona wished, as she watched the flames take hold in the shaggy wooden walls, that she knew the right words to lay to rest the souls of the dead. These people were all strangers to her. She knew nothing about them, how they'd lived, whom they'd loved, what they had liked to do after work, if they enjoyed music or art or tri-dee video. And then she thought of Altuine. She had known the young woman only a day and a half, but Altuine had impressed her with her courage and determination. It was unjust that she should not have survived after working so hard for the sake of others.

I can cry for you, Shona thought, her eyes stinging, as the climbing smoke mixed with the waving branches of the treetops.

Karela's last funeral pyre burned fiercely most of the night, falling to embers and ashes just before dawn. The crew were afraid the fire might spread and consume the rest of the village, but it didn't. The moist greenery of the creepers shed hot red sparks that flew out from the pyre like a dog shaking off droplets of water. By the time the last glow had gone out, Shona's tears had dried. The living needed her now.

"How about it?" Gershom came up to her while she was standing outside the door of the small hut where the girl slept on the morning of the third day. "Will she make it?"

"She'll make it," Shona said, arching back with her hands on her hips. Her cramped spine emitted a sharp crackle, and she sighed.

"Is she stable?" he asked, tilting his head toward the house.

112

"Just barely."

"Then let's get her out of here," he suggested quickly. "You shouldn't stay here any longer if you can help it. It feels unhealthy here. She has to come off-planet with us."

Shona nodded. "I'll set up a quarantine zone for her in my module until I'm sure she's disease-free. It won't be the very best place to care for her, but it'll do until I'm reassigned."

"Better than a planet of the dead," Gershom said firmly.

Shona went inside and knelt down beside the girl, who lay on her mat staring expressionlessly at a spot on the wall.

"Hi, there. We're going to take you away with us," Shona told the child. "We want to take care of you. Would that be all right with you? We want to take you somewhere you can grow healthy again. Is that a good idea?"

Slowly, the little girl turned her head to meet Shona's eyes. Shona, her heart contracting with pity, smiled at her encouragingly, and the child nodded.

"Good! Will you tell us where you live?" No response. "I know. Let's have you show us. All right?" She scooped up the frail little body in her arms, covers and all, and carried her out into the sunshine.

The side of the hut had become a mass of creepers almost overnight. When the child saw them, she hid her eyes against Shona's neck.

"They do look like they're coming right down at you," Gershom acknowledged. "Hey, Lani, look. C'mon, look." When the girl raised her head timidly from Shona's shoulder, Gershom showed her his laser sidearm. "Watch this."

The red spotting beam picked out a curtain of creepers festooning the side of the main building, and swept slowly across them at the roof line. One by one, with a sigh like a summer shower, the severed vines fell to the ground in a cloud of leaves and tendrils. Leilani stared at them with wide black eyes, and smiled very tentatively at Gershom, who smiled back.

"See? We can slice them up, and they can't do a thing to us. Do you like that?" he asked. The child nodded, her grin widening.

"Now, where's your home, honey?" Shona asked.

The child still wouldn't speak, but she pointed the way.

Her family home was on the edge of the compound opposite the trelasi warehouse. It was a modest dwelling. The family had poured their wealth into the decoration of the inside of their home and the garden beyond. Colored wall hangings of brilliant jungle hues were tacked up everywhere inside. In one of the rooms was a loom with a half-finished tapestry still stretched across it. Shona

113

mourned for the loss of a talent who could weave the rainbow like that.

Leilani directed them to a room at the back of the house. It wasn't large, but it was full of sunlight. In the middle of her small, low bed was a doll, made by hand with great care, and dressed in what have been leftover scraps of woven fiber from the tapestries in the center room. Leilani began to sob quietly when she saw it. Shona set her down on the bed and stepped back.

"We'll be outside, honey. You pick out what you want to take with you, and we'll be waiting. All right?"

Without looking up, the child nodded her head. Shona signaled to Gershom to withdraw quietly.

"Give her a chance to say goodbye," the doctor said.

Once they were outside, Gershom gave a huge sigh of relief. He stood beside Shona and wrapped an arm around her shoulders.

"I feel as if I'm tiptoeing through someone's private life. I hate it. That garden must have been a marvel," he said, wistfully surveying the yard. "It figures anyone who lived here would have a green thumb."

It had been as much a work of art as the wall hangings. Under the ever-present mat of creepers, Shona caught glimpses of formal paths and archways, and the bright gleam of flowers in well-tended beds, all but blotted out by the trelasi.

"It's wonderful. They probably couldn't help it," Shona said, admiringly. "I think if you throw seeds at the ground here, you can jump back and watch them grow."

Leilani reappeared from the house with a small bundle wrapped in a shawl hanging from her shoulder. She said nothing, but put her hand into Shona's and looked up at her. The girl's eyes were dry now, but they were red from crying.

"Ready?" Shona asked energetically, squeezing Leilani's hand. "Come on. Let's get to the shuttle. Ready? Go!"

The shuttle lay just beyond the edge of the compound, its hard-wheeled landing gear resting on what remained of the path leading out of the village. Creepers had grown up to the tires and had begun to wind tendrils around the struts. With unmasked irritation, Gershom burned the vines off.

The child was very shy about boarding the shuttle, until her youthful curiosity took over when Shona told her about her collection of animals. Leilani went big-eyed at the idea that there were dogs and cats and rabbits orbiting above them in a big ship, if only she would come on board to meet them.

"You're going to have to live in here for a while, Lani," Shona said, carrying her into the lab module, and setting her down on the bed she had made on the examination table. She pulled off the fiber booties the girl was wearing and replaced them with a new pair. "Until you're better, you'll see my animals through a window, but after that, you can play with them all you want. Will that be all right?"

The long walk to the shuttle from her parents' house had used up what little strength the girl had. She nodded sleepily, and lay down. Shona pulled the sheet up to her neck, and fastened thick, padded impact straps around her for the flight to rendezvous with the *Sibyl*. With a sigh, Lani gathered a fold of sheet in her fist and went to sleep.

Smiling down at her, Shona gave her a soft pat on the shoulder, and went forward to be with Gershom.

"The report on Karela, sir," the administrative assistant said, setting a datacube down on the sector chief's desk.

It was relatively unusual for his efficient assistant to draw attention to herself, Mitchell thought, looking up from his screen and reaching for the cube. There must be something unsettling in the report.

"Thank you, Ms. Stone," he acknowledged. She paused before leaving the room, also a break in routine. Without hesitation, he pulled the report he was reading, and set the new cube into its place.

The face of young Dr. Taylor appeared on the screen. She looked very solemn; the corners of her attractive mouth were turned downward, and had the suggestion of a tremble. The news she had to report was more than unsettling; it was downright disastrous. The entire population of Karela was dead, wiped out by a bacterium that moved too quickly to be stopped once it was detected. Another colony reduced to the last man, or in this case, child. Mitchell heard the report through, scrolling through the recorded images of the dead settlers, and examining Shona's analysis of the organism itself.

She informed Mitchell that all precautions had been taken to avoid carrying the contagion on board her transport. The little girl was subjected to quarantine until she was clear and healthy. "I'm still puzzled," she said, "as to the source of the infection. I've analyzed samples from the areas surrounding the village, and even some from remote reaches of the continent, but there is no sign of the organism, nor even a similar bacterial form. The vector of transmission is a puzzle, too. It's a plague-like bacterium, but I found no parasites or vermin capable of carrying it from human to human.

"I'm also including Leilani's medical profile for your records. Taylor out."

"Very thorough," Mitchell murmured to himself.

He reached for the intercom patch. "Ms. Stone."

"Sir?" His assistant appeared at the door. He realized that she must not have gone very far, probably anticipating his call.

"Will you inquire if Mr. Verdadero can see me for a moment? There's something I'd like to bring to his attention." *Before someone else does it for me,* he thought, and knew the thought was in his assistant's mind as well. He glanced down at the frozen frame of Shona's serious face.

"I don't know what I'm going to do with her next." He glanced quickly up at the secretary, who was waiting for instructions. "She's had such an unfortunate time, you understand. But her reputation as a functional physician has suffered, being on a colony with such a hefty death count—not that she is to blame for it. It might well make her hard to place."

"Yes, sir."

"I must find her a position that's appropriate to her talents," Mitchell said, almost to himself, as he pulled the datacube out of the reader and dropped into his pocket. "It's what she deserves, after all."

"A tragic occurrence, Manfred," Verdadero said, sitting back thoughtfully in his majestic desk chair. It was more of a throne than a simple workseat, Mitchell thought, not for the first time. He stood before his senior's desk, trying to appear at ease, but feeling the agitation down to his toes. This incident would not look good before his fellow sector chiefs. It was possible they would accuse him of not handling the situation swiftly enough or with greater competence.

"Yes, sir," Mitchell acknowledged.

Verdadero looked at him with something approaching suspicion in his eyes. "This is the third such calamity in your sector in recent months. Is it an error in screening the colonists for infectious disease before they are placed on planet?"

"No, sir, not at all," Mitchell interjected quickly, hoping to lay suggestions of sabotage to rest before they began an inquiry. "This was also a colony of long standing. Twenty-four years, in fact. I am at a loss to explain why this should have happened now."

"Were there any survivors?" Verdadero asked.

"Just one, sir. A little girl. Dr. Taylor removed her from Karela when she departed, and put her on her transport."

"Dr. Taylor, eh? She seems to be very unlucky with her assignments. Beginner's luck?"

"Or lack of it, sir. I am sending her to Glory Station II for the time being. The miners out there are due for biennial examinations. I am considering where to reassign her afterwards, and what to do with the little girl. I would appreciate your input."

"The child? Get her here, Manfred, get her here! The Corporation takes care of its own, you know. And prepare some publicity to be released on her arrival, why don't you? We like to show the public that we care about each of our people."

"My feelings exactly, sir," Mitchell said, with some relief. "And now, if you'll excuse me, sir?"

Regally, Verdadero waved him away. "Go on, Manfred. Keep me posted."

CHAPTER

WITH ADEQUATE FOOD and care, and the resilience of youth Leilani recovered good health in a couple of weeks. There was color in her thin cheeks, and tone as returning to her skin, which had been of a pallor that rivaled the shining white walls of the lab. She stopped looking so much like a stick insect, and more like a little girl. It took longer before she began to lose her haunted look, but soon she started showing more interest in her surroundings and talked more when Shona spoke to her.

"Can you tell me how you got sick?" Shona asked one day.

"I don't know," Lani said, looking puzzled but interested.

"Did you get sick before your parents did?" This was daring, and Shona knew it, trying to persuade her to talk about her lost family. She held the girl's hand tightly to give her support.

"One day Mam and Dad had it," the girl volunteered. "Then I felt bad, too."

"Did you have a bug bite, by any chance?" Shona asked.

"No," Lani said, after some thought. "Mam kept the electronic repeller on all the time. She went crazy if she got bitten."

"Ah."

"I don't like them either, but I'm not as bad as Mam."

"How about your friends? Were any of them bitten?"

"No."

That seemed to scotch the possibility of the ordinary mode of transmission. Shona had to rearrange her notions about the spread of the disease. She had done tests, checking for the bacteria in the child's lungs, but there were none. It was her conclusion that the infector must have been introduced in some other way, perhaps in the food or water, or through tissue contact.

"Dr. Shona?" Lani asked.

"Mmm?" She was running one final test on a sample of Lani's blood to confirm the results she had found the day before. The bacterium had been wiped out of the girl's bloodstream. The child was unlikely to be infectious any longer. Shona considered that it was about time to lift the quarantine. The tapestry-scrap doll could just survive one more auto-claving. If she'd been Lani, Shona would have been going mad with cabin fever. She raised her eyes from the eyepieces of the microscope.

"You promised I could meet your pets when I got better."

"Well, a whole sentence," Shona said, smiling at her. "Yes, I did. I think I'll keep the mice out of your way for a while. They're prone to catch anything, but I think you'll be all right with the others." With a twinkle in her eye, she turned toward the door, and let out a loud whistle. On cue, Saffie started barking and dashed into the module from the corridor where she had been waiting. Lani clapped her hands. Saffie balanced her front feet on the top of the exam table, one to either side of the girl's hips, and barked again, lolling her long pink tongue in the girl's face. The child let out a cry of joy. Shona smiled.

"Saffie I wouldn't have to worry about, even if you were still ill. I kept her out because she can be a handful even for healthy people, and I hated the idea of giving her an antibacterial bath every time she visited. But that super-immune system of hers has yet to meet an infection it couldn't throw off." Lani was still regarding the big dog with an expression of awe. Saffie dipped her head and stuck her nose into the child's hand, which broke the spell. The girl started stroking her fur, and buried her face in the dog's neck. Saffie whined with pleasure.

"I am not either also worried about Terran diseases," Chirwl said, scurrying in and scrabbling up onto the lab table to be at eye level to their visitor. He was curious to meet a human who had lived in a jungle much like his own home. "I will be happy to be companionable. How do you do. I am called by the name of Chirwl."

Leilani turned to face the new voice, saw the alien face of the ottle gazing at her, and screamed.

"The spirit stealers!" she cried. She scrambled off the table, and crouched in the corner farthest from the strange creature.

The ottle's curiosity was piqued, and he waddled closer to the cowering girl. She screamed. "Spirit stealers?" he asked, academic investigation coming to the forefront. "What are spirit stealers? Instruct me in this matter, if you pleased."

Shona picked him up bodily and carried him out. "She does not need to deal with superstitious fears on top of recovery from a virus and the loss of her whole family," she scolded the ottle.

"I apologize for making breach of manners," Chirwl said contritely, his limbs splayed in the air. "I only want to know about the customs and legends of other worlds."

Shona sighed and set him down. "It's not your fault. Stay away from her for a while, and I'll ask her if she feels like talking about it later," she promised him. "Go talk to Kai, all right?"

She sat down on the floor beside the panting child and spoke to her in low, soothing tones. "He's gone now. Chirwl wouldn't hurt you. He's not a monster. He's an ottle, and a good friend of mine. It's all right. I would never let anything happen to hurt you. Do you believe me when I tell you that?"

Lani, trembling, nodded. In a little while, Shona persuaded the girl to let her carry her out of the module and into the main body of the ship. She introduced her to Harry, who accepted homage in typical catlike fashion, with much stretching and preening, and to the rabbits, but the girl preferred the exclusive company of the shaggy black dog. Lani showed the most animation at the sight of Saffie, and was soon engaged in a vigorous game of tug of war over an old rag with her.

As he had promised, Chirwl kept his distance. He observed Leilani through the viewtank on the bridge, and made copious notes on his wooden disks about her play, the things she said and did. She never mentioned the stealers of spirits again. The ottle mentioned his unsatisfied curiosity to Shona.

"Don't ask her! She needs to recover at her own pace," Shona chided him. "She's blossomed so well over the last few weeks from a plastic doll to a live, eager child that I'm thrilled. You'd hardly know she had just been through a catastrophic illness that claimed her whole family."

"Why does she play so hard?" Chirwl asked. "She is active many hours every day."

Shona sighed. "She's trying very hard to keep from thinking about her loss. I want her to handle her feelings in her own way. When she wants help, I think she'll ask for it."

"I regret having caused disturbance," Chirwl said, ducking his head.

"I think it'll be all right in a while," Shona assured him. "She just needs to learn to separate you from the campfire stories she learned on Karela. She's got a lot of healing to do."

The child, torn away from her own environment, was eager to bond with anyone who would provide her with a measure of stability. Shona she saw as her new mother, who fed her and bathed her, and gave her a calm explanation about the series of inoculations which made her arm sore but which she had to have, but it was Eblich, and not Gershom, who took the place of her father. The laconic bookkeeper was the first of the crew to make friends with Leilani. With five children of his own, he had the most experience as a parent, and understood Lani's disinclination toward talking. He played skill games with her, and under Shona's direction, devised exercises that would help build up her shrunken muscles. Gershom was seen in a very different light by the little girl. Shona suspected she had a crush on him. She caught Lani looking at him from under her long eyelashes when she thought he wasn't watching, and did little favors for him, like bringing him fresh tea while he was on duty. Her dark eyes glowed whenever he paid her the slightest compliment. Gershom was embarrassed by the girl's attention, but Shona assured him it was perfectly natural behavior.

"It shows she's recovering," she told Gershom. "Besides, I understand why she feels that way. I'm crazy about you myself."

The sleeping arrangements settled themselves. Expending the most syllables Shona had heard her use to date, Leilani begged to have Saffie sleep with her.

"She will protect me. She is my friend," the little girl said, her arms wrapped around Saffie's neck. "Please don't make her go away from me."

"Well," Shona considered. "Why not? You sleep in here from tonight on," she said, showing her the bedroom. "If you need anything, just call." She tucked the child in. As soon as the light coverlet was patted smooth around her, Saffie jumped up and settled down beside her with a noise between a sigh and a groan. Leilani threw her arm across the big dog's back.

"Sleep well, you two," Shona said, turning off the lights as she left.

A little while later she came in to see how they were doing. At first, she thought they both were asleep. Leilani, lying very still, had her face buried in Saffie's thick coat, her black hair blending with the dog's fur. Shona was about to leave as silently as she came, but she heard the girl's breath catch in a sob. Saffie's large brown intelligent eyes met hers over Leilani's back, and they, shared a moment of sympathy. The dog thumped her tail once on the bed as Shona sat down on Leilani's other side.

"Anything you'd like to talk about?" Shona asked, laying a gentle hand on the child's back. "Someone who's been through as much as you must have plenty to get off her chest."

Leilani looked up. Her mouth worked as she tried to decide what to say, and ended up mute with fat tears rolling down her face.

"I know, I know." Shona picked her up and rocked her for a few minutes, until the racking sobs passed. "There's my brave girl,"

Shona said, stroking the child's smooth hair. "Is that better? Stay here a moment, won't you?"

She went to the food preparation area, and came back with a warm cup of fruit-flavored liquid nutri and a Crunchynut bar. She put them into the girl's hands and sat down beside her on the bed.

"There, I'm spoiling you," Shona said, pointing to the bar. "These come all the way from Earth. Very special candy. My very favorite. Do you like nuts?" The girl nodded. "These have all kinds of nuts and caramel under the chocolate coating. They're Chirwl's favorite, too."

The child looked worried.

"Will the talking animal come and take it away from me?"

"He's on the bridge," Shona assured her. "He won't come in here. You'll be just fine."

"It's nice to have her aboard," Gershom said softly, when Shona returned to the bridge. He almost echoed her own thoughts. *It's what it might have been like in a few years if our child had lived.* She smiled at him, meeting his eyes.

Eblich coughed politely, interrupting. "You had a message."

"That's right," Gershom said apologetically. "The Corporation sent us the coordinates for your next destination. It isn't a planet, its an asteroid belt."

"What?" Shona asked. She leaned over Eblich's shoulder, who made room for her as he called up the message from the com-unit. "I'm being sent to a Corporation space station to give physicals to the crystal miners out there," she said with a sigh. "It's a lot like what I was doing on Mars."

"What about Lani?" Gershom asked.

"Nothing yet," Shona shrugged. "But I'm taking her with me, no matter what they say."

As her living module was attached to an arm of the space station, Shona mused about how few places in the galaxy were really suited to human existence, and how humankind shifted to make itself comfortable on the edge of such inhospitable environments. Corporation Space Station Glory II was small, unprepossessing, and had few comforts to offer the independent men and women there other than an assay office, a supply depot, and a bar. The barkeep, a lean, tough woman in her fifties named Girelda Baker, instantly offered to buy out any video cubes, reading matter, and snack foods Gershom had on board the *Sibyl,* without quibbling about the price.

"When the miners are out there"—she pointed at the asteroid belt, visible through a broad glasteel viewport that made up the rear wall of the bar—"they're busy. When they come in here, they want to be entertained, and they don't want nothing they've seen before, neither. But they ain't too particular what it is they watch. You got quilting lessons, they'll watch that too." The woman glanced over the edge of the bar at Saffie.

"I'm here to give them their annual physicals," Shona said. "Didn't anyone from the Corporation notify you I was coming?"

The woman waved a hand. "They told me, but it ain't gonna make a toot's worth of difference in an airlock to them. When they come here, they want a drink and a little company, not a poke and a prod."

Saffie, disliking the woman's tone of voice, barked warningly. Instead of being upset, Girelda peered over the bar at her thoughtfully. Lani, waiflike in one of Shona's oversized jersey tunics and a pair of her exercise shorts, stood silently beside her friend, her arm over the dog's back.

"Dog, eh? You'll get patients quicker if you advertise you've got a pet. These folks like animals, but no one can keep 'em on a mining scout. Kid'll be popular, too," Girelda said, smiling at the girl, who returned the gesture shyly. "Lots of miners miss their families."

"That's a good idea," said Shona.

"Remember," Girelda reminded her with a grin, "I want ten per cent of the gate."

When miners began to return to Glory II in the next few days, there was a sign in the bar directing them down the corridor to "Dr. Shona's Traveling Menagerie and Medical Clinic."

As the bar owner had predicted, no one was too interested in meeting a doctor, especially not one giving inoculations, but the attraction of cats, dogs, rabbits, and children was irresistible. From the first two miners who followed the sign out of curiosity, word spread, and Shona and Lani found themselves in the middle of a budding social center.

Shona had felt instantly lonely when the *Sibyl* detached from the airlock and threaded its way out of the asteroid belt. It had been therapeutic for her to have months together with Gershom, relearning each other, sliding back into the comfortable routines they had established during their courtship and early marriage. If it wasn't for the fact that he would be coming back when this assignment ended, she would have been miserable. Once again, Shona was thankful to Manfred Mitchell for suggesting that Gershom and the *Sibyl* be her transportation from billet to billet.

She was glad to have Lani for company. The little girl responded to Shona's love with affection and trust. Shona found herself thinking of her lost son with regret and longing, but without so much of the pain as before. Since Lani now had no family and Shona could have no children, she determined to ask Gershom if he would approve of adopting the girl. She was certain he'd agree. They'd have to inquire of the Corporation as to the protocol for getting custody of one of its wards. It would solve a lot of problems all around, fulfilling both their needs and those of the girl.

The animals' presence in the examining room was good for an immediate drop in blood pressure. One female miner with a haze of fuzzy black hair clipped almost to her scalp kept Harry on her lap throughout her entire examination. "When I retire," she said, dreamily, as the blissfully purring cat rolled over and exposed his belly for scratching, "I'm going to get a cat and sit like this for three weeks straight."

"That's only a week less than the cat'll want you to sit there," Shona commented. The miner laughed. Harry, affronted, turned a fox-colored back on both of them and whipped his tail up and down in agitation until the tension was stroked out of him again.

Other patients waiting for examination or treatment sat or lounged in the corridor. In Lani, they found a fresh audience for their tales of adventure and narrow escape from explosions and crushing in the belt mines. The little girl thrived under all the attention. Her shyness began to wear off, though she still spoke very little. Chirwl often translated her few sentences to spare her having to explain herself. The girl and the alien were becoming fast friends. She was no longer threatened by his strange face.

Chirwl considered himself the unofficial host for the clinic, taking names and loping back in to tell Shona who was waiting. He also looked after Saffie and the two rabbits, who were passed around from hand to hand, and collected choice bits of gossip, while sharing the latests thoughts in his burgeoning thesis with the visitors.

"Gandwright, Loyol, is here," the ottle reported, lolloping in to see Shona. He climbed up on the table beside Shona's current patient, a young metal-processing specialist who worked in the plant on the lower level of the space station. "He tells me he will get oiled in the bar until you want him for his tuneup and plug replacement. Does me mean what he says?" the ottle asked, fascinated. "Is he not a human being, but mechanical?"

"No," Shona laughed. "That's a metaphor. He's using machine terms to refer to his body. When he comes back, you might ask him why he does it. There might be some material you could gather in it."

Chirwl brightened. "Perhaps a subtopic of my thesis. I shall so do. To also say, there are three more patients before Gandwright, but they will wait where they are. What kind of entertainment is an extravaganza?"

"Usually a tri-vid movie," Shona said, after some thought. "Why?"

"A new extravaganza has opened humangalaxywide," Chirwl said with satisfaction, "earning one and one half billion credits on the first day. It is called *Innermost Being*."

"Sounds very existential," Shona commented, listening to her patient's heart.

"I saw the trailers for it," the young man said. "Its about a group of scientists shrinking down and traveling along the synapses of someone's brain, trying to prove the physical existence of thought."

"Sounds interesting," Shona said. "I wonder when we'll get it out here."

"Not for ages," the young miner said. "We get everything last, unless some trader brings it out here. This isn't exactly Alpha Centauri."

"Not within many light-years of said star," Chirwl acknowledged.

"You can say that again," the young man said.

"You're behind on your sepsanus boosters," Shona noted, perusing the miner's medical profile on her terminal. "Chirwl, would you mind turning on the synthesizer and pushing number four? I need a one cc. dose."

The ottle's whiskers twitched as he climbed down from the table and waddled over to the small device on the shelf behind it. He whistled to himself, looking the device over as if it were a strange animal he couldn't trust not to bite. Getting no response, he patted the top of it with a hand, and reached for the controls with the other, but he stopped short of pushing the buttons. Watching him out of the corner of her eye, Shona waited, containing the laughter that threatened to bubble out. He was one terrific theorist when it came to machinery, but it was clear he was terrified of the actual objects. They were far beyond his normal experience, and it was brave of him to try.

"Well?" she asked gently after several minutes.

"I cannot make it work, Shona," the ottle admitted.

"Never mind," Shona said, picking Chirwl up and putting him back on the table. She switched on the machine and waited for the little capsule to pop out. Shona slipped it into an inoculator and applied it to the miner's arm.

"Those things make me nervous, too," the young man admitted. "I use laser drills all the time, but stuff with chemicals, not on your warp drives."

"You are most kind," Chirwl said. "I admit to being more theoretical than practical."

"Aren't we all," the man said, putting on his tunic. "Nice to meet you, Doctor, friend Chirwl."

"Good to meet you also, friend." Chirwl whistled happily, leaping off the table and turning a flip in the air. "I will alert the next patient who awaits."

"I'm going to suggest to the Corp that they bring in a couple of animals to live here permanently," Shona told the bar owner later that afternoon. "They'll be pleased to have an idea that would help morale."

"Don't do it," Girelda warned her, "or the next Corp doc won't be able to attract patients. Keep it as a trade secret."

When the other animals were overstressed from too much aggressively friendly company, Shona took her diagnostic equipment to the bar with Chirwl or Harry, and sat in there with a beaker of mineral water from her own supplies, chatting with customers, and doing examinations on a more casual basis. Girelda refused to allow Lani to sit in the bar, saying that the presence of an innocent little kid put off the serious drinkers. There was no hurry. Between the time the first call went out for physicals and the time every miner and technician would check in from the far arcs of the belt, weeks or months might elapse, and Gershom would return no sooner. The *Sibyl* wasn't due back for three months.

Her patients were a dour group. It took them some time to warm up to Shona, but in time her sunny personality and patience won them over.

The chief health risks to the miners were bone calcium loss and complications from radiation poisoning, as well as the usual round of injuries and ailments men and women working with heavy equipment in hazardous surroundings are prone to. In addition to comprehensive physical examinations, Shona had to check each miner's suit to make certain the rad shielding was still intact, and that the counter functioned. As for bone loss, all she could do was caution them to take supplements and spend as much time under gravity as possible.

"Can't do it, missy," one of the oldest miners said, regretfully shaking his head when Shona showed him his readings on her scanners. "If I'm not out there, I'm not making money." He squinted at her. Shona observed how thin his facial bones were.

"But what good is money if you won't be around to spend it?" Shona asked. "You have to take care of yourself so you can survive."

"Well, indeed," the old man said, "you might ask that of the poor folks I heard about. At least I'm here to tell my tale. Did you hear the news? Eh?" Shona shook her head. "A whole colony wiped out. A Corporation colony right in the middle of nowhere. Some mystery sickness."

"That's terrible!" Shona exclaimed. "What was the name of the colony?"

"Can't rightly remember," the man said, gratified to find someone new to tell. "Traveling merchant gave me the word over a drink. All dead. Struck 'em quick, it did. I remember now. It was called Carl or Carla, or something like that. Heard of it eh?" he asked, when Shona winced. The nightmare faces of the dead flashed before her eyes once more, and she nodded. "See, could happen to anyone. So I'll go on doing my job, and if I live, I'll have the money to spend, see?"

With a sigh, Shona put aside her memories and launched once again into her lecture about calcium/magnesium supplements. There were easier jobs than persuading a group of stubborn individualists like these miners.

Her personal messages had caught up her within a few days of arriving on Glory. Her aunt was full of fussing advice on how to take care of herself in space. Shona messaged to her family, thanking her aunt and gave them the news about Karela, reassuring them that she was all right. It wasn't possible to tell them how she felt after that assignment.

It was different with Susan. Her best friend's message was full of cheerful news about her job. The date showed that she couldn't have known yet about the Karela disaster. Shona filled her in. "It's frustrating knowing that I had the knowledge and the technology to save those people in my hands, but I couldn't get to them in time to use it. I feel guilty and angry. If only the messages they sent to Mars hadn't gone astray! Dai Minaukan could have synthesized a vaccine himself, and he would still be alive. And so would Altuine." She stopped, and swallowed. "You'd have liked her, Sue. She was a hero. I would have given anything to have saved her. It's only because we were able to save Lani that helped me keep in perspective. We've cried together a few times. She's a joy. She has a puppy crush on Gershom. I think its funny, but he's mortified. I've forgotten what it was like to be ten. Do you remember?

"So far so good here, though," she assured Susan. "You have

never met such stubborn, individualistic people in your life! I get to hear every spacer's life story. I could almost write a book, but no one would believe half the stuff. One of my patients repeated the news about Karela to me as if it was old data. We're at the buck end of nowhere, but news seems to travel faster to Glory than anywhere else I've ever been."

Shona woke up to the sound of rapping on her module door. "Shona?" Girelda called. "You in there?"

Shona threw off the thin coverlet and displaced Harry, who was sleeping between her knees. The cat mewed in protest, but Shona ignored him. "Coming!"

Instantly alert, Saffie scrambled to her feet and galloped to be beside Shona when she opened the door. Girelda looked agitated. Her short graying hair was ruffled in all directions.

"What's wrong?" Shona asked, drawing the bar owner inside.

"Don't have much time," Girelda burst out. "I just got a message for you. Medical emergency on Celtuce. They need a doctor, and you're the closest. Corporation office relayed the message and said they wanted you to go. They've co-opted one of the scout transports to take you to meet your regular transport ship. Shuttle's just big enough to hold your lab. How soon can you be ready to leave?"

Shona was suddenly fully awake. "All I have to do is lock down the glassware and drain the tub," she said. "Fifteen minutes at the most."

"You've got twenty," Girelda said, seizing her hand. "Won't have time to tell you goodbye later. It was good to have you here."

"It was nice to know you, too," Shona replied, and then released Girelda. She tried to collect her thoughts, to put things in order. "Will you let everyone who had appointments today know where I've gone?"

"I sure will. They won't be sorry, but they'll be disappointed not to meet your animals. Good flying, and good luck. Bye-bye, kid," she said over Shona's shoulder to Lani, who, awakened by the disturbance, had come out of the bedroom behind Saffie. The woman hurried away. Shona whirled on her heel and considered what had to be done in the module. Twenty minutes was all she had.

"What's happening?" Lani asked.

"We're being picked up for another mission," Shona said. "An emergency. Can you get dressed right away?"

The girl nodded, staring as Shona hurried around the room, putting lab equipment into cabinets and securing the doors.

An emergency! Shona was grateful for Lani's help in keeping the lab immaculate. Who knew how much time she'd have to prepare

128

herself before having to dive in to help the colonists on Celtuce.

She tried to remember if she knew anything about that world. The name sounded somewhat familiar, as if it had been part of a history lesson. Her memory linked the name with the word uranium. It was a mining colony, one of the established ones. She wondered what was wrong, She hoped the scout picking her up had a briefing for her, and she prayed that it wouldn't be another Karela, the situation too far advanced for her to be of any help.

Against Harry's verbal protests and the wistful expressions of the other animals, Shona put off feeding anyone breakfast until the module had been sealed and detached from the side of Glory II. She herself couldn't eat anything; she was too worried about the people of Celtuce.

The last glass beaker had just been locked down when she felt the tremendous wrench that meant the transport had kicked away from the space station. It threw her off her feet, and she slid across the floor to land against Saffie's cage. The animals protested the sudden jerk. Harry set up his usual wail. Chirwl huddled down into his pouch and flattened himself against the wall.

"Dr. Shona, are you all right?" Lani shouted.

"I'm fine, sweetheart," Shona called back. "You stay where you are."

Shona clutched the padded mesh of the cage with her fingers. The dog whined at her worriedly, until the initial pressure had eased somewhat and she climbed cautiously to her feet. She wasn't bruised anywhere, but carefully kept a hand within grabbing distance of permanent fixtures. The transport's acceleration was not smooth and frictionless, like the *Sibyl*. There was a subtle vibration, like standing upright on a speeding platform.

"Can you sleep in the straps?" Shona asked the girl, who nodded. "I'm going forward. I'll come back and let you know when it's safe to get up." She pulled herself out of the door of the module and handed herself along the narrow corridor to the pilot's compartment.

"Come on up," the pilot called. Shona climbed through the framed doorway to the small bridge. There wasn't much room on the scout except for a tiny galley and sleeping quarters. The whole ship was taken up by its hold where the module lay and the airlock where the mining compartment was stowed. "Good morning, or whatever your shift is. Have a seat." The pilot was D'Auria, the dark-skinned miner Shona had seen in the early days of her stay on Glory II. She patted the co-pilot's chair and gestured to Shona. "I was closest when they sent out the Mayday, so I came back for you. We'll get you to your ship in nothing flat."

Shona dropped into the seat and strapped herself in. "That's good of you, pulling yourself away from your claims to go on an emergency mission."

"Oh, its okay," the woman said, waving away any suggestion of heroism. "I'm on contract. I get paid whether I bring in crystals, or bus doctors up and down. Claim's not mine, it's the Corp's. The Corporation's been good to me. I make less than if I worked a personal claim, but I don't have to worry about marketing or making a contract for marketing. Or empty strikes. And there's the benefits."

"That's what I'm here for." Shona remembered the pep talk Manfred Mitchell had given her about supporting the Corporation's personnel, and her personal commitment to it. "I'm part of the benefits. Do you have any details on the emergency on Celtuce? What's wrong with them?" she asked.

"Don't know," D'Auria said, her hands moving deftly over the controls as she calculated the coordinates for a jump. "We got the word that they were having fevers and flu." She nudged a button on her control panel, and turned a small screen to face Shona. "Here, this is the message that came in to Glory. You can listen to it while I try to find us a piece of clear space to jump warp from."

"This is to Corporation Headquarters," said the man on the screen. He had a pleasant, bony face and big ears outlined by a thinning fringe of fine, light brown hair. "Robert Derneld, leader of Celtuce Colony. We've got a lot of people starting to come down with fevers and upset stomachs, and frankly, the situation's getting out of hand. It's spreading all over the colony, and we don't have a clue how to control it. Two people have died so far." The man stopped and mopped his face. "There are a few others who are on shaky ground, and I'm worried about them. Our doctor's down with it himself right now. I want you to send someone to help us, as soon as possible, before it gets worse. Derneld out."

The image faded, and the face of Manfred Mitchell appeared. "Shona, you see the situation. You're close enough to get to Celtuce quickly. The *Sibyl* is on its way to take you from the end of your third jump point. I apologize for cutting short your assignment on Glory, but an emergency takes precedence over routine physicals. I appreciate your cooperation." He smiled suddenly. Shona was held by his eyes, even though she knew consciously that it was only a recording. "You've been doing a fine job for us, Shona. I want you to know that I comprehend and will note in the record that the decimation of Karela was not in any way your fault. A

130

problem of missed communications, and help arriving too late."

"Thank you," Shona said gravely.

"In the meantime," Mitchell continued, "please keep me posted as to the developments on Celtuce. In service to the Corporation. Message ends." The screen faded to black.

"Nice guy to work for," D'Auria said, breaking the silence. "*Mmm*-hm!"

"Yes, he is," Shona said, with a sigh. "I wish I could have done more on Karela to help."

"He makes you feel like surpassing his expectations just to please him, doesn't he?" the older woman said, with a knowing expression. Shona nodded agreement. She recorded a quick message to Celtuce asking for more details of the epidemic, and sent it off.

"Hold tight, now," the pilot instructed her. "We're going to jump."

Shona watched the viewscreen. The ship was just breaking free of the asteroid belt, dodging between the last spinning shards of rock and ice and passing into empty space. She became aware of the silence around her as the repulsors, which had been protecting the sides of the ship from collision, switched off, leaving an audible void. The belt disappeared behind them. D'Auria pointed the nose of the scout toward and over the primary in the center of the broken ring described by the belt, and nodded meaningfully to Shona. The doctor braced herself in the impact padding, and held tightly to the armrests. D'Auria punched a control and jerked her hands away from the board just as the ship bounded forward, throwing them both backward. Shona felt her chin snap up, and she fought it down to see what was happening on the screen.

Normal space was folding around them, compressing and contracting until a tear in reality opened up to admit the scout. The system's primary raced by beneath them in a flicker, and then all the stars went out.

"Hope you didn't have any more urgent letters to mail," D'Auria said, "'cause we just went incommunicado. We're going to be frequency-dead for about sixteen hours."

"How long until we rendezvous with *Sibyl*?"

"This bucket can't go too fast," D'Auria warned her. "Takes it some time to work up to a jump, and then it has to rest. It's likely to take me more than three jumps to those coordinates so I don't overtax the engines. It's old, like me." The pilot seemed resigned but not apologetic. "Two weeks."

Shona whistled. "Seems like forever when you're in a hurry."

"Yup," D'Auria said, finishing her calculations. She hit a control and tilted her chair back. "That's no lie. Well, it's nice to have company for once on one of these hauls."

D'Auria was eager for a chat. Shona answered a few questions about herself but D'Auria did most of the talking. Shona encouraged the miner to open up, asking for details of her close calls and successful strikes, out of genuine interest not only in the events, but in D'Auria herself. She understood that most of the scout miners grew lonely out on their remote claims. Places like Glory, besides being a central point where the ores were collected for processing and shipment, provided space workers with a place where they could meet and talk with other living beings once in awhile. No doubt the Corporation wrote off maintenance of the space stations as a necessary expense in keeping their employees' level of productivity high, or some other cold term, but they were vital to the spacers' sanity. Conversation would also keep Shona's mind off the emergency towards which she was traveling.

Shona went back to get Lani and Chirwl. Lani was willing to come forward and meet D'Auria, but Chirwl huddled in his pouch and couldn't be persuaded to leave it.

"I do not like the discomfort of this small, noisy box," he said. "I feel the walls too close around me, and they hum. The soonest we arrive in something more larger, happy it will make me."

"That is a fine sentiment from someone who lives in a handbag," Shona said. "All right. I'll bring you something to eat in a little while."

Lani sat with D'Auria while Shona put together a meal in the tiny ship's galley. It was breakfast for the two of them, and lunch time for the scout pilot. From her supply of nutri, Shona made patties which she braised in a creamy sauce suitable for either meal. While the food cooked, Shona fed her animals and let them loose within the lab module to allow them some exercise and a chance to stretch. After having lived on the stuff for over a year during her two previous assignments, she had become expert at preparing nutri in interesting ways. D'Auria pronounced it delicious.

"Of course," the spacer said with a grin, "anything I don't have to cook for myself is always delicious."

"I'm going to get some sleep in a little while," Shona said, after she'd cleared away the empty bowls. "When do you want me to come in and spell you at the controls?"

D'Auria waved away the offer. "You don't have to. Eighteen hours isn't that much of a stretch for me. I've got a clutchful of trelastadin pills. Isn't science something? I'll be awake until we break out of warp, no problem. Sleep well."

CHAPTER

— 10 —

WHEN SHONA AWOKE, feeling as if she had only just caught up on her lost sleep, she made a list of jobs on the console screen. She was anxious, but there was no point in overstretching her nerves. No matter what she did, it would still be two weeks until she reached the *Sibyl*. She began prepping her lab and taking inventory of supplies. More general antibiotics would need to be synthesized. Final cleaning of the lab room itself had to wait until the very last minute, to avoid having to do it over again in a rush. The animals, Chirwl, and now Lani would need to be isolated in the module until she found out if the environment was safe for them.

Her monitoring equipment was in good condition. It had been cleaned, disinfected, and cleaned again after she had left Karela. She checked off tasks as she completed them, and added more as they occurred to her. When Lani walked out of the bedroom with Saffie after sleeping a good long shift Shona realized there was a job she'd neglected that wasn't even on the list. The girl was still wearing Shona's casual tunics, which hung to her knees. She hadn't a stitch of her own to wear.

"Good grief, child," she exclaimed, abashed. "You can't go on wearing paper nighties indefinitely. We're going to make you some clothes of your own. Would you like that? If you don't mind cut-down hand-me-downs, that is."

"Clothes?" The girl's eyes shone eagerly. "Yes!"

"For underthings, we'll stick with the isolation supplies for now. You ought to have new ones, but for outer garments, I have enough to share." Shona went back into the bedroom and began to rummage through her closet, holding up garments against the child's thin chest, trying them for color and style. The girl exclaimed happily over Shona's wardrobe, touching the cloth with respectful fingers. Shona found several possibles, but the best was a rich, deep-green dress trimmed with gold that looked terrific with Lani's natural bronze complexion.

"I think you'd look good in this," Shona said, rocking back on her heels with satisfaction. She pressed the waist of the frock along the girl's sides and calculated how much needed to be taken in. "Wonderful. It'll look better on you than it ever did on me."

"So pretty," Lani said, fondling the fabric between loving fingers. She let a fold of cloth drift over her wrist and admired herself wistfully in the mirror. Shona let her hold the dress while she thumbed through her casuals. There were a couple of soft cloth pantsuits, one of cream and iridescent blue, and one of pinky-peach with chocolate-brown trim, that could be cut down without ruining their line. The girl was thin, but she had long legs, which meant the pants didn't have to be shortened too much. Shona decided, after giving Lani a critical look, only to hem up the surplus. Before too long, Lani would need the extra length.

"After this, you'll only have to wear my exercise clothes if you *want* to. Kids on Mars think those're the height of style."

One of the pantsuits was ready within an hour after breakfast D'Auria watched Shona's deft stitching with envy.

"I don't have any talent like that," she said. "I can hardly fix a tear, myself."

"I just think of this as surgery on cloth," Shona joked. She shook out the garment and surveyed it for mistakes. Shona was grateful for her aunt's insistence that all of the children in her house have at least a rudimentary knowledge of clothesmaking. Most of the alterations had been done by laser-sealing the cloth fibers, using one of her older scalpels, but the smaller nips and nicks had had to be done by hand with a needle. They weren't too uneven. The chief thing was that the outfit looked stylish enough for a ten-year-old girl's taste but was tough enough for play.

Lani noticed none of the flaws. She romped off to try on the suit in front of the bathroom mirror, and came back with her face glowing.

"Looks good, kid," D'Auria said approvingly.

"It certainly does," Shona agreed. "Wait until we get to Celtuce. I'll make you something pretty from scratch."

"Thank you, Dr. Shona!" Lani exclaimed. She ran off to find Saffie.

"Run Saffie up and down the hall for a while," Shona called after her. "She needs some exercise! And," she confided to D'Auria, "it won't do Lani any harm to get her blood moving."

"That was a nice thing you did for that child, giving her all those pretty things," the pilot said.

"It could never be enough. After what she's been through, no amount of kindness could make up for it," Shona said, watching after Lani thoughtfully. "She forgets about it now and again, but she watched her whole world die around her."

With her duties in the module out of the way, there was time to spare. Shona caught up on her correspondence, recording messages to her family and friends, telling them where she was going to be transmitted when they left warp. She was preparing a message for Susan when the sound of the scout's engines changed. The vibration slowed, almost imperceptibly at first until it was down to a deeper rumble.

"Got to go, twin," she told the screen. "We're dropping out of warp. I'll put this on the beacon to you as soon as possible, and send you the vectors for Celtuce when I know them. Love." She shut down the program.

"Are we arriving at the *Sibyl?*" the ottle's voice asked from inside his pouch.

"No, that was just the end of the first jump," Shona said. "Only two or three to go."

"Let them be swift in coming," Chirwl pleaded. "This machine's rumblings give me an ache in the head. It is destructive to natural organisms who occupy it. I shall note this in my dissertation."

"Evening, there," D'Auria said cheerfully. There were half-circles under her eyes but she was still alert. Shona looked into the viewscreen at the constellations. They were unfamiliar to her, and in spite of the seriousness of her mission, she felt a small thrill at the sight. "Jump concluded on schedule, and about where I thought we'd be. I'm tying into the local beacon for news. The Corp's got our flight path, if anyone wants to find us. We'll be out of warp for about two days while my engines recharge themselves. Want to give me your comm number? We'll see if we've got any mail."

Shona recited her number, and waited for a few minutes while the beacon processed the information. "That's my husband's code!" Shona exclaimed, reading the lone entry that appeared beneath her number on the screen, and the short line of beacon codes that followed it. "He must be fairly close by." Eagerly, she downloaded the message and played it.

"Hello, darling," the image in the tank said. "I miss you."

D'Auria scrambled out of her chair. "I was just going to the galley for some coffee. Back in a few minutes."

Shona grinned at D'Auria's tactful exit, and went back to Gershom's message. His expression was playful and a little sheepish.

135

"You don't know how nice it was having you on board for the last few months, and what a wrench I felt when we left you on Glory. I'll be seeing you shortly after you hear this, but I wanted to send to you as soon as possible." Gershom's image in the tank straightened its back as he got down to business. "You must already have heard from Mitchell about your assignment The message from Celtuce went the long way around, to Corporation Headquarters, and then routed out to you as the nearest available physician. Instead of having the *Sibyl* double back and pick you up, they shortened the trip by having a courier bring you out to meet us. They've determined to the square centimeter where we will rendezvous. Pity I'm not getting back to Glory, because I traded in a load of music and entertainment disks for Girelda Baker, but good planning on their part." Gershom nodded his approval. "That's the upside of dealing with the Corp. The downside is the peremptory drop-everything tone that your boss fired at me, ordering me to get my butt moving. I'm only a piecework contract employee, not an indentured servant. If it was anyone but you I'm supposed to retrieve, I'd have told him what to shove up his afterburners. He's used to getting his way—now!"

"There's another part to my assignment and I don't know if you know about it since it doesn't directly affect you—they think. My orders are to drop you on Celtuce, and bring Lani back to Mars with me. Sector Chief Mitchell's expecting her. They've turned down our request for custody temporarily until they assess her legal status as a Corporate ward." Gershom looked apologetic. "I sent him a message asking if she could stay aboard the *Sibyl,* but they want her there."

"No!" Shona said, banging her hand angrily on the console. Her first reaction was to record a message to the Corporation insisting that Lani stay with her, and then she began to consider the reality of the situation. It was difficult to accept, but she had no legal claim to the girl. Until she and Gershom could present a united, stable family unit, it was unlikely a court would award her to them. That would take another two and a half years. She sat fuming, drumming her fingers on the edge of the keyboard when D'Auria returned.

"Anything you want to talk about?" the pilot asked, noticing Shona's agitation. "Lover's tiff?"

"No," Shona said glumly. "There's nothing wrong between us."

"So what's the problem? You're all antsy, and you don't get to Celtuce for another month."

"They've dumped a rotten job on me that I have to do right here, and I'm not looking forward to it. *I'm* going on to Celtuce, but Lani has to go back to Mars with Gershom."

"What? You poor thing!" D'Auria exclaimed sympathetically. "You're just about cemented to each other. That child looks up to you."

"Poor both of us," Shona said, shaking her head. "I promised her I'd look after her. I don't know how to break it to her, but I had better just get it over with."

"Man proposes but the Corp disposes," D'Auria said with resignation. Shona went astern to find Lani.

"But why may I not stay with you?" Lani demanded, holding tight to Saffie. The two of them huddled in the middle of the bed, an island of security. Saffie's ears sagged, sensing the unhappiness of her two people. "I love all of you. Even the strange animal and I are friends now. I don't want to leave." Shona put her arm around the girl's shoulders.

"I don't want you to go," Shona said. "But I don't really have a choice. I'm going on to an assignment where people are very sick. I couldn't expose you to them, because you could catch whatever it is they have. I need the lab, so that would mean that you'd have to stay locked up in the bedroom all the time. Possibly for months."

"I won't mind," Lani offered desperately. "Don't send me away."

"I have to, honey. Gershom will be taking you back to Mars, where I used to live. That'll be nice, won't it? We'll still have some time together before I have to go," Shona said.

"You promised you'd take care of me," the girl wailed, clutching Saffie with one arm and Shona's neck with the other.

Shona put her arms around Lani and rocked her. "I would never let you go if I thought something terrible was going to happen to you. You're going to be under the protection of the Corporation. You'll have a good time traveling all the way to Mars. Have you ever been on another planet?" Lani, muffled in Shona's tunic front, mumbled a negative. "You're going to meet the man I work for, Mr. Mitchell. He's very nice. He'll find you a new home and a family."

"Aren't you my family?" Lani asked.

"Only unofficially," Shona said, resting her chin on top of the girl's head. "I would love to keep you with me forever, but I'm not my own boss yet; I won't be for many months yet, but after that, Gershom and I *will* try to get you back. It doesn't mean that I love you any the less. I'll be lonely without you around. You're good company, you know. It's been wonderful having you with me. Promise me you'll send messages to me?" She shifted her head so she could meet Lani's eyes.

137

"All right. Is Mars nice?" Lani sniffed.

Honesty fought with diplomacy to warn her against the dreariness of the domes. Diplomacy won in the end. It would be wrong to frighten her out of going. She would not sabotage the girl's chances for a happy life. "It's different from Karela. People live under domes. Have you ever seen tapes of a dome world?"

"No."

"There, you see?" Shona asked drying the girl's face with a handkerchief and making her blow her nose. "It'll be an adventure. You only have to stay there until you grow up a little more. Then you can go where you want to." She felt the trickle of tears on her own cheeks.

"Why are you crying?" Lani asked, her eyes welling up anew. She offered the handkerchief back. Shona blew her nose in embarrassment.

"I don't want you to go, either," Shona admitted. "But the sector chief is right to do this. It's best not to bring you into a strange biosphere. Your resistance is down. You could catch a new kind of cold, or flu, and that would be bad. I want you to be in a place where are good health facilities, and schools, and all the things you'll need to grow up. I'll miss you, sweetie."

"I'll miss you too, Dr. Shona," Lani said. "And Saffie."

Shona embraced her. Once again, she felt as if a part of her was being wrenched away. For a moment, she considered sending in her resignation and refusing to let Gershom take Lani away with him. But she couldn't give in to such an infantile gesture. She couldn't give up her job, and Lani would be well taken care of on Mars. Shona could offer her no definite future, no stability while she was being transferred place to place. This was for the best. She'd have to update Lani's file so the medical team on Mars could give her a proper vetting.

Because they knew their time together was reduced to mere days, the time aboard D'Auria's scout rushed by for Shona and Lani. The little girl continually offered to help Shona get ready for her assignment, straightening up supplies and running through checklists, trying to prove that she wouldn't be in the way on Celtuce. Shona found it touching, and continued to reassure Lani that it was for the best that she go on to Mars with Gershom. Chirwl was kind to the child, admitting he would miss her, too.

A message from Robert Derneld hit the beacon after their third jump. Shona brought Lani forward to the bridge to listen to it.

"Pleased to hear from you so promptly, Doctor," the colony leader said. "I still don't know what it is that's ailing us. We've got bellyaches and fever, and a kind of general weakness. We've got people who are sick nursing people who are sicker, and more are coming down with it every day. Haven't pinned down any specific virus yet, but I've got to tell you it's unusual for us to be ill like this. I hope we'll see you here pretty soon. Derneld out." The man's calm delivery belied the anxiety in his eyes.

"Do you see why I can't take you with me, dear?" she asked Lani gently. The girl nodded, staring at the ground. She refused to meet Shona's eyes. Shona tried to put a hand on her shoulder but Lani shrugged it off and went back to find comfort with a sympathetic Saffie.

Fifteen days after leaving Glory, D'Auria called Shona up to the bridge. Lani trailed behind her. "That yours?" she asked, pointing to the viewtank.

Shona peered at the tiny three-dimensional image floating at the perimeter of a red-star system that warp jumpers used as a marker. It drifted on its axis, projecting a growing arrowhead silhouette against the orange glow of the star.

"That's the *Sibyl*," Lani pointed out poking a finger into the tank field.

"That's mine, all right," Shona confirmed with a grin.

D'Auria tuned her communication unit to general hailing frequency. "*Sibyl*, this is Scout G.L.C.-Fifteen A. Got a package for you!"

An image of Gershom's face replaced the holo in the tank. "Ho there, Scout Fifteen A! Ready and eager to receive it. Hi, love!"

"Hi, sweetheart," Shona said. "Give me a few minutes to lock down, all right?"

"You give the word," Gershom said cheerily. He sat back in his seat and made himself comfortable with his hands behind his head.

"I'd better get moving." Shona rose from the co-pilot's chair. D'Auria rose, too. "Thank you for everything. It's been wonderful traveling with you. If you ever want a job as a courier, use me as a reference," she said playfully.

"Well, shucks, ma'am," D'Auria retorted, twisting up the corner of her mouth. "Hope when they next send someone to give us shots, it's you."

"Oh, I hope so, too," Shona said, clasping arms with the pilot. "Stay in touch, will you? You have my comm number."

"Sure will, when I get clear space to send from. Chin up there, little thing," D'Auria said, kneeling down to look Lani in the eye. "These are good people. You'll be okay."

Lani threw her arms around the pilot's neck and gave her a violent hug, then pulled back and dashed down the corridor to the module.

"I guess that's goodbye," Shona said. "Safe going, D'Auria."

"Safe going, Shona." D'Auria gave her a casual wave, and spun her chair around to face her console. "Okay, *Sibyl*, let's work out positions here."

Shona hurried back and strapped herself into the jumpseat in her module. She smiled at Lani's long face. The girl had pulled the straps across the bed with her and Saffie under them. "Hang on tight! They're going to transfer us between the two ships in midspace."

Lani's mouth dropped open. "Are you scared?"

"A little," Shona admitted. "But I'm more interested in what it's going to be like. Aren't you? Good! I'll defog the skylights, and we can watch."

She reached for the dial on the wall that controlled the opacity of the clear panels in the top of the module, and turned it all the way down. There was nothing to be seen above them yet. The lights inside the module illuminated only the ceiling of the cargo hold, inches above the roof. Shona stretched over a little further and switched them off.

There was a bump, as the mechanical arms which manipulated ore or crates in and out of the hull latched on to either side of the module. They were dragged along noisily over ballbearing-loaded skids until the lip of the hatch became visible. It drew back smoothly like a shutter, and Shona could see the stars above her, twinkling blue-white and gold and red against the ink-black void. In the other chamber, Lani let out a gasp of wonder.

Their view was cut off by a vast, arrow-shaped shadow. It was the *Sibyl*, maneuvering into position. Shona sensed the vibration rather than heard it as the arms extended to the end of their reach, holding the module out for the *Sibyl's* to take it aboard. She felt a keen thrill of terror, knowing that it was at that moment they were most vulnerable. If the robot claws let go before the others had them, the unit could go drifting off into space.

The shadow slipped away, and they lay watching the stars wheel gently over. It seemed like the passage of eons before the *Sibyl's* tractor arms clamped around the sides of the module. The scoutship jerked and began to rotate in the opposite direction, with the momentum of the larger ship. For Shona and Lani, the transfer took place in the most eerie silence. Only the near-imperceptible burr of motors and the hum of the air-recirculation system broke the stillness.

Another lip of metal appeared on the other side of the skylight, gradually wiping out the stars as the trading ship swallowed up the module. Outside, there was a loud clank, and the *whoosh* of pumps. The cargo bay had been sealed, and was being filled with air. No sooner had the pumps ceased their sound, when there was a tiny tap on the door.

Shona scrabbled at her straps and pulled herself free. She flattened her hand against the door panel and it slid out of the way into its niche. Gershom, his ears and nose red with cold, stood balanced with each foot on a metal rail and his arms extended toward her. She nearly knocked him down with the enthusiasm of her embrace.

"Hello, love," he said. "Let me get my breath!" Contritely, she loosened her clasp a little. He grinned, and pulled her forward into a passionate kiss. "Welcome aboard," he said, when he came up for air. "Hi, Lani. Come on forward. Eblich has been waiting to see you. I've got some surprises for the two of you."

Chirwl popped his head out of his pouch and looked around. "This is much better. It is a calmer machine. The angry buzz noises are gone."

"Chirwl is right," Shona observed, as they went forward into the living quarters. "This ship is a lot quieter than D'Auria's. The constant hum does begin to get to you after a while. I felt more at ease right away when you brought us on board."

"Then all the money we've been pouring into her has been worth it," Gershom said.

"Oh, but I'm not saying that the hum is the only reason I feel more comfortable," Shona said, tucking her hand into Gershom's arm. "Brr! Your skin is cold."

"Well, warm me up," Gershom suggested, his eyes gleaming wickedly.

Lani and the ottle bundled past them in the narrow passage and raced toward the pilot's compartment with joyful shouts.

"I feel guilty," Shona said. "It's almost a betrayal sending that child away after I promised her we'd take care of her."

"We're not going straight back to Mars," Gershom declared. "There's not a thing the Corporation can do to compel me to do it. I've still got a business to run. Lani will just have to stay with me until I get there in my own good time. Sooner or later, she'll get used to the idea, and it won't be as much of a wrench. In the meantime, I have a surprise or two set aside for her, to ease her over the rough spots."

Shona squeezed his arm. "Your thoughtfulness is only one of your many charms."

Gershom peered down at her through the soft locks of his hair. "Doctor, are you trying to seduce me with sweet talk?"

"Honey, you don't know the half of it," she said, grinning up at him. "I've *missed* you."

Lani's surprise from the crew was a communications terminal of her own.

"It's really mine?" she asked, amazed. She looked up at the three men, who were smiling a little self-consciously at her. "It's too nice."

"It's not too nice for you," Kai assured her when she went speechless trying to think what else to say, "so don't fret. Now you have to learn how to use it."

"That *is* nice," Shona said, examining the unit. The console keyboard was small but the controls were clearly marked, and the tank's resolution was enviable. "You can use it to send messages to me on Celtuce. I'd like that."

Lani remembered their upcoming separation and became solemn. "I will, Dr. Shona."

"Oh, don't bog down in tears," Shona said brightly. "This is a reunion. Cheer up!"

Encouraged by Eblich and the others, Lani wore herself out telling her adventures to the crew. They made her welcome when they sat down to their late shift meal, asking questions about life on the space station: who she'd met, where she had explored. She was almost asleep before her plate was half empty.

Shona carried Lani off, long legs dangling limply over the doctor's arm, and put her to bed in one of the spare bunks. "It's all those words," she told the men. "She's not used to talking so much."

Gershom pulled Shona aside after she came out of Lani's room. He had changed into a formal tunic that emphasized his slim frame. "This one's for you," he said, presenting her with a small package wrapped in spangled tissue Tearing open the paper, she found a bundle of red silk gauze. She caught her breath as she shook out the dress.

"Oh, Gershom!"

"Try it on," Gershom suggested. "I want to see how it looks on you—and don't you dare insult me by asking what it cost You can dress up and we'll have an intimate little evening all to ourselves. I want to tell you over wine and candlelight how much I've missed you."

"Oh, love, you've taken the thoughts right out of my mind. It's getting harder to leave you every time I do it." Shona took the dress out of the package and shook it out. She held out the shoulders so she could see how it draped. She had never seen such exotic fabric. It was shot with light without sacrificing any of the richness of color. The folds of the full skirt swirled against themselves with a sensual whisper. The bodice was made of bands of cloth that swept across and around, but she didn't quite see how they were put together. She smiled up at him. "It's gorgeous, but it looks awfully complicated to put on."

"Ah," Gershom said with a twinkle. "But it comes off very easily."

CHAPTER

⟶ 11 ⟶

THE HEAVY SHUTTLE glider hit the ground rolling. Shona sat in the copilot's chair beside shuttle pilot Ivo, rapt, watching the scenery of a new world spiral before her, growing larger until it filled the viewscreens. Celtuce was gigantic and covered with swirling white clouds, as if it couldn't make up its mind at the moment of creation whether it would be a gas giant or a solid planet. The thump under her spine was solid enough. Her menagerie, in the compartment immediately behind the pilot's cabin, set up its protests as they hit. She could hear Harry's yowl of complaint almost nonstop from the time he was locked into his protective landing capsule. The cat's ululation was briefly interrupted by a sound like a hiccup as the shuttle's wheels hit the ground, then modulated into affronted cries that he couldn't get out. Shona ignored him.

Saffie was unusually quiet. The dog had been subdued since they had said their goodbyes to Lani. When Shona closed her up inside her impact cage, she settled down with her nose on her crossed forepaws, as if uninterested in anything that was about to happen. Shona felt sorry for both the girl and the dog, realizing how close they had become over the last months. She, too, missed Lani already. They had cried, clinging to one another, each reluctant to be the first to let go. Shona wondered how the girl would adjust to life on Mars, thrust once more among strangers. She promised to send messages to Lani as often as she could, and to visit whenever there was a chance for her to come back to Mars. It wasn't enough for either of them, but it would have to do. Shona had a job, and having arrived on the scene, could put off parting no longer.

She stared out the windshield at the terrain. She had to admit that Celtuce wasn't the Earthlike paradise that Corporation Colony Services featured prominently on its recruitment posters, but it was interesting. The shuttle's huge, soft tires climbed extensive hills of torn stone, some of it melted into crevices and fissures. There was nothing alive out there that she could see.

The first thing that imparted itself to her senses was that the gravity on Celtuce was heavier than Mars or even Earth standard. She was glad she had insisted on daily, full-gee exercise programs, and regretted that they hadn't been more intensive. The muscles in her thorax fought just a little bit more than usual to draw in air, and every movement of her limbs required more effort. It would be tiring to work here until she became acclimated.

The gauges told her that the heavy atmosphere was unbreathable methane, flavored with a quantity of sulphur and other trace elements, including iron. Ambient temperature, at 10° centigrade, was cool but not unpleasant for human beings. It was certainly warmer than Mars, whatever the Terraforming Council there was promising as its end result. The clouds of gas swirled and parted coyly, like translucent veils, revealing parts of the landscape and hiding them again as swiftly as snapshots. Celtuce showed the scars of its unstable core's activity in long, jagged tears that zigzagged across one another on the surface of the land and the surrounding mountains. She thought that some of them had the truncated tops of volcanoes, but the mist hid them again before she could be sure. The milky clouds made it impossible to see where they were going.

"I have a large mass on radar scan," Ivo said, growling under his breath as their way became entirely obscured. "It seems smooth. Sure hope it's the colony dome, and not another of those peaks. Give me good, clean space travel any time."

A hint of red flashed in the fog ahead of them, and five degrees above the level of the shuttle's windshield. As they moved towards it, the light became a steady beam of color. Whirling clouds shredded and parted to reveal the side of a residential dome. The beacon was on the inside, pointing directly towards them. The small craft began to climb the slight rise toward it. The ship's communicator crackled into life.

"Shuttle, welcome to Celtuce! I'm Robert Derneld, First Leader of the colony. Is Dr. Taylor with you?"

Shona seized the pickup, beating Ivo's grasp. "That's me," she said. "What's the situation in there?"

Ivo lifted an eyebrow, pretending distaste for her impatience.

"We'll brief you as soon as you're attached, Doctor. Now, if you'll just follow the beacon around the side of the dome, it'll lead you to an airlock where you can hook up your living module. We'll be waiting for you. Derneld out."

Shona almost bounced in her seat with impatience while the shuttle rumbled around the perimeter of the dome in the glow of the red light. At last, the beacon stopped, and blinked slowly twice. Ivo acknowledged the signal with a grunt. He turned the controls and reversed the shuttle until the laboratory module was touching the dome. The rear hatch opened, and there was the sound of suction and ventilation fans as the unit's seals extended and adhered to the city wall. The moment the screen on the control panel read "All Clear," Shona was out of the co-pilot's chair and through the rear door into her living unit. Her animals and Chirwl clamored for attention.

"It's all right!" she shouted, over Saffie's excited barking and Chirwl's eager questions. "Calm down. I'll let you out in a minute."

She took a quick moment to seal up her environment suit, centering the clear face panel and settling the helmet's rim on her shoulders. All the suits had been irradiated and cleaned to prevent carrying any strange organisms into the colony.

Gershom, clad in an isolation suit, followed her slowly, his rangy step covering the distance from the pilot's compartment without the appearance of haste, and stood amused, patting Saffie's head through the mesh of the cage, while he watched Shona compose herself to open the door.

This is it, Shona thought to herself, as she pressed the control. She wasn't afraid of work, or challenges, but she had no idea what to expect. She was thankful that she was able to reply to this call for help in much better time than she had before. It was up to her to keep the situation from worsening, put an end to whatever was wrong here, and prevent another Karela.

The door swished open, and she was face to face with a crowd of people. Now that the methane fumes weren't blocking her view, she glimpsed over the heads of the people the soaring height of the main dome, and glittering, brightly colored façades that were the decorated fronts of individual dwellings. She was struck by how clean and new everything looked. Another thing hit her with the mix of atmosphere strained through the filters: the shocking smell of methane mixed with sulphur. The air within the dome reeked of it.

As soon as she was in view, the crowd began to cheer. She glanced back at them, looking from face to face, expectantly. There were young people and old people, children and babies in arms, and they all looked very healthy.

"So," Shona asked, her voice a little breathless in her own ears, only partly from the sulphur. "Where are my patients?"

The tall man in the middle of the group looked just a little sheepish. He cleared his throat. "Actually, ma'am, no one's sick anymore."

Shona's round brown eyes echoed the shape of her open mouth.

"I'm sorry to spring it on you like that, but we're mighty glad to see you all the same," the tall man said, stepping forward and extending a hand to her. "I'm Robert Derneld, by the way. Call me Bob. On behalf of the whole colony, I welcome you." He touched a small gray box attached to his tunic shoulder.

Shona knew the shock had to be showing all over her face. The crowd dispersed before she could entirely recover her composure. Only Derneld along with a shorter, older man, and a couple of other colonists remained outside her door. She gathered herself up and presented a hand to the colony leader.

"Pleased to meet you. I'm Shona. Forgive me if I'm a little taken aback," she said slowly. "After all, it was only a few weeks ago that I received your message."

"Closer to three months since we asked the Corporation for a specialist," the leader said. "Maybe a little less."

"That's plenty of time for an illness to run its course," the older man said. Derneld introduced him as Dr. Franklin, and presented the other man and two women as other administrators of the Celtuce colony. "We are very glad to see you, Dr. Taylor. No one's shown any symptoms of the fever for the last couple of weeks, but I'd be glad to describe to you what they had, and get your impressions."

"I'd be happy to hear about it," Shona said, still feeling lost. Her sense of great purpose and excitement had been abruptly deflated. "It's not that I'm upset that I don't have to work. Believe me, I'm delighted the epidemic's over."

Gershom appeared behind her, and smiled at the colony leaders, interrupting when he sensed Shona's discomfiture. "How do you do? I'm Gershom Taylor, captain of the *Sibyl*. We're a trading ship, but we do occasionally deliver doctors." The three men shook hands.

"Any relation?" Derneld asked, looking from Shona to Gershom.

"Only by marriage," Shona replied. She squeezed her husband's arm for thanks.

"Interesting place you've got here," Gershom said, sweeping the city with a calculating eye. Shona could tell by the way he squinted that he thought there was money here. "What's your business?"

"Radioactives," Derneld said. "We've been mining this world for some forty-five years. It's been a lucrative field, in spite of some natural drawbacks."

"The, uh, smell?" Shona said, searching for polite synonyms and failing to come up with one that didn't sound forced.

Derneld nodded. "Well, that too. It is pretty bad. Nauseating, in fact, but it isn't harmful. It would be worse if we didn't have the filters, but they cost the colony a bundle, and they have to be replaced every four weeks."

Gershom's ears perked up almost visibly. "Perhaps we can help each other. I'll see if I can't find you a supplier that can undercut the price you've been paying," he offered.

"I hope you can," the colony leader said. "We're running down to the scrapings on high-yield pitchblende, where we get our supplies of uranium and other radioactives. There won't be any more accessible ore until the next geologic age of this planet. Pretty soon, the colony will have to go it alone. The Corporation will only have to keep us afloat until we create a viable economic infrastructure, but then it's up to us. As soon as the last shipment of ore goes, and that could be as early as next month, we get our exit bonuses from the Corp."

"That's right," one of the female administrators said, with avid anticipation. Derneld introduced her as Dana Murye. Like all the others, she was wearing a small gray box on her shoulder. "Me, I'm about due to retire. I've done everything from supervising blast sites to accounting for thirty-eight years. My pension, on top of my bonuses, should be generous enough to keep me in filters for the rest of my life, and set me up with a fine dome out there on the range."

Shona stifled an urge to break into song. "That sounds very nice," she said, trying not to giggle. She chided herself for her suddenly frivolous mood. It had to be a form of shock having the emergency vanish abruptly when she had spent weeks preparing for it.

"Our latest Corporation contract has about two years to run. Good thing, too. We're ready to retire and start living our own lives," Dr. Franklin said. "On the other hand, nothing will change for me. A doctor sees the same patients forever."

His fellow colonists laughed at Franklin's expression of suffering from over-work and imposition. It was obviously a complaint of long standing, and just as obviously, they were fond of the old curmudgeon.

"Let's talk about filters, Captain Taylor," Derneld said, leading him away toward a street that led between rows of residential domes. The other leaders trailed behind them.

"You know, your location would be good for warehousing on the trading routes," Gershom began, looking around. "You're not that far off the main route between Alpha and all that new construction out by Sector's End. You might consider establishing yourselves . . ."

148

"I don't suppose you can join me for dinner?" Dr. Franklin asked Shona, politely, seeing that the two of them were left out of the new topic under discussion. "We're proud of our culinary skills here."

"I wish I could," Shona said with regret. "Until I check things over—I am supposed to be your epidemiologist even if there's no epidemic—I can't even go about in the domes without this suit. I'm supposed to eat and drink only the provisions from my module. Rules of the game. I would be happy to sit and talk with you while you dine, though."

"I'd be delighted, under whatever circumstances," Franklin said gallantly, escorting her toward his quarters.

Frenzied barking from inside her module distracted Shona's attention.

"Wait please!" she called to Franklin over her shoulder, as she hurried back inside. "I've got to go let the animals out!"

"Is this all the people there are on Celtuce?" Shona asked, scrolling through the employee file. The entire population roster, including dependents, covered only four screens. She ran through it again, wondering if she'd missed a reference to a larger file. Franklin leaned away from his saffron-tinged risotto and glanced over her shoulder. A hint of the aroma from his meal reached Shona's nostrils. She wished the circumstances of her visit were different. She had nothing better to look forward to in her module than chicken-fried nutri. It was a temptation to break training with such delicious inducements as real food at hand. But she was too well trained to give in to mere temptation, and she knew it. *The sacrifices I make for science*, she thought regretfully. *Just my luck I've fallen in with excellent cooks.*

"No, ma'am, that's all of us. It only takes one worker to operate the big lifts," the doctor explained. "All computerized. Very easy. That's how we have been able to keep up such a tough production schedule with such a small work force. We've exceeded quota by a minimum of five per cent every month for the last four hundred and thirty."

"That's extraordinary! The Corporation must be proud of you," Shona exclaimed.

The doctor smiled modestly. "We think so. But on a more tangible level, the bonuses we've been promised are better than any praise. As Dana mentioned to you before, radioactives pay very well. I don't know what we'll do to replace the income when the mining is gone, a couple of years from now. We're discussing some kind of technical manufacturing. We have a highly educated, intelligent work force, and we don't want it to migrate off-planet."

Shona looked out at the unfriendly landscape beyond the domes. This was no placid plain, like the rusty expanses of Mars, but a brutally rent land, ripped apart by some insane force. "How do you feel about children growing up here? Constrained by the lack of space to play, the radiation risks?"

The doctor showed her his radiation counter. "We're all right inside here, and we are very careful about contamination. The children have adapted well, so far as I can tell, but I'll be happier when we can afford to finish the new recreation center. It'll give them some place that is particularly their own. You young people need more active occupations than us old folks."

Shona turned back to Franklin and mentally drew herself up. She thought she saw disappointment in the older doctor's eyes, probably because of her youth. She was determined to impress him with her thoroughness and knowledge.

"Should we discuss the epidemic?" she asked briskly. "After all, that's why I was sent here in the first place."

Franklin cocked his head, remembering. "Well, the symptoms were a high fever, delirium, and disorientation in the people with the highest temperatures; flush, lack of appetite, and upper respiratory impairment that was due more to deeply swollen tissues than surface inflammation. It was very unpleasant. Everybody had it."

"How much of the population actually had the fever?" Shona inquired, making a note.

"Everybody had it," Franklin repeated with emphasis. He reached over and flipped on his computer screen. "Every single person in this colony."

Shona's brows drew down in a puzzled expression. She looked up from her stylus. "That's statistically improbable. How many deaths?"

"Only two," Franklin shrugged. "They were both older folks. One of them was my superior. She was eighty-two years old. She thought there was something funny about the extent of the infection, too."

"Any clues as to the infector?" Shona asked, running over Franklin's notes. "I've got a list of possibles that match the symptoms Bob described to me in his message. What was your conclusion?"

"None, really, as you'll see in my file," the doctor said.

Shona read his report over again. His documentation was clear and precise. The colony physicians had treated the symptoms empirically, limiting contact the patients had with healthy colonists, reducing fever and aches with analgesics, forcing liquids to deal with dehydration. The epidemic was over as swiftly as it had begun, leaving them none the wiser as to its origins.

"We're usually a healthy bunch," Franklin continued. "In fact, it's been, oh, fifteen years since there's been any kind of pandemic infection. We thought we'd cleared everything out. With an environment as unfriendly as the one out there"—he tipped his head toward the curved observation window that made up the outer wall of his office—"and we make it a point to limit contact strictly, and check everything over frequently. We started careful. That's why everyone wears these radios." He pointed to the box on his shoulder. "Don't really need this tight communication anymore since no one is wandering out by themself in search of hot strikes, but old habits are hard to break. You'll need one, too."

The notes bore out Franklin's assertion. "Everything seems fine," she said. "It looks like you've handled it very well. Perhaps the fever was caused by a strain of E. Coli that mutated and spread, something that you're already carrying with you, perhaps through the water filtration system. You've all been together a long time, without a lot of outside input. That'd give you all the symptoms you mention, plus maybe intestinal troubles for good measure. Your resistance is down to new strains. The two people who died were elderly and frail. It happens. Everyone seems healthy now."

Thoughtfully, Franklin pulled at his lower lip with a forefinger and thumb. "Yes, now. But it was strange, when it happened all at once."

Shona sighed, agreeing. "It seems that way, sometimes. That kind of thing can spread by touch in a few days. The symptoms might appear a little while later, and pow! No one's expecting it, so no one has guarded against it." She felt curiously let down. "It seems I came here for nothing."

"Oh, no, not for nothing," Franklin said, smiling. He took her hand and squeezed it warmly through her glove. "To tell you the truth, Shona, having you come has done wonders for the morale of the colony. It's better medicine than anything I could have prescribed. The specialists they sent with us to help set up the colony left after six months, but that was a long time ago. What remained was myself and another general practitioner, an OB-GYN who doubled in surgery, and what assistants we've been able to train among the young folk. We were afraid the Corporation had forgotten about us. We've been out here a long time, and never asked for anything fancy, not in forty-five long years. We weren't sure they'd respond if we did call. I'm sorry you had a long journey and find yourself here with nothing to do, but you've made us all very happy."

"That is something," Shona admitted, feeling a rueful smile begin in spite of her disappointment. Firmly, she stomped down the little moan of selfishness that still insisted she hadn't needed to come all this way and cut short her time with Lani and Gershom. "Nothing I can help with? Food poisoning? Bug bites?"

The doctor's ears seemed to prick up. "Now that you mention it, there's been a few complaints lately about chiggers."

"*Chiggers*? Here?"

The doctor shrugged."That's what we called 'em where I grew up. Same exact symptoms. A small and painful welt that takes days to go away. I haven't a real clue. We've done cultures, but I'm not picking up a damned thing. We think they're coming in from outside."

"Well, that's strange. There haven't been any chiggers for the last how many years?"

"Forty-five. Not since the beginning, when we had an outbreak because of a few supply shipments from an agricultural world. But we get shipments in every week from other sources. Maybe the little pests rode in with one of them."

"Of course, where there're chiggers, which is a larval form, there are insects. What do they look like?"

Franklin shook his head. "I've never caught one to have a look at. It falls off the site before I can tell it's been there. Though I haven't been bitten yet myself, I should say, I've been treating little red bumps the appearance of which my patients tell me are accompanied by a hot, burning sensation. One young lady had to be treated for something like anaphylactic shock. Funny, because there isn't that much life on this planet that bothers with carbon-based forms. What little there is seems to be silicon/chloride-based, and primitive."

"Since you don't have much else for me to do while I'm here, I might work on that," Shona said. "Sector Chief Mitchell didn't say how long I was to be here after the epidemic passed, but in my last job specialists were usually assigned to a colony for six months."

"If you wouldn't mind, there's a truly important job I'd like you to take on, although it can wait until you're acclimated and out of that suit," Franklin said tentatively, and studied Shona, waiting for her reaction. "I haven't had a vacation in six years—six long years. Would you mind acting as my locum tenens for, say, two weeks or so?"

Shona threw back her head and laughed. "I would be delighted, Dr. Franklin. Take as long as you want. I'd be happy to do it."

152

"Wonderful. But please," the older doctor man said, patting her on her gloved hand, "call me Al. If you come by tonight I'll start getting you acquainted with our patients. A few of 'em might have been auding us right here, so don't be surprised if they already know what we've been saying!" He touched his shoulder radio.

Shona looked shocked but Franklin winked at her.

"This place is information-crazy, my dear. If you don't want a thing known, don't say it out loud!"

He invited some of Celtuce's leading citizens to his home to become acquainted with the Taylors. Over wine and cheese which neither Shona nor Gershom could sample, they chatted with a few dozen men and women with almost absurdly ornate manners. All of them were careful to call both the Taylors by title and surname until invited to use given names. Shona found it amusing, and mentioned it offhandedly to Al when he came over to the punch table to refresh his drink.

"They're sticklers for the old-fashioned ways. In fact, they don't easily take to any kind of change. Once you get the social leaders on your side, you'll have no trouble at all with anyone," Al confided to Shona, with a cynical squint at a couple just coming in. "Charm these two, and they'll wonder why they didn't abandon the old bastard"—he thumped himself on the chest—"years ago."

"Well, I want them to call me Shona," she said, and leaned forward to bawl into Dr. Franklin's radio unit. "*Call me Shona*!"

"That's taking the buffalo by the horns," Franklin said approvingly.

"This is one rich colony." Gershom whispered to Shona when they were alone. He'd made appreciative 'ching-ching' cash register noises behind the backs of a fashionable woman and her children who had come to meet the new doctor and her trader husband. "That youngster's tunic must have cost eight hundred credits! You know," he continued, "there's a ready-made market here for a trader who has fancy goods to sell and a good line of patter. There's almost too much money lying about here, and they're desperate to spend it."

Within a week, Gershom had to leave and resume the trade route toward Mars, where he would drop off Lani in Manfred Mitchell's care. He was still awaiting word from higher up concerning permanent arrangements for the child. Shona missed them already. There was more than a twinge of regret that she couldn't

153

take up his offer to stay on board the *Sibyl,* but a contract was a contract. He'd given her a parting gift, which he made her take an oath not to open until he was gone.

"It'll cheer you up," he promised.

She waited a decent interval until the shuttle had rolled away for the last time, and tore open the box. On top was a note. "Sweets to the sweet, or an occasional break from the never-ending nutri." Beneath it was a transparent package of beautiful dried fruit, a selection of exotic spices, and at the very bottom, a box of Crunchynut bars. Shona held the package of goodies in her arms and laughed until she cried.

Tachyon mail brought the first message from Gershom and Lani only two days after they had left. When Shona downloaded it to play, the screen showed Lani sitting, hands folded, in the co-pilot's chair on the bridge. She was wearing the green dress, and had painstakingly braided her long black hair into a bundle of small plaits pinned back over her ears.

"Hi, Dr. Shona," she said. "Hi, Saffie. How are you? I miss you."

The dog barked, hearing her name, and came over to whine at the screen while Shona waited for Lani to say something else. The child had apparently exhausted her store of conversation, and sat fidgeting uncomfortably until the screen faded to black. The video came up again on Gershom, who was shaking with stifled merriment.

"That's the best we could do for a first effort on her new board," he said, his warm eyes twinkling at Shona. "It took her hours to work up to that much. She speaks for all of us. We miss you. Here's our schedule for our stops en route to Mars." The screen changed to a flat two-dee printout. Shona marked that part of the transmission for transference to a quick-ref file. "No trouble leaving the system or jumping warp," Gershom continued. "I'll stay in touch. You take care of yourself. All of my love to you, every day." The screen cleared to show his face smiling at her just before the transmission ended and the screen went blank.

That's it then, Shona thought to herself, squaring her shoulders. *This time I'm really on my own, without Gershom to fall back on. Let's see what kind of job I can do. The isolation will be good for me.*

Mitchell went to see his superior as soon as Shona's notification reached him.

"The child is on her way, sir," he announced.

"Child?" Verdadero asked. "Ah, yes, the tot from Karela. Good. Very good. We'll have to arrange an appropriate welcome. Have you the final figures on the Karelan economy?"

"Yes, sir," Mitchell said. He had the account report ready, and offered it. "I thought you might like to see it yourself."

"No need." Verdadero waved away the datacube with a regal hand. Data-crunching was for underlings. "How much does this tragedy return to the Corporation? Less the child's inheritance and survivor's pension, that is."

"None at all. The settlers of Karela made an unusual arrangement sir. They arranged a tontine. I'm certain that the contract is an unbreakable one."

"Tell me about it, Manfred." Verdadero planted both hands on his desk and straightened up to meet Mitchell's eye.

"It's an ancient contract sir. Legal seemed to be very amused by the whole thing. In the event that some calamity would befall the colony, the sum of their profits, resources, bonuses, insurance policies, what have you, goes to the last survivors or survivor," Mitchell explained. "In the case of Karela, it amounted to millions of credits, and there is no one else to share it with. This child, Leilani, is rich beyond reason." He let the corner of his mouth turn up. "She'll need a home when she reaches us. The Taylors have offered to adopt her legally. Perhaps I should adopt her myself. I hear they're about to raise taxes again. It wouldn't hurt to have an heiress for a daughter."

His chief laughed, emitting a short sound like a bark. "Practical! Well, we'll see what will look best for the Corporation's image when she arrives. It might seem a little self-serving in the public eye to sequester her for ourselves."

"What should I do about the arrangements for publicity?"

"Hold everything for now, Manfred. No sense in crossing a bridge until we come to it. Too much attention is likely to frighten the child." Verdadero tapped his cheek with a thoughtful finger. "How curiously old fashioned of them. A tontine. Hmm."

CHAPTER

~12~

AFTER A PERIOD of time had elapsed during which there was no recurrence of the fever, and Shona's repeated battery of tests continued to come up negative, she was able to abandon the weight of her isolation suit, which was a relief. It had taken weeks before she didn't go to bed feeling sore performing her daily normal tasks in the heavier gravity. She was still bound to eat and drink only her own supplies, but being rid of the enveloping garment lowered an off-putting boundary between herself and the colonists. The animals, who had no suits, had to remain sequestered in the module. Only Chirwl had his own custom garment, but he declined to go out alone.

"It was like wearing free-weights all the time," she told Chirwl. "On the other hand, carrying the extra load helped strengthen my muscles. I wonder what it was like in the early days of the colony when the domes were under construction, battling the radiation and atmosphere as well as the gravity."

"I am most anxious to examine this place," Chirwl said. "Here is perhaps my greatest example of where living beings should not belong."

"For pity's sake, don't suggest that to my patients," Shona said.

Franklin began his long-awaited vacation, leaving Shona in charge of the entire office. Al's notion of a vacation was to stay at home with the comlink and doorbell turned off, and to take it easy. Once he'd acquainted Shona with his office and staff and outlined the daily routines, he disappeared, refusing to answer any calls, virtually forcing his patients to turn to Shona. She went gently, taking time for a consultation with a patient before the examination. Fulfilling Franklin's prediction, some confided that a polite, young physician made a nice change.

Celtuce's wealth of minerals returned a sufficiency of credits to its workers. Shona felt like a poor relation every time one

156

of the colonists came in to see her. Their clothing was made of very expensive fabrics and draped in the latest styles, which made the fine garments Gershom had brought her seem dowdy and lifeless. If you were paying a premium to have your clothes brought from light-years away, it made sense to get the best for just a little bit more. Even the children had costly jewelry as well as custom-made electronic toys. Without many outlets to spend on, Celtusians applied their plentiful capital to personal adornment and amusements. Shona had an urge to start wearing her fancy clothes during office hours.

"Maybe I'll blend in better," she suggested to Chwirl playfully. Her duties were not time-consuming or difficult. As the older doctor had said, Celtusians were a healthy lot. She had a lot of free hours to fill.

Some of that time was taken up by social calls. The colonists were delighted that someone new had come to stay, and each household took turns inviting Shona over to visit. Small as it was, the colony was spread out under a joined trio of domes, giving each individual domicile a pleasing sense of space. Each home within was expensively decorated, and had every labor-saving device Shona had ever seen, and some she hadn't. She was puzzled as to why everyone in a dome with less than two thousand colonists had to have a high-speed copier capable of producing ten thousand copies a minute, or what they would use them for, but what one Celtusian had, the others wanted. She heard from one hostess that the copier craze had started when one young man started self-publishing hard copies of his own poetry, and distributing the booklets to his friends. It sounded rather like keeping up with the most socially advanced citizen had gotten out of hand. If it hadn't been for the mandatory recycling laws imposed by the Galactic government, there'd have been 'outdated junk' heaped up in craters everywhere on the planet as updated versions of appliances came along in the Corporation traders' ships. As it was, the colony sent a lot of its hand-me-downs and trade-ins as though they were discarded toys to younger, less-prosperous cousin colonies.

It was like wandering into the wealthy side of the Martian Domes. There was no unemployment, no temporary or transient housing, no poverty or middle class, only well-to-do and wealthy. "You don't have anything if you don't have your health," her mother used to say. It was the one commodity that couldn't be bought, which was why they had sent for her. Everything seemed all right now, though. Barring the occasional industrial accident or domestic injury, she had nothing to look forward to but the mind-numbing round of social calls and bingo.

Shona found the concept of serious bingo-playing highly humorous, but her neighbors were serious in their pursuit. Some of them were addicted to it. To her amazement, they played for money, large sums of it. Credits didn't seem to be real to them. Gershom was right. There was so much capital here that they treated it like play money.

The social schedule was as intense an occupation. Shona was eager at first to get to know other people, but it was very disconcerting talking with someone wearing a shoulder unit. She didn't know if she was speaking to one person or sixty. She gave a lecture at the community college to thirteen, and found later that the entire colony had heard it. The radios had a whole range of uses she had never dreamed of. A child who wanted to skip school could hear the day's lectures courtesy of a cooperative friend. And the radios were a wonderful way to hear gossip, with or without the knowledge of the wearer.

"What a very interesting field you're in," Berna, one of her hostesses, began after they had sat down with steaming cups of tea, inadvertently repeating almost to the syllable what Shona's previous hostesses had said to her. Shona wondered if she had overheard it from listening in on another of Shona's social calls, or if the archaic etiquette manual everyone used demanded the formula. "You seem so young to take on such a responsibility. What made you go into it?"

Resisting an impulse to recite the query along with her, Shona smiled. She talked about herself, her work, and her family, trying to make her reply interesting and slightly different than the version she had recited the day before, and the day before that. She wondered if the electronic eavesdroppers ever checked. "My father had encouraged me to go into medical school so I could work with him one day."

"How lovely! And will you?"

Shona just shook her head regretfully. "He's dead."

"Oh, I'm so sorry," Berna said, and gracefully turned the conversation to another topic. "I've just redecorated. Tau Ceti modern. What do you think of it? Eberhard doesn't like all the chrome, but I think it adds a touch of elegant light to the room, don't you?"

For all that they were unimaginative, the colonists were kind and considerate. Shona could never bring herself to talk about the details of her parents' deaths or what she'd undergone in the year immediately before she signed on with the Corporation. She felt both to be private matters, not to be trivialized by casual conversation. One was a long-standing regret, with which she had never really come to terms, and the other was too fresh. It still hurt to know that the child she had carried under her heart would never grow up, never be more than a brief memory and a small hologram which she kept on her computer console. Shona couldn't yet talk about it even if she had wanted to. Lani had filled the gap for a little while, but now even that comfort was gone.

"I think it looks marvelous," Shona said, searching for words that would please her hostess. Despite the brilliant chrome curves of its frames, the furniture was spare and simple of line. It belonged in a more intimate setting; a den, perhaps. The arrangement made the large room seem empty. "You get a tremendous feeling of . . . of *space,* don't you?"

"Oh, yes, that's exactly what *I* felt," Berna said, delighted with her guest's perspicacity, knowing that all her neighbors had just heard the new doctor praise her choice. Shona breathed an inaudible sigh.

Beyond her social schedule, she had a lot of time to herself, which, after the utter lack of privacy on Mars and the ships, she prized and enjoyed. Living in a closed dome and unable to take a pressure suit and walk by oneself out on the surface as the Martians could, Celtusians had an instinctive understanding of the need to be alone. It was impossible to 'get away' anywhere, so they learned to be alone within crowds. When Shona strolled around the marbled floors of the colony during planetary evening every day, she had to make direct eye contact with curious passersby if she wanted company. Otherwise, they went along their way as if they hadn't seen her, usually talking on their shoulder boxes to an unseen friend still at home. She appreciated the custom. It gave her time to think. She was still avoiding dealing with her miscarriage and hasty escape into work, leaving even Gershom behind. She needed to prove herself, but she still missed being with those she loved. If any of her Celtusian neighbors observed the tears on her face after one of her long walks, they never said anything about it.

To the delight of the many children in the colony domes, Shona took Harry and Saffie for frequent airings every day. Pets were a limited commodity. With no crime, there was no need for watchdogs. Vermin were unknown, so there was no need for pestcatchers.

Her animals settled into Celtuce reasonably well once they had become used to the press of extra-gee. After pleading to be let out of the module for the duration of Shona's self-imposed isolation period, the dog refused at first to step out of the module into the dome when at last she was allowed. Shona finally figured out that the animal's sensitive nose was going on overload because of the noxious slap of dome air. Gradual acclimatization helped ease her out into the domes.

On the other hand, the cat loved it. Because of his special breeding, his sense of smell was even more well-developed than the dog's. He walked around with his mouth slightly open, tasting as well as sniffing the strong aroma. Harry couldn't wait to get out and explore. Chirwl was nonplused by the sulphur smell, declaring that it made him sleepy, but Shona enjoyed his company on her walks, and often carried him on her back in his sleeping pouch, like a papoose.

Celtuce's surface was unstable. At least twice a day there were ground tremors, some barely more than a distant vibration, but some of such ferocity that they threatened the integrity of the domes. The marbled patterning in the floor, Shona had learned, was not a planned design, but the remains of surface minerals that became entrapped in the glasslike complex when cracks caused by the earthquakes were fused together. For the first few weeks, the vibrations were gentle and eminently ignorable. Her neighbors insisted that it meant a serious quake was on the way, citing examples from the colony's long history, and cautioned her to be careful.

"Are the gray boxes pets, like those you have?" Chirwl asked, while they were taking a walk.

"No, they're just machines," Shona assured him.

"But they behave to them like precious," Chirwl insisted. "These people are saying words talking to them all the time."

"They're just talking to other people through them," Shona said, amused.

"It is most peculiar to speak to people who are not there," Chirwl said, severely.

When the rumbling began, Shona did not at first recognize it for what it was. The sound grew louder and louder, echoing off the inside of the dome until it drove her to her knees in terror with its intensity, and made her very skull shake. Under her, the ground tossed crazily from side to side. Harry fell out of her arms, and she grabbed for him. The cat yowled and batted at her hands.

As if anyone in Celtuce couldn't tell what was happening, alarm bells began to ring, and her shoulder box squawked, "Earthquake! Take cover!" Saffie barked and tried to grip Shona's sleeve in her teeth, pulling her toward a semicylindrical building on one side of the enclosed street. The cat, terrified of the noise and confusion, retreated a little way out of Shona's reach.

"Harry, come here! Saffie, stop it!"'

160

With difficulty, Shona drew herself to her knees, and scrambled toward the nearest doorway. Chirwl stuck his head out of the pouch, which had swung around off Shona's back and was hanging down, bumping the floor.

"A tremor?" he asked glancing around, blinking. "Seek a stable archway!"

"I'm trying!" Shona snapped, scooping up the pouch. With a cry of protest, Chirwl fell inside the bag as she swung it around out of her way. The swaying stopped for a moment, and she regained her feet. Suddenly, there was a violent thrust that threw them all to the ground and pried open a long crack in the floor. While klaxons rang the alarm, Harry sniffed the split with feline delicacy, and then discharged a hairball on the floor with appropriate sound effects. Then he began to scratch backwards at the crack, attempting to bury the smell under the floor.

"Oh, thank you," Shona said disgustedly. "Thank you very much." She hooked her free arm under the cat's body and swung him up. He yowled a complaint, to which she paid no attention.

"What's wrong with him?" demanded a man, running up. Shona recognized him as Len, one of her neighbors who lived in a dome close to her quarters.

"Nothing," Shona snapped, kneeling down and applying her sensor to the crack, just before she was elbowed aside by the repair crew. The man caught her arm and steadied her, guiding her away from the crack as the emergency team converged on it. "Nothing, Just traces of sulphur and the usual mineral soup. Too bad. I hoped we'd have something here that would solve the mystery of your epidemic. I hate unexplained illnesses."

"That old thing? But it's over. It was just a mutated virus," Len said. "Nothing to worry about."

"No. It puzzles me." Shona shook her head definitely. "Not after all this time. Not after you've been so careful to keep the outside out there. It's got to be something that originated in here or was brought here recently."

The emergency team, clad in suits and hoods, sprayed a thick foam from canisters with hoses over the break in the floor, and spread out to cover smaller cracks that etched outward from it like a fractal. A huge machine, like a steamroller but with a flat blade similar to an iron, rolled up. The first team got out of the way, and the operator lowered the big blade over the break. Hot steam rose around the machine. When the blade rose again, the surface was restored to its glassy, cobbled texture. The only trace of the breach was a new line of brown and yellow in the marbled swirl.

The short-lived fever was still making Shona's whiskers twitch. There were a million factors to be considered as to why, after half a century of normalcy, the people of Celtus were reacting to their closed environment. Common sense dictated that such reactions would have likely turned up at the beginning, from exposure to the local water supply or atmosphere, or more likely come on gradually. This sudden, lightninglike intrusion was very strange. Of course, there was Franklin's opinion, that the problem had come in from another world. Still, even cargo entering from outside was subjected to irradiation or fumigation to prevent infiltration. If a new bacterium was in the water or air, she wanted to find it. Shona's equipment analyzed the myriad chemical and organic components from air samples trapped in aerogel and vials of mineral sludge scraped from the sides of the water-recycling plant's filters, and spat its opinions out on disk. There wasn't a suspicious microbe, bacterium, or fungus in any of them. Shona carried portable testing equipment with her whenever she went out for a walk, just to see if any variations ever turned up. It was unlikely to have been caused by a mass allergy among the settlers. So far, though, she hadn't found the enzymal footprint of any unusual virus. Harry hadn't sniffed out any overt pollutants yet either. So where were the 'bites' coming from, and what had made everyone sick?

The Celtuce communications system pulled messages off the local beacon addressed to its denizens. Shona's comm number turned up with several entries, which were duly transferred from the computer center to her personal unit. Susan had replied to Shona's most recent messages, but owing to what Shona could only guess must be anomalies in the beacon system added onto her frequent travels, her letters arrived out of order. After some confusion over the state of Susan's documentary project, Shona began to read the dates on the tachyon encryption. One, which turned up in the latest batch, had been recorded while Shona was on Mars, waiting for her transport to Karela, offering her loving sympathy and wishing her good luck on her new assignment. Shona felt a strong surge of sisterly love for her friend.

"Congratulations," she replied to Susan. "I've just received the oldest one yet. It's been bouncing around, following me across the galaxy for nine months. It feels like I've been off Mars longer than that—several lifetimes, in fact. Thank you, belatedly, for your kind words. They mean more to me now than they would have if I'd gotten them when you intended. Every time I think I've healed, something comes along and tears the scar open again, but I know I really am healing now because I can look objectively at the loss of my baby. My body's bounced back to just about normal. One good thing you can say about endometrial scarring is a less onerous curse every month." She emitted a wry chuckle. "It's an ill wind, or some such bromide. Love to you, twin. Hope your project is going well. I'd like to see it someday when it's finished!"

The next message was from Gershom. "Hello from Tau Ceti. Miss you, of course. We stopped here to pick up some supplies and dine with Ivo's sister. Lani wore your green dress. She and Eblich sat and beamed at everyone like a pair of searchlights, but they had a good time. She's becoming a regular little member of the crew. I'll hate leaving her behind on Mars, and so will the others. Tell your colony leader that I've got a line on his filters. He should be happy to hear that. By the way, I didn't know it, but Celtuce is famous in shipbuilding circles. Their processing plant turns out some of the highest quality raw materials for drive systems in the galaxy."

"Hmm," said Shona. "You learn something new every day."

For the primary occupation which had caused the formation of the entire colony on Celtuce, the mining process was carried on almost sub rosa. Once the suits were off, no one mentioned work, or yield, or the problems encountered in excavating radioactive ore from the surface of an unstable planet. When Shona asked about the processing plant, one of her hosts laughed hilariously.

"What do you want to know about that for? It's dull. It's work!"

"I'd like to know, that's all. I'd like to go down to the plant and see what happens there," Shona said defensively, feeling a little silly to have her interest denigrated. She didn't want to mention out loud that it was also the only place that hadn't been checked as a source of the virus. "Why, is it top secret?"

"Far from it," her friend said. "Just watch out for Larrity. He's the head of Mining Services, and he doesn't like anyone."

"I'll avoid him, thank you!"

"If you hang around at the plant, he'll find you," her friend warned.

The way to the processing plant was the only part of the domes which was not carefully landscaped or decorated. If anything, it made Shona think of the blocks of windowless manufacturing buildings in Mars Dome #4. Instead of the cheerful bustle of the living quarters, the semicylindrical passage seemed dangerous and remote. Even though the walls were made of the same plexiglass, transparent to the white fog outside, it felt darker.

163

At the end of the corridor, Shona passed through successive sets of pressure doors and decontamination chambers. At the urging of flashing warning signs in the first chamber, she donned a white protective suit, somewhat like the ones she used to wear at the Space Center, but heavier and with double-sealing seams. She observed that the dome-shaped transparent helmet was equipped with a rebreather circuit, in case of an emergency in which the wearer was forced to outlast his or her small airpack. A tinny recorded voice like a gloomy conscience at the rear of the collar informed her of these facts. Shona kept walking, ignoring the chills that went up her spine.

Shortly, the transparent walls were replaced by solid walls of dark gray titanium alloy. Light-strips, at either side of the passage and in a single line overhead, provided illumination. She passed through one more set of doors, where she donned a pair of disposable booties over her suit boots, and emerged into a gigantic chamber filled with machines rolling back and forth, busy at their tasks. It was almost a shock to find life, after the isolation of the corridors. Shona decided to explore. This chamber contained approximately the same area as one of the three domes that made up the residence section. There was a small office block on one side of the chamber, but otherwise it was given over to the factory.

The process was well-organized. The ore came in through baffles at the rear of the huge dome, and went through several processing stations, progressing from tumblers that broke up the boulder-sized chunks to crucibles that poured out neat ingots of metal. Scrap rock was tumbled out of the side of the dome through chutes. The din was deafening, even though much of the machinery was shielded behind thick transparent walls of plasteel and insulation.

There was a sirenlike hoot behind her, and Shona turned to see what it was. With a squawk, she jumped back against the wall to avoid one of the biggest machines of all, almost a building on treads, carrying a small moon's worth of broken rock. Her suit's rad counter went wild until it passed.

There were human beings working in the dome, but they seemed so tiny atop their engines that Shona almost had to squint to see them. Dr. Franklin had been right when he told her a huge work force was unnecessary. Most of the processing was handled by automation. It was the mining itself which needed human minds and eyes.

The "building on treads" dumped its load into a long hopper, and as soon as it was empty, reversed swiftly across the dome toward the baffled gate. Another lift the same size, carrying more rock, zoomed inside from the surface almost before the first one had gone. It rolled past Shona, and the heavy boulders clattered against the metal sides of the chute with a noise like an avalanche. Shona watched with fascination. Robot hands suspended above the conveyor lines sorted through the rock as it was broken up, and graded it, transferring some of the pieces onto two other lines for special treatment.

"Hey!" A man's voice on her collar radio cut through the racket. "Isn't that Dr. Taylor?"

"Yes!" She looked around. "Where are you?"

"Up here. It's Len," the voice said. Shona turned around, and saw that the small figure in the cab of the earthmover was waving. Swiftly, it swung down the ladder, and descended the distance to the floor. Shona marveled at the scale of the machine. "Hi. Decided to take the tour?"

"I wanted to see what you do back here," Shona said. "You handle that thing amazingly well."

"Thanks, ma'am," Len said, his cheeks turning red inside his helmet. "I've had more than twenty-five years of practice."

Shona gestured around her. "You're all moving so fast. I thought you were near to the tap end of your source. Is there that much left to do?"

"We're going to work hard right up till the last load, ma'am," Len assured her proudly. "We're going to go out with the same level of productivity we began with."

"I am very impressed," Shona said definitely. "Do you just pick up loads from other workers, or do you mine the ore yourself?"

"There's fifteen of us earthmovers," Len said, patting the loader's tire nearest to him. It was more than double his height with grooves deep enough for him to stick in an arm up to the shoulder, but he managed to seem protective of the giant machine. "We do it all, from rock face to the return trip."

"That's amazing. Could I come out with you on the next run?" Shona pleaded. "I'd love to see how it works."

"Well, I wish I could," Len began, "but—"

"But you can't because she's leaving," a new voice growled. "Now!"

"Uh-oh," Len muttered, under his breath, as a tall figure in a bright red pressure suit strode toward them. "Larrity."

"What is this woman doing here?" the man demanded peremptorily, confronting Len and cutting Shona dead as she tried to introduce herself. Larrity was a big man, with a burly physique that belied his age, which had to be nearly that of Dr. Franklin's.

His thin hair was gray, and his eyes were bitter, sunk into a face lined with anger and disappointment. He loomed over Shona like a building, glaring at her.

"She's just visiting, Mr. Larrity. She's the doctor from the Corporation—" Len tried to explain.

A slice across the air from Larrity's hand stopped his explanation. "I don't care if she's Galactic President. She's unauthorized. Throw her out of here," he ordered Len with the same heated growl that the bad guys on the Old Time 2-D movies said, "Terminate with extreme prejudice."

"Doesn't he have trouble walking upright with a chip that big on his shoulder?" Shona asked Len sourly, as he escorted her toward the entrance. She didn't care if the supervisor could hear her through the shoulder link. She was shaken by the unpleasant incident. "I don't mind having him enforce the rules, but has he ever tried a spoonful of sugar? It might make all the difference in the world!"

Dana Murye came out of the office and ran over to them. Like the others, the accountant was dressed in a neck-to-heels protective coverall. She pushed the two of them into the first airlock. "Oh, Shona, I thought that was you on the radio link. I should have warned you about Larrity, but I never thought you'd want to come down to the plant. I don't know why I didn't think you might be curious, like anybody else. I'm sorry. He's rude to everyone, but I think he has a special grudge against doctors."

"It's all right," Shona said, slipping off her disposable booties. "I'm going. Where in the myriad planets did you get him? Everyone else I've met on Celtuce is so nice."

Len shrugged. "I don't know how he got assigned to the colony in the first place. I think the Corp forced him on Bob Derneld. He's not married. He's not sociable. But he knows his job inside out and backwards. I guess," Len said dubiously, "that we're lucky to have him. I think."

As the planet swung closer to its primary over the course of the following days, Shona could see that under the milky sunlight and in the protective shelter of the domes, Celtuce was a pleasant enough place to live. There was enough of interest within the domes to keep the population occupied. Its leaders deliberately kept going a multitrack program of continuing education, and encouraged discussion groups, which Shona was invited to join. There were sports teams that sponsored ongoing tournaments. Basketball season was just ending, and Shona was there to witness the championship game, a crushing defeat to that year's challengers. The parabolic antenna brought in all the latest entertainment programs from the system beacon and beamed it down into the domes with surprisingly little interference. Shona found she was only a few days behind on her favorite series. But the Celtusians favorite entertainment was still socializing with one another, gossiping with each other, and eavesdropping.

"We don't like to travel. All of our contact with the outside world comes in on videodisks, books, or in magazine cubes. You might call us sticks in the mud, but we're happy this way," Dr. Franklin said one day when she managed to tear him away from his self-imposed exile. The senior doctor was enjoying his time off. He resisted, irascibly, any efforts by his neighbors to drag him back into society, but he liked Shona, and didn't mind coming out to see her as much as he pretended he did. "Maybe I won't ever come back to work. I'm an old man. Tell anyone you like. That'll give the gossips something to think about for at least a week or two. You'll see. They'll come up with a thousand reasons why I don't want my job anymore, and none of them will be that I'm old and tired and want to rest."

Shona went out for a walk later that day with Leader Derneld, and mentioned Franklin's proposed resignation. "He said to tell everyone he's an old man and he's just not going to come back. . . ."

Derneld dismissed her report without waiting to hear all of it. "I know the rest. He says that about once every year. I'm ignoring it until the day I get a datacube in hand with his holo on it. It's just a rumor he likes to keep going."

"Rumormongering seems to be the national sport," Shona said with a chuckle. "With everyone in and out of everyone else's house all the time, spilling secrets they promised sincerely only half an hour ago to keep forever, how do you keep from having blood feuds?" She had three of her menagerie with her. Chirwl dozed or muttered to himself in the pouch on Shona's back, and Harry ranged from a tucked position in her arms to an obstinate drape across her shoulders; anything rather than be put down and walk on his own power. The combined weight of the cat and the ottle on any extended walk was enough to give Shona a fine aerobic workout and leave her aching at the end. Saffie pulled at the lead tied to Shona's wrist, eager to sniff out their path. She had gotten over her dislike of the air, and enjoyed every outing as if it were in the filtered streets of Mars.

Derneld laughed, and kicked at a rough place in the cobbled, glasslike floor. Shona found the translucent floor swirled with brown, black, and red, slightly sinister but attractive. "Sheer volume of data, I think. Since everyone has their own version of all the latest news, it's hard to take any of it seriously. You're quite the subject of talk just now." Derneld spread an imaginary banner on the air with a sweep of his palm. "You're the 'Lady Doctor with Mystery Past and Personal Zoo.' I want you to know you're making thousands of people happy here. They have a new subject to pick to pieces."

She laughed. "They're going to be very disappointed when they find out how ordinary I really am. By the way, I'm still curious about your *real* bug problem."

"Oh, that. Nothing but a rash of little red bites," the colony leader said with a grin, waving a vague hand. "Excuse the pun. Some kind of no-see-ums. Chiggers."

"That's what the doctor said," Shona told him. "And that's exactly what I find hard to believe."

"Don't worry about it. We're going to take care of those ourselves. Let me show you." Taking her elbow, he guided her into a semicylindrical-arched building not far from his office. "The traders brought this to us with the latest shipment." Against one curved wall was a cluster of high-pressure gas canisters. "They said it's guaranteed to do the trick no matter what kind of bug it is. We'll be rid of them in no time."

Shona bent to look at the label, and looked up at Derneld, horrified. "By the Blue Star, no! You can't use this."

"Why not?" The colony leader looked a little hurt. "This is the very latest and best in pest control. I've got to tell you, young lady, we're pretty frustrated by the damned biters. They've scored on practically everyone."

"But you can't use a pervasive chemical like that in a small, closed residential dome. Whoever told you you could misled you terribly. It will have side effects and long-term effects that you won't believe! It'll wipe out life forms all right, human beings among them."

Derneld listened with growing concern. "Are you certain we can't use it? This chemical cost a lot of money."

She read the labels on the tanks and nodded grimly. "I am very sure. This molecule's got a wanted poster on the wall of every environmental tech in the galaxy. It's a guaranteed killer. One of these canisters is enough to spray a continent. It's for open fields on atmosphere worlds, not a small closed system like this. It might begin to break down your nervous systems, too, in a matter of weeks! People's immune systems could be affected and they'd become allergic to everything. They'd end up living in dark rooms, and subsisting on unspiced nutri the rest of their lives."

The colony leader made a playful face. "Ugh. Nutri. Now, there's a horrible fate."

"You're so right," Shona said, with an equally expressive grimace. "I ate nutri through the first half of my pregnancy. At least now I can use flavorings on the stuff."

The colony leader smiled down at her. "I didn't know you had any children."

"I don't," she said with a sad smile.

"I'm sorry," Leader Derneld said. If he was curious, he didn't pursue the subject. She was grateful. "How are your friends today?" he inquired as they emerged from the building. He stooped to pet Saffie, who wagged her tail. "My neighbors have been telling me how much they're enjoying your delightful pets. I regret that I've been too busy to come calling."

Shona smiled fondly. "They're my team of experts. Saffie's a vaccine dog. Saffie, this is Leader Derneld. Friend."

The big black dog strained forward to sniff the man's hand. Satisfied with his scent, she looked up into his face and whined expectantly. Derneld, glanced at Shona for enlightenment. Shona laughed.

"Don't fall for that unless you like scratching dogs, Bob," she said. "At Saffie's size, it's an occupation rather than a hobby."

Derneld grinned and rasped his fingertips between the dog's ears. Saffie closed her eyes and crooned. "Well, maybe once in a while. I'm a busy man, but there are very few animals here. Our people don't seem to go in much for pets, though they like them. It's nice to have yours here. And the others?"

"This is Harry," Shona said, setting the cat down on the street. The cat immediately pointed one leg toward the sky and began to wash under his tail. Shona shook her head in mock exasperation. Harry had a cat's sense of occasion. "Hmph. Cats. Have you ever met an ottle, Bob?"

"Never," Derneld said with interest. "I've heard of them, though."

"Chirwl?" she called over her shoulder. The ottle wasn't paying attention. She heard the characteristic scratching of the alien's claws in inscribing minute calligraphy on a resin chip. Shona poked at the pouch on her back. "Chirwl, may I introduce First Leader Derneld? Leader, Chirwl."

"How do you do?" Derneld said, staring with open fascination at the sleek creature that poked its head out of the knapsack.

"How do you do," the ottle inquired pleasantly, lifting the upper half of his body and bowing with boneless fluidity. Then, fixing intelligent eyes on Derneld, he extended a paw, which the leader took delicately in his big hand. "I have observed the atmospheric and tectonic conditions of this planet over the course of some weeks and find it much active for too little comfort. Do humans belong here?"

"I certainly hope we do. We've been here for over forty-five years." The number bounced off the leader's tongue like a rubber ball falling down stairs.

The ottle waved a claw. "A brief moment in the Great Year. I am studying whether machinery is an affront against nature, or an offshoot thereof. It is my theory that—"

"Chirwl!" Shona said, warningly. "He's a philosopher, sir. I believe he's trying to figure out where humans fit in the scheme of things. Up until five years ago, all his people knew about was other ottles."

"We must discuss it some time," Derneld said, smiling and turning toward the door of his module. "In the meantime, I must get back to my office. It was a pleasure chatting with you."

"Please, Bob, let me investigate what's causing the welts. There's surely a harmless way of dealing with them."

"The council's going to be upset to be deprived of their fancy new chemical," he said flippantly, "but I agree. You seem to know what you're talking about. I'll send the next case to you, and we'll see what you come up with."

Chirwl nodded absently, his attention already back on his work. The humans went on talking. The whole character of this colony had the air of normality in the midst of machine-made sanctuary. Very strange, when it was surrounded by danger. Humans liked to live in unnatural places.

There was a sudden change in the air, an imperceptible alteration from the norm of balance or pressure. The fierce land outside was making its presence felt. His heart started pounding.

"Seek shelter," he cried to Shona, his data chips scattering all over as he attempted to duck down into the pouch. A shock wave hit, making the ground heave, and Shona staggered. She and the leader hurried toward the warehouse archway. Chirwl's pouch swung, flinging the ottle out. He hit the ground shoulder first and rolled hooplike across the glass floor. Alarm bells began ringing, echoing crazily against the ceiling of the dome.

"This is not a place suited to living things!" the ottle wailed, scrabbling back toward Shona and the leader. His claws slipped on the glass.

Another tremor hit, a strong one that tore through the translucent floor with a report like a thunderbolt, almost underneath his tail. He chittered, scrambling for safety.

The alarms got louder, joined by the breach siren. The cat in his agitation was trying to climb Shona's shoulder. Shona yanked him down against her chest and held out her free arm to the ottle. Chirwl climbed her legs and huddled in a tight ball against the cat. As soon as the heaving of the ground stilled, the emergency team, clad in protective suits, hurried through with repair equipment.

"Are you all right?" Shona asked him.

"I am . . . better," the ottle opined shakily. He hung limp as a kitten as Shona put him back in his pouch.

"Here, Shona," said Dana Murye, calling her over when the alarms had died down. "Len has one of those bites coming up on his arm."

Shona recognized the earthmover operator, who also worked on the repair teams. He had yanked off his gauntlet, and was scratching furiously.

"Let me see it."

"Right here." Len grimaced, holding out his arm to her. "It's burning. The little monster is there, all right. Look, he's bitten me about a dozen times already." There were numerous small, angry bumps rising on the man's skin. A new one rose while Shona watched.

Quickly, she fumbled in her kit for a curved sample glass, trapped the portion of skin underneath it, and chivied the surface cells with the edge of a slide. "Come with me to my office, and I'll put cream on it We'll see what we've got here."

The others waited while Shona looked at the contents of her sample glass under a microscope and examined Len's arm with a magnifier.

"Well?" asked Derneld.

"There's nothing there but skin cells and a little chemical sludge," Shona said. "It isn't an insect bite. It looks like a localized allergic reaction, probably to that sulphur soup coming up through the floor. Look—" she picked up Len's gauntlet and handed him a magnifying glass. "There's a pinhole puncture piercing your protective suit. Hmm. Try saying *that* three times fast."

Len scowled. "I can't be allergic to that stuff! I work with it every day. I operate loaders!"

"Sure you can be allergic. You can become sensitized to any compound over a long period of exposure," Shona pointed out. "I'll bet that everyone who's been 'bitten' has a leak in their decontamination suits. This stuff could make an armadillo itch."

"You'd be wrong," Derneld informed her. "Plenty of people have complained about the bites, and they don't handle anything that comes in from atmosphere directly."

171

"Unless the dome breaks!" Shona pointed out. "As it just did. Maybe I should be checking for surges in the reaction right after a breach occurs. Then we should have someone run a scan over each new seal to see that the contaminants don't make it into the air or water supply."

"Ahh." Derneld nodded, enlightened. "That makes sense. We've had poor old Al Franklin looking for bugs all this time. From now on, teams should be wearing something as well-sealed as mining suits to handle dome breaks. I'll talk it up on the net."

"But I've been exposed to that stuff for years," Len said.

"You're older," Derneld said, clapping his friend on the back. "You might react faster to things that didn't bother you before. Well, Shona, thank you for clearing up another mystery. It was a good thing you came to Celtuce after all."

CHAPTER

⟞13⟞

"WAKE UP, SHONA." Chirwl's voice interrupted her dreams. "It is a beautiful sunrise. Wake up and see it." Something nudged her in the side of the neck. "You have fallen asleep at your desk. Did you know that?"

"What I do in the name of duty," she muttered, refusing to open her eyes. Now that Chirwl mentioned it, she wasn't very comfortable, but she was too tired to move.

"Shona. It's a beautiful morning," Chirwl insisted, loping to the other side of the porcelain-topped table to face her when she turned her head to avoid him. "Come, look up. Shona." She turned her head again, and Chirwl thundered back the other way.

"Stop that," she said drowsily. "You sound like a herd of rhinoceroses. Rhinoceri."

She heard Saffie whine a few inches from her ear, and relented, opening one eye. The dog's warm brown eyes pleaded with her to get up. Harry stood right next to Saffie on the floor, tail and ears erect, waiting. "Did I sleep through breakfast time?"

"Not yet," Chirwl said. He rolled back on his tail with his front paws clasped over his chest. "It continues to be early. I observed the handsome prism effect of the light, and thought you might appreciate it, too."

"Not as much as you do, I'm sure." The ottle's eyes were capable of picking up more color variations than hers. "Well, you're nicely recovered from your adventure."

Chirwl's whiskers twitched. "I have recorded it in my thesis. It was at least an act of *nature*."

Shona grinned. The muscles in her back knotted as she straightened up, and her teeth tasted like vintage hiking socks. She didn't remember dropping off over her files. The data she was reading when she fell asleep just blended right into her dreams. They'd been very strange dreams.

Her pets were all staring at her from their post beside the food cabinet, waiting for their breakfast, which was probably a long overdue supper.

"I'm sorry, all," she said contritely.

As she dished out various preparations of nutri, she watched the effect Chirwl had mentioned. The sunrise through a methane atmosphere attained an unexpected beauty as the yellow-white primary struck rainbows off the shimmering residence dome amid the swirling gases.

"Just goes to show you what the Terraforming Committee would do if only it had money," Shona wisecracked. "On Mars, it's just bang, and up over the horizon."

"Did you learn what you sought last night?" Chirwl asked, eating kibbled and nut-flavored nutri out of hand from his bowl. She yawned.

"Well, the bumps aren't caused by bugs or allergies," she said definitely. "It seems to be dermatitis caused by that soup out there." She gestured at the mist, fast becoming a homogenous curtain of white as the sun rose further behind it, flooding it with light. "I got a low-concentration distillate of the atmosphere, and did allergy testing on half the population. The reaction to it is a completely local thing. The population must be fairly sensitized to it. I tried it on myself, and it only reddened my skin. I couldn't even raise bumps on the mice, and you know how sensitive they are. The stuff is faintly corrosive. Nothing I'd want touching me on a long-term basis. But also nothing that I'd need Saffie's talents for. The substance itself could have eaten those holes in the protective suits over time, let alone unprotected skin, another good reason to keep a closer eye on suit and seal integrity."

"Well done," the ottle cheered her.

"Not yet," Shona said. "Not until I can figure out how to prevent recurrences."

The next few days she spent treating a dozen people who had welts. Any suggestion that they were an isolated skin condition, or sociogenic in nature was quickly dispelled. None of the subjects appeared to have anything in common except for the 'bites.'

"They're pernicious," one man complained as Shona examined his arms and shoulders, which were thickly covered by the angry red bumps. "Never had anything like that before. It's an allergy. Or a curse."

Antihistamines and cortisone cream brought down the swellings before the man was even out of the office, but that didn't stem the problem at the source.

174

Shona discovered her solution when one woman came in for treatment. She had had chronic symptoms every few weeks since they began to appear.

"Like a chronometer, Doctor," the woman said desperately. "I'm at my wits' end. I've tried sprays and electronic bug-catchers. Nothing works!"

"You'll be happy to know that the condition isn't caused by insect bites. It would seem to be chemical in origin. When are they the worst?" Shona asked. The welts were the same as all those she'd been treating on her ten previous patients, so she applied the cortisone cream to the woman's skin. Within moments, the redness began to subside, and the woman sighed with relief.

"About the beginning of every other fortnight," she said, after a quick query over her shoulder unit to her husband. "Yes, now that I think about it every four weeks. I noticed that the bites came up before payday, every time. It might be from tension, because that's when my bills all come due." She laughed. "The pay's good, so I spend too much."

"I know what you mean," Shona said with a grin. "I always have too much month left at the end of *my* money. Can you stay in a room for the next few days that has its own air-filtration system? I have an idea what might be causing the problem."

She took her findings to the colony leader's office.

"What happens every four weeks right before payday?" she asked Derneld.

"What?" the colony leader asked, staring at Shona. "Where did that come from?"

"I've treated a dozen chronic cases, and they all claim that's when the 'bug bites' come up, without fail. Not at the same places everywhere in the domes or the same times, but all at four-week intervals."

"Four weeks," Derneld mused, glancing through his records. "Oh, yes! That's when the air filters are changed. We rotate the locations weekly where the filters will be pulled and replaced. And yes, there are four sites."

Shona nodded. "Uh-huh. I think you're going to have to change them more often. They're not doing the job toward the end of their life span. You ought to do it every two weeks. Every week would be better."

"We can't change those filters every week!" Derneld squawked. "They're too expensive, even taking into account the bargain your husband found for us."

"You have to filter out those chemical irritants," Shona insisted, "or the reactions will only get worse over time. Some chemical

175

damage is cumulative. Think of it as an experiment. If it doesn't work, and the patients continue to complain about the same time every month, you can slow down the schedule again. Please, just try it. And open the hydroponics center, or get a lot of potted plants out there. They'll help clear toxins out of the air. Trust me."

Reluctantly, Derneld complied. After a few days, the air even smelled cleaner, and the complaints ceased. Derneld had to admit that she had been right to insist.

"This is going to use up the air filters even faster," he said. "But it was a good piece of detective work on your part, and I'm glad you persisted. We're not gonna enjoy our riches with the itches. I hope your husband gets back here soon with a shipment."

Shona chuckled at the leader's joke. She, too, hoped Gershom would be coming back again soon, for purely personal and selfish reasons. It only made matters worse if she thought about the months they'd had together on the *Sibyl*. It was no consolation for what she needed now. Pushing erotic fancies to the back of her mind with a firm mental hand, Shona concentrated her thoughts on the day's work.

When she arrived, Dr. Franklin was in the office going over the patient files. "Couldn't take it any longer," he explained, a little sheepishly. "I thought I'd be good for at least eight weeks of time off, but no. Couldn't even finish off a paltry six. A fellow can have only so much privacy, and then he begins to go buggy, if you'll excuse the expression. I'm not at as sure my friends and neighbors will be overjoyed, but here I am. I read over your notes and recommendations that you sent on to Bob Derneld. You did a nice job. That was a good thought, having the filters changed more frequently to cure the itches. Now I can barely smell the stink. The air smells almost . . . nice."

"Do you know the worst thing about it?" Shona told Franklin. "I think I'm getting used to it."

With Franklin back on the job, Shona found herself with nothing useful to do. She didn't really enjoy video games or gossip. None of the current continuing education courses appealed to her. She was bored with bingo, and she'd failed for the last time to wheedle a ride on one of the gigantic mining machines so she could see more of the outer surface of Celtuce. The domes were shrinking around her, constricting her mental space as they had at one time on Mars. It would be a good time to move on to another assignment. On impulse, she went to see Derneld, and explained that she didn't think she was serving any purpose by remaining.

"You admitted six weeks ago that once I arrived I was already too late to do my job. I was happy to take over for Al while he took a vacation break, but now that he's back I cease to have any useful function."

"I suppose I'd have to concur," the leader said, with regret. "You've obliged us by coming out here, which to tell the truth was all we wanted of you. There's no need for you to sit here for the entire length of your contract. I'll get in touch with the Corporation and see if we can't get you reassigned."

She thanked Derneld profusely, and hurried back to her module to send a message off to Gershom. If there was a chance that the *Sibyl* was close enough to come back for her, she wanted to let him know at the earliest possible moment.

Within days, the colony leaders had an answer for Shona. Having served her purpose and more, she would be permitted to go. After receiving her initial report that the situation on Celtuce was under control, the sector chief must have been anticipating her request to move on. Details of her next assignment were in a separate message coded personally to her.

Mitchell's handsome face appeared on her tank screen. "Shona, I've got a special assignment that I need you to take. Erebus is a research colony. It is important to the Corporation. They need a general practitioner for permanent assignment. You'd be the sole physician for a group of forty scientists, all adults. I'm not asking you to remain there forever. You would only need to keep the posting for two years, while I find someone else for the job. After that, you can be moved to an assignment of your choice."

"I certainly will be on an assignment of my choice by that time," Shona said to the screen. "Don't try to sneak a new contract in past me. This one expires in a little over two years, and then I'll be permanently attached to the Taylor Traveling Medicine Show!" Erebus, she mused, replaying the message. It didn't sound at all bad to her. A colony of research scientists would be an interesting place in which to live. Chirwl would certainly be pleased to be among fellow theorists.

Mitchell's message continued. "I regret that you won't be able to use your customary transport, as it has not yet completed its present assignment. We are still awaiting the arrival of the *Sibyl* here on Mars." There was gentle but evident reproof in his voice, to which Shona paid no attention. If she could have been on that ship with Gershom, she'd have delayed delivering Lani as long as possible. The transport ship that was to bear her away was only a short distance from planetfall. It had just made its last drop within two warp jumps of the Celtuce system. She wondered why she suddenly felt defiant, and decided it was because the executive

177

made the assignment sound like a request but had already sent a ship to pick her up as if she'd already accepted. High-handed, indeed.

"Gershom was right," she grumbled. She put her anarchistic thoughts aside while she recorded a reply to Mitchell.

A message from Gershom arrived with the same batch. "I'm sorry to disappoint you, love, but no go. We're already committed to taking a load of perishable chemicals from Lazenby VI to Alpha. Luck of the spacelanes. I miss you and love you. Good luck on your next job, whatever it is."

She sent a copy of Mitchell's briefing to him along with details on Erebus's location. Even if she wasn't going to be traveling with Gershom, a permanent assignment meant that he'd be able to visit her more often.

Shona waited in the midst of the crowd at the side of the transparent dome until the big-tired vehicle appeared over the rise through the white mist, then reversed itself to envelope her living module. She made sure the animals were secured in their crash cages. Harry tried to climb through the padded mesh, but the rabbits sat placidly chewing on their chow. Saffie went into her box without complaint, and Shona stepped outside one more time to make her final farewells to her friends. Derneld was the first to say goodbye.

"We're very sorry to lose you, Shona. We were starting to think of you as one of our own."

Shona was touched. "Thank you, Bob," she said sincerely. "You have no idea how much I appreciate that. Goodbye, Al," she said, speaking directly into Derneld's shoulder box.

"Caught me," Franklin's voice chuckled from the little square. "Safe journey."

Many of the colonists pressed small gifts on her, which she felt awkward about accepting since she had nothing to give them in return. She'd done a lot of healing on Celtuce from being able to deal with her loss in private, to do a lot of thinking and self-searching among sympathetic people who didn't pick at her for every fault. Her time here had been a real success, and all her own. With a self-deprecatory chuckle, she realized she'd miss their passionate taste for gossip and charming, stilted courtesies. She regretted not being able to introduce a child of her own to the joys of space travel and meeting kind people like these. A fresh start, patience, and consideration were the real gifts they had given her. She was more than grateful to them. As she sealed the hatch of the module and it detached from the dome wall, she found there were tears running down her face.

"You're too sentimental," she chided herself as she wiped them away.

The executive meeting room was simple in its grandeur. A gigantic oval table of genuine Earth woods, burnished softly in a rich golden-brown, dominated the indirectly lit chamber like a planet hanging in the night sky. A circle of efficient-looking men and women sat or lounged in the springform seats ranged about its circumference, reading report data on the individual screens discreetly placed beside each chair at the level of writing tablets.

Verdadero's chair was the same height as the others, but his imposing presence made it seem as if he were sitting above them. He glanced at his screen. "Our net profits per sector for the quarter are slightly more modest than last quarter," he said, expertly conveying disappointment rather than disapproval. "There were a few exceptions. Prime Sector, for example, showed a rise in profitability, for the seventh quarter in a row. That's good news. Well done. Can you share your secret with us, Manfred?"

Murmurs from his fellow sector chiefs served for applause. Manfred Mitchell cleared his throat. The corners of his mouth lifted briefly, then dropped, leaving his face a blank mask, as if he hadn't the will to maintain a smile.

"You'll have to forgive me if I don't agree that it is good news. Gains were only marginal on our new product lines. We took a slight loss in the setup of Tachyon Communication Systems in the outer quadrant of the sector. The addition to the books was caused by a tragedy of which I've only just had word. Over ten billion credits are reversion to the Corporate accounts of bonuses set in an escrow for the workers on the colony of Celtuce, and all other benefits that belonged to employees who died without issue on that world. Most of them were wiped out in a plague which suddenly struck its population. It was the oldest colony in my sector. Celtuce survived under incredible hardship for so long it's difficult to believe that it's gone. The colonists will be replaced by salaried workers for the brief time until the claim is worked out."

There was a susurrus of horror among the other executives around the table.

"That's terrible, Manfred," Verdadero said, speaking over the others. "Your sector suffered another killing plague only two quarters ago. The entire population of our most profitable agricultural colony."

"Yes, sir. These things happen," Mitchell said blandly, concealing his agitation at having the matter brought up again. "When a species is not native to a biome, there are likely to be reactions I am surprised it doesn't happen more often."

Verdadero considered the truth of Mitchell's statement and nodded slightly. "Well, death benefits are to be made available to the survivors of Celtuce. We owe them that. How many are left?"

"Twelve," Mitchell said shortly. There was a heavy silence. "They had reported a fever some months ago. We sent a specialist out when there was a complaint, but it had abated by the time she arrived. The tech was inexperienced, but thorough. She stayed long enough to satisfy herself that all traces of the original infection had gone, and then requested a change of assignment. At the time, I saw no reason to believe her incorrect. She claimed there were no signs of illness when she left for her next assignment. We should have sent a team out there, not one lone doctor, but with space travel so slow, there wouldn't have been time to get anyone else. The killing plague occurred after she left."

"It's not as if teams of plague doctors are available," the big boss said understandingly. "You responded as was appropriate. The Corporation is proud to offer any assistance to a colony that requests it." The others all nodded. "What will happen now? Twelve is hardly a viable colony."

"I know, sir. We've picked up the rest of the colonists and are relocating them, wherever they want to go. Five said they'd prefer to stay on Celtuce, but that would be impossible," Mitchell said flatly. "There's no other developed industry there, and we can't justify running the domes at a loss for two more years for five people. I'm having them brought here. The remaining benefits total only about two hundred million. The difference will be placed in the general fund."

"That will help with the notes we were discussing earlier," the comptroller broke in.

"Acknowledged," Verdadero cut him off brusquely and then forced a smile as he turned to face Mitchell. "Give the colonists priority placement on other colonies."

"Yes, sir. I'd already given Dr. Taylor another assignment. I think it's more on her level. She's young, but I think she's a winner. It is not unreasonable that given the interval, a more experienced hand might have come to the same conclusion, and departed on the eve of the disaster. Might even have left Celtuce sooner."

Verdadero conveyed disapproval with a slight lowering of his eyebrows, a discreet gesture not lost on Mitchell. "Dr. Taylor eh? Well, you have autonomy in your sector. I am sure you will do what you think best on the Corporation's behalf." He turned to the next sector chief, a man who straightened his tie with a tug from below the edge of the table. "Cardenza, you also showed a profit this quarter. Would you share with us the reasons behind that?"

CHAPTER

~14~

SHONA SETTLED INTO her third colony with anticipation tinged with nerves. There was nothing difficult in the job she was expecting to do there, but she was concerned that she might be operating under some kind of jinx. The complete devastation of Karela still haunted her, though it was mitigated by the uneventful stint on Celtuce. Shona had been horrified to have been too late to have saved more than a single child on Karela. Her bright and shining vow to save lives, reaffirmed on Mars after the stillbirth of her son, had already suffered some tarnishing. It was only a small success to have saved one life, however lovable that little girl was.

She could see immediately why Erebus needed a doctor on staff the moment the shuttle hit the ground. The planet was hot. The briefing she had received on it had said that temperatures during the day ranged from a low of 26 degrees centigrade just before sunrise to a blazing 170°C or worse later in the day. Planetary dawn was only a few hours behind them when the transport set down. The airy domes that rose over the shuttle reminded her less of Celtuce than of her old neighborhood on Dremel—if the whole town had been placed inside a ceramics kiln. Instead of airlocks, there were single portals, and she thought she glimpsed breezeways cut into the walls. She couldn't wait to get the module hooked up to the colony power supply so she could run the refrigeration system. The sun baked the little shuttle. All the fans in the pilot's compartment were running full blast, and she was still hot. Shona thought of her poor animals, sweltering in their crash cages. At leash the gravity didn't weigh them down. Erebus's was 20 per cent lighter than Celtuce's.

It wasn't possible to keep out all of the heat, though the heat-exchangers on her little module tried to bring the temperature down to a bearable level. She was thankful that there wasn't an emergency situation here, obviating the need to use an isolation suit. Her short-sleeved tunic alone felt too warm. Once she got the air-conditioning running for the animals, Shona opened the door of her module onto a wave of hot, moist air that nearly knocked her over. A man and a woman were waiting for her outside.

"How do you do, my dear?" the woman said, taking her hands and grasping them warmly. "Everyone else is busy, so we are your reception committee. We're a very casual group, as you'll find out. I'm what passes for the administrator here. Veronica Wheatley. This is our project manager, Dr. Alf Tettenden." She gestured to the man, a charming gentleman in his seventies, tall, with a white walrus mustache. "We're very glad to have you here."

She and the man were dressed in very light, loose-fitting garments of white and beige. Her gray, curly hair was cut sensibly short to keep her head cool. Shona noticed that the man's white hair was clipped very short, as well.

"Thank you," Shona said, putting a hand to her own hair, which had grown out into ponytail length in the months since she'd left Mars. She could already feel sweat starting at her nape. Hastily, she pinned the limp tresses up flat against the back of her head using a stylus for a hairpin. It might be well to clip the excess off before it began to be a bother. "How do you do, Doctors."

The two scientists looked at each other, and Wheatley cleared her throat. "I wouldn't bother with titles here, dear, or you'll be doctoring all day long. You can call me Wheatley or Ronnie, I don't mind which. I answer to both."

"Please call me Shona," Shona said. "I'm very pleased to meet you."

"Well, as no one else will be back until dinnertime," Tettenden said, extending an arm to her, "perhaps you would like to have a look around? We're just a small scientific community, a lot of old fogies fussing around with our bits and pieces. You're likely to be the youngest person here."

"I'd be delighted to have a tour, Alf. Thank you." Shona smiled up at him, and the old man harrumphed and smoothed his mustache with a knuckle.

"I'd join you," Professor Wheatley said, looking at her wrist chronometer, "but I've left something on the boil. I'll see you at siesta-time, then?"

"To say 'this is it' is simplistic," Tettenden said, spreading his arms out to the main hall, "but this *is* it. Our little world. Our oasis in the desert."

The basic style of building was like those on most other colony planets, relying mainly on the building block of geodesic dome and cylindrical towers. They stood in the midst of a gigantic semi-cylinder set on its side, off of which clusters of smaller domes opened out. Shona's module had been attached at one end of it. "This is the main hall. That side"—Tettenden pointed to a huge dome at one end of the hall—"functions as the communal mess hall and social center.

"These small domiciles are each living and working spaces for our various members. We're not very original in our designs, I'm afraid," the project manager said. "Utilitarian to a fault. We reserve our creative thinking for our work."

Shona looked around at the soaring white enamel and plexiglass arcs, and disagreed with her host's assessment. Not a little care had been taken in ornamentation that went beyond mere structure. Archways were decorated with filigree tracings in silvery gray that owed as much to the ancient art of arabesques as it did to the transcription of printed circuits. Shona admired the conceit. She thought she recognized the symbols for resistors and capacitors amidst the charming asymmetrical whorls. Climbing plants, some familiar but most alien to her, grew up inside shining white walls ten meters high, to the level of the transparent windows. Shona guessed that the windows were purposely slick so that the twining suckers couldn't attain a foothold and shut out the natural light which illuminated the long room.

Light also came into the hall through open doors from the private living spaces. What she could see of the rooms inside had been decorated or not, according to fiercely individualistic and independent tastes. One room was plastered to the ceiling with colorful tapestries not unlike the work she had seen on Karela. The next was furnished in what her mother had always called "Post-Modernistic Clutter." If there was a flat surface unoccupied by piles of equipment, sheaves of notes, clothes, or eating utensils, Shona couldn't see it from the door. Tettenden's own room, close to an enameled spiral staircase at one end of the hall, was tidy and spotless, decorated simply with personal mementos. Holos of smiling children stood in a line on an ancient desk under a sedately curtained window.

Unlike the domes on Celtuce, the structures were open here and there to the outer atmosphere, which meant the air had been tested and adjudged safe. Shona felt a faint breeze brush her clothes, carrying with it the scent of sand. Erebus had sufficient oxygen for humans to breathe, but the heat gave it a presence like the air inside a greenhouse. According to the reports, the O^2 content was just barely at the level to sustain human life.

"This way," Tettenden said, taking her arm. "We'll go up to the observation tower. You'll get quite a marvelous view from there."

Halfway up the spiral flight of stairs, Shona collapsed against the rails, panting. "I feel like I've been climbing mountains," she said. The old man waited patiently for her at the top landing. She wondered at his endurance. His skin was pouched with age under his eyes and around the corners of his mustache, and his calves stuck out pipe-stem thin from the legs of his walking shorts, but he showed no signs of exertion. She, much younger and in reasonably good physical shape, in a lighter gravity than she was accustomed to, was in a flop sweat, and the muscles in her legs and back pinched. In a moment, she forced herself to finish the climb.

"Don't go too far too fast until you're acclimated, my dear," Tettenden told her, gently helping her over to the window. "Erebus developed an oxygen-nitrogen atmosphere based largely on photo-planktonoids in the oceans, which are surprisingly vast. They're the only feature that kept the whole planet from ascending to the blazing temperatures of Venus-Sol. No one is certain yet why the oceans didn't bubble off long ago, but it provides us with a fascinating laboratory for high-temperature experiments. Why don't you rest here a moment, and I'll tell you what you can see."

The planet's fanciful name had been well-chosen. The landscape spread before them shimmered blindingly under the sun. She could make out ranges of mountains, sharp-edged crevasses, and empty, open plains, but not a single speck of green. All the colors there were—browns, yellows, bones, golds, and oranges—blended into a dry, yellow haze.

"For the three hours before noon every day and three hours after, the transparent domes are made completely reflective to keep out the rays of our sun," Tettenden said. Erebus's primary, a giant yellow star, hung hugely in the sky. "It's mid-morning right now, as you can see, and already you can feel how hot it is. You've arrived at a good time to see things.

"Our day may take you some getting used to. It's thirty-six standard hours long. Means four or five meals per diem. There is a study going on," Tettenden began, then laughed deprecatingly. "There's always a study going on, but this one is based on the premise that humans do better on a longer day-night schedule than the short twenty-four-hour one we were subject to on Earth." He sighed. "And that gives rise to the old argument that *homo sapiens* didn't originate on Earth. We hear both sides. If you're here very long, our devil's advocates will try to drag you into our ongoing disagreements."

"I'm looking forward to it," Shona said, and laughed. "With every breath in my body, which I admit at present isn't a lot to offer. But I have with me another social scientist, who will likely charge madly into the middle of any philosophical fray."

Tettenden regarded her curiously. "Thought you had come alone. Is there someone else in your living quarters?"

Shona chuckled. "I'm the only human here. I'm hosting an ottle. Are you familiar with them?"

"Oh, yes!" Tettenden said enthusiastically. "I've read a great deal about the species. How very fortunate for you. I am looking forward to meeting it. It?"

"I call Chirwl 'him,' mainly because his sex doesn't carry young, but I admit I'm not clear on how their species does reproduce. I've approached the topic, but though he's surprisingly open about some things, there are others he considers strictly private, and that's one of them." Shona turned away from the sun's glare and peered out over the top of the main dome toward the flat, tan plain. "What are all those small buildings out there?"

"Way stations, you might say," Tettenden replied. "Cooling-off places for the scientists who are investigating their own little studies. Most of them were built by Professor Novak, our geologist. The features you see out there in shades of brownish-gray are hydrothermal pools—superheated mud flats. They're not unique to Erebus; in fact there are similar pools on Earth; but they bear examination as they have remained undisturbed by mobile life over the eons. In very old ones, Novak's found natural crystal formations created by heat and pressure. They're rather curious. You should let old Novak tell you about them."

"Are those volcanoes?" Shona asked, pointing at flat-topped hills in the distance.

"Um-hmm. Some are, some were. They've slid off the cracks in the mantle fairly recently, geologically speaking. Erebus has a fairly active tectonic life. I'm surprised we don't have more earthquakes, but perhaps the mantle layer's polished smooth from all its activity, eh?" Tettenden laughed at his little joke.

"Earthquakes?" Shona asked cautiously.

"Mere hums," Tettenden assured her. "Never a real shaker. Would you care to have a bit of a look around outside before it gets unbearable? It's safer if I take you out for a quick view while it's still relatively cool."

Shona followed him eagerly down the steps. The descent was far easier than the ascent. It took less time to get her breath at the bottom.

"This is cool?" she wondered aloud, as they passed under one of the ornamental archways into an uninsulated hangar. With no air moving inside, the heat felt stifling.

"Yes, rather. Erebus describes a true elliptical orbit around the sun. There are four seasons: first spring, first summer, second spring, second summer. We're just leaving second spring. You should be well used to the temperature by the time second summer comes. At least," the old man said with a glint of humor, "I hope so. Else we'll have to pack you in dry ice."

He helped her into an open-sided aircar that had a silvery domed canopy suspended over the whole vehicle. "It's good that you're wearing white," he said, noting her medical tunic with approval. "Anything else seems to attract the heat."

"Cuts down on my wardrobe choices," Shona commented. "I haven't got much else that is light-colored."

"Oh, only during the day," Tettenden assured her. "Things liven up considerably at night. You'll see." The hangar doors parted, drawing back soundlessly into the walls, and the brilliant light blotted out everything in the chamber.

Tettenden handed her a pair of plastic eye protectors that also shaded her nose and cheeks. "You'll want these. If we get out of the car, orders are for full coolsuits. You can burn in an instant out here, a mere instant. For a brief look round, you won't need anything else." He touched the controls, and the car, humming, rose half a meter off the ground and sailed out through the door into the sunshine.

"Oh, that breeze feels good," Shona sighed, wiping sweat off her face under the eye protectors. The glare suffusing the landscape vanished, and she could see detail. "Why, it's wonderful out here. It's stark, but I like it."

"It's possible to come out at noon, but I try not to," her host said, as he guided the car along a path marked with rocks. "We take siestas when it gets hot, but the local wildlife is liveliest then. I'm always afraid they'll get out of hand. Our exobiologist tells me I'm too cool to be interesting to them, that I have nothing to worry about, but I take leave to doubt him. There's one!"

Tettenden slowed the car down, and the smooth engine hummed louder as he forced it to hover in place. "There's your first native, Shona."

At first it didn't look all that different from the smooth tan stones jumbled beside the road. Shona was wondering if she was looking at the wrong thing, when the round rock moved. It elongated slightly, and compressed again, having gained a distance of five or six centimeters. It stretched again, and Shona caught a glimpse of shimmering color in the folds of its skin before it became a dull rock again.

"The life forms here are based on silicon," the project manager told her. "We call those hummocks. They feed in a sort of thermosynthesis. No teeth; in fact, no mouths. Very simple, but aren't they beautiful?"

"Very," Shona agreed. Leaning over the side of the car, she held her hand over the hummock so that her shadow fell on it. Feeling the sudden lack of warmth, the hummock stretched, groping its way out of the shadow and into unobstructed sunlight. The glistening rainbows appeared and disappeared as it accordioned further off the pathway. "Wonderful! Aren't they cute?"

"Don't ever pick one of those up," Tettenden advised her. "They look smooth and appealing, but their body temperature is up in the hundreds. Several hundreds. That shell concentrates and absorbs the sun's rays like a magnifying glass, stores the heat for the nighttime. Here, you'd better have a whole nature walk, hadn't you?"

Tettenden guided the car over the ground with a practiced hand, pointing out items of interest. "You'll find most of the geologic features have been named after all the scientists here. No one else seemed interested in competing for place names on Erebus, so it'll be our little version of immortality.

As they came over a high ridge, named, her host informed her, for Ronnie Wheatley, the car's smooth dome lowered slightly to deflect the sun's glare. Shona tapped the inside of the dome with her fingernails.

"You can sure see this top at a distance," she commented. "It would make rescue easier with a beacon like this."

"Yes, well, it serves more of a purpose than mere visibility. It reflects the light and most of the heat. Otherwise, we wouldn't get far. Even though we can use the heat as a power source, no engine will last long if it's directly exposed to these ambient temperatures."

On the other side of Wheatley Ridge was a steep slope. Tettenden guided the car down it toward the dark pools at the bottom. "Here we are, my dear," he said, regarding the thick, bubbling mud with affection but at a respectful distance from the stinking fumes. "Erebus's own health spas. The planet's surface is covered by these hydrothermal pipes. We've only a few up here in the temperate zone. There's an astonishing collection of them at the equator. Here we have an easy source of pure molten lead, tin, sulphur, and a host of other minerals, including some raw crystals, with rather interesting properties, as I mentioned before. As scientists, we're proud that the Corporation saw the merit of putting a laboratory here. We like to think we're pulling our own

188

weight." He smiled, a wry little grin. "I'm afraid that on the ledger sheets we still look like a liability. This project overstepped its ten-year budget in only four years, with little perceptible return. Scientific knowledge is not, per se, valuable. We hope our little observations have some merit."

"Those are very pretty," Shona said, pointing at clusters of blossoms. "Are those silicon, too?"

"Oh, yes. If you tap the petals, they resound like glass. Which, come to that, they are. But don't touch them," Tettenden warned again, with a smile. "Hot, hot, hot."

The project manager was an amusing companion. Shona enjoyed the rest of her tour. Though she was beginning to feel dehydrated and tired, she was reluctant to bring the jaunt to an end. Tettenden noticed that she was beginning to flag, and gallantly turned the car around toward the domes. "No sense in overdoing. I'd be most delighted to escort you out again very soon. You have but to name a day, and I'm your man."

"Thank you so much," Shona said, grateful for the offer, and the professor's observant eye. "I'd really like that. Can I come out here on my own, too? I hate being cooped up. I've . . . been confined in some pretty small spaces for long intervals lately."

"One thing Erebus has in plenty is wide, open space. I don't advise you to stay out here often or very long," he said, "but if you remain under a sunshade with a lot to drink, and wear a coolsuit, it's possible to come out now and again to enjoy a good hike. We find it a pleasant change from the domes."

They circled in toward the domes from the other side. "So you can have a full view," her host said. "There's your little home. It is made of ceramic, isn't it?"

"Well, it's titanium and fiberglass underneath, but the shell is spacegrade ceramic, yes."

Tettenden nodded approvingly. "Good thing. Summer's coming on. During our summers, even some denser metals melt. And everything retains the heat. Hence the heat exchangers."

He nodded toward a cluster of comblike machinery in the outer corner of the social center where it met the main hall. "They give us cool air in exchange for waste heat, which is belched out, if you will excuse the crudity of the expression."

An especially abundant growth of the silicon flowers closely surrounded the machine housings, and Shona could see the low, rounded shapes of hummocks moving slowly between them. Shona mentioned them.

"Yes, we've created a comfortable little attraction for the hummocks. They like to curl up around the exchangers. It's nice and warm to them. Don't laugh," he warned, holding up a stern finger. "They dissolve the insulation. We have to go out with nonconductive rods from time to time, and shoo them away, or we'll soon lose our air conditioning."

Shona laughed in spite of herself. "I'm sorry, but it's a funny mental picture. Those cute little things?"

"No, most seriously. They may look cute, but they're a damned pest."

"I'm feeling a little faint," she said suddenly, as Tettenden guided the car into the hangar. "Is there somewhere I can rest for a bit?"

"There, there, my dear." He helped her out of the vehicle, and guided her inside through the main hall to the other end of the complex. "You'll like this. It's our hydroponics lab. It's nice and cool in here. Have an extra shot of oxygen. Do you good. I'll get you something to drink."

"No, thank you," Shona stopped him before he turned away. "I'll get something from my module in a moment."

Light filtered curiously through a meshed series of white enameled shutters. Shona peeled off the eye protectors and gazed around at the chamber, which was filled wall to wall with greenery. In the center, trees intertwined their limbs, mixing conifers with deciduous, and tropical with temperate varieties. All around the miniature forest, a garden of smaller plants bloomed. At first Shona thought that most of them were flowers, and realized only after close inspection that the majority were food producers. What she had seen as blossoms were brightly colored fruits and vegetables.

"We pride ourselves on eating well, even in the midst of a desert," Tettenden admitted. "The hydros also make life itself more comfortable for us. If it wasn't so moist in this dome, the oxy concentration would probably give rise to spontaneous fires every day at noon. You can see that the greenhouse dome is heavily shuttered. Only a small percentage of Erebus's sun is needed to make Earth-style plants grow, even tropical fruit. Here!" He reached up to rattle a tree branch, and a round fruit fell heavily to the floor. "Mango. Don't pick one green. They're ripe when they fall."

"I shouldn't," Shona said, eyeing the orange-tinged fruit guiltily. Its perfume tantalized her, and she felt her mouth water. "I'm supposed to eat only the nutri supplies in my module until I get acclimated. I'm going to be here a long time. I'll have some another time."

"Oh, a bite shouldn't hurt you. Go on," Tettenden urged. "Hydroponically grown, and perfectly pure."

"Well . . ." The fruit was cracked slightly from its drop, and the flesh showed golden and juicy through the break in the skin.

Without further hesitation, Shona pulled it apart and bit into one half. She offered her host the other. They stood in the blessed coolness, eating fresh mango that was flavored as intensely as its brilliant orange hue. Shona looked around her in wonder.

"How can you grow so much in such a small space?"

Her host surreptitiously wiped mango juice off his chin with a fold of handkerchief. "Miracle, isn't it? Our exobiologist is also the botanist. He's got quite a green thumb. I don't know what he feeds them, but the results are worth almost any effort, I can assure you."

Shona shook her hands, looking around for a sink to wash up in. "That was delicious. I should *not* have done it, but I haven't had fresh fruit in months. I've been on ship food, nutri, and ship food again."

"Over there, my dear," Tettenden pointed to a molded terra-cotta bowl full of greenery. Shona walked over to take a look. She noticed the garden herbs were suspended in an ornamental pool of water. The whole cluster covered only half its surface, leaving plenty of room open. Shona began to plunge her hands in and clean off the mango juice.

Her fingertips had barely brushed the surface when she was gripped brutally around the upper arms and yanked backwards away from the pool.

"Hey!" she protested, twisting her head around to see who had grabbed her. The hollow-cheeked old man had sprung out of nowhere.

"I'm sorry," Shona began, trying to break free. "I was just—"

"You were just about to upset the chemical balance of my system," he growled, glaring at her. With his hands locked about her upper arms, he walked her firmly to a sink and released her to flip on the tap. "There. Wash in that. It runs to the purification system. You can pollute that all you want." He stalked away without another word and sat down in a chair sheltered by broad-leaved ferns. He must have been observing Tettenden and Shona the whole time they were there. Keeping a wary eye on him, Shona hastily ran her hands under the water.

"What a grouch," Shona observed under her breath, as she and her host left the dome.

Tettenden shrugged. "George Hood. A sound scientist but I admit not a terribly nice man. It's all stuff-and-a-yard-wide about you throwing off his precious ecosystem. Nature's not that exact, and he knows it. We pay no attention to his tantrums. You mustn't, either."

"All right," Shona promised, doubtfully.

"I'll let you alone for now to rest and become acclimated," Tettenden said, escorting her to the door of her module. "You must join us all in the observation tower at sunset. We foregather there following our daily grind, and usually dine together thereafter. Tonight will be a little special because you have arrived among us. We've planned a small party. I hope you don't mind. Until this evening." He sketched a stiff half-bow and left her.

By twilight, the temperature altered dramatically, falling so quickly that Shona felt chilled. She kicked on the heating unit in her module, and donned the tunic she had discarded earlier.

For the first time all day, her menagerie showed signs of life. The rabbits picked themselves up from the shavings on the bottom of their cage and shook out their fur. Marigold began to chew the edge of the door busily, twitching her nose at Shona.

"All right, all right I get the hint," her mistress exclaimed, rummaging in the cupboard for rabbit chow. The second the cat heard the sound of food being prepared, he was underfoot, winding his way around her ankles, and yowling. Saffie just thumped her tail on the bed and looked expectant.

"You're probably going to need a haircut to survive here," Shona said, glancing at the dog. "So am I. Where's Chirwl?"

She hadn't expected an answer from her pets, but the module was only four small rooms. The ottle should have heard her voice wherever she was standing.

"I can't believe he went out into the hall," Shona mused. "Now, wait, I know." She went into the bathroom.

The tub was full to overflowing, and there was a faint eddy of movement on the surface. Shona peered over the edge into the depths. Chirwl looked up at her through the water, and she beckoned to him. He kicked upward, and broke the surface of the water with his nose.

"What a terrible place is this hot world," Chirwl said, as soon as his mouth was above water.

"Well, it's cold at night," Shona said, helping him over the edge so that not too much water slopped to the floor. "Besides, you'll like it. We've landed among a bevy of philosophers. If you were hoping for an opportunity to brush the dust off your theory, these are the people to air it for. They're having a little party for us this evening."

"That is most joyous gracious of them." Chirwl kicked free of her arms and shook himself vigorously, spraying water everywhere. Shona backed off hastily.

"It's a good thing I haven't changed yet!" she exclaimed, heading for her closet. "Come on. We don't want to miss sunset."

Because they were in a hurry, Shona had to carry him, which taxed her unacclimated muscles in the thin atmosphere. The shape of his body made him an awkward bundle for his weight. As they reached the top of the stairs in the observation tower, she was puffing for breath. Tettenden spotted them and waved them over.

"So this is the ottle, is it?" the old man said jovially. "Nice to meet you. Alf Tettenden."

"How do pleased to meet you, Alftettenden," said Chirwl. "Chirwl I am called by you humans. I trust your health is well?"

"Very well. We'll get acquainted later. You're just in time. Come along and have something to drink. It's our little custom. Mineral water bottled on Mars. Should be perfectly safe for you."

Shona had never seen anything quite like an Ereban sunset, even on Mars. It didn't take very long. Since there was no pollution diffusing the light in the sky, the sun disappeared behind the horizon without fanfare. One moment the red disk burned at the edge of the world, and the next, it was gone.

"Most amazing," Chirwl said.

"Cheers, all," Ronnie Wheatley called. "To life."

"To life," the others echoed, and drained their glasses. Shona followed suit.

"I like your custom, Alf," she said. The old man patted her on the shoulder.

Without the sun, the air became very chilly. Shona and Chirwl trooped downstairs behind the others. The floor below them seemed to be heaving and swaying. Shona clutched the banister, fearing an earthquake.

"What's that?" she exclaimed.

"We always get fog in the evenings," Alf said. "Warm moist air hits cold air. At aphelion, we even get a little snow. Doesn't last. When it hits the ground it's gone, but it's rather homey in the meantime to those of us from Old Earth. Listen," he said, as a low rumbling noise began, vibrating in the walls, "there's the defrosters going on in Hydroponics."

Shona waded through waist-high fog toward the dining hall with the others. The main hall was illumined by small, hidden elements that provided just enough light to see their way.

"Who needs auxiliary glares after a day here?" Wheatley pointed out.

There was more light in the dining room, but it was dimmed to make the surroundings intimate. Tettenden escorted Shona and the ottle from table to table, introducing them to the community.

"Dr. Taylor called Shona, and Chirwl, meet Dr. Maling, Dr. Spiegel, and Dr. Novak."

"I'll never remember all the names the first time through," Shona protested.

"Nor I," Chirwl asserted, his round eyes bright.

"There are only half as many of us here as there are elements in the periodic table," said Novak, a tall sturdy man of thirty-five, with bright blue eyes and a pink, boyish complexion. "Try to think of the names as genus and species. You must have memorized names like that in a night in med school, like the rest of us. Let's see, that would make me a *Novakus Guillermii*, but call me Bill," he said, and grinned as Shona broke up.

"That's worse. I'll remember everyone's name backwards if I do that. I'll just have to hear them a few times."

"That's the spirit," Maling said. She had very dark skin, against which her white teeth gleamed. "Don't let anyone pretend to you that you must learn all our names tonight. There is no exam to follow."

Chirwl was the immediate center of attention for these naturally curious people. Shona left him at one of the round tables in the midst of a group who wanted to ask him questions. Shona set him down on a chair. He was instantly absorbed, and never noticed when she left. She heard one man's voice raised over the others.

"Saint-Exupéry points out that 'the machine does not isolate man from the great problems of nature, but plunges him more deeply into them.' "

"No, no," Chirwl disagreed at once. "Does it not put one body at a further remove yet?"

"See you later," Shona called, and shrugged when the ottle didn't respond.

"He's a most interesting character," Tettenden said as he escorted her to a table where there were unoccupied chairs. Wheatley and three others were already seated there. "It must be quite something to travel with him."

"Sometimes he's like a companion. Sometimes, he's more like another pet. I love my pets, even though they can drive me crazy." She turned to the others at her table. "I have several Terran animals in my module. Anyone who would like to meet them is invited to come by any time. I'm not bringing them out for a while. They'll need time to get used to the heat, so I'm keeping them in with the air conditioning. I'll get them acclimated before too long, but I don't want to rush things. When that hot air came in, the cat and the rabbits went down like they'd been ironed flat."

"A cat?" one of the men said absent-mindedly. "Used to have a cat. I wonder what became of him."

"Well, come and meet mine," Shona invited. "He won't let you forget about him."

A peal of laughter erupted from the table behind her, and Shona glanced over. A group of diners were sharing some joke, seemingly at the expense of one of the people at their table, who was taking it with a sheepish grin. Dance music came out of the walls, and between courses some of the diners got up to glide around with a partner.

"This place certainly comes to life after dark," Shona observed.

"It certainly does." The languid Dr. Wheatley was livelier and more cheerful than she had been that morning. "Sometimes I can't think in all that heat," she told Shona. "But I'm doing a study in optics, so it's impossible for me to work in the dark."

"Physically or philosophically?" another woman scientist asked, on the opposite side of the table. She had been introduced to Shona as Margo Chan, a specialist in sonics, and the person who ran the planetary communications system. Her fine-grained skin was butter-yellow in the low light and her shining black hair, in defiance of the Ereban climate, was kept long and coiled up at the back of her head.

"Oh, thank you very much," Wheatley said, grimacing playfully at her friend as the others laughed.

Unable to eat the meal, Shona chatted cheerfully with everyone except the man opposite her. She recognized him as the botanist who had frog-marched her away from the hydroponics tub that afternoon. Dr. Hood ate his dinner in silence, ignoring his tablemates entirely.

"Dr. Hood," Shona addressed him. "I'm so sorry about this afternoon." The botanist didn't even look up when she spoke.

"What happened this afternoon?" Wheatley demanded.

"A Hoodian bee," Tettenden explained, circling his temple with a forefinger, "in the bonnet. She nearly touched the hydro tanks. My fault entirely."

After the meal, the party started in earnest. The tables were pushed back against the walls, and lighter refreshments were brought out. When she wasn't dancing with one man or another, Shona found herself hanging around the punch bowl, chatting with her new friends. She stayed with her mineral water, wishing that she'd had the forethought to supply her module with wine or some other festive beverages.

She talked with Dr. Novak at length about shared experiences in medical school, until he was dragged away to the dance floor by one of the ladies. Shona watched them for a moment, then looked around for a free partner to dance with. As she turned to put down her glass, a hand clasped her wrist.

"Oh!" she exclaimed, jumping. "Is this how you make everyone's acquaintance, Dr. Hood?"

The man glared at her from under his eyebrows, and let go of her.

"I suppose now that you're here you'll be poking us full of holes for blood samples," he said sourly.

"You seem very healthy," Shona replied. "I only do that to sick people."

"We do well enough," he admitted. "Nothing here but what we brought with us. Except for fiberglass rash and burns, not a lot happens to us. So I don't expect you to pull us in for unnecessary nonsense."

Shona raised an eyebrow. "I'll take that under advisement, sir."

"Professor Hood," Tettenden said jovially, coming up with a female scientist on his arm and Dr. Novak behind them. "Do try to cheer up. Just once. As a personal favor."

The exobiologist spared him a glare, and marched away. The others watched him go without concern.

"Never mind, my dear," Tettenden said, smiling at Shona from under his magnificent mustache. "Hood wears a chip like other people wear a watch. He takes care of it, carries it everywhere he goes, and examines it frequently. May I introduce Professor Margaret Davis? She's a seismologist from Alpha University. Also our writer of grants and contracts. An expert in legal language. We count on her expertise to keep the funding coming in."

"I'm not as important as all that. It's a formula," Davis explained. Her voice was low and musical. "The Corporation keeps asking us very politely if we wouldn't like to pull out of Erebus, and I continue to explain all of the benefits they are gaining by having us here. They're like anyone else; they don't like funding scientific research unless there's a very specific goal in mind. What we came to do was to test out a lot of theories in this very natural laboratory."

Tettenden harrumphed, and tipped a sly wink to Shona. "Our friend here was thoughtful enough to get the Corporation to sign a long-term contract, and we'll hold them to it. If there's anything a scientist is good at," he said humorously, "it's setting down the terms of a grant in a manner which will stick."

"We have the opportunity for other income, if we needed it," Dr. Novak put in. "There is an easy source of pure molten lead, tin, and sulphur, as well as a host of other minerals in the hydrothermal pools, which we could use to produce income, in a small way. And from the pipes, we're harvesting small crystals, both quartzites and a crystalline matrix which is almost the perfect superconductor. It's unique to this planet. It will probably never be more than a curiosity, because it would be very expensive and time-consuming to seek out in its natural form, but we feel that it's the only truly superconductive crystalline matrix not made in outer space. It's worth a study to find out why it works here and not elsewhere. I published a paper on it which was read at the Geological Consortium last year. I feel we're giving value for money," he concluded.

"Hear, hear," Tettenden cheered him. The music changed to a rumba, and he held out his hand. "Care to dance, Shona, my dear?"

Shona went back to her module after the party and dictated a long and enthusiastic message to Gershom.

"It's a strange group, but with the exception of one crank, everyone is very friendly. Chirwl is still in the mess hall, arguing some part of philosophy with half the party. I think I'm going to enjoy this posting, everything except the heat. The next time you see me I'll have short hair, out of pure self-defense. I hope that we're on a trade route to somewhere so you can stop by and visit me sometime. Any time. I miss you. All my love to you, every day."

CHAPTER
⫷ 15 ⫸

IN HER FIRST full day on the job Shona unearthed what medical records there were for the scientists in Ronnie Wheatley's office. To her surprise, the data files were spotty and incomplete. They hadn't been thoroughly updated since the first weeks the settlers had spent on Erebus four years ago, and then only to note what reactions they had had adapting to the hot climate. She was exasperated by the haphazard organization and lack of system. Wheatley had been accurate in describing the community as casual. From the assortment of handwritten documents and printouts, she guessed that the data on each had been entered by the person to whom it belonged, when and if they felt like it. Some people were more assiduous than others; some records bore no new information at all.

"Casual is an understatement," Shona grumbled, taking a list of the names and entering them into her own database. The histories had to be updated, and that included medical examinations for everyone.

"These records should be kept current," Shona explained to Professor Wheatley in her optics lab on the south side of the complex. "It's been four years since there were entries in some of those files. If there was a medical emergency and the patient was unconscious, you'd have effectively tied the hands of any physician who came in. He or she would have to guess at allergies, past sicknesses or injuries, chronic conditions, and that could be fatal. Can you order everyone to come in for a physical? That would help me straighten all this out."

"I'm afraid I can't order compliance, Shona," the administrator said. "I don't think I would if I could. I'm only the manager here, not a policewoman. My job is to facilitate the organization and operation of this outpost. But if it'll help you do your job," Wheatley added, noticing the dismayed expression on Shona's face, "you can tell people that I think it's a good idea that they come in for a checkup. I'll be first, and get the ball rolling."

Creating an organized file system helped keep Shona busy over the first few weeks. Most of the scientists said they were happy to comply with her request for an exam, but mere willingness didn't seem to get them into the office. After getting vague promises from some as to when they would appear, she took a no-nonsense stand and scheduled appointments for anyone who agreed to come in. Others she trapped as they appeared.

"We're opening up another mud bath day after tomorrow," Bill Novak said, leaning in at her door one day. "The sonograms show what I believe to be a significant quantity of crystals in the pipe. It's an important find—if nothing goes wrong. Would you like to come out and watch?"

"Wonderful!" Shona exclaimed. "Come in, take off your shirt, and tell me all about it."

"Caught," Novak said guiltily, complying. "Starts early morning, before the sun gets too high. Wear your grubbies. We're going to get really filthy. Hey, boy! Here, boy." He held out his hand to the dog, who was being inconspicuous in a corner.

"Girl," Shona corrected him. "Her name's Saffie. Say something nice to her. Anything will help. I think she's a little upset with *her* haircut. I'm a doctor, not a barber." The thick coat had been reduced to an even, two-centimeter length all over. Novak ruffled the dog's ears.

"You both look fine. On my honor as a scientist." He grinned, also eyeing Shona's new short cut. Saffie whined reproachfully at her mistress. Shona stroked her head when she reached for her stethoscope. "Didn't barbers use to do both jobs, hair cutting and surgery?" At Shona's command, Novak sat up straight on the edge of the examining table and breathed deeply.

"Thank heavens for specialization," Shona said. "I'm a self-confessed flop as a hairstylist. Ooh! Sorry if that's cold. It's an ancient tradition for stethoscopes to be freezing. Don't ask me how, considering how hot this room is. One thing about the people here, the thin air has made you develop excellent lungs. You have diaphragm muscles you could use for trampolines."

"You'll notice we don't have an intercom system," Novak joked, patting his rib cage. "We have to make do somehow. One or another of us is always hollering from one end of the hall to the other. Chan keeps threatening to kill us when we goof up her sound recordings. The only way I can placate her is by keeping her in native crystals."

"Well, you pass all your tests," Shona said, tapping the last data into Novak's file, and slapping the Enter button smartly. "Twenty-three down, and twenty to go."

She didn't want to harass the remainder of the scientists, but as time went by and they still showed no signs of acknowledging her request for checkups, she began to seek them out.

She started with the exobiologist, running him down while he was filling one of the hydroponics tanks with a nutrient solution. "Oh, come on, Professor Hood. I want a perfect score, and you're one of the few holdouts. Come in for a checkup. It won't hurt you, promise."

Hood didn't even look at her. "No. Unless you've thought of some means to compel me?" He moved away.

"That's childish," Shona replied, hurrying after him. "Of course I can't force you. I could call the Corporation, but that's expensive and silly. I'm only asking. I'll simply point out that it is practical to have a complete and recent medical record on file in case of an emergency."

"And what emergency do you foresee?" he asked, turning to peer suspiciously down his thin nose at her.

Shona forbore to say that she was going to strangle him personally, after which he would need resuscitation. Instead she chose diplomacy. "I couldn't say, sir. What if you slipped and banged your head? If you had an allergy I didn't know about, I'd be risking your health to give you pain medication."

"Oh, putting responsibility on me, are you?"

"If you want to think of it that way," Shona replied. "It's your health, not mine. How about tomorrow, during siesta?"

"How about when hell freezes over?" Hood retorted.

"Fine," Shona said, without a pause. "This dome ices up at night, doesn't it? After *sunset* tomorrow. See you then." She spun and sailed out of the done, listening with small satisfaction to Hood sputtering behind her.

She wasn't surprised when the day came and went and Hood failed to show up. She would simply seek him out again.

Novak's digging party assembled in the vehicle hangar just after planetary dawn the following day. Shona, next to Maling in the seat of a miniature earthmover, hugged herself against the morning chill. Novak was in a merry mood as he prepared his team for departure. He was clad in an amusing combination of coolsuit, strapped-on goggles, and a broad-brimmed, white cotton hat. Everyone else wore helmets or hoods.

"Now, Petrie and I are driving the laser drill out to the site," he explained, indicating the other man in the party. "Wheatley, you and Chan take the lighter equipment, and the water. Maling can drive the dozer. Taylor, you stay with her, all right?"

"Sure," Shona said, her teeth clenched together with cold.

"You'll warm up as soon as we get outside," Novak assured her.

"Now, I'm only doing this to get a hold of some of the crystalline matrix for my experiments," Wheatley warned. "Don't get the idea that I'm going to come out here and grub any time you want to dig up a pipe."

"Done," Novak said, handing her a shovel, which she stowed beneath the seat in the hooded hovercar. He passed up more tools. "Here, Shona, take these." He gave her a handheld laser drill and helped her take on board the two pieces of the lifting rig. "The hovers can't carry that much cargo. All right, let's move out!"

Novak led the way down the roughly graded road leading south.

As the sun ascended, steam rose from the warming land. They followed the road to its southernmost end, where the two hover vehicles left it and veered off to the southwest. The earthmover followed, less gracefully, lurching over stones and upthrust edges of rock. Unlike the other vehicles, the dozer couldn't manage any speed on the rough terrain.

"We'll catch up to you," Maling called, when the others pulled away. The protective sun hood over the dozer made her voice echo eerily.

"Aren't they going to leave a trail of bread crumbs?" Shona asked.

"Oh, I've been to Bill's site," Maling said, indicating a directional dial on the control board. "It's straight along this vector, south-southwest. We will simply take longer to get there than they will. That is good. They'll get the cutting underway before we arrive. I'm not fond of flying chips."

The area beyond the road's end was active geothermically. The spreading pools of bubbling hot mud overlapped one another, making it heavy going for the earthmover. The dozer's wheels became gummed up with thick clay until they bumped it off on rocky, dry stretches.

At one point when they tried to skirt a pool of mud fifteen meters across, the dozer's wheels stopped turning altogether.

"Aha, I thought that one might be a little deep," Maling said.

She forced the throttle, but they didn't move forward at all. The engine whined dangerously. With an exasperated grunt, Maling threw the throttle into reverse, and they climbed backward up the hill they had just come over.

"We can't go this way. Not to worry." She edged the heavy vehicle backward until it was facing the other way. "There's a depression we can drive through to the east."

It was more of a small ravine than a depression, Shona noted. The steep sides rising jaggedly around them were touched here and there on the north wall with blooms of the silicon 'flowers.' Shona leaned further in under the hood when the vehicle brushed too close to the wall, splintering off a few of the sharp-edged flakes of glass.

"I don't want to have to do that again," Maling said, looking back over her shoulder at the narrow culvert.

They emerged onto a spit of sand that had been formed by two upthrust strata grinding against one another when the plates of the planet shifted. Rubbernecking under the hood for a glimpse upward, Shona stared wonderingly. A tiny sprinkle of sand trickled down on the roof of the dozer, and she ducked inside, brushing it out of her hair.

"That's one of the things I like about this job," Maling confessed, watching Shona with a smile. "You see things no other living eye has ever seen. Uh-oh."

Beyond the cliffs was an open stretch, smooth enough for the earthmover to roll unhindered, if it hadn't been for the small, round boulders clustered and scattered on its surface. As Shona watched, one of them moved, a corruscation of color flicking off its back and vanishing again.

"Hummocks!" she exclaimed.

"Dammit," Maling ejaculated. It was the first profanity Shona had heard her use. "I can't drive over them; they'll melt the treads. And if we wait here too long, they'll come and nest in the mechanism. The engine's nice and warm. They're still cold from the night. They could surround us."

"What can we do?"

Maling leaned an arm over the back of the driver's seat and tried to reverse, then stopped hastily. "They're coming from behind us, too. Can you steer me between them?"

Shona climbed over the seat and looked down over the rear of the dozer. "They're too close. You'll hit one of them." It was hard for her to be afraid of the little things on sight, but she knew they were dangerous. She could push them away one by one with a nonconductive rod, but she might miss one climbing into the engine or the treads. She needed to create a diversion to get their attention.

An idea came to her. She rummaged through the tools Novak had loaded on board and came up with the small laser drill.

202

"What are you going to do with that? Shoot them?" Maling asked. "I warn you, it'll do no good."

"I wouldn't hurt them," Shona said. "They need something more attractive than our engines." She climbed out on the hood of the earthmover and looked for a target. At the side of the clearing, she found a smooth-sided boulder.

"I hope that thing won't spray burning rock all over the place," Shona said as she took aim with the drill as if it were a rifle.

"I hope it won't reflect that beam right back," Maling retorted. "Please avoid hitting the side facing us."

The drill was weighted to face downward. Bracing the barrel on her feet, Shona fought to keep the nose facing her target as she sighted along its length and switched it on. There was no framing red beam, so the only way they knew that the laser was working was when the side of the boulder began to smoke. In moments, the rock slagged and dribbled a small stream of lava onto the ground. Even at a distance, Shona could feel the growing heat in the skin of her face. The hummocks, roused by the sudden wave of warmth, inched across to absorb it, ignoring the vehicle.

"Resourceful, aren't you?" Maling said admiringly, as Shona crawled back into the cab, dragging the drill.

"I saw the same thing in a two-dee adventure show once," Shona admitted. "The hero was afraid of snakes crawling up to get warm against his body, so he set a fire to attract them away from him. Erebus reminds me of the setting where the story took place. That's what made me think of it."

"Well done," Maling applauded. "I should watch more historical dramas. Please make certain that thing is off, and we'll continue our little drive."

"Where've you been?" Novak cried as they rolled into sight "You missed all the fun."

"Really?" Maling asked. "Good." Her eyes begged silence from Shona, who nodded.

The large drill was propped up on a lightweight scaffolding suspended above the center of a huge, steaming pool. It was just finishing describing the circuit of the pipe, its invisible beam's point of contact demarked by hissing and flying globules of mud. Wheatley and the others were standing well back, sheltering from the spray behind the canopy of the hovercars. Suddenly, the drill head stopped moving, and the hissing died down.

"That's it," Novak said, cheerfully. "Now the exciting part begins."

"This is where I begin work," Maling said, zipping up the neck of her protective suit and putting on a heatproof helmet.

Stopping to let Shona off, Maling began to dig out the pipe. She started from one edge of the pool, scooping up hodloads of hot mud and carrying them over the slight rise beyond where the hovercars stood to dump them out. The pool was very shallow at the sides, and deeper in the center.

"I believe these pools started off very small," Novak explained to Shona. "Just a little break in the surface for the heat and molten mud to escape. As more liquid bubbled up and filled in the depression, the chimney had to become taller so it could continue to vent. Over time, it's filled this entire depression, maintaining astonishing temperature levels. This colloid really holds the heat, and the pressure contributes to help form crystals in the chimney. By clearing away the pool and breaking off the pipe, we're returning this site to the way it was thousands, perhaps tens of thousands, of years ago, when this geyser first surfaced."

Shona retreated back behind the hood of a hovercar as Maling passed with another load. The dozer blade was becoming shiny in patches with streaks of tin and lead from the pool solidifying in the cooler air. The black scientist was surprisingly deft with the shovel of the earthmover, turning it delicately around the laser-cut, shiny curves of the pipe to clear away matrix rock without damaging it. When she had exposed a meter and a half of pipe, Novak signaled to her to stop.

Donning protective suits, the others waded across the sticky bottom with shovels to clear away the remaining debris of clay and rock. Shona was impressed by how well Novak had estimated the depth of the pool. There weren't more than a few centimeters of mud left in the stone bowl. Petrie knelt at the base of the pipe and attached a chainlike apparatus around it, then helped Maling and Wheatley with the braces for the lifting rig to be attached to the earthmover.

"All right," Novak said. "Everybody back at least a hundred meters. It may spray when we cut it." He waited for the others to climb into the hover cars and drive away, and then signaled to Petrie. "Hit it!"

From a safe distance, Shona watched as the chain began to revolve around the pipe, throwing chips and sparks in every direction. Steam began to escape at the cutting line. Novak stood between the chain of the saw and the earthmover with his hand raised like an old-time film director, watching and waiting.

Shona heard an explosive *crack!* and saw steam spurt out at several points around the base of the pipe. Novak dropped his hand, and Maling began to back the dozer away, pulling the rig taut around the pipe. At first the chimney resisted, but as the saw cut away more of its support, it leaned almost imperceptibly toward the dozer. Suddenly, it flew off its base, and a ball of hot steam catapulted into the air, nearly knocking Novak and Petrie over. The pipe, severed, dangled in the air for a moment until Maling got control of it, and lowered it into the shovel bed of the dozer.

Everyone cheered. As soon as the first geyser of steam abated, Novak and Petrie gathered up the chainsaw and ran to where the hovercars waited.

"I feel like I've been steam-cooked!" Novak exclaimed, climbing up into the cab. His normally pink cheeks were red. "Eureka, folks! Have we got everything? Well done. We'll take the pipe back to my lab intact so I can do soundings on it before I break it up. Drinks are on me!"

The hovercar delivered Shona to the dozer. More congratulations were shared all around.

"Wonderful job, Maling," Novak called, from the hovercar. "Sure you wouldn't like to take up earthmoving as a career? You've got a knack for it."

Maling's eyebrow rose, but she grinned at him. "Thank you so much. I didn't realize my present job was in jeopardy. Now, shall we get away from here before that steam attracts every hummock in the surrounding area?"

"What's all the commotion?" Tettenden demanded, closing in on the noisy party as it entered the settlement hall carrying the length of rock like a prize catch on their shoulders.

"A celebration!" Novak called, ducking his head to see under the heavy pipe. "Come and join us!"

"What? A celebration? Certainly." The old man strode into Novak's lab behind the high-spirited group.

"Okay, down slowly now," Novak directed, guiding the carriers over to his lab table. Moving carefully, the pairs of bearers edged around alternate sides of the table until the sample, well-supported, was poised above the padded surface. "Easy . . . easy . . . good!"

Novak superintended strapping it onto the bench, directing the others with the air of a nervous symphony conductor, and then stepped back to operate the ultrasound scanner. The group of scientists exclaimed over the masses of crystals that appeared on the video screen as the heavy device hummed over the length of dark stone.

"We did it folks! Look at those clusters," Bill said happily, pointing out various masses as they appeared. "The best we've ever found! This calls for a drink!"

"Hear, hear!" Tettenden seconded.

"I bag that one," Margo Chan said, poking her finger decisively at the image of a thin crystal which even on the ultrasound appeared transparently clear and unblemished. "Could I get resonances out of that!"

"Whatever you want, my charmer," Novak said, putting his arm around her plump shoulders. "But first a toast to our success."

From a cold cabinet, he drew out two glass beakers filled with a brilliant orange liquid.

"Is that mango juice?" Maling asked.

"Yes, ma'am, pressed by yours very truly. Fruit courtesy of Mr. Sunshine himself."

"Hood gave you all those mangoes?" Wheatley asked, plainly astonished.

Novak shrugged his shoulders, his boyish face mischievous. "Well, not all of them. Not exactly *gave*." He poured the juice into clean cylinders that Chan arranged on a tray, and handed them around. "He was surprised when I asked, but what he let me have was not enough, so . . ."

"Oh, naughty," Maling smiled, as she sipped from her mango juice.

"Aaah. That cuts the dust."

"A toast," Novak said, holding his drink on high.

"Just a moment!" Shona pleaded. "I need to get something *I* can drink."

Shona dashed back to her module to get a container of mineral water out of her refrigerator. The floor next to it, below Chirwl's pouch, was liberally strewn with his miniature chips of resin, and she could hear busy humming. Evidently, the nightly debates with learned minds had spurred inspiration again. Saffie stood up and came to stick her nose in Shona's palm, begging for a walk.

"Later, honey," Shona said. "I'm going to a little celebration."

She hurried back. As soon as she appeared, Novak raised his glass again. "A toast to our enterprise and hard work!" He drank deeply, draining his glass. The others followed suit. Shona tipped up her flask, feeling the desiccated tissues of her throat open up at the healing touch of cool water.

"So let's see what we've got," Petrie urged, grinning.

Novak brushed away the mud on a loose chunk of rock which had cracked when the pipe was severed, and yanked it loose from the matrix. "There you have it, folks. The only naturally occurring room-temperature superconductor in the galaxy."

It was passed around from hand to hand, and admired. Chan took the hunk of rock in one hand and struck it with a small, metal implement she kept in the pocket of the coverall under her coolsuit. The crystal gave off a musical whine, which continued on and on until Chan stilled it by touching its surface.

"Marvelous," she said. "This could revolutionize communications. Do you know the theory of congruent harmonics?" she asked Shona, who shook her head. She plunged into an explanation peppered with references to sonic and supersonic frequencies, of which Shona couldn't comprehend one word in three. Novak appeared from behind them and snatched the sample she was brandishing out of her hand.

"Yours will be free of the matrix by tomorrow. In the meantime, don't drop this one!" he pleaded. "I need it."

"Oh, you're such a baby," Chan chided him. "You always think people are going to damage your things."

"That's because they always do," Novak returned cheerfully, making off with the chunk of matrix.

CHAPTER

— 16 —

WITHIN DAYS SHONA found that she was becoming more acclimated to Erebus's weather, which allowed her to roam further
afield. In her free hours, she went out on tours of the surrounding
area with any of the settlers who were checking their data. Petrie
was the settlement's meteorologist. He had weather stations set
out at thirty-mile intervals running due south from the colony
base. Shona rode with him frequently when he went out to check
on them. She also went for walks, clad in a coolsuit, with Bill
Novak and Alf Tettenden, her two closest friends in the settlement.
Harry still refused to set foot outside the module before sunset,
but after the daily heat abated, he made himself welcome in the
colony, wandering in and out of any living quarters he chose as if
he belonged there. Following shipboard confinement, Saffie was
eager to get out no matter what the temperatures. The dryness of
the daytime climate diminished both animals' ability to follow
scents, which was probably a relief to Saffie after the stench of
Celtuce. Shona hoped it wouldn't lead either animal to investigate
a hummock up close, because the little creature was hard to smell
from a distance.

Shona's correspondence caught up with her within a week, and
she spent the hottest midday hours, known as siesta times to the
colonists, answering messages. There was a kindly, concerned note
from Taji Chandler, wondering how she was doing after her ordeal
on Karela. Gershom had transmitted during an ion storm or some
other disturbance that interfered with the signal, causing his image
to break up on screen, and making Shona replay it several times.
She wasn't sure she understood everything he said, but she was
so glad to hear from him it didn't matter. And, as she might have
guessed, there was a month's worth or more of messages from
Susan.

"You can't believe some of the stuff I've been hearing about
what's happening to you. I'm so sorry about that colony. The

news reporters try to make it sound like it's your fault everyone died, but I know you. I know there's nothing you didn't try to make it come out all right."

More old messages, undoubtedly from ricocheting beacons. This must have been sent after she'd heard about Karela. Shona grinned at her friend's sweet overestimate of her talents. Since she couldn't reach Susan, she hugged Harry, who was curled up as usual in her lap. He grunted. Susan went on to enumerate her own woes.

"Meantime, twin, I wish you could be out here to heal my documentary. All of a sudden, the government agents have gotten stinky about releasing footage, and it's their rotten project, Before, everything they didn't want for the survey was waste tape. Now, just because someone wants it—me!—it's worth something. But don't worry. I'm not going to give ground, not unless they claim me as a regular employee and pay me mileage for all the flying I put in on the *Rust Bucket*." Susan wrinkled her nose, but her blue eyes were full of humor. "You could heal that too, if you've got time and a *lot* of patience. Poor old thing. Well, back to Project X! Wish you were here. Tell me what you're up to and where you are. Love. Over and under and around and out."

A rap from outside distracted Shona as she started to record a soothing reply to her friend.

"It's open," she called, then hit the button that would store the rest of Susan's messages for later and went out into the main lab room.

"Hello, dear," Wheatley said, poking her nose around the edge of the hatchway. "I wondered if you would give me a look-see. I'm feeling a little off."

"Sure," Shona said, gesturing her toward the examination table. "That's what I'm here for. What's wrong?"

Wheatley shrugged. Shona noticed her skin was slightly moist and puffy, unusual for the dry heat of Erebus. "I'd say, if it weren't a joke in this hot climate, that I'm feeling feverish. Might be coming down with something."

Shona ran a scanner over the administrator. The woman's temperature and heartbeat were elevated. "How long has this been going on?"

"Oh, a few days." Wheatley frowned, trying to remember. "I'd say, not before we all went out to paddle in the mud with Novak. Perhaps around then. Wonder if I caught some microbe from Novak's bit of rock. We all handled it before it'd been sanitized."

Alarmed, Shona tried to recall who had touched the crystal pipe, and if she had been among them. "You could be right. I'll look into it. In any case, let me prescribe a broad spectrum antibiotic. If you've contracted some kind of amoeba, that should help knock it out. And drink a lot of liquids."

Wheatley grimaced. "Antibiotic. That means no alcohol, is that right, dear?"

"I'm afraid so," Shona said, following the line of her thoughts. "You can join me in a split of mineral water at the sunset salute for a while."

"It just won't go down the same," the administrator said, wrinkling her nose playfully, "Not that it's much in the way of sunset nowadays." With the approach of second summer, the sun seemed to hover almost directly overhead for most of the day, disappearing entirely for a mere hour or two around midnight. The period known as siesta time, when the settlers avoided going outside, lengthened from five hours to nearly eight, and the evening toast was set by the clock, not by the sun. "Many thanks, dear."

Novak appeared later that afternoon. "Hi, there," he said, brightly, popping up on the examination table. "I'm not sure why I'm here."

Shona bent to the small refrigerator and offered him a bottle of mineral water. "What were you thinking of when you suddenly found you were coming this way?"

Novak turned up his palms helplessly, and took a long swallow of the drink. He swept the cold container across his forehead, leaving a trail of condensation droplets that ran down his pink face. "I'm not sure. I guess it's because I don't feel a hundred per cent. I know it's been hotter than usual lately, but normally heat doesn't bother me."

"But now it does?" Shona moved in to pick up his wrist and take his pulse. It was a little elevated, but not out of normal range. "What else?"

"Oh, it's nothing," Novak said, waving the other hand. "Little things. I'm not sleeping well. I don't feel rested when I wake up."

"Have you adjusted the cooling system in your quarters?" Shona asked. "Petrie said that this summer is the hottest season you've had since the settlement was founded."

"Maybe," Novak acknowledged, but he didn't seem satisfied. He finished the mineral water and set down the container. "Still, all of us have been here from the beginning, too. I should be able to handle significantly higher temperatures than I would if I'd just arrived. I come from a pretty warm homeworld. By the way, it feels like an icebox in here. At least to me. That's no way to get acclimated."

"It's for the animals," Shona sighed. "This is their only haven from the heat. I've been dutifully going outside with anyone flying afield, to get used to the climate. Petrie calls me in the morning when he's going out to check his weather stations. I tag along. I do it as much for getting acclimated as for sightseeing. But I can wear a coolsuit, and the rabbits and cat can't. Harry's been waiting until after sunset to make his presence known."

Novak grinned. "I've seen him. Bold little feller. That skinny tail of his has been spotted going in and out of every single room in the place. You never know where you're going to find him. I don't think I mentioned it, but I rescued him from Hood, who caught him drinking out of one of the hydroponic tanks. Mr. Sunshine was threatening to use him for fertilizer."

"Oh, thank you! That cat!" Shona exclaimed. "On Earth three hundred years ago, they'd have said he was born to be hanged. Well, let me give you a quick going-over. It's probably no more than heat fatigue. I've been feeling flattened myself. Wheatley was in earlier. She's a little under the weather, too." Shona was struck by a thought. "She said she's felt bad since the day we came in with the rock sample. You handled that, too, didn't you?"

"Sure I did. What about it?" Novak asked. "I handle them all the time. It's my job."

"Well, how many people were in contact with it?"

Novak thought for a moment. "I don't know. We brought it around to nearly everyone to gloat over. It's a prize find. I'm still crowing about how much crystal was in there. That must have been a grand-daddy pipe. I haven't found nearly as much in any of my other cuttings. It's worth a small fortune."

"Is it possible that you brought in a bacterium or an amoeboid in the mud? We were handling it before it was cleaned."

Novak's eyes went wide. "I don't think so. I hope not. Normally I'm pretty careful about limiting exposure to the native organisms. But nothing's ever happened to me before." He looked worried. "This was a new pool, in a new area. I just don't know."

"I'll have to have a look at the pipe and take some samples," Shona said. "In the meantime, don't worry. Just take it easy and rest when you're tired. I'll put you on the same general antibiotic Wheatley's taking. If its a bug that fancies human tissue, maybe it'll respond to the same antibodies that Earth-type bacteria do."

"Sure," Novak said. "Come with me. I'm sure there's a chunk left I haven't cleaned."

At dinner that evening, Shona made a general announcement "Two of the people who handled the crystalline matrix brought in

211

by Novak have come to me over the last couple of days with similar symptoms of fatigue. I'm not showing any symptoms myself, but then, I can't remember specifically if I touched the sample, so I don't know if I'm immune or not. If anyone else starts feeling under the weather, please come in and see me. Thanks." She nodded to Dr. Spiegel, one of the metallurgists, who had a finger raised.

"Any specific symptoms?"

"Exhaustion, low-grade fever, low tolerance to the heat, perhaps difficulty in respiration," Shona said. "That's all so far. Anyone want to ask anything else?" Murmuring filled the room, but no one else put up a hand. She sat down.

"Given 'em something to think about," Tettenden said, smiling through his moustache at her. "Funny you should mention feeling tired. I thought it was just the heat. Summer cold, you know."

Shona received a few more complaints of fever and fatigue, all from people who had been on Novak's mining party that morning. Concerned that a native bug might be to blame, Shona delved into the mineral samples Novak found for her, running complex analyses on the claylike mud that clung to them. It seemed strange to her that there should be any organism on this world that attacked carbon-based life forms. It was curious, since there were no carbon-based natives. She found nothing that she could recognize as a bacterial or viral form.

"It's nothing but mud!" she told Saffie, who was watching her from the cool surface of the examination table with head propped on paws. "Colloids, quartzite compounds, that's all. It's virtually sterile. You could spread it on toast and eat it, and it wouldn't do a thing to you." The dog whined in sympathy.

At last, she put aside the samples, giving them up as useless. It might not have been anything in the mud itself. In open environment suits, they were exposed to the local flora and fauna, such as it was, as well as the mud.

"And you know what that means," Shona said aloud, pushing back from her lab table and standing up. "I've got to go ask Mr Sunshine for his files. After all, he is the exobiologist for this colony. I mean, what can he do to me?"

Shona found George Hood in the midst of the herb garden. He resembled a cranky Death as he clipped stalks of mint with a short curved knife and laid them in a disk-shaped, curved basket.

Hood glanced up as she approached, and went immediately back to his work. "What do you want?" he demanded.

"I've had a few patients come in showing flu-like symptoms," Shona began, watching his hands as they moved deftly through the stand of herbs, choosing or rejecting which leaves to take. "I wondered if they might have picked up local bacteria."

"Why ask me? You're the doctor." The long, bony hands folded the knife blade into its handle and laid it on top of the sheaf of mint.

"I have to check every possible source of infection."

"*Every* possible source?" Hood asked. "Phah!"

Shona met his eyes. "I'd appreciate your help. You've been studying the native flora. I want to look at your files on the native microorganisms, particularly anything that tends to be airborne. And if you have any insights on potential troublemakers, I wish you'd tell me."

"It's all in the public record," Hood said shortly, turning away from her and making for his office. Just as she was ready to form a sharp retort, she saw that he had activated his computer screen and was punching buttons with his free hand. "There. The files have been ported over to your quarters. Now, if there's nothing else?" He gave her a brief look, pursed his lips sourly, and walked off.

"Thank you," Shona called after him. She had the satisfaction of seeing the set of his shoulders stiffen. Hood deliberately went out of his way to be irritating to everyone. On her way back to her module, she wondered again how a man with his contentious personality had managed to be assigned to a group this small.

Whatever Hood's personality flaws, he was a careful and thorough researcher. His files were in good order, and included spectroscopic and microscopic analyses. Everything that the exobiologist had discovered was silicon-based. Shona could almost hear her computer groan as she typed in the commands to do a comparison search for likely invasive organisms. It was going to be a big job.

Saffie's growl awoke Shona in the middle of the night. She opened her eyes, and stared at the dark, wondering what had alarmed the dog. The growl came again, low and insistent. Shona listened closely, but she couldn't hear anything. Who would be disturbing her at this hour?

A thought alarmed her suddenly. What if one of the heat-loving, silicon hummocks had become attracted to the exhaust vent coming out of Shona's air-conditioner system, and was ambling around inside, away from the cold night? Saffie could be burned! It could set fire to the whole place. The dog's snarl came louder, from the laboratory room. There was definitely something in the module that shouldn't be there.

"Saffie! Guard!" she snapped, ordering the clog to watch but not advance on the intruder. Stumbling to her feet, she felt in the dark for the light switch. The dog responded with a savage growl and a warning bark. "Saffie! Behave!" Shona turned on the light.

A figure hunched quivering by the door, protecting its throat with both hands. "Get it away from me!" Hood cried. Saffie stood on guard in front of him, snarling, head lowered and white teeth bared. Her mistress stared.

"Down, Saffie," Shona commanded, letting out a gusty breath of relief. "Dr. Hood, what are you doing here in the middle of the night?"

The old man straightened up, glaring from dog to doctor with undisguised fury. He lowered shaking hands. "I have a cough. I came looking for a cure, not to have the life frightened out of me by a wild beast."

"Saffie, bed!" The dog retired to her bed in the corner of the main chamber, and settled down with crossed paws, keeping an eye on Hood. "Come in, Doctor. Let's have a look at you."

With ill grace, Hood sat up on the examining table. Shona went for her handheld monitor.

"Will you at least close the door?" Hood asked peevishly, but Shona suspected that he was embarrassed to reveal weakness to anyone.

"Certainly," she said, hitting the control. "How did you get in here without setting off the door signal?"

"Never you mind that," he said. "What about a cure for my cough?"

"I don't hand out drugs until I know what you're going to need," Shona said. "Just give me a moment, please. I'll go as quickly as I can."

As Hood fidgeted under the whining instruments, Shona ran a complete diagnostic on him. The results were surprising, and dismaying. He had a degenerative nerve condition that she had seen only once before, as an intern. It was painful, and invariably fatal. So far as she knew, no cure had yet been found.

"This isn't a new condition, is it?" she asked. Her sympathetic gaze made him turn away his face uncomfortably. "It's been going on for several years, and getting more painful by the day, hasn't it?" Hood didn't answer. "I suppose you know the condition is considered terminal."

"Yes, I know," Hood snapped. "I haven't got that much time left to live that I can waste any yammering with you."

Shona decided to keep expressions of sympathy to herself. In his place, she would want to keep on working, too. "How in the galaxy did you get on the mission in the first place?"

214

"They needed my skills, and there wasn't any intruding snoop like you telling me I shouldn't go."

"Even if you were the last exobiologist-botanist-whatever in the galaxy you were supposed to have a full physical before departure. I bet Wheatley doesn't know about your condition, does she?" Shona eyed him, wondering what kind of lever she could use to keep him coming back to her for treatment. Persuasion and charm didn't work; maybe blackmail would. "That data in your medical file is all phony. I ought to tell her, and have you evacuated back to Alpha on the next supply ship."

Hood looked frightened and angry. "Don't you dare. I haven't got that much time left. I'd die on the ship. Do you want to have that on your conscience?"

That struck a very tender nerve with Shona. "No, of course not. I won't tell her *if* you let me monitor you."

"A devil's bargain," Hood said, but with a note of respect. Shona prepared an injection of the lowest possible strength that would do the job. She didn't want him building up resistance to a drug he might need later on. She operated the synthesizer and produced a package of tablets of the same medication.

With a look of recognition, he reached for it. Before she put the packet in his outstretched hand, she eyed him squarely. "You come back to me when you run out of these, Dr. Hood. And I want you to let me examine you from time to time. Say, once a week. Your condition could change at any time, and I want to be on top of it if it does."

Hood nodded, and she gave him the tablets. "You got what you wanted in the end, didn't you? I could almost come to like you," the old man said, narrowing a speculative eye at her. "Huh! But why bother? There isn't that much time left."

"How am I?" Wheatley asked the next day. "Effluvian fever? Galactic rot?" She bestowed a humorous grin on Shona, who scrunched up her shoulders sheepishly.

"I am forced to conclude," Shona said, "that you're probably down with a summer cold, brought on by coming and going between chilled rooms and the heat. The only culture that turned up positive was a cold virus. I'm only surprised it hasn't happened to me yet."

"It has been rather hotter than usual," Wheatley admitted. "I could have told you that it was a bit of a cold myself."

"I hope you'll pardon me for jumping to dire conclusions," Shona said contritely. "I tend to take things too seriously. How do you feel today?"

"Just fine. I'm not cross, dear. I'd rather have you jumping at shadows than not."

The heat grew more oppressive as summer advanced, even at the poles. With the temperature gradient between indoors and outdoors increasing the settlers' resistance dropped. Shona saw more cases of low-grade fever, and several cases of borderline dehydration.

"I feel like a broken record telling you this," she said, as Spiegel jumped off the exam table and put his tunic back on. "You've got to bring adequate supplies of drinking water with you when you go out in this weather."

"Taylor, I appreciate what you're saying," Spiegel said patiently, "but the water's got to go someplace after we drink it and we can't spend all our time going around behind rocks."

With a rueful smile, Shona spread her hands. "I'm only the doctor. I just give advice. I get paid the same whether you take it or not. How's the operation going?"

Spiegel grinned. "Pretty well. It's so hot out there that we've got molten lead and tin pools right up around Novak's latest dig. It's amazing how much the matrix holds the heat. That's farther north than we've ever seen in four years, though the geological evidence is that the effect can be present up to within ten degrees of the poles when the volcanoes are active."

"Are we going to have an eruption?" Shona asked. "I've never seen one."

"Got no indications as yet, but I'll let you know." Spiegel eyed her. "You want to come and watch?"

"You bet! I've never seen a live volcano."

"Wait until the middle of next spring. I'll take you down with us toward the equator. There's always a few down there. Nothing showy," he warned. "More radiant gases than explosive."

"I don't mind." Shona smiled. "Thanks. I'll enjoy that."

Spiegel grinned wickedly. "You going to come right up on the slope and stand between the lava streams, while hot ash and clouds of smoke rain down on you?"

"Certainly not," Shona said. "I intend to sit under the canopy in the hovercar and watch *you* stand on the slopes. Adventures are always more interesting when they happen to someone else."

During the fiery height of summer, the metallurgy teams made more frequent trips to the equator, bringing back ingots of metal from the molten pools for analysis. Before a team dispersed to its labs to make their tests, Shona took samples of the dust on their suits, and scrapings from each of the ingots to ensure there was no hidden carcinogen to which the settlement at large would be exposed.

"Of course, breathing hot fumes isn't good for you, either," she pointed out to the teams.

The samples of metal were suffused with dissolved gases. "Each region has a different mix bubbled through it in the pool," Spiegel pointed out to Shona. "You can tell where each one of these ingots came from by the gas signature. It makes the job more interesting."

The pools of molten metal even began to appear close by at midday. Shona found nothing harmful to Terran-based life in any of the mineral samples brought in from outside. She was convinced that she had overreacted to the first round of summer colds.

"Uh, Taylor?" Shona turned away from the rabbit hutch, not recognizing the hoarse croak.

"Hello, Spiegel," she greeted him, setting down the bag of chow. "What can I do for you?"

The metallurgist hung back in the doorway of the module. He ran a hand through his dusty curls, and coughed sheepishly. "Got room for another hypochondriac, Taylor? Can you take a look at my throat?"

"Sure," she said. "What's wrong? No, wait until I check. Then tell me." Shona pressed down Spiegel's tongue with a sterile swab and peered into his mouth. "Hmm, swollen tonsils." Swiftly, she dabbed the swab at the back of his throat and transferred the sample to a petri dish. She tweaked the skin of his arm between thumb and forefinger, and the pinched flesh stood up for a brief moment before smoothing out. "You haven't been drinking enough, Spiegel. You're dehydrated."

"I know," Spiegel croaked. "Started feeling lousy yesterday. I came back ahead of my team because I got lightheaded. Can't do that around hot metals. Too dangerous."

"You're running a slight temperature. You need to give your system a chance to catch up with you. I prescribe three days of bed rest and lots of liquids," Shona said firmly. "I'll see if anything develops in your throat culture. Is there anyone else on your team I should meet with an IV bottle when they return?"

"All of them, maybe," Spiegel admitted. "It's been extra hot down there. Never seen anything like it in four years."

It was the next day when one of the other metallurgists came to her with swollen glands and a light fever, almost certainly a virus, probably brought on by lowered resistance and dehydration. Shona prescribed bed rest and lots of liquids, and took a few blood and tissue samples. Nothing surfaced. Shona began to test for fatigue syndromes, and analyze samples which the technicians brought in to her for reactive histamines.

Wheatley's symptoms returned, this time with a new wrinkle. "I can't seem to keep anything down, dear. Everything's been disagreeing with me."

Shona, concerned, put her on a bland diet and did another blood workup, hoping for clues. Wheatley was only the first. Other patients began to show sensitivities to food, though none so violent as that of the members of the crystal-mining party. Most of these new patients had been out in the fields, working amidst the noxious fumes of the thermal pools. The hot, coppery aroma hung in the air everywhere. She was still puzzled over why she hadn't been afflicted with the lassitude or fever that affected everyone else.

"They're behaving as if the fumes in the air are exacerbating a condition they have from being exposed to a pesticide or another toxic substance," Shona said when Novak asked her about it at the evening meal. "I can't imagine that I have any natural immunity, so is it possible I just wasn't here when you were exposed? How long ago might that have been?"

"No noxious chemicals have ever been used on this planet," Novak assured her. "Unless you count the bad food." Complaining of a sensitive stomach, he had shifted to a bland diet. He and Wheatley were calling themselves the Culinary Exiles. Novak was down to a diet of potatoes, rice, and hulled grains, with supplementary nutrients, and had joined Shona in her daily suppers of prepared nutri. "Everything else makes me sick," he complained with a grimace.

Shona was worried about him and the others. Wheatley was the worst off. She had gone over to a diet of nutri with the barest hint of seasonings. "I'd get more flavor out of sticking my finger down my throat," the administrator said, "and pretty much the same reaction. Just can't take strong spices lately. Anything I try comes hurrying back."

Dear Alf Tettenden had been philosophical about cutting back on his food choices. "Just like being in the service," he'd told Shona, with a gallant smile. "You got what they were serving that day, and liked it. I'll get by."

Novak was skeptical. Making a face, he took a forkful of scrambled nutri colored with annatto. "Ugh, this is dull! How do you stand months of it?"

"I fantasize about real food," Shona joked. "But seriously, it would explain why I have no symptoms."

"Would that mean it's treatable?" Wheatley asked. "I don't want to eat unflavored nutri forever."

"Probably," Shona said. "If you aren't exposed again."

"Could such compounds be naturally occurring?" Chan asked from across the table. She was in what Shona was calling the first stage, headaches and general fatigue. Shona was concerned that if she didn't find what was causing the ailments, Chan, and the rest of the scientists, would begin losing their tolerance for food.

"In such a volatile environment, it's possible," Shona speculated. "I've been checking for bacteria and other organisms. I'm going to go and take another look in the morning. Otherwise, I'm going to begin assuming it *is* the food."

She got up early, and picked up the cat from his comfortable nest of cushions. He murmured a protest.

"Come on, Harry," she said, hoisting him onto her shoulder and scratching him behind the ears as she walked. "You might as well earn your keep for once. If anyone can sniff out something I've missed, it's you."

The sun was still below the horizon. Shona was grateful that second summer was passing. The constant heat and bright sunshine had become enervating.

In the dark hangar she found an available hovercar and signed it out, using the clipboard hanging on the wall behind it.

"Here you go, puss," Shona said, setting Harry into the car cab. "Stay there a minute."

She selected a coolsuit from the racks, and put it on. The puffy, silver garment was all one piece, but inside were tapes that had to be fastened around knees, thighs, waist, upper chest, and upper arms to hold the suit in place. Just before she zipped up the neck, she checked inside the oversized collar to see that all the little function lights were on green. The power packs were attached to the upper-leg casings like saddlebags. Shona reached down to the right one and hit the control. Goose bumps ran along her chilled skin as the cooling units kicked on, filling the suit with a blast of cold air. She shivered violently once, and took a deep breath, waiting for relief. In a moment, the temperature warmed up and stabilized. She put another coolsuit on the cab floor, and switched it on for Harry. Disdainfully, the cat ignored it.

She stepped into the hover and glanced over the controls. Harry jumped up onto the seat beside her to watch what she was doing, until Shona opened the hangar doors and the outside air flooded in. Once the hot air hit him, the cat flattened out on his side like a mat and refused even to switch his tail. Shona glanced at him before donning her goggles.

"I'm sorry, sweetie. They don't make these suits in your size. If you don't stay by it, there's nothing I can do. I'll make this trip as quick as I can, I promise." The very end of his tail flicked up and settled down like a flower petal falling.

The sky was clear, glittering with stars. Shona knew from experience that the day was going to be a scorcher. She was grateful for the protective canopy of the hovercar.

On command, the vehicle lifted up and moved out of the hangar. Everything seemed to be functioning well. Since it was her first outing alone, she had been concerned about knowing what to do, but, as Novak had promised, the car practically drove itself. He had volunteered to come along, but until his condition improved, Shona didn't want to expose him to extremes of temperature. She was concerned enough about the cat. If Harry didn't scent anything double-quick, she would turn around and bring him back in.

She went back to the mud field from which Novak had taken his crystal pipe. Everyone's health problems dated from that day when the crew, including her, had churned up the mud and been exposed to the mineral-heavy steam geysering up from the heart of Erebus.

The sun came up just as they came over the rise, peeping under the edge of the shimmering canopy. The mud pool had partly refilled since the day she and the others had gone out there. Using an extending tool instead of tracking into the hot sludge, Shona put one of her sampling tubes into the steam coming up from the minute caldera in the center. She took dozens of other samples of clay and air from the field.

"I hope I find something," she told Harry. "It's beginning to make me think I'm imagining the whole thing. It can't be the weather affecting everyone's metabolism, but something is slow-ly breaking down their resistance to normal strains of bacteria. Normally I'd say this would be the ideal world for someone with chronic allergies. Nothing I've found so far even *interacts* with carbon-based tissues. No high-power or magnetic emanations, no native plant life. It would make the ideal health spa."

His eyes narrowed to knife-edged slits, Harry seemed unim-pressed. Shona put her samples under cover in the vehicle, and wrapping a fold of the spare coolsuit over the cat's head and body, carried him around the site.

"Think you can do your job under these conditions?" she asked him. "I'm not putting you down on this hot ground, so I'll try and read you." She brought him, legs dangling, to the edge of the thermal pool, and watched curiously as his nose began to twitch. An abrupt kick in the stomach from one of his back feet told her he wasn't interested in the pool. She carried him from point to point in the area, trying to remember where everyone had been standing, what they had touched. The cat showed no signs of recognizing any of the dozens of chemical compounds he had been trained to identify by scent.

At last Shona gave up. "Either you're not talking, or there's nothing here," she said. "That's the same conclusion I reached." She brought him inside the car and poured water from a thermos jug into the cup-shaped lid for him to drink. The cat lapped it noisily and looked for more. Shona gave him another ration, and drank some herself.

"Come on, it's getting hot," she said. She put away the bottle, and the cat settled down underneath the passenger seat away from the spare suit. Giving herself a moment until her eyes adjusted to the shadow under the canopy, she hit the starter.

Nothing happened. She pushed the button again, glancing at the motion-control lever to see if she had inadvertently left the vehicle in drive. It was in the center, neutral position. Hopefully, she pushed the lever forward and back, hoping the car would move.

"Uh-oh," she said, biting her lip. "What did I do wrong?" Forcing herself to calm down, she started over, and over again. Nothing she did made the power plant respond. The indicator lights all went on, but nothing else worked. "I'd better call for help." She reached for the commset key.

It wasn't there. The thin bracket which held the commset was empty. She hadn't noticed it when she drove out. It looked like all of the other modular units in the control board. Shona gulped. This looked remarkably like sabotage with the radio missing, except she didn't know enough about engines to tell if this one had been tampered with. But who would want to strand her out in the desert? Shona felt close to panic.

Underneath the seats, Harry began to pant. He was becoming overheated in the still, hot car.

"Do you want some water, kitty?" she asked, getting down on her knees beside him. He had flattened out on the floor, and his breath was going in and out rapidly. "Oh, no. Oh, no."

She tucked the sides of the spare coolsuit around him. With a weak snarl, he batted at her hands and snaked out of it, resuming his position on the floor. She looked around for shelter but there was no more-protected place anywhere on the plain. In a very short time the increasing heat could kill him, and the sun was rising higher in the sky. If he refused to stay in the refrigerated suit he could die. Shona was getting hotter, too. She could start walking back toward the settlement, but it would take hours, and they had very little water with them. They would have to wait until dark, almost twenty hours away, with the heat of noon yet to come. Sweat broke out down her back, and the small motors in her coolsuit speeded up. An idea struck her.

She zipped down the front of her suit. The heat slammed into her like a wall, and she knew how much the cat had to be suffering. "Come on, kid," she said reaching for him. "In with Mama." He protested, but she had a hand hooked under his belly, and snaked him toward her.

Packing a cat into your coolsuit with you, she thought, was like trying to put a five-meter decapod into a shopping bag. If she wasn't so upset about her situation, she would have laughed. Eventually, she got Harry zipped up inside the roomy suit braced on top of the folds of fabric fastened around her waist. Soon, his breathing slowed down to normal, and he emitted a complaint. She kept the collar unfastened so he could get enough air, and sat down with the spare suit over her head to assess her situation. If she left the car, she would eventually reach the settlement, *if* she didn't get lost. That thought alone was enough to dissuade her from trying. She wished there was something she could use as a signal flare, or to set fire to some handy brushwood, if there was any around. Which there was not. She groaned. There was a definite disadvantage in being lost in a desert. Even if she was willing to risk it, she wasn't willing to bet Harry's life—or her own—that she knew how to find her way back. Her best chance of survival was to stay here with the car, and pray it wasn't long before someone noticed she was missing. She hoped it was before she died of thirst. Her heart pounded against the cat's back.

The questions remained: what was wrong with the car, and was it deliberate? If so, who did it, and why?

Verdadero relaxed in the red plush of an armchair and snapped his fingers for the drink server. The sun was just dropping below the horizon, illuminating the incandescent soap bubble of Dome #4, far below the broad picture windows of the club. "Have anything you like, Manfred. I can't believe this is the first time you've set foot on Mons Olympus."

For all his natural poise, Mitchell looked like a schoolboy caught at a cocktail party. He looked around the luxurious room with guilty interest. "First time, sir. This is an occasion."

"I've been remiss," Verdadero said, flippantly. "You're a top executive; you should have been made a member of the Olympus

Club a long time ago." For himself, Verdadero enjoyed the exclusivity, the extraordinary deference shown by envious colleagues who would have killed to be put up for membership. He smiled. The Corporation paid *his* dues. It had been a long, miserable climb to the top for him, and he reveled in every perquisite his lofty office allowed.

"Sir, since we can't be overheard, I wanted to discuss with you . . ." Mitchell began, leaning forward.

"I won't hear a word, Manny," Verdadero insisted, making an imperious gesture. It wouldn't do for his subordinate to forget his place. "No business here. This is a social occasion. You're my guest. Enjoy yourself. Relax," he said, leaning back and enjoying the knowledge that Mitchell could do no such thing. He meant to show him the heights, and demonstrate that the younger man did not yet own them. *Perhaps one day*, Verdadero thought, *he can take over my office when I no longer want it. Unless he proves to be more ruthless than he seems.*

Chirwl, left alone in the module, fielded visitors politely. "No, Shona is away from here. She is investigating."

His fellow scientists were equally polite, though amused. "Full of activity, our Shona," Alftettenden said. His cheeks were very pink, an unnatural color for him. "Will you ask her to stop by my hovel when she returns?"

"I will most certainly do so," Chirwl agreed, shifting around in his pouch to get a better look at his friend. "Are you well, Alftettenden?"

The old man harrumphed. "I'll do," he said. "It's Wheatley I'm worried about."

"I will so tell her," Chirwl promised. Alftettenden left, and Chirwl returned to his note-making at the bottom of his pouch. Based on his studies, he had a new facet to add to his theory: that of character. Machines were different depending not only upon the maker, but the user. He had not yet decided whether the changes visited upon the mechanicals were permanent or not. Margochan had complained that nothing Billnovak used was ever the same again—had he instilled his character into it?

A noise disturbed him. He popped his head out to see. "Shona?"

Hood stared at him from beside Shona's food-preparation console. This human did not like any other human in the colony, nor did he speak decently to Chirwl, though the ottle had gone to lengths to engage him in conversation. "May help be given to you?" he asked.

The exobiologist started, dropping a cooking utensil Shona used for boiling nutri. "You startled me," he said accusingly.

"May I ask forgiveness," Chirwl said contritely. "Shona is not in at this time. How may you be helped?"

"Oh, nothing, nothing," Hood said quickly. "I . . . I wished to talk to *you*, about the plants on your homeworld."

"True words?" Chirwl said, with delight. "I would find most honor in that. Please, be comfortable." He waved a claw at Shona's office chair, and climbed down to sit by his guest.

Chirwl had a most satisfying conversation on the subject of botany. It was some time after Hood had departed that Chirwl considered it odd that Shona had not yet returned. The day was becoming uncomfortably hot. Had she not told him that the temperatures outside the structure were dangerous to humans?

CHAPTER

17

THE CHRONOMETER SAID that two and a half standard hours had passed since Shona realized she wasn't going anywhere. The sun had lifted above the hover's canopy, and was shining its full face on the surrounding terrain. Shona could see the heat haze rising from the ground around the steaming pool.

She felt her cheeks. In spite of the cooling units, her face was hot and clammy, and if she could see it, was probably pink as a candy apple. She had decided firmly not to think of water. Defying her, her truant imagination had summoned up memories of waterfalls and rivers on Dremel, rain on Karela, and the swirling waters of her bathtub as Chirwl dived into it to escape a scolding when she discovered he'd eaten her whole bag of Crunchynut bars. She licked her lips. They were dry and cracking. Her vision changed to the contents of a pot of soup her aunt asked her to stir. The steam from the pot left moisture on her face. She wiped it off. On the whole, she preferred cooler memories. Inside the suit, Harry shifted to his feet, walked around her belt line to her back, and flopped heavily to his side. One sharp toe poked her in the spine.

Shona had turned over a lot of ideas in her head about her predicament. It was most likely that the car was faulty, or that she had blown the power plant through inexperience. Least likely was the theory that someone had deliberately fiddled with the mechanism to strand her alone and helpless in the desert. After all, what was the guarantee that she would take this particular car? And what did she know that was worth killing for? The only thing she knew that someone wanted kept secret was that Dr. Hood was a dying man, and it was a fact more likely to hurt him than anyone else.

Twenty minutes more passed. She shared the last of the water with Harry, who crawled back into her suit as soon as he drank his ration, and lay curled around her stomach. Her lips and tongue felt swollen. If they didn't get more water soon, they would become dehydrated. Harry, unable to comprehend privation, might become desperate, savage, before dropping into a coma. The burning landscape around her seemed intensely brighter. She felt scared. What if no one came to rescue them?

She looked down at the bulge in her suit where the cat huddled. It was almost as if she were pregnant again, with a helpless life there dependent upon her for safety and sustenance. Tears rolled onto her cheeks and dried there before she could wipe them away.

"There she is!" A shout interrupted her self-pity session. She looked up. Cresting the rise was another hovercar, with Novak in his ridiculous cotton hat standing up next to Chan, who was driving. Shona sprang to her feet. She cried out a greeting to them, her cracked lips and dry tongue making it incomprehensible gibberish.

"Oh, Taylor, look at you!" Chan said, climbing out and hurrying to her. "You're red. Are you all right?"

Shona tried to assure her she was fine, but her voice was a croak.

"Something to drink is indicated, I think," Tettenden called, pouring liquid from a thermos to a cup as he walked. He extended the cup to her, changed his mind, and proffered the thermos instead. Shona drank its entire contents of cool water without lowering her chin.

"Oh, Taylor, I am so sorry!" Chan said contritely. "The comm-unit in this car was faulty. I pulled it yesterday and neglected to leave a note on the car. I came down to the hangar this morning and found you'd taken it out."

"I'll testify to it: Chan went absolutely spare," Novak said, clapping his colleague on the back teasingly. "We didn't worry about it until Chirwl came looking for us and said you'd been gone a long time."

"How did you find me?"

"I knew you'd revisit my mud pool," Novak explained. "Just stood to reason you'd be somewhere nearby."

His face was ruddy with the heat. "You shouldn't really be out," Shona protested.

Novak raised an eyebrow. "Oh, should I leave you here and go back until it's cooler?"

"No!" Shona said. "I'm very glad you're here. You have no idea how glad!"

"Great. Let's see what we can do with this hulk of a machine."

"Good heavens," Tettenden said. "What's wrong with your tummy?"

226

Hearing other voices, Harry had awakened. He pawed at the inside of the suit, trying to get out. A rusty mew came from beneath the padded panel. "It's my cat," Shona said, unfastening the front of her coverall. She hauled the limp bundle of fur out of her suit and began to feed him water by pouring it into her palm from the thermos lid and letting him lap it up.

"Come on, sweetie," she coaxed. "Just a little more for me. That's a good kitty. Come on, another mouthful."

After some banging and swearing, Novak extricated himself from the bottom of the console and hit the starter button. The hover began to hum.

"Your lead was disconnected from the power plant. There was probably just enough juice left in the batteries to get you out here and no further. I'll drive this one back," he insisted. "You two get into the other car. It's cooler!"

Escorted protectively by Tettenden, Shona carried the cat to the other vehicle and climbed aboard. Harry was recovered enough to complain weakly when the big hangar doors boomed shut behind the returning car. "You are back," Chirwl said, full of concern as Shona came into the module. "Where is my friend Harry?"

"Right here," Shona said, holding out the exhausted cat, who fell asleep as soon as the cool air in the hallway hit him. "Don't harass him. He's had an adventure." She set Harry down on his cushions and went right to the water cooler. Stopping midway only to take a handful of salt tablets, Shona drank two liters of water. "Whew! That's better. I'm pooped. I might use siesta time for a siesta, for a change."

"Ronnieorwheatley needs to see you," Chirwl said.

"What's wrong?" Shona asked, putting down her beaker.

"She did not look well," the ottle replied. "Her scent was not of the best. Too much acid."

"Acid?" Shona wondered hurrying to the administrator's cubicle.

Wheatley's room was in total darkness. Shona stopped on the threshold and peered in, trying to make out shapes. "That's all right, dear. Come in. Is it Shona?" The older woman was lying on her bed with a cloth over her eyes.

"Yes, Ronnie. What's wrong? Chirwl told me you needed me."

"I've got a nonstop headache, dear. I can't look at the light. Can you give me something for it?"

"Sounds like a migraine," Shona said. "How about a cafergot?"

"Nothing by mouth, please. I've been rejecting breakfast from both ends, and I've got no taste for lunch."

"That does it," Shona said. "I'm putting you on an IV. You're not getting enough nutrients with all that upchucking."

Wheatley nodded, a gesture Shona sensed more than she saw. "Whatever you say, dear. Could you ask them to keep it down out there? Noises are bothering me, too."

Shona had barely heard the soft footsteps and conversation passing by. Wheatley was in serious trouble. This was in store for the rest of her patients if she couldn't do something.

After giving Wheatley an injection to help her sleep, and attaching a glucose drip, Shona went back to her module and recorded a message to Manfred Mitchell.

"There's a catastrophe arising here on Erebus," she explained. "I hope it will turn out to be nothing serious, but I am very concerned that I haven't been able to identify the cause. All the symptoms point to exposure to an infector or pollutant in the past which is causing secondary reactions now. They're suffering from vomiting, chronic diarrhea, sudden allergies, and becoming unable to tolerate foods. I am forced to treat the patients empirically according to need, but some of them are becoming very weak. I am especially concerned about Veronica Wheatley. Her senses have become unusually sharpened, and she is becoming allergic to practically everything. It's very strange for Erebus, because there's almost nothing to be allergic to here.

"This is a serious epidemic. It is possible that this might have been caused by something recently introduced into the environment I suspect a cumulative rejection of a local irritant, but nothing I have examined has panned out. The colony is very young. It's possible that something carrying infectious bacteria was inadequately sterilized and hadn't been opened and used until now. It's also possible that the problem is coming from a recently discovered local source. It's even possible that the problem could have come in with me, though I assure you that everything, including my module, was sterilized and disinfected inside and out. It's impossible for me to say the same thing about other transports that have dropped off shipments on Erebus. I believe that it is vital to track down the source and see if the effects can be reversed. If not, everyone could be reduced to eating nutri and staying inside during all daylight hours. I will keep you advised."

She put an "Urgent" flag on it, ensuring it would get priority handling when it was downloaded, and alerted Margo Chan to send it off to Corporation Headquarters immediately. Then she renewed her search for the source of the problem.

Hood had stopped eating his meals in the dining room. No one had seen him since breakfast the previous day. Shona suspected that the disease from which he was suffering had recurred, making it too painful for him even to walk the length of the compound. She went to the hydroponics section.

The huge chamber had a kind of sinister look with the shutters fully closed. All she could see was a sort of black-on-black wash of the jungle she knew was there: vast, tentacular shadows. "Dr. Hood?" she called. There was no answer. She ran back for a torch and her medical bag.

His office was empty. She tried the other small chambers surrounding the greenhouse one by one. She'd never had an opportunity to explore the section unimpeded. The doors around the left arc of the dome led to a potting shed, a root cellar, and a cold room for fruit and herbs. At the far end of the greenhouse was a locked door. She banged on it with a knuckle.

"Dr. Hood?"

"Go away!" a hoarse voice yelled.

"Dr. Hood, it's Shona. I have your medication."

There was a long pause, and the door slid open. The chamber was dark behind him. Shona turned the flashlight up into his face, and was taken aback by the nightmare visage caught by the yellow glare.

Hood looked terrible. She was used to his gauntness. This was a shocking extreme. Now she could see the bones of his face, and the veins under the skin as well. "You've got it, too," she whispered.

"This ought to be a great satisfaction to you," he sneered.

"It isn't," she said, stifling the pity she felt because she knew he found it contemptible. In her bag was a prepared package of his pills. She handed it to him. Watching her with the very greatest suspicion, he took one and choked it down with a glass of water. While he took the tablet, she uncoiled an IV.

The medication worked very quickly. She could see the easing of the deep lines of his face, and the trembling of his lips stopped. "What's that for?" He pointed at the clear plastic bag.

"You. If you have what everyone else has, you'll have been vomiting up anything you try to eat, isn't that right?" she demanded. "You need nutrients. I know you have it. You're hiding out in a dark room. All the pumps in the hydro section are off to stop the noise. Please, take it."

"I can't lie still all day for a drip feed," Hood protested.

"You can wear it around your neck if you like," Shona said. "Don't fight with me. I want to help."

"Leave me alone," he said. "That's all I want from you." He broke away and shut the door on her. She heard the lock engage.

"Poor silly man. Dr. Hood!" she shouted. "I am leaving the IV on the bench out here. Just slap the patch on the back of your hand. It's already adjusted to the correct flow. I'll come back later and leave another one."

"Stay away from me," the hoarse voice said. Short of breaking down the door and taking him prisoner while she treated him, Shona could do nothing more than she had. The pills would enable him to operate at the top of his strength. She suspected the IV would vanish as soon as she left. Her other patients needed her.

Her other patients, in the genuine manner of scientists, were philosophical about their sudden sensitivities when she went around to ask how they were doing. Each of them handled the discomforts and inhibitions of the ailment in a different way. Spiegel had plunged his room into darkness, but Shona could hear a thread of music from his sound system. Incredibly, he was practicing guitar by ear.

"I'd go stir-crazy if I didn't have something to do," he said. "I'm all right at night, but in the daytime, I can almost hear the sunshine, if you know what I mean."

Alf Tettenden attempted humor for her, though Shona could tell that his stomach was hurting him. He was now on a bland diet too, and had given up his sunset drink. He was more concerned about Wheatley.

"I'm not going to quit working just because I don't feel my best. I'd have expected *you* to get a touch of tourist tummy, landing in a new place, not the people who've been here all the time. Just shows how backwards things are in these foreign parts," the old man said.

"Just so long as you don't think it's something I put in the food," Shona joked, noting with dismay that his temperature was up a few points. "Keep pushing liquids, and I'll come and see you later. I'll find out what's causing this if it kills me. Did you know that Dr. Hood is sick, too? He's back there in Hydroponics, hiding out. Someone else is going to have to keep things going. He's shut off all the pumps and closed the skylights."

"Novak can do that. He's a born tinkerer." Tettenden pushed out his lower lip and prodded it thoughtfully with a forefinger. "What haven't you tried, my dear?"

Shona raised her shoulders. "The only thing that everyone has in common is the food supply or the water-purification system. It's also the one thing I haven't shared with all of you. It might explain my immunity. I kept thinking that it had to do with the crystal matrix. I didn't touch that, but neither did half this colony; and most of you were already sick when the metal teams began to

230

come down with it. I'm going to have a look at the filters as soon as I finish seeing everyone."

When she returned to her module at the end of her rounds, her console alerted her that a message had been downloaded. The graphic on the screen was whirling and flashing, indicating an urgent transmission. "Now, what?" she asked, plumping down to listen to it. "My letter can't have reached Manny already."

The data chain had the official seal of the Corporation on it. Instead of one of the faces she knew from Marsbase, the man on the screen was a stranger, dressed in the Corporation uniform. Behind him, Shona glimpsed a ship's control room.

"Dr. Taylor, I am Captain Cipriano of Transport Ship Twenty-Two. I have top-level orders to pick up you and your lab, for an emergency assignment. We'll be moving on a tight schedule, so I request that you have everything battened down and ready to go in forty-eight hours from this transmission. This is a mandatory order from Corporation HQ."

"What?" Shona squawked at the screen. "I can't go. I have an emergency on my hands right here!"

She sent a message to Mitchell, and coded it double Urgent. "Why am I being moved? I notified you that there was a medical emergency here. I can't go. Please, call off the transport. I have to stay. Two days will not be enough time."

Forty hours later, Wheatley, weak and dehydrated from constant vomiting and purging, unable to tolerate food, developed a rash on the arm where the glucose IV was attached. Shona switched her to a simple saline solution, and gave her a low dosage of an antibiotic to bring down the swelling. The reaction was swift and devastating. Wheatley's whole body became covered in a thin, red rash, and she began gasping for breath. As Shona and Maling, Shona's press-ganged aide and one of the few who was reasonably healthy, worked to save her, Wheatley went into cardiac arrest and died.

CHAPTER

⟞18⟝

THE CREW OF of the *Sybil* waited inside their ship in Bay Seventeen with half a dozen other small cargo ships while port officials fumigated the whole dome's worth, then went over the cargo manifests and checked paperwork one ship at a time. Several crews were still waiting ahead of them for processing, including fourteen shuttles that were in Bay Sixteen, next door, that were stuffed with Earth tourists from a luxury liner orbiting overhead.

"I've said it before," Kai complained, leaning on the back of Gershom's pilot couch and watching the tourists through the transparent walls of the landing bay as they filed out toward the Space Center. There was a brilliant flash of light as one of the travelers noticed the *Sibyl* and took her picture. Gershom grinned, knowing it would come out as a blank white spot on the woman's tape of her vacation. "I'll say it again. Mars has the worst backups of any known planet in the galaxy. You'd think they'd sign up more personnel to handle space traffic."

Ivo flicked the controls on the screen tank to hook into the planetary news channel. A menu of stories appeared. "What's anyone want to see?"

Gershom leaned over to read the list. "What's that one? 'Plague strikes mining planet.' I wonder if it's anywhere we do business." He selected the story and settled back to watch.

The dancing graphics cleared to show an empty street intersection inside a dome. To either side of the camera's view, the houses were large, ornate, and silent.

"Tragedy struck the uranium-mining colony of Celtuce two months ago, when a mysterious plague killed nearly all of the two thousand people who lived there," the announcer's voice said.

"Wait a minute," Ivo said. "Celtuce. That's where Shona was."

"I wonder if she's heard about it," Gershom said. "She'll be devastated. She liked those people."

More video followed, of a handful of exhausted men and women in white coveralls filing aboard a shuttlecraft. " . . . only twelve survivors who do not understand why they were not stricken when all of their neighbors and friends fell ill and died. A doctor on temporary assignment had just left the colony when the disaster occurred." Tape of Shona talking with some animation was laid under the voiceover. "The colonists are left to wonder if she had anything to do with the tragedy, or if she just left too soon. The survivors have been transported to Mars and are awaiting relocation by the Corporation."

Gershom was stunned. "Good grief! They makes it sound like she's responsible!"

"You take it up with that Corporation man who's meeting us," Ivo advised.

"You better believe I will," Gershom said furiously.

Eblich came forward with Lani. She was wearing a coverall and carrying a suitcase in front of her with both hands. Eblich held her comm-unit clutched under one arm. "Ready," was all he said. Written eloquently on his face was the sorrow and disappointment he felt that the little girl was leaving them.

"I know how you feel," Ivo told his crewmate. He picked Lani up, suitcase and all, and gave her a big hug. She buried her face in his mass of fuzzy hair. "Don't cry, kid. We'll come back to visit, all right?"

"All right," Lani said, her eyes big and solemn. The other men hugged her goodbye. Eblich was the last to wish her farewell. The inspectors rapped on the cargo hatches for entry, and Kai hurried out of the cockpit to admit them.

"We're clear," he called forward a few minutes later. "Goodbye, Lani. Safe landing."

Gershom escorted her down the ramp and across the vast floor. Avoiding the small motorized carts and ground crew in environment suits, they skirted gigantic cranes and containers. Lani looked warily at all the strange things around her. Gershom knew she'd never seen so many machines in her life. He squeezed her hand for confidence, and she looked up at him adoringly. "I'm going to miss you, Lani," he told her.

"Me, too," the girl said simply.

Clad in an environment suit marked with the G.L.C. logo, Mitchell waited near the entrance doors of the landing bay. He recognized Gershom Taylor walking toward him with a little girl by the hand. He checked his handheld comm-unit. Yes, that was Leilani of Karela. You never knew if someone was going to attempt to pull a switch and turn in a ringer. Considering that both husband and wife had contacted him asking to adopt the child, it was fair to assume it might happen. But the Taylors seemed to be honest in spite of their fiercely declared affection; they were turning the girl over to him as agreed.

"Captain Taylor?" he said, approaching them. "Good to see you."

"How are you, Mr. Mitchell?" Taylor said, setting down a black case and holding out his hand. "This is Lani."

After shaking hands with Captain Taylor, Mitchell offered his hand to the girl, and she took it. She looked healthier than she had on the message transmitted to him by Dr. Taylor. She had put on weight, and her hair had grown glossy. She'd look good in publicity tri-dees. Mentally, he went over the list of arrangements to be made on her behalf. Decisions had to be reached immediately as to her upbringing and education. Mitchell began to make plans for some publicity to accompany the girl's arrival on Mars. It would be very good for the Corp to be shown helping an orphan to make a new life, aided by the fortune she inherited. It could even be a documentary.

"My name is Manny," he said. "What should I call you?"

"Lani," the child said.

"Are you hungry?" he asked. Leilani shook her head. "Well, you've come a long way. There are a lot of people who want to meet you."

"She's a good little one, but she doesn't say much," Taylor said, patting the girl on the shoulder. The child smiled up at him trustingly. They looked disconcertingly alike, the tall, thin man and the child, with their straight dark hair and black-brown eyes. "Shona didn't want to give her up. Neither do I."

"I don't blame you, Captain," Mitchell said. "I promise you, I'll take good care of her." He waited.

"These things are hers," Taylor said, and from his pocket removed a disk which he extended to Mitchell. "Here's her medical records. Shona gave her all her inoculations before we left."

"Very thorough," Mitchell said. "Thank you. Thank you for bringing her here safely. There's a ten-thousand credit bonus for you and your crew on top of the fee for transporation. I can have it added to your credit account if you prefer."

"Mr. Mitchell, I'd like to talk to you for a moment, on another matter," Taylor said, looking a little uneasy.

Mitchell was curious, but he had another duty to perform first. "Certainly. If you can wait here a moment, I need to make a call. Then we can talk." He walked toward the bank of telecommunicators along one wall, leaving the man and girl standing alone under the bright glare of the dome lights.

"Sector Chief Mitchell on line, sir," Verdadero's aide reported.

The CEO leaned over to his console. "Put it through." Mitchell's face appeared on the screen. "Manny! What news?"

"The child is here, sir," Mitchell reported. "She's with me now." He glanced back over his shoulder, past which loaders and the edge of a cargo ship were visible.

"Excellent," Verdadero said. "Manny, I want you to stay right there, if you would. I'm sending one of Lodge's people with a video team. We'd like to record this moment for the media."

"Very well," Mitchell nodded. "The girl's a quiet child. She doesn't look like she'll be any trouble. We're in Bay Seventeen near the entrance."

"Bay Seventeen. Good. See you later, Manny." Verdadero severed the connection, put the security lock on the comm-unit, and dialed another number. "They're in Bay Seventeen. You know what to do. Get them both, if you can."

"My boss is sending a publicity photographer to take a little video of Lani here in the landing bay," Mitchell explained, returning to them. "The Karela tragedy has remained in the news. People are interested in the story. By bringing this child on the last leg of her journey, we can put a reasonably happy ending to the whole mess. Now, what may I do for you?"

"Mr. Mitchell, what's this about Celtuce?" Gershom asked. "My wife was stationed there a few months ago. When she left, everyone was fine. I saw the news report while we were waiting back there. I'm astonished that you let such a report go out!"

Mitchell regarded him with bemusement. "The disaster on Celtuce is public information, sir. We can't suppress the fact that two thousand people died."

"But it makes it sound as if it's Shona's fault that the plague hit the colony. This is ruining my wife's reputation. Your office implied that she caused the plague or allowed it to happen through negligence." Lani said nothing, but she clung to Gershom's waist, staring at Mitchell reprovingly. Gershom wrapped a protective arm around her shoulders.

"That's not what the report from my office said," Mitchell told him. "I assure you, our press releases on tragedies are intended to be as neutrally written as possible. I reviewed the press release myself."

"That's exactly what it said on the news," Gershom said, feeling his face get hot.

"I assure you, it was never our intention to suggest that she was to blame," Mitchell said, taken aback. "This did not come out of my department, Captain. I'll arrange for the correct facts to reach the press myself."

"I'd like confirmation of that, if you don't mind, sir," Gershom said. Mitchell could see how angry the trader was, and he answered him soothingly.

"Certainly. As soon as—"

A huge shadow cut off the light over the empty expanse of concrete on which they were standing. Gershom looked up. Above them, a rectangular shape, a cargo container, was hovering above them. There was something wrong with the way it hung there, almost as if it was going to drop on top of them. Gershom knew suddenly that it would. He heaved Lani to his hip, and hooked Mitchell with his free arm, shoving him out of the way.

"Run! Run! It's going to fall!"

They scrambled toward the side of the loading dock, hurrying into the light. Behind them, there was a splintering crash as the container hit the ground where they had been standing. From the split sides of the container, debris flew in all directions. The three of them narrowly missed being flattened by a man-sized box which blew out of the interior and slammed down onto the ground. Smaller containers sailed into the wall of the landing bay ahead of them and rebounded to crash in front of their feet with a report like a series of firecrackers. Mitchell, his customary self-possession gone, gaped panting at the wreckage. Lani began to cry.

"What's the matter with that crane driver?" Gershom demanded. He looked up. The cab of the gigantic vehicle was invisible from where he was standing. Checking to see that Lani and Mitchell were unhurt, he ran to the ladder on the side of the machine and scaled it.

At the sound of the crash, people started running from all over the landing bay, and someone hit the alarm siren. From twenty meters up the metal ladder along the crane's flat sides, Gershom could see that not one of the hemicylindrical containers had fallen, but two, one on top of the other. No wonder boxes flew!

Five meters more, and he was climbing into the glass-sided cab. There was a short man at the controls. Gershom grabbed his arm to spin him around.

"You nearly killed three people, man!" The crane operator fell onto Gershom's feet. He was unconscious, or dead. Gershom started to feel for a pulse, and caught a sudden glimpse out of the side of the cab of another man, standing between the giant cable guide and the crane derrick and aiming a pistol down at Mitchell and Lani. Scrambling out of the control house, Gershom ran at the gunman.

"Hey!" Gershom yelled. The pistol went off, missing its target.

The man turned and brought the weapon to bear on him. Gershom threw himself down behind a metal lip as the pistol, an old fashioned slugthrower, went off again. He made a leapfrogging bound over the cable house, ducked another slug, and jumped to catch the metal beam overhead with his strong spacer's arms. Luckily, the gunman was not expecting an attack from above. Gershom kicked him solidly in the chest and the face, drawing blood from nose and lip. The slugthrower went flying over the side into the heap of debris on the dock.

Gershom dropped down out of reach, preparing to grab the would-be assassin and hold him until the authorities could get up there to take him away. The man must have guessed his thoughts. Eyes narrowed and face dripping with his own blood, he crouched over, daring Gershom with a flick of his hands to come and get him. He was a burly brute, and the way he moved told Gershom he was a practiced fighter. Gershom, who used a martial arts workout only to keep in shape on board ship, would be no match for him.

Suddenly, the man feinted right, then headed left. Gershom dove for him, but the move was just another feint. The gunman gave him a quick elbow in the ribs and a kick as he hurried past, and slid down the ladder. Gershom followed after him, but he wasn't quick enough to stop him before the assassin disappeared into the crowd.

"Stop him!" Gershom yelled. "He'll be the only man in the corridor with blood on his face."

The port authority force ran out after him. A few minutes later, a guard with several stripes on his shoulder came over to speak to Gershom and Mitchell. "He's dead, boys. Shot himself with his own laser. What's all this about?"

"An accident," Mitchell said, quickly. "The crane driver dropped his load. He must have been horrified by what he did, because he ran away after it happened. My associate here was trying to bring him to you."

"Can you give us a description, or a card number?" the lieutenant asked Gershom. Puzzled by Mitchell's prevarication, Gershom responded with a brief physical description. "Sounds like a new one," the guard said.

"Why didn't you tell them he was trying to kill us?" Gershom hissed when they left the dock area.

237

Mitchell's handsome face was set and white like a marble statue. He pulled Gershom aside, leaving Lani a little distance away. She started toward them, and he held up a hand with a friendly smile. She stopped. "The facts don't match. The guard said he killed himself with a laser. He shot at you with a slugthrower. There was someone *waiting* in that corridor for him with a laser. No one knew we were here," Mitchell said in a whisper. "No one except my superior."

"An assassin and a backup killer. Why would he try to have you killed?" Gershom asked.

Mitchell spread his hands. "I don't know if I'm a specific target, but Lani would certainly be. She's heir to billions of credits."

"*What*?"

Mitchell nodded. "She's the sole beneficiary of a kind of cumulative bequest set up by the leaders of Karela. She's worth a fortune, more than some colonies, and it all devolves to the Corporation if she dies. Not to mention the planetary exploitation license, which she also owns."

"What should we do with her? I could take her away with me," Gershom offered. "It would be no problem."

"No," Mitchell insisted. "Too much chance you'd never get off the planet, or someone would plant a bomb in your next cargo if they knew she's on your ship. I want her here on Mars, where I can keep an eye on her, and where no more mysterious accidents can befall her. I have an idea where she will be safe."

The transport shuttle landed within a kilometer of the community. As Shona watched from the observation tower, a hatch opened and a shuttle rolled down the ramp.

"They're not wasting any time," she said to Chirwl. "I wonder what's going on."

She found Tettenden reading in an easy chair in the main hall. "That Corporation transport is here. I messaged them saying I couldn't leave, but they're here."

The old man shook his head. "Duty is duty, my dear."

Novak spotted them as he came out of his module, and made a beeline for them. "Whose ship is that landing out there? They're disturbing one of my sample pools."

"It's from the Corporation," Shona explained. "They want to take me with them, but I can't go. I told them so."

Novak stared. "Why you? Aren't there other doctors on the payroll?"

A tall, muscular man with bristly black hair entered the hall and strode up to them. He was attired in a Corporation uniform covered by a transparent isolation suit.

"Captain Cipriano. Which one of you is Dr. Taylor?" the captain asked without preamble.

"I am. Look, Captain, I'm not going with you," Shona said, putting her hands on her hips. "I've got an emergency situation on my hands here right now. Didn't you get my message? People are dying here."

"Doctor, I have my orders," Cipriano replied, his bristling brows meeting over his nose in a scowl. "This order comes from HQ. If you're still working for the Corporation, I suggest you get it together. We lift as soon as your module is secured."

"Say, who do you think you are?" Novak protested. "She was assigned to this unit. I'll call for clarification."

"And now she's been unassigned," Cipriano said, turning on Novak. "They need her elsewhere. Call all you want, it won't change anything."

"Where am I going?" Shona asked.

Cipriano hesitated. "I can't divulge that. It's classified."

Shona folded her arms. "Then I'm absolutely not coming with you. I refuse to leave a genuine emergency for a mystery tour out to who knows where!"

"You'll stay without equipment. The module belongs to G.L.C. services," Cipriano warned.

"Then take it," Shona shot back "I'll strip what I need and they'll find us somewhere else to live." Novak nodded vigorously in Shona's support. "You're treating these people as if they don't matter. There's been one death already, and there'll be more if I don't stay here."

"I'll just shut it down right now." Cipriano flicked on a hand-communicator. "Durgen, hit the override codes."

The lights went out suddenly in Shona's module, and the door slid shut. Inside, she could hear Saffie's frenzied barking. "Wait what are you doing?"

"Repossessing the module," Cipriano said. "I'll take it on board with you or without you."

Shona looked at him in horrified disbelief, and ran to pound on the door control. "Let my animals out of there!"

Cipriano struck an impassive pose. "Are you coming with me?"

She spun on him. "That's blackmail," Shona hissed. "If you don't put the air on again in there, they'll suffocate. It's over fifty degrees Celsius out there!"

"You're the one holding things up, ma'am. As soon as you tell me yes, I'll have Durgen turn everything on again."

"Now, wait a minute," Novak said. "We need her here."

"I'm only going to remind you people once," Cipriano said warningly. "She goes where the Corp wants her. Unless you wish to break your contract. That'll mean no transport will come here with supplies, no pay, no support system."

Not only was he pressuring her to go, he was also using force on the colonists to make her leave. Shona felt trapped but she stuck out her chin in defiance. "I won't even consider it until you tell me where I'm supposed to be going."

Cipriano appeared to make a decision. "You're bound for Borderline," he said reluctantly. "It's in a classified system. I can't say any more than that. They need you. They've had a series of deaths, too."

"Symptoms?" Shona demanded.

"Bellyache, weakness, fever. That's all they told me."

"Why isn't their own doctor taking care of them?"

"I've told you all I know. Are you coming or not?"

Shona wanted to tell this imperious blackguard off, but she could hear Saffie barking and Chirwl wailing inside the locked module. It wouldn't take long before the heat began to build up. She was torn. There was no doubt that Cipriano would do what he said, taking the module away and opening it when he pleased if she didn't do what he said. Her pets, and the ottle, whom she had promised to care for and keep safe, would be terrified, possibly even die of maltreatment. On the other hand, she was obligated to save the lives of her patients.

"I suppose you enjoy bullying people?" Novak shoved in front of the Corporation captain and stood nose to nose with him, but Tettenden laid a hand on the young geologist's arm and drew him away.

"If you don't have a choice, you don't," the old man said to Shona. "He's got all the aces, my dear."

"But you all might . . ." She couldn't finish the sentence.

The old man smiled, lifting the ends of his moustache. "And then, we might not. Luck of the draw, my dear. You can't be all things to all people, I'm afraid. It's all right. None of us are very bad right now."

He was right. Except for Wheatley's death, there had been no further deterioration in anyone else's condition. It would be fatuous to assume that everyone had suddenly stabilized. Still it looked hopeful. "I can monitor your progress by transceiver," she offered. "Or can I?" She rounded angrily on Cipriano. "Will I have access

240

to the communications board to keep in touch with my patients, or will you pretend they don't exist when we leave here?"

"You will," he said grudgingly.

She took a deep breath and let it out. "All right I'll be ready to go in half an hour. Now, open that door!"

Novak followed a shaking Shona into the module. She fell to her knees among her pets. "Sweeties, I am so sorry!" Harry climbed into her lap and hung on to the cloth of her trousers with all four feet. He was trembling. Saffie leaned her weight against Shona's side, and let out a sigh.

Chirwl was upset. "The module ceased to function working," he said. "It would not let us breathe or flee."

"It won't happen again. I'm so angry, I don't know what to say." Shona consoled her pets, clutching them to her.

"He's got us by the short hairs," Novak agreed. "We can't do without support. We stand a chance of getting another physician if we play along. It's in our contract, you know."

"What occurred?" Chirwl demanded. "The machines stopped humming, and it became dark, and the air grew stuffy. Is it the fault of the machines?"

"No. We've been blackmailed into changing assignments," Shona said bitterly. "Your lives were part of the bargain. This Captain Cipriano isn't afraid to play dirty to get his job done."

"Is it safe to go?" the ottle asked. "Not only do I ask on behalf of the welfare of the patients, but also our own, when we are in the ship of this Captaincipriano."

"The patients," Novak insisted, helping Shona to her feet, "will be fine. Give me your records, and recommendations, and we'll obey your instructions to the last punctuation mark. It's all right," he assured her. "We'll do what we can, follow your lines of research. I'm pretty good at picking up on other people's reasoning." He grinned at her, his boyish face earnest. "That's why I'm a researcher."

They were both being so brave, Shona realized. "All right," she said at last. "I am going, but under protest. It's got to be against the law, pulling a physician away from one emergency case for another." She downloaded a copy of her files from the computer net. "Everything here is duplicated in the settlement's mainframe, but I want to make sure you have it all in one place. Try to treat the problem like an allergy. Pull everyone back to nutri and water, and gradually add on one food—"

"I know, I know," Novak said. "Before you go and put on an isolation suit, there's one more thing." He pulled Shona into his arms and kissed her full on the lips. She stood stunned when he

241

let her go, and he smiled apologetically. "I've always wanted to do that. I hope you don't mind. Goodbye, Shona."

"Goodbye, Bill," she whispered. He gave her a cheery wave over his shoulder. She felt a chill run up the middle of her back and settle inside her heart. This might be the last time she would ever see any of these people alive. They had become dear to her. She wanted to run after Novak, calling out more instructions, but that was insane. Against her will, her better judgment, and her oath, she was going to have to turn away and let them try to handle the situation on their own.

The farewells were hasty and very sad. Cipriano permitted her fifteen minutes to find everyone and tell them she was leaving. Tettenden remained near her module door, and was the last to say goodbye. Alf's large moustache drooped sadly on either side of his mouth. "Don't you worry about us, my dear," he said as the door closed. "Safe landing."

Once her animals were secured, Shona zipped herself into an isolation suit, and flopped heavily into her impact seat, careless of bruises or discomfort, and fastened the straps. "I'm going to miss them," she said. It was an inadequate phrase for the longing she felt to stay on Erebus.

"I, too," Chirwl agreed solemnly. "They would be respected even among ottles, for their brave as well as their think."

CHAPTER 19

SHONA IRRADIATED THE exterior of her suit thoroughly before emerging from the module into the transport ship. The module had been placed in an unused sports court. Her footsteps echoed from wall to wall as she surveyed the empty chamber. Cipriano assured her that the room would be entered by no one else for the duration of the journey. It had been cleaned and disinfected by maintenance machines only hours ago. She was at liberty to use it all if she liked. As soon as the ship went into warp, she let Saffie out to run. Chirwl, Harry, and the two rabbits followed more timidly. The big black dog ran around and around the simulated wooden flooring, sniffing energetically. She seemed to have revived in the cool ship's air. The cat and little ottle began a spirited wrestling match, evidently enjoying the way their cries echoed off the ceiling. A cinnamon and sable blur, they whirled around the room happily, regardless of others' toes and paws.

"Back soon, guys," Shona called. "I'm going to go find out who else is aboard here, and see if I can't get some answers regarding this assignment."

The vessel appeared to be a standard transport. Its living quarters were a series of broad cylinders that rotated to simulate gravity, joined by stationary access chutes at the top and bottom that surrounded the rotation axes.

Her fellow passengers, four men and two women, were all bound for Borderline as well. She found them in the recreation lounge spinward of her quarters. They glanced up as she entered. The isolation suit gave them some pause at first; then one man slapped his knee with a hand.

"You're the new doctor? You've got your work cut out for you. I'm Den Selby." He put out a hand, and she shook it. "This is Carter Sordyzs."

"I'm Shona Taylor," she said with a friendly smile. "I don't suppose you have any details of what I'm going to find there, do you?"

"Shona Taylor? The Angel of Death?" the other asked, his face a disbelieving mask. He had started a hand forward to grasp hers, but he whipped it back as if afraid of her touch. "You're kidding. They're sending *you*? Now we *are* in trouble."

Shona was horrified and affronted. "What are you talking about? I was too late to save the people of Karela. I've had a very good medical record."

"Oh, really? Then what about Celtuce?" Sordyzs asked.

"What about Celtuce?" Shona asked, puzzled. "I treated them for chemical rash."

"Some kind of plague took them. There's only twelve left alive on the whole planet. It was in the news."

Shona stared at him. "I don't believe you," she replied desperately. "I was just there a few months ago. They were all healthy. They'd had the flu, but they were well. There wasn't a single reason why a plague should have arisen. There was hardly a stray bacteria in the domes."

"If that's true, then you must have given them the plague yourself. They're all dead. All but a dozen of them. Check the news archives," the man said, and turned away. Shona looked at the others, who refused to meet her eyes. Only Selby nodded solemnly, affirming what Sordyzs had said.

Without another word, Shona went to find proof. The control center was encased in its own spin-cylinder for stability. Shona made her way up there to the communication center. Through the floor of the transparent access tunnel the dizzying spectacle of the white pillars turned slowly, like so many giant rollers, against the black sky under her feet. It was a disorienting sight, reflecting the turmoil of her thoughts. Celtuce, so many dead? Derneld, Franklin, Dana! Impossible!

In the viewing room, she accessed the Universal Press International feed database, and found that Sordyzs's cruel taunt was true. Dated only weeks after she left, the report said that the plague, thought at first to be radiation sickness, had spread from the mining complex to the residential domes. Sufferers reported symptoms of vomiting, high fever, delirium, dry mouth, and marks on the skin like burns. They sent for help, but it was too late in coming. In no time, the population was reduced to a dozen survivors.

She sat back in the chair, shocked speechless. "I should have stayed," she whispered. If she had been there, she might have been able to save them. What had happened? The report indicated that the earliest infections were in the mining facility. Dr. Franklin had assured her that they had always been careful to limit contact to the outside, but someone must have let in a killer organism. If she had stayed, she might have been able to help track it down. She felt like resigning.

And what good would that do? the mocking voice inside her sneered. She hadn't heard that cold mental tone since Gershom had come in take her off Mars. *You'd be out of a job, and they'd still be dead, dead, dead.*

Shona went back to her module, and sent an angry message to Mitchell.

"Why wasn't I notified about Celtuce?" she demanded. "And why am I being blamed for it? If word had been sent to me of the epidemic while I was en route to Erebus, I would have returned. Moreover, why was I pulled out prematurely from Erebus, where I was handling a genuine emergency?"

Her anger spent, she lay on her bed staring up through the skylight at the gym ceiling, wondering what had gone wrong. She wished Gershom was there to give her confidence. She felt as if all control of her life had slipped gradually out of her grasp, leaving her helpless, but she didn't know to where it had gone.

Shona felt cold all the time after that, and it wasn't simply from the ship's low ambient temperature. It wasn't only the heat she'd grown used to on Erebus; she'd also come to love the eccentrics who lived there, squeezing grant money out of the Corporation and coming to life when the sun went down. She was afraid for them, wondering if the jinx that seemed to be following her would work against them. A horrible thought niggled at her, making her wonder if the disease that struck the scientists on Erebus had been the same as that which swept Celtuce. Could she have brought it with her? She listened to the news report again and again. The symptoms were not the same.

Durgen, who proved to be Cipriano's first officer, signaled to her that she had messages waiting in the communications center.

Gershom's message had been sent by special tachyon burst. "I hope this beats the news reports to you. I've seen Mitchell, and he swears blue that the Corporation understands you're not to blame, though that was the way the news bureau picked it up. He's supposed to have them broadcast a retraction. I think he's sincere, honey.

"Something else came up while I was on Mars," he said, and held up his hand to forestall her outburst almost as if he could see it coming. "Lani's fine. She's safe. I wish I felt I could say more, but I can't be sure someone else won't hear this. We're on our way out to Erebus to see you, and I'll talk with you then."

I won't be there. I wonder why Manny didn't tell him I'm being moved? Shona mused to herself. She recorded a letter to Gershom, letting him know her new destination, and went on to the next message.

Novak's cheerful face appeared in the screen tank, with his workshop in the background. He looked pale but chipper, and Shona felt a surge of relief that he was able to tolerate light "Hello, Taylor. Just wanted to let you know everyone's holding on. We've had a couple more people sign in from the south range with stomach troubles. The Culinary Exiles are increasing in number. Biochemistry's not really my line, so the others are pitching in on your suggestion, to check out the food synthesizer and the waterworks. You covered a lot of ground, lady, but I'm beginning to agree with your contention that the problem lies right here in the complex with us. I'll let you know what we find when we find it. Chan sends her best and since she's in charge of making sure this message gets to a beacon, I figured I'd better say so."

In spite of her worries, Shona grinned.

The transport ship went into warp a few hours later, cutting off communications with the outside. Shona made a few attempts at conversation with her shipmates. After a few pointed snubs, she spent the rest of the day in the empty sports court with the menagerie.

At first, she was able to keep in regular contact with Erebus between jumps. After the first cheerful message, conditions there began to deteriorate. Novak couldn't hide the concerns he felt; his plump cheeks were getting thinner, and Shona was becoming increasingly upset that she had been pulled away. The lag time between sending and receiving a reply grew longer and longer as the journey to Borderline dragged on.

On the twenty-third day out, Novak sent word that Hood had died. Shona had been expecting it, since the botanist's already serious condition made him especially vulnerable to the new illness. She immediately informed Novak of the botanist's long-standing neurological disorder, and told him that it should be noted on the death certificate. It was inhumane to remove a doctor from an emergency situation. Surely someone else could have taken over the post she was going to. She grimaced, thinking of Sordyzs and the others. Someone else might have had a warmer reception than she was enjoying.

"By the way, how is the detective work going on the food supply?" she asked. "It frustrates me having to conduct research by long distance, though I'm sure you're doing everything properly. Chirwl sends his regards to everyone, and so do I."

The lag time had increased to nine days. It would be eighteen before she heard from them again. On the nineteenth day, she waited impatiently in the communications center for the anticipated message from Erebus. On the twentieth day without news she was so agitated that she forced herself to run laps around and around the abandoned gym, until she collapsed from simple exhaustion. On the twenty-first, she knew she wouldn't ever receive a message from them again.

She sent a frantic communiqué to Mitchell, asking if he'd had any word on Erebus, and sent him a copy of Novak's last message.

Mitchell's reply came several days later. The image wavered and broke up somewhat, but she could see clearly that his strong jaw was set. He looked as if he had been under phenomenal strains. "I have had no transmissions from Erebus in some time," Mitchell said carefully. "Until I have more information, I must conclude, as you have, that they are incapable of transmitting further messages. A ship has been dispatched. I'm sorry they moved you. It was beyond my control. I knew you were concerned for their welfare."

Shona spent the rest of the trip to Borderline very subdued, robbed of her normal vivacity.

"I should have stayed on Erebus," she said to Chirwl, not for the first time.

"You had orders. This is an emergency, too."

"Well, they should have gotten someone else." Shona laughed, a bitter sound. "That's what *they* think, too."

After the friendly openness of the community on Erebus, Shona found that Borderline was like going into solitary confinement. Allegations of misconduct, however spurious, had tainted her reception there. It was clear that she was being tolerated only because the Corporation had sent her.

"No situation is so bad that we're willing to take a chance on Typhoid Mary," said the colony leader, at their first meeting in her office. Dr. Monique Bayeaux was taller than Shona and model-slim, with black hair and very pale, creamy skin. Her office, like her, had an air of elegance, even though it was cluttered with disks and information cubes. Shona felt short, dumpy, and stuffy inside her enveloping isolation suit. "I'm sorry. You're not going to be permitted to see patients. I'd like to give you a chance to prove you're as innocent as you say, but we're running scared here. I've notified the Corporation to send us a replacement, and set up a general quarantine notice. Until then, I'd be grateful if you didn't make a fuss."

Furious at being rendered helpless, Shona was determined to make the best of a very bad deal. She set her jaw. "Dr. Bayeaux, I hope I'm too much of a professional to take offense at false accusations. I wish I could assure you that they *are* false, and I promise you, that's the case. If I can't examine people directly, will you be willing to make the exam tapes available to me? I'll offer you my diagnoses, at no extra charge," she finished lightly.

That won a tiny smile from the colony leader. "You're acting with grace, and I appreciate that."

"I'm not here to make things harder, I promise. It would help, for example," Shona began, "if I knew what the colony's purpose was. The transport pilot had only a list of symptoms. You have to take context into account."

"I'm sorry," Bayeaux repeated, with a flick of her eyes toward her tank screen. "According to your dossier, you don't have a sufficient security clearance for me to give you that information. You'll have the run of the 'strangers' dome,' the entertainment center, and the food preparation areas, but that's all. I can't even hint at our activities, and I'd appreciate it if you don't ask again."

"Whatever you say," Shona said amiably. "Is there a spare room somewhere I can use to exercise my pets? Since neither of us knows what's troubling your people, I can't risk exposing them to you. Or you to them."

Bayeaux prodded a console control with a delicate finger, and perused the floor plan that appeared on the screen. "There's an office and storeroom next to your module I can have vacated and cleaned by this afternoon."

"That would be fine," Shona said, rising. "My door will always be open, if anyone wants me." The last was the only hint of wistfulness she would allow to show in this hard place. She went back to her quarters, inwardly seething but refusing to give the colonists the satisfaction of knowing that they had gotten to her.

The colony was under domes in the middle of an airless, swampy landscape. The swamp she knew about because the shuttle had rolled through kilometers of squelching mud from the time it landed until the time it hooked up her module to the side of the colony complex. She knew it was airless, because she had been warned not to open the rear hatch of her quarters. Other than that, she knew nothing about Borderline itself. No pictures hung in the lounge; no books or tapes on the system were in the library.

The loneliness she had suffered on the trip over had been enough for her. She attempted to make friends among the colonists. The distrust expressed by Carter Sordyzs had spread like a virus. No one exactly fled in panic when she appeared; it was more as if she was simply not there. Her solitary meals of nutri grew tedious, then unpleasant, then unbearable. She missed Gershom terribly. It only made matters worse if she thought about the months they'd had together on the *Sibyl*. Memories were no consolation. She pushed erotic fancies to the back of her mind with a firm hand. Poor old Dr. Franklin had been right. A person could have only so much privacy.

"If I could leave, I would," Shona messaged furiously to Gershom. "But there's no transport due for weeks, and you can't go in and out of a secure location like going home in a huff from your Aunt Mabel's. They sign me in and out of different parts of the complex as if I were a prisoner. Chirwl's used to being without his own kind, but even he's getting bored. The news is edited before we get it, and I don't know why. I suspect the mail is screened, too. If you don't get this, that's why. I haven't heard from Susan in weeks."

Occasionally, she sent another message to Erebus, hoping that since she had seen no news about the demise of the colony there still might be a few of them left alive.

Once or twice a day, she viewed patient examinations that were taking place in another dome. The colony leader had been right to ask the Corporation for help. Whatever was troubling them struck as quickly and as devastatingly as anthrax. The physicians, a married couple named Chaudri from Tau Ceti, whose credentials Shona found impressive, had no more warning to guide them than a slight rise in a patient's temperature. Within twenty-four to forty-eight hours, the patient would die of respiratory distress, lungs filled with fluid. The condition resembled pneumonia. The team managed to save two sufferers by introducing surfactants and anti-inflammatories to the diseased lungs, but usually patents suffocated before they were found.

Pulmonary involvement suggested an airborne organism. The Chaudris had isolated the pneumococcus that was present in each of the patients who caught the disease, but were puzzled as to the vector by which it spread. With Bayeaux's permission, Shona set up aerogel traps in the ventilation ducts at face level throughout the public areas and windowless corridors of the complex. Some of them were defaced by an unknown hand during the first dark shift they were in place. Doggedly, Shona cleaned out the holders and put up new gel slides.

Gradually, her patience and good nature won defenders from among the settlers. Not too surprisingly, the first to make friends with her was Den Selby. During a shift when no examinations were going on, she decided to watch the news in the entertainment center instead of the slowly encroaching walls of her module. He and a group of his cronies came in and gestured to her to join them. She welcomed the overtures of friendship as a driftbound spacewalker clutches a lifeline.

"Do you have to wear that atrocious suit all the time?" Den asked.

"I wish I didn't have to," Shona acceded, smoothing the crinkling cloth over her midriff. "But rules are rules. You have an emergency situation here, and I can't afford to catch whatever's going around. I may be carrying something you're prone to. I had to leave my last assignment before solving the problem there. The suit protects both of us, but I do admit it makes socializing difficult. Looks like I'm in personal, mobile quarantine, doesn't it?"

"I can hardly tell what you look like," Den protested.

"Men," complained Tevia Bruns, a tall, big-boned woman with close-cropped blond hair. "You can see her face; isn't that enough? You have lips to kill for, my dear. Delicious. Natural or enhanced?"

"Only my plastic surgeon knows for certain," Shona quipped, pursing her mouth into an outrageous knot. She grinned widely, and Tevia chuckled. The others laughed, an artificial sound at first, but quickly becoming real and relaxed.

"You *are* trying to help, aren't you?" Tevia asked.

"I am, with all my heart," Shona said.

"What can we do to help you?" asked Wilson Nimak, a slim, black-bearded man with the look of a poet. "This epidemic thing is scaring hell out of everyone. You never know who'll be next."

"Nothing," Shona sighed. "I've promised I won't examine patients."

"Well, what would you do that the Chaudris aren't doing?"

"The three of us suspect that the virus is getting around in the air, which is recirculated and filtered to remove all pollutants. That means that there's a carrier, who is constantly spreading the infection without becoming ill herself. Those gel traps are supposed to pick up samples. It would help if we could learn who the carrier is."

"Is? Why can't the carrier be dead?" Nimak asked.

"If she's dead," Shona pointed out, "she's out of the biosystem, and that should be the end of the epidemic. Everyone could help by contributing a breath sample, and we'll find who's carrying the germ. The funny thing is, it's not really an airborne type."

"The damndest things are unlikely," Den said thoughtfully. The others laughed, and he grinned.

"The trouble is getting everyone to cooperate," Tevia pointed out. "If they knew the suggestion came from you, they would probably refuse."

"I have to go," Den said. "I've got a meeting." He glanced up at the big screen Shona had been watching, and his face lit up. "Say, I have a brilliant idea. This receiver taps into the comm system. We could sit here and talk to you in your quarters on your screen, and you wouldn't have to wear the silly suit. How does that sound?"

"Wonderful," Shona said. "The ottle who lives with me has been itching to talk to someone beside me. He'd love it."

"Perfect. Meet you this time tomorrow, on screen." Den waggled a couple of fingers in the air for farewell.

"I will try to persuade people to give breath samples," Tevia promised. "Without telling them where the suggestion came from."

"Thanks, Tevia," Shona said. "It will help, truly, it will."

The idea that the doctors were collecting breath samples to pin down a key to the fatal pneumonia went around the colony over the next few days. Collection of aerogels was beginning in Shona's appropriated lab, when the whole notion was rudely shut down. The rumor spread that Shona was trying to take over the medical investigation. In protest, the Chaudris went to Dr. Bayeaux. The leader demanded to see Shona in the colony office immediately.

"You've overstepped your bounds, Doctor," Bayeaux told her severely.

"I'm only trying to help," Shona protested, starting forward toward the desk. The suit crinkled around her legs, distracting them both and causing them to look down at it. Shona cursed inwardly. It was a nuisance.

"No more active interference from you, Dr. Taylor, if you please. I'm rescinding your advisory status and making you an observer only."

None of Shona's protests did any good. "I think pleading my case only made things worse," she confided to Den and the others. She and Chirwl leaned over her screen. The rec room gang sat at theirs, but the hologrammatic process made it seem that they were in the module with her.

"Hard going," Den said sympathetically. "Still, we were half expecting it weren't we?"

"I wonder who guessed?" Tevia asked with a lift of her head.

"Probably Sordyzs," Shona said sadly. "I've tried a dozen times to talk to him, but he's not seeing me at all. He's seeing the Angel of Death."

That night, five people, all from different parts of the complex, went into cardiac arrest. The Chaudris worked to save the ones they could. In the middle of the night, they summoned Shona to help them, first with patient care, then, after three fruitless hours, with the autopsies. She assisted the male Dr. Chaudri with the operations while his wife did microbiological analysis. The holo screen, echoing their movements at one-eighth scale in the tank, took a running record.

"Lungs, obstructed. Heart"—Dr. Chaudri paused, peering over his mask as Shona extended a gleaming metal dish for the organ—"shows signs of myocardial infarction. Of course. Poor thing beat itself to death."

The process of autopsy, repeated five times, had an air of the macabre.

"Danson: lungs, heart, stomach, all show signs of pneumococcus X," Madam Chaudri said aloud for the recorder.

"Why stomach?" Shona wondered.

"Postnasal drip?" the microbiologist suggested.

After an interminable period, Shona was excused. She staggered back to her quarters and stood under the ultraviolet decontamination light as if it were a shower. She stripped her garment off inside out and stuffed it into the sonic cleanser.

"You have been gone a long time," Chirwl said, leaning out of his pouch.

"I have been gone forever," Shona groaned, pulling off her clothes. She shrugged into her sleep robe and dropped flat on her back onto the bed. "Why do I seem to be falling into colonies where there are so many fatalities?" she shouted. "When I was with the GG colonial service, it was rare for settlers to drop dead. I can't believe that the health screening is that much poorer in the Corp."

"Not from what you have observed to me," Chirwl said. He climbed down the wall and waddled in to join her. "The Chaudris appear to take great care."

"They're good doctors," she said. "I just wish they and Dr. Bayeaux didn't think of me as just another liability. Somewhere else, we might have been colleagues and friends."

"You have friends," Chirwl assured her. "Myself included in that number."

Shona stroked the soft, wiry fur of the ottle's stubby forearm. "I value that. Thank you."

"It is still most interesting being a companion to you," Chirwl said. He leaped headlong off the bed and rolled in a hooplike somersault to the door. "Good sleep."

The comm-unit summoned her early the next shift. Shona, blearily serving the menagerie breakfast, activated the screen.

"Dr. Taylor." It was Bayeaux.

"Morning," Shona said, hastily pushing her hair back behind her ears with her fingers. Bayeaux always made her feel like a fashion refugee.

"Good morning. I wanted to thank you for your help last night during the crisis," Bayeaux said, and paused. "I also wanted to make certain that you don't take the request for aid as a cue to go off and take unilateral actions."

Shona sighed. At least the woman had said thank you first. "I won't. I've already said I won't."

Bayeaux, also aware of the awkwardness of her duty, nodded curtly and signed off.

"An insult first thing in the morning really gets you going," Shona said. "Oh, well. Where's my copy of those autopsy reports?"

Shona spent most of the day reviewing the tape of the postmortems. It was depressing viewing, but she hoped to gain some insight into pneumonia X even if she couldn't share it with anyone else. Something didn't quite add up. She had a germ which shouldn't be able to fly, but obviously, it did.

A quiet, burring sound intruded itself into the quiet of the lab. Shona looked up, her brow wrinkled, trying to place it.

"The machine next to your bed summons you," Chirwl called from the tub in the bathroom. He hung out of it halfway, his arms dripping water to the floor. "Who calls?"

"My communicator?" Shona asked. She hurried in to answer it, wondering who in the colony had the code for her personal transceiver/transponder. It didn't have much of a range, limited to a million klicks, give or take a hundred. Her fingers fumbled excitedly over the buttons as she pushed the receive switch.

"Hello?" she said. The tiny screen cleared, and Gershom's face looked up at her.

"Hello, darling," he said.

Shona's breath went in sharply. "Gershom! Where are you?"

"On the moon above you. I've missed you."

Shona no longer cared that her hair was uncombed or that she was wearing her saggiest tunic. "But how did you find your way here? Everything about this place is classified."

Gershom grinned. "They didn't classify the beacons. I calculated the vector from the tachyon codes on your messages from the ship. That's surprising, considering. If I had a secret installation, I'd

253

route my messages off through the Crab Nebula. Anyone who wants to, can find you here."

Shona's hand flew to her mouth. "I wonder if I'll get in trouble for that. They're against me about everything."

"Too bad for them. I haven't heard from you lately, and I was getting worried."

"You haven't?" Shona said. "I've been sending to you every couple of days, but I haven't heard from *you*—No, wait a minute, I bet they've been stopping my outgoing mail as well as my incoming. These people are paranoid. Oh, Gershom, I've missed you so much."

"When can we get together?"

"I want to, but we can't." Even as Shona said it, the temptation to defy authority nearly overwhelmed her.

Gershom's eyes became pleading. "It's been months since we've been together. I think of you every day and every night. When I'm alone, in my bunk at night, I remember all the times we've been together since we met. I imagine running my hands along your body, feeling your lips against mine, your hands . . ."

"Stop!" Shona cried. She'd been imagining the same things, and having him enumerate them in his sweet voice just made the longing worse. "I want to see you, but I'm confined to this section of the complex. I'm not supposed to leave."

"Sweetie, I miss you so much. Only the atmosphere separates us. We're so close. Are you sure you can't find a way to come up here?"

"Well, there are lift shuttles. I saw them when we landed . . ." Shona began. "No, I shouldn't really. I'm in enough hot water with the leader. The people here hate me. Wait until I tell you . . ."

"*I* love you. Look." Gershom held up sealed flask to the video pickup, just close enough so she could read the label. "See what I brought along? I traded in a shipment of your favorite wine. And I've got all sorts of special things waiting for you. Besides me, that is."

"All right, you've convinced me," Shona said, debating with herself whether it was worth censure to meet illicitly with her own husband in a secret rendezvous. The answer was obviously yes, but her conscience made her work for it. "But I'm not coming up for the wine, you know. I'll be there in a couple of hours."

"I'll be waiting. Love you." Gershom smiled as his image faded from the screen.

"Love *you*."

She was so excited, she could barely contain herself. All of the ill feelings dropped away as if they had never existed. She could

254

hardly wait to see him. And how like him, how very thoughtful of him, to bring her favorite treats, as if she needed inducements. It made her feel precious and sought after, instead of the despised Angel of Death.

"Chirwl, mind the store. I'm going out."

"Where out?" the ottle wanted to know. "You are restricted only to the public areas and this module."

She smiled wickedly, pulling the red gauze dress out of her storage closet. It was the sexiest thing she owned, and fit her like another layer of skin. She stripped off the floppy tunic and dropped it on the floor as she came into the bathroom. "I'm going to see Gershom."

The ottle was interested. "He is here?"

Shona stood under the sonic shower, impatiently waiting for the signal to go off. "Yes. He followed the tach-signal codes here, would you believe?"

"I do believe. Gershom is a clever human."

The red dress swirled around her hips as she settled the bodice in place and did up the fastenings on the side, then slipped the isolation suit on over it. "Don't tell anyone where I'm going."

"Then do not tell me," the ottle said, reasonably, kicking the water with his feet and flipping over onto his belly. "Give Gershom my best wishes and regards."

CHAPTER

20

SHONA KNEW FROM Den's gossip that the lift shuttles were available for use by anyone in the colony who had the know-how to operate one and who had unrestricted access to the exterior of the planet, so she was breaking only half the rules. When she called up the specs, she was pleasantly surprised to find the shuttles were simpler to fly than the *Sibyl's*.

Technically, the shuttle bay was in the "strangers" part of the dome. She skirted the sign-in book when she left her corridor, feeling a small twinge of guilt for defying Bayeaux's instructions, but she didn't want to have to find herself explaining Gershom's presence, or asking permission to meet with him. It was only inviting the answer 'no.' She was taking appropriate precautions to shield the two biospheres from one another; in her opinion, that ought to be enough.

Casually, she slipped into the bay, which was not locked, or even assiduously patrolled. Not wishing to repeat the experience of being stranded, she chose a craft that had all recent stamps on its maintenance records. When the shuttle lifted, the technician in the control booth glanced up from his screens. Counting on his not being able to identify her at that distance, Shona waved to him. He waved back, and went back to his instruments.

Shona's flight path took her into the night sky overhead. The little vehicle drove as easily as Susan's old jalopy, safe as an easy chair. As she gained altitude, she took in a loop around the dayside of Borderline. The frosty mass of clouds parted before her, and the sky turned black as she left Borderline's thin atmosphere. The irregular moon was full. Shona found herself whistling lunar love songs as she straightened out her trajectory for the glimmering orb.

The shuttle bay of the *Sybil*, set above and between the two cargo bays, slid open as she approached. Shona set the little flyer down, and clambered out. She stripped off the enveloping isolation suit, and fluffed out her skirts just as Gershom appeared. He wore a soft tunic in a deep purple, edged with the same kind of gold trim that adorned her dress. He ran to her and swept her off her feet in a circle, swirling the folds of red gauze in the air.

"Oh, love," Shona said, holding his face between her hands and kissing him over and over again. "You cannot believe how good it is to see you. You look wonderful."

"Come and see the others," Gershom offered. "They want to make sure you're alive, and then I want you all to myself."

"Absolutely," Shona agreed, wrapping an arm around his waist as he set her down. "I'm looking forward to all those treats you promised me."

"Oh, yes," Gershom said, amused. "The wine's decanted, and I've got your favorite foods all ready."

"Well, thank you," Shona said, her eyes dancing. "I am so sick of nutri, I could scream, but that's not the sort of treat I was hoping for."

A real wax candle puddled in its holder in the center of the table between glasses tinged with the dregs of the wine. In the flickering light, Shona's skin gleamed like a pearl. Gershom's hands smoothed her over and over again, running his fingers gently over her shoulders, breasts, and ribs, his thumbs stopping to massage away the tension. She sat astride his hips with her hands playing over his chest, letting the wiry hair tickle her palms. She felt herself melting, all the worries of the past months gone.

"If I could purr, I would," she said. "*How* I've missed you."

He stretched up an arm around her shoulders and pulled her down to him. They made love once more, and fell asleep snuggled together, with Gershom's arm curled around her rib cage. She felt safe and content for the first time in ages.

"Thoughtful?" Gershom asked softly. Shona had awakened and was running her fingers along the nap of the thin coverlet underneath them. He leaned over to kiss her, and his soft hair caressed her cheek. She turned her lips to meet his. The initial passion was sated, allowing her brain to switch on again. And her memory. A corner of her wide mouth turned up, and he kissed it.

"Mmmm. I was wondering about something. Something in your last message."

"Which one?" Gershom asked. "I don't know what you got and what you didn't."

Shona wriggled around so she was lying on her back, facing him. "You'd just left Lani off on Mars. You said that something came up, but you couldn't talk about it. What?"

Gershom's face turned grim. "Someone tried to kill us in the landing bay. Not me, but Mitchell and Lani. He dropped a couple of containers on the dock on our heels. If I hadn't looked up just then, I'd be flat as a photocopy. It happened just after Mitchell made a call to his office. A press videographer was supposed to come and take some tape of Lani. He never showed up, but a thug did—one who knew how to operate a crane. When the load missed us, he fired a slugthrower at Mitchell."

"Oh, no!" Shona's eyes were wide with fear.

"I gave him one to remember me by, but he was shot to death a minute later. New concept," Gershom said dryly. "A backup assassin. Someone is planning these things to the letter."

"Where's Lani?" she demanded.

"Mitchell and I took her out to the remote domes and set her up with a couple of the refugees from Celtuce," Gershom said soothingly. "We said it would be a personal favor to you if they'd keep the child hidden, and not tell anyone she wasn't theirs. The fellow we left her with, his name was Len, told me to tell you he's all right, and he knows it wasn't you. Mitchell said the same."

"Oh, thank heavens for that," Shona said fervently. "Oh, Gershom, all those lovely people on Erebus! Why did he pull me out of there?"

"Mitchell didn't send you here," Gershom said.

"Then who?"

The cold look appeared on Gershom's face again. "The same person who arranged for a container to fall on our heads."

"Verdadero? He wanted the people on Erebus to die? Why?"

"I don't know for certain."

Shona bit her thumb. "I've been thinking about it and what you say pulls it all together in my mind. Doesn't it strike you as strange that every assignment I've had has been a colony that had, or was about to be struck by, a fatal plague?"

"You think they might be deliberate?"

"It suggested itself in the back of my mind when I couldn't find a chemical footprint for the problem on Erebus. Everything was too sterile, too *clean*. It never occurred to me precisely that it was deliberate. It never *would*. But it would make sense. And the welts that the people on Celtuce had? They had chemical irritation rashes. The stuff was mostly sulphur and the other elements from the external atmosphere, but there were other trace elements. It looked familiar. I think it was the residue of a toxic chemical used for pest control. Leader Derneld had a canister of it in a warehouse. It's highly volatile, which when applied to the skin affects the nervous system. It evaporates, leaving practically nothing behind."

258

"You don't think that Derneld sprayed that stuff on his own people?"

"No, but someone did." Shona stared at the wall, trying to bring back a stray thought. "Those deaths were not my fault but someone was trying to make it look like they were."

"Someone's making you the scapegoat for a load of engineered plagues!"

Shona nodded.

"Carrying this theory to its logical conclusion," she said, "you know, I wonder if Karela had been the same. Like the closed environments of Erebus and Celtuce, it was virtually sterile to humans. All of the indigenous species, though they resembled life that had originated on Earth, were alien. Karelan biology didn't have much in common with Terran-based life. I remember mentioning it at the time. It was so unlikely that anything on that very alien world would affect human life forms, but I accepted it. Where else could the disease have come from so suddenly? In fact, I should call it incredible that human beings so far from humanity's cradle had encountered a bacterium so similar to the deadliest disease in history. It was not like American humans getting smallpox from the European humans. It would be as if the Europeans had managed to infect the trees. They could poison one another, but their genetic material would have been unable to interact."

"It couldn't be mere coincidence," Gershom agreed. "It's monstrous. But what you're saying is that someone actually spread the diseases, or the poisons, in each of the colonies. Who? It couldn't have been Verdadero. He never left Mars."

"There must have been one assassin on every planet I visited. I'll never know who it was on Karela, but I bet I could put a name to the one at Celtuce at least: Larrity. He was deliberately antisocial. I told you about him." Gershom nodded. "I don't think there's any doubt who was responsible for Erebus. George Hood. I suspected a sort of genetic sabotage when everyone started to show signs of environmental illness. He had access to the food supply. I was just too late in checking that lead when the Corporation ship came for me. I thought back again and again to the day the trouble all started. We were all blaming the sickness on the crystal matrix and the mud, and forgot completely about the mango juice! Novak said that Hood had given him some fruit for squeezing. It had undoubtedly been laced with a chemical that left the blood once it had done its damage to the nervous and immune systems. My question is why? Why murder the populations of harmless colonies? You've never met people as harmless as my scientists, Gershom." Shona appealed to him with saddened eyes, and he hugged her tightly. "Poor old Alf. Poor Bill."

"Why, I think, Mitchell will have to tell us. He's on our side, Shona. The attack by Verdadero's thug shocked him blue. Lani's in no danger, but Mitchell went back to his job. He's pretending that she's dead, in a tragic dockside accident, but if Verdadero suspects he hid her, Mitchell's a dead man."

"He's a good man. I'm so glad none of you were hurt. I've got to think about all you've told me, and what it could mean. I still wish we knew why." Shona stood up and looked at the chronometer. "Good grief, I've got to get back! They're going to be spitting comets when they discover the shuttle missing." She smiled fondly as she slipped her dress on and pulled up the folds of the bodice. "The animals are going to be jealous when they smell your scent on me. They'll wonder why you didn't come to see them yourself."

"Well, they'll see me soon enough," Gershom declared. "I'm taking you away from here. Go back and get packed, and I'll send Ivo down with the shuttle."

"Gershom, I can't just leave. I'm assigned here. Why?"

"Think it *all* the way through. He got you assigned here. What if this is just like all of the others, and he's about to push the button on them? It must mean Verdadero figured you've caught on to the system by now."

"He meant me to die here," Shona said, horrified. "All of those people are going to die, too."

From the bed in Shona's room where he was watching the news, Chirwl heard Saffie barking. Coming out to discover what the fuss was about, he saw the dark-haired human fend off the dog with one arm, then stick a can in her face. Colored smoke poured out of it. Saffie lost her grip on the man's arm, and slid whimpering to the floor. Her head fell over and she lay still.

"How did you come in?" Chirwl asked. He recognized the man.

"Just came to visit," the human said, showing his large flat teeth.

"We are quarantined," Chirwl reminded him. The human, instead of leaving, ran at him with the little can. Recognizing his danger, Chirwl dashed into the bedroom. The human chased him, dodging around Shona's furniture after the ottle. Chirwl jumped to Shona's chair seat and down again, hoping to evade his pursuer. The man stamped down on the ottle's foreleg making him squeak with pain. Fearful of further injury, Chirwl scooted

260

under the bed. The human flung himself to the floor, and sprayed the smoke after him. By then, Chirwl was already over the top of the bed and into the small bathroom. He ran silently, on his pads, ignoring his throbbing foot, and hid inside the sonic shower. The human rose slowly.

As Chirwl watched, the dark-haired male came into the bathroom. Chirwl cowered, thinking that the human knew of his hiding place, but the man went instead to the water-filtration unit, and opened it up. The ottle squinted, making a mental note of everything the human did. He had committed evil, Chirwl was certain of it, but he could not undo it himself. It was machinery. He would have to wait for Shona to help him.

After the man left, the dog began to come to. Saffie staggered unsteadily to her feet and made for her water container. She panted, as if the colored smoke had made her very thirsty. Chirwl was alarmed. The dog's dish worked by pushing a lever that made fresh water come out of the tank, the tank which the human had adulterated.

"No, friend Saffie," the ottle pleaded, getting in the dog's way. "Do not drink. You may become ill." Saffie ignored him, trying to push past him to her dish. He grabbed her collar and pulled back. The dog, much stronger than the ottle, tossed her head and threw him aside.

He could not keep her away from the poison for long. If only Shona would return and make the machine cease to give water. He could not. Saffie made for the dish, sticking her nose forward to hit the lever. Using all his strength, the ottle pulled her head aside. Saffie growled at him! His friend did not understand he was saving her life.

He must be the one to turn off the water. Chirwl did know where the shutoff lay, but had never dared to touch it, to risk becoming involved with dangerous machines. It was on top, above the drinking-dish backsplash. Keeping his flat body between Saffie and the spigot, Chirwl boosted himself up and touched the shutoff valve. It did not protest. With an apology, he wrenched it to one side. The little green eye beside it turned to red. From behind him, Saffie nudged him aside and put her nose to the lever. Nothing came out. Chirwl felt hugely relieved, and most heroic at his own bravery. Now he had to wait for Shona.

Shona fidgeted on the drop into Borderline's atmosphere. Gershom's conclusion frightened her, because it was one with which she had been toying herself. How unconscious she had been of the danger around her, never realizing that she had been maneuvered into a death trap. If Gershom was right, and she was certain he was, who knew when the killer would strike? Her breath sounded loud in her own ears inside the confining isolation helmet.

Entering atmosphere, the shuttle set off the approach alarms. The computer automatically responded with its identification code, and the alarms shut down. With trepidation, she set the shuttle down among its fellows.

Incredibly, no one was paying much attention to the return of an illegally borrowed shuttle. She sneaked past the control room, where a handful of technicians and guards were arguing about something. Shona listened closely as she passed the inset speakers. It sounded as if the plague had struck again. There was no time left. The killer was on the loose now! She had to find Bayeaux.

She located the colony leader stalking back along the corridor leading to the module. Bayeaux stopped when she saw Shona and pointed an accusing finger at her.

"You! Where have you been?"

"I can explain," Shona began.

"No explanation will be good enough!" Bayeaux shouted. "Twelve more people are dead. The Chaudris could have used your help, but you decided to take illicit leave from your quarters and your post for the last sixteen hours!"

"Please!" Shona interrupted her. "I've just had news." Quickly, she explained the theories she and Gershom had been discussing, and the conclusions they'd reached regarding the pneumonia epidemic. "The killer has just been warming up. Any time now, he could unleash a full-scale plague and kill the entire colony. You're all in terrible danger," she insisted.

"*We* are," Bayeaux snapped obviously not having heard another thing Shona had said. "If only from medtechs who don't remember that they have jobs and they've been restricted to unclassified areas! You're confined to your quarters as of now until the Corp sends someone to replace you. Is that clear?"

Shona protested to no avail. Bayeaux summoned security guards, who escorted her back to the module, and waited until she was inside before they left.

"You've got to listen to me," Shona insisted, as the door shut between them and her.

The dog and cat ran to her as soon as she was past the UV lights. Sadie barked, dropped her chin to the ground, and bounced up again.

"What's with you?" Shona asked. The black dog repeated the action over and over again. "You want to play? No, you want me to follow you." Harry yowled, and she picked him up. "All right!"

Saffie led them to the bathroom, where Chirwl stood hunched on all fours before the door. As the dog appeared, Chirwl's back fur went up in an attempt to make him seem larger. It only served to add to the agitated expression he wore. Saffie barked at him.

"No one must go in," he said reprovingly. "Please! Shona, you are returned, I am glad. This has been most distressful."

"What's wrong?"

"They are thirsty. I will not let my friends have any water, and they are upset with me," the ottle explained. "They want to drink from the tub, but they must not! A man came in and put something into the tanks."

"Show me what he did," Shona demanded. She pulled the barking dog away from the door, and locked her and Harry in the bedroom.

Chirwl waddled into the bath, and pointed his whiskered nose toward the storage tank. "There. He put something in."

"Show me how."

"I should not," the ottle said, emphatically. "I do not use machines. I only touched the other to save Saffie."

"Now you have experience," Shona said desperately. "Come on, Chirwl. It's important."

Behaving as if it believed it would bite him, the ottle gingerly patted the water purification mechanism, and talked soothingly to it in a low voice. Shona cleared her throat. Deftly, he unfastened the bolts holding the filter assembly in place and removed it. Four small, round vacuum filters fit inside the pipes that processed all the water in the module. They glistened in their frame. Chirwl started to reach for one with his claws. "It feels most peculiarly strange, as if I am a part in the machine instead of an independent being, repeating the motions exactly of the being that came before me."

"Wait," Shona said. She ran for a sterile drape, and knelt with it before the ottle. "Lay it on this, and don't touch the wet parts." He complied, his whiskers twitching nervously. "Now, which one did he change?"

"I do not know. He his back was to me."

"Did you speak to him?"

"Yes." Chirwl was offended. "He kicked me!" Though it was not broken, the injured paw still hurt. He sat beside Shona and nursed it.

"Chirwl, you were very brave, and I'm grateful," Shona pulled the filters one by one and put them under the microscope. The images of the first two were nothing out of the ordinary. The third was filled with the images of small, round organisms with defined nuclei. "Gotcha!"

She ran a sample of tap water into a slide, pushed it into the field, and adjusted the eyepieces. "Chirwl, you're a hero. If you had let anyone drink this stuff, they'd have died."

"A hero? I did well?"

"Wonderfully," Shona assured him. "You got over your fear of machines at exactly the right time. Now I've got to go see Dr. Bayeaux. There's a maniac running loose."

She stopped to take a water sample from the sinks in the food preparation area. Ignoring the shouts of the security guards, she ran down the corridor toward the colony leader's office. Panting, she dodged past Bayeaux's secretary, and into the rear chamber.

"You're confined to quarters," Bayeaux stated, reaching for the intercom.

"You wanted proof of a killing plague," Shona said, putting the slides on the desk. "I have proof." She showed the colony leader the autopsy report with a notation of the bacteria found in the digestive system. "I checked all of the reports. Every one of those corpses had P.X. in his digestive tract."

"How did it get there?"

"They've been *drinking* it. Someone's been poisoning people one by one. He's decided to step up the pace, and go in for mass murder. Even if you could explain it away, you couldn't make me understand why it was present in such concentrations in their stomachs. Nothing here is safe to drink, and probably not to eat. You've all been marked for death."

"How diabolical it all sounds," Bayeaux said, sounding a little bored.

Shona put both hands down on the desk. "Pneumococcus X was introduced into my water-recycling system last shift while I was out. I've also brought you a sample of your own water."

"Well?"

"Well, look at them," Shona barked. "At least give me the courtesy of a hearing. Someone is trying to kill me, but it would do no good unless he killed you all first, so it could be blamed on the Angel of Death. I'm sure your water is tainted. I'll stake my reputation on it."

"Your reputation," Bayeaux reminded her, "is worth nothing here."

Shona groaned and shook her head. "Please, I am concerned only for the welfare of the people here. Look at the slides. Please, just look at them."

Shrugging, Bayeaux carried the slides into the lab next door, and put the first one under the lens. "That is P.X. What about it?"

"That one came from the filters in my water system. The next one"—Shona handed it to her—"came from the water itself. The third one came from the kitchen on my corridor. The public kitchen. On your system."

Bayeaux looked up at her, wide-eyed. "It must have been contaminated by your supply."

Shona shook her head. "Mine's a closed system. I've been drinking the same water for over a year now."

Bayeaux gestured toward the microscope plate. "If anyone drinks this, he will die."

Shona nodded. "That's what I've been trying to tell you."

"But we must all drink sometime. We can't go without water indefinitely."

"We have to leave this place," Shona said. "It's dangerous. There must be liters of the live bacteria somewhere. If you avoided it today, one day you'd come into contact with it. It's inevitable."

Bayeaux was still stunned. "Who could have done this? Can you put a name to this killer?"

"I can't, but Chirwl can."

"Who is Chirwl?"

"The ottle."

"The alien? He can barely distinguish one of us from another."

"That's not true," Shona said. "He's a marvelous observer."

Bayeaux switched on the public address system, and made an announcement.

"Attention, please. This is Dr. Bayeaux. Do not eat or drink anything. We have uncovered the possibility of mass contamination in the food systems. Repeat, do not eat or drink anything. No exceptions. Please stand by for further announcements."

They were leaving the lab when the security guards caught up with them and took Shona's arms. "Come on, citizen. You shouldn't have slipped your leash."

"Let her go," Bayeaux said, gesturing them away. "Come with us. We might need you."

Shona unzipped her isolation suit and threw back the helmet while they were on the way back to the module. "Whew!"

"What are you doing?" Bayeaux asked, watching with horror.

"If I'm right," Shona said, "neither of us has anything that can infect the other. If I'm wrong, we're hours from being dead anyway. I'm willing to take that chance. We're dealing with a disease that someone wants us to think is airborne. It isn't. It can't be. Chirwl will tell you what he saw." She opened the module door, and they all stepped in through the UV lights.

"Chirwl, this is Dr. Bayeaux," Shona said, feeling a trifle foolish making formal introductions at a time of crisis.

"Most pleased," the ottle said, bowing to the leader.

"The pleasure is all mine," Bayeaux said graciously. "Please, let's not waste time on chatter. Tell me, who was the human that tainted the water supply?"

Chirwl glanced over at Shona. "It was the one who does not like you."

"Sordyzs," Shona exclaimed promptly. "He's still thinking I'm the Angel of Death."

"No. The man with the brush face," the ottle said. "The one who was on the screen. He says cheerful things, but he does not mean them."

Shona's mouth dropped open. "Nimak?"

Bayeaux turned to her guards. "Find Nimak."

"Every moment we delay here, we're in danger," Shona reminded her.

"Dr. Taylor, we have nowhere to go," Bayeaux said pathetically. "If nothing is safe to eat and drink, we will starve before we can get help. The next transport isn't due for a month."

"Well," Shona began. "My husband's trading ship is out there on your moon."

"If I dump everything from the cargo bays," Gershom said, when they called the ship, "I can load four hundred people. It won't be comfortable, but it's clean, and the air system's good for that many for a limited time. We'll be on very short rations."

Shona glanced at Bayeaux. "I don't know how many people there are on Borderline."

"Three hundred and forty," the colony leader said, looking relieved.

The security guards returned. "Nimak's not in the compound, ma'am."

"He's outside, then," Bayeaux said. "Good, let him stay." She turned to the guards. "Begin to gather everyone from the complex. Everyone. We are evacuating as of now. Remind them to eat or drink nothing and take no food along. Everyone is limited to small personal items. We'll come back later if we can."

By the time the approach alarms went off, signaling the arrival of the *Sibyl*, most of the colonists were gathered in the landing bay, protesting the situation. Most grew quiet when Bayeaux explained the need for emergency evacuation, but a few refused to understand. More of them were cross about the ban on removing household goods. Bayeaux allowed them to bring one small bag apiece of personal possessions. Shona sacrificed all of her personal goods in favor of the drug synthesizer, which fit in a case she could sling over her shoulder. She went past her clothes closet with a twinge of regret, but decided on a utilitarian coverall that she could wear for several days and wash over overnight. As fond as she was of pretty things, she was a doctor first. It was more important to get the people and her animals to safety.

"It's her fault, isn't it?" Sordyzs asked, pointing at Shona, who had her hands too full with cages of mice and rabbits and Chirwl's pouch to confront the angry man. "Something she did caused our biosystem to go toxic."

"She's trying to kill us!" cried another angry voice. There was a murmur of agreement throughout the crowd. Shona's few defenders were nearly set upon for asserting her innocence.

"Dr. Taylor is providing us with the means to save our lives," Bayeaux explained calmly, raising her voice over the hubbub. Her luggage consisted of a file box of disks and a cushion, and she held Saffie's leash. Chirwl hunched beside her, hanging onto Harry, who was stuffed protesting into his harness. "I've seen sufficient proof, and I am satisfied. This colony is no longer safe."

"I'm not going with her," Sordyzs said.

"You won't make it here," Shona informed him emphatically. "This bacteria is resistant to every antibiotic and antibacterial I've tried."

"I can vouch for that," the female Dr. Chaudri put in, her black eyes flashing. "It is not a natural organism."

"I'm staying! Who's with me?" Sordyzs backed away from the crowd. A few people joined him, looking askance at both Shona and their leader.

Gershom's ship landed, her engines backfiring with a roar like cannon. A toddler began to cry, and kept it up while the passengers were filing onto the *Sibyl*. Pushing her burdens into Den Selby's arms, Shona went over to help the overburdened mother comfort her child.

"He's hungry," the woman said, her eyes haunted. "I was just about to program a meal for him when the announcement came. Is it true?"

"It's true," Shona said. "The water system was infected. Dr. Bayeaux checked the food-synthesizers herself. They use the same water we drink. If you'd eaten that meal, it would have been your last."

"Thank you," the woman whispered.

"It's all right. Come on, sweetie," Shona cooed to the child, who looked up at the new voice. "We're just going for a little ride. We'll find you something to eat in a few minutes, all right? I hope you like nutri."

"All aboard, folks," Gershom called. "Conditions are going to be a little cramped, but we'll manage."

"They'll be just fine," Bayeaux assured him, "when you consider what our alternative would be."

"Come on." Shona reached out a hand for the holdouts. "Last chance?"

Reluctantly, sheepishly, the protesters joined the queue into the ship. Sordyzs passed her with an expression that was a cross between distrust and fear. Shona allowed herself a half smile when he was safely in. *I'll save your tails whether you want me to or not*, she thought to herself.

There was room for three hundred-odd people to settle down in the echoing cargo bays, using their meager luggage as padding. Bayeaux, the Chaudris, and some of the more elderly passengers were assigned the spare berths in the forward section. Shona divided up the animals between the crews' bunks, and brought Chirwl forward with her into the pilot's compartment.

"Having to run with the life-support system on full-recycle all the time makes us a little heavy," Gershom observed, checking the gauges. "It'll be rough taking off since we can't do it vertically."

The *Sibyl* taxied away from the dock. She thundered down the short runway, and over the edge of the paved stretch into the broken rocks. Eblich eased over the thrusters, slamming in the main force just before the hurtling ship squelched into the mud beyond the barriers. Shona could hear the engines strain, but the ship dipped only once, and took off at an oblique angle toward the sky.

"There's a government installation in the nearest system, you know," Gershom said, glancing over at the course Eblich was plotting. "I think we can do it in four weeks. Maybe a little less."

"We'll have to," Kai said. "The nutri supply won't hold out quite that long, and I can't say more for the waste disposers."

The portmaster of the new government trading center sat with the independent videographer in his office, going over details of the personal interview he would give her to flesh out the disk and make the documentary she was doing much more interesting. Tomaso Orzi, a plump man with strands of dark hair plastered to

268

his egg-shaped skull, never liked to let an opportunity for publicity slip away. The young woman seemed fascinated by all that he had to say about running a space station, or anything else he said. She was all leg, and he liked women's legs. He kept his gaze on her very attractive knees while he spoke. "You might also stress the personal angle, Ms. MacRoy. For example, where the various people came from who will be running this installation. I myself—"

"Excuse me," Susan interrupted, pointing at the board at his elbow, and shifting her recorder to a wider angle. He glanced up, and she fluttered her lashes at him. She had very attractive blue eyes. "You've got customers. I'll just sit here and run tape. It might be interesting. For that personal angle. How things work."

Frowning, Orzi leaned over the board and read the data on the ship that was coming in. "Attention, *Sibyl*, this is Station FEX-245. I don't have a flight plan for you."

Susan's ears perked up, and her blue eyes went wide when she heard the reply over the speakers. That was Gershom Taylor's ship, and Gershom's voice. "Station FEX-245, we have an emergency situation here. We are bound from Borderline system, where we were forced to evacuate the population of the colony. We're carrying over three hundred people who have been eating unflavored nutri up until three days ago when we ran out of food completely. The waste system is on the fritz. The air recycler has almost had it. Permission to dock, please?"

Orzi tapped in the reference, and his eyes widened at what he read on his data screen. "Permission denied, *Sibyl*. That system's under quarantine."

"The quarantine was a fake," a woman's voice broke in. "We're not carrying a plague. We're running away from a poisoner. Our life-support systems will not hold out much longer, and these people are getting bedsores from sleeping on metal plates. Our situation is becoming desperate. We request humanitarian aid, under the Alpha Centauri Convention if we have to."

"Shona," Susan demanded, leaning over the pickup, ignoring Orzi's grunt of astonishment. "Is that you?"

There was a pause. "Susan?" Shona asked disbelievingly. "What are you doing there?"

"What am I doing here? Don't you know where you are?" Susan laughed. "You're nearly home! This space station is on the edge of the system—Dremel! Don't you remember, I messaged you about it when you said they were moving you to Borderline."

"I never got your letter," the voice said plaintively. "How's your documentary?"

"If you come down here, you can see it," Susan said promptly.

"If they let us!" Shona replied. "They haven't given us permission yet."

"I hate to interrupt this happy reunion," Orzi said, "but the fact that you are acquainted does not change the fact that we cannot let you land here."

"Portmaster, how can I prove to you that we're harmless?" Shona asked. "I'd like to transmit to you all of my data on the so-called plague, including a diagram of the bacteria. I've done an analysis of what I believe to be genetic tinkering on it." His screen filled with technical information and scrolling pages of printed data.

"And to whom am I speaking?" Orzi asked, recording it all.

"Shona Taylor." She read him her government identification number, and he brought up her employment record, including the character analysis she had undergone at hiring.

"I seem to remember your name, Dr. Taylor," Orzi said, his face clouding. "In connection with a series of plagues."

"All lies, Portmaster," Shona said. "It was a smear campaign, designed to cover up someone else's machinations."

"I'll vouch for her," Susan put in. "We've known each other all our lives. She takes her job seriously. And you know me, Portmaster," she added coaxingly. "You also don't want to be the man who refused succor to an entire colony in need. Though it would make for an interesting story, probably get carried galaxy-wide. I can see the story lead now: 'Four hundred die in orbit vacuum due to bureaucratic cowardice!'" She smiled at Orzi, who twitched his fingers nervously, trying to make a decision. He was a cautious man, uncomfortable with taking chances, but he didn't care to be labeled a bureaucrat or a coward.

"Well," he said, after some thought. "Your character analysis isn't the profile of a serial killer, I'll grant that. I'll allow you to land, but you'll all stay in secure quarantine until I can check this out."

"That's fine!" the woman's voice agreed jubilantly. "Just have some food waiting!"

The human cargo, frightened, uncomfortable, and unhappy, were allowed to debark into an isolation center, where isolation-suited medics were giving examinations and dispensing hot food. A stiff-legged dog and a cat were running around between the passengers, sniffing and investigating, followed by a hunched shape with sable-brown fur. Clad in protective suits, Orzi, followed by

Susan, made their way into the center. Two of the figures detached themselves from the crowd and headed toward them.

"Susan!" The small woman, clad in a coverall that was baggy at every seam ran the rest of the way to embrace Orzi's tall companion. They hugged one another so hard the cracking of bones was audible. "Hi, twin."

"Hi, twin, how ya doing?" Susan replied. "You're going to have to tell me all about it. Wait till I get my recorder going."

"Me first, if you don't mind, Ms. MacRoy," Orzi said with a bow.

The man caught up with them, and put an arm around Orzi's shoulders. "I would appreciate if you would treat everything we're about to tell you as confidential," he said in a low voice. "It could be dangerous for you otherwise."

Tomaso Orzi listened with growing amazement and horror to the Taylors' story. He shook his head at the end of it. "I have to tell you, Captain, I am not comfortable being in the middle of this."

"The important thing," Shona said, sitting contentedly wedged between Susan and Gershom on a couch in the medical wing, "is that this has be stopped. The person pulling these strings can't be allowed to snuff out lives if they become inconvenient to him, for whatever reason."

"It's like a tri-dee thriller," Susan put in.

"Too rich for my blood," Orzi said, shaking his head again. "I'll keep the data confidential, but I don't have the authority to take action, and frankly, I'm glad. I am going to pass you up the line to my superiors on Mars. Let them handle the situation for you. The refugees may stay until what we know what to do with them. They must have relatives or homes somewhere."

"Thank you," Shona said.

"Don't let anyone know they're still alive," Gershom suggested.

"Well keep their presence as quiet as we can. I suspect that you will be ordered back to Mars as soon as we can restock the *Sybil*."

"Then we're taking Dr. Bayeaux along with us to corroborate our testimony. I want this cleared up," Shona added with more vehemence than she intended. It was hard for her to contain her anger now that her charges were safe.

"I'm going, too," Susan said. "Someone has to get this on tape."

CHAPTER

—21—

ON MARS, THE *Sibyl* was met by the portmaster and an official of the Galactic Bureau of Investigation. As soon as Shona, Gershom, and Susan were clear of decontamination, the GBI agent hustled them to a secure meeting point. Waiting for them there were Manfred Mitchell, with Lal and Harry Elliott, who were upset to learn what terrible danger their niece had been in. Also present was the girl Lani, escorted by Len. It was a happy, but brief reunion.

"Your story is very interesting, Dr. Taylor," Agent Jaco said. "I've had plenty of time to analyze the data while you were in transit to Mars. But all we have so far as to the motive is conjecture. This man wanted to sweep these colony planets clear of personnel, why?"

Mitchell cleared his throat. "I've been doing a little quiet investigation of my own," he said, smiling at Shona. "I have to thank your husband once again for saving my life so that I might be able to help put a stop to this criminal intrigue. Tomorrow is the day that the senior officials of the Corporation meet with the banks who hold notes written twenty years ago to finance colonial programs. Hundreds of banks are involved. I doubt each one is aware of the total due within a few months. The total amount, with interest, is staggering. It is far more than can be paid back from G.L.C.'s normal profit flow. If the facts which I have unearthed are accurate, you should get an earful that is positively admissible in court."

"For that, sir," the GBI agent said, turning to Harry Elliott, "we need your help."

"Me?" Uncle Harry said. "Anything. What?"

The next day, Harry Elliott, loan officer for Galaxy One Bank, became Harry Elliott, government spy. He stood nervously in Mitchell's office while he was wired for sound and video with a button camera attached to the fabric of his tunic just under his plump chin.

Shona and the others were sneaked into the office complex one by one, and given chairs. They clustered around the screen on Mitchell's desk, waiting. The GBI man gave Harry the thumbs-up as he left the office trying not to play with the device on his tunic throat. "With any luck," the agent said, "this'll be the end of it. We'll have evidence, testimony of witnesses, and a confession of motive. And here's our last witness."

The GBI man stood to one side as a skinny old man with a rolling gait strolled into the room. With disbelief and delight, Shona flew up out of her chair and gave him a rib-cracking hug.

"Alf! You're alive!" She burst into tears as he patted her hair in an absent-minded, fatherly way. "I thought I'd never see you again."

Gershom smiled, and offered the elderly scientist a hand. "So this is your beloved scientist. Pleased to meet you."

"Little scout ship picked me up," Tettenden said, sitting down between Shona and Len. "Said she was a friend of yours, my dear. Bumpy ride, but I met a big transport ship coming this way. Much more comfortable. Shh, my dear. I want to see the show. Video's not bad, is it? We'll talk afterwards."

Mitchell straightened up as he entered the conference room, and nodded to his employer. Verdadero threw him a casual wave from behind his vast, polished desk. Mitchell shook hands gravely with the representatives of the bank, greeting each one by name. Harry Elliott's palm was sweating. The plump little man looked nervous. Mitchell considered whether it was out of character for Elliott to look so agitated, and decided it was appropriate. He was only a minor loan officer, here to act as a clerk for his superiors.

"Friends," Verdadero said genially, clapping his hands together, "let's talk."

"Willingly," said one of the bank officers, a prim woman with short, frosty-white hair framing a dark skinned face with smooth, chiseled features. "I represent a consortium of fifty-seven of the banks holding notes against G.L.C. assets. The time has come due for a payment against your debt. How are you planning to handle it? We understand that the Corp is rather cash-poor this quarter."

"But we are rich in other assets," Verdadero assured her. "I am prepared to offer you certain of them in partial payment."

"And what are they?"

"Property rights to some very interesting planets." Verdadero tapped a control, and a holotank screen came to life, displaying a planetary landscape superimposed with a bar chart. "A mining

273

planet, proven over the last forty-five years to have superior veins of radioactives. Currently uninhabited. Look at these figures. We set them a high quota, and they surpassed it every single quarter. Twenty billion credits."

The woman examined the data. "Good. Eighteen point five."

Verdadero was smooth. "Madam, I won't quibble. Nineteen."

"Done. Next?"

The scene in the tank changed. "We were using Erebus as a research outpost, but it is capable of more than that. We have found on it a natural source of superconductive crystals. You might also consider it a health spa. The extant structures suggest one. Natural oxygen/nitrogen atmosphere and H_20 seas without a single allergen.

The bankers conferred, and the second one answered. "Very well. Next?"

The CEO brought up another graphic, which showed a small village in the midst of a cluster of thick jungle. "An agricultural world, also uninhabited. All the equipment is there. We were raising a cash crop, trelasi root, but as you know, we've developed a substitute, so it was no longer financially viable to continue. The question never was put to the population, as they all died of a plague. But the soil is first-class, and the climate would allow you to raise three or four crops a year. We would deed the entire planet to you. Enormous profits if you sell it off piecemeal. With no original population left, you'd have a free hand."

"Ah." The associates conferred. "Fifteen billion."

Verdadero nodded, allowing his seamed face a slight smile. "Done, and done. Lastly, and this one has only just become available, a manufacturing complex. We were using it for specialized manufacturing for the Galactic Defense Department. Can't tell you what it was for; the data is still classified."

"Also depopulated?" the woman asked. Harry Elliott pulled at his collar. Mitchell shot him a glance, and Elliott's hand fell.

"Alas, yes." Verdadero tented his hands and rested his elbows on his desktop. "You've heard of the Angel of Death, the doctor in the news who was responsible for destroying the population of planets? We don't know if she was insane, but she was most certainly a murderess. The four planets whose dossiers you have before you were all victims of hers. Safe now, by the way. She miscalculated on Borderline. Her machinations killed her as well as the population."

"That is actually incorrect," Mitchell spoke up. The others turned to glance at him, and Verdadero stared incredulously at his subordinate. "Dr. Taylor is no more a murderess than I am.

Nor is she dead. Though it is obvious who the murderer is!"

Verdadero was dumbfounded. His face reddened for a few seonds until he regained control. His eyes were hard as he stared at his subordinate. "What? Mitchell, you're out of line."

"No, sir, you are, and have been for years. I wish to tell our creditors now that this man's actions are not representative of G.L.C. Have you heard enough?" he finished, turning his head toward Harry Elliott. Everyone stared at the little man as if they were expecting him to do something, and he squirmed uncomfortably.

"Yes, sir, we have." Through the door came the GBI men, followed by Martian police. "And a very interesting little speech it was, too."

"But it's all true," Verdadero protested. "My friends, this man is insane. All of what I just told you is the truth."

"No, it isn't," Shona said from the door. "Not a word. I'm Dr. Taylor." She came in, followed by Len, Tettenden, Gershom, Bayeaux, and lastly Lani. "Let me introduce you to some of your intended victims." Verdadero goggled at them as she introduced each of the colonists the CEO had minutes earlier casually pronounced as being dead. Shona put her arm around Lani. "You're a monster, trying to kill an innocent child for the billions of credits she'd inherit as sole survivor of Karela." She turned to the bank officials. "If you're interested in the planet, you'll have to talk to Lani here. She owns the colonization license. She might even consider loaning some of the money back to G.L.C. to help preserve the colony program, at a good rate of return."

"Who handles her financial arrangements?" the woman from the consortium asked.

Uncle Harry cleared his throat, and exchanged glances with Shona and Lani, who nodded vigorously at him. "Well, I suppose I do, if Gershom can help me with some of the more exotic details."

Mitchell was obviously angry, but pleased as they hauled his former boss away in restraints. Susan and a full news crew were in the corridor outside the room. The bankers departed hastily, leaving Gershom, Shona, Mitchell, their GBI liaison, Chirwl, and the former colonists in the board room. The G.L.C. executive was explaining what he had been doing since the attempt on Lani's life. Muttering happily to herself about exclusives, Susan had her video recording every word. "The Corporation couldn't be seen to be murdering unwanted personnel, so an amoral murderess was a clever invention. Verdadero knew where Shona was being sent next, even steered my hiring and assignment of her. She was placed where a colony was to be 'deactivated,' thereby killing two birds with one stone: the colony dies after she leaves, ridding the company of that millstone, and the blame is attached to her for the deaths. When word got out, she wouldn't be considered trustworthy or even sane any more. She would have no authority, possibly making her placement ineffectual. Somehow, she managed to overcome her lack of authority and save the lives of many people, on four different worlds."

"And ottles she has saved, too," Chirwl chirped in. "She is teaching me machines."

Mitchell showed a glimmer of humor. "I'm certain I was justified in hiring her. She's saved thousands of lives. She's a credit to the spirit of the Corporation, if not its weaker and more corruptible body. I didn't know she had been moved from Erebus until I got a message from her, furious and spunky. I started checking around, and found things I'd been blind to up until now.

"All those people died just so Verdadero could look good and keep his position as CEO of G.L.C. The Corporation had discovered long ago that the minerals and other resources it needed were not in themselves intrinsically valuable, but they were irreplaceable. The megacorp needed huge quantities to keep the manufacturing facilities occupied. Demand, of viable spaceships, drives, space station modules, always outstripped supply in those early days of space colonization. G.L.C. allowed the establishment of as many mining colonies as they needed, accepted the shipments of minerals from their happy employees, and then began to kill off the colonies as a way of closing up operations when they had ceased to be useful to the company. Trade they had aplenty—elsewhere. Millions of Corporation employee/colonists, with unbreakable contracts, reproducing millions more company dependents, were a deficit to the figure on the bottom line.

"We couldn't—particularly Verdadero couldn't—appear vulnerable. With a large part of our debt coming due, he needed to get money or assets free and clear to offer to the banks. Verdadero was creative as well as greedy. A very secret branch of the Corporation manufactured toxins and viruses plausible in the exotic environment of each planet. Because the viruses were designed to affect humans primarily, the indigent life forms rarely succumbed, which was a great disguise for 'tourist sickness.' I don't know where they were coming from. It is as you guessed. There's one or more people in each colony armed with the means of wiping out the rest of the population, and in most cases terminally ill or sociopathic, who would not care if they commit mass murder. I've warned the GBI to keep Verdadero away from any communications devices, to prevent the loss of any more lives. If all went well, and the colony was profitable, the human 'bomb' was never detonated. If it was, well . . ."

"Like old Hood," Tettenden finished. "He had a neurological disease that must have been very painful to endure. Fortunately, my dear Shona's notes gave us the clue to where the poison was hidden—in the very food we were eating. We went on nutri, and everyone started to perk up. Petrie was out getting a suntan within a week. Couldn't let Shona know because, poor young Chan died only a day or so after Hood. Turns out, she was the only one who knew how to run the beacon system." He coughed, embarrassed. "You'd think a cluster of scientists with an average of three degrees apiece could figure out the phones, but I assure you, we were helpless. It was Novak who finally broke down and found the manuals."

The GBI man broke in. "You will be required to testify at Verdadero's trial as to your findings, Dr. Taylor."

"Under two conditions," Shona said. The man looked surprised, then his face lost all expression, waiting. "One, Gershom and I want to adopt Lani. Right away. If there's any red tape, cut it. And I don't want any difficulties about taking her off-planet with us."

"That might be difficult," the man said. "Colonies have autonomy in these matters."

"Find a way," Gershom said pleasantly. "You can point out that none of us are permanent residents of Mars, to begin with."

"There should be no problem with that," the government man said carefully, after some thought. Lani cheered. It was the loudest noise Shona and Gershom had ever heard her make. They stared at her, and she clapped a hand over her mouth in embarrassment. Shona smiled and winked. "And second?" the agent asked.

"I'll be available by prearrangement only. We have trade routes to cover. If you let me know when to appear, I'll be here, but I can't sit around and wait. We've got to earn a living, you know."

"Doctor, you might be in danger. It will be months before we'll be able to bring this to trial. Verdadero still has agents all over the galaxy, and you'll be a target. You should go into hiding," the government official said. "We'll find a nice place to put you. We have a number of safe-houses all over the galaxy, where you can remain hidden, and with a new identity. We'd prefer you to stay here on Mars."

"Oh, no," Shona declared, folding her arms. "I will not be trapped planetbound again. I've got a better idea. They can't find me if I don't stay in one place. Gershom and Lani and I are leaving on the *Sibyl* as soon as possible. You'll forgive us if we don't file a detailed flight plan. The Corporation has too many connections. Susan will always know how to reach me, but—no offense, Manny—she's the only one I can trust."

"Understandable," the GBI man said, pursing his lips. Mitchell nodded.

"That is, when I get back to Dremel," Susan said, with a grin. "I'm going with them, too. I intend to get at least one documentary out of this."

"We'll be stopping on Erebus before that," Shona said. "I have patients to see there. Besides, Alf needs transportation back."

The old man smoothed his moustache with a knuckle. "I'd enjoy nothing better. Everyone will be very happy to see you."

"And we have a few loads of untainted food for the colonists," Gershom added. "I'm trading for some of that crystal matrix. It sounds intriguing to me, even if the Corporation isn't interested in it."

"Professor Tettenden," Mitchell put in, "I want to assure you that the Corporation will continue to fund Erebus's researches, but can I impress upon you the need for staying within your budget?"

"Do my best to persuade the others," the old man said, with interest. "Don't know how much good it'll do. We're scientists, not accountants."

"Shona," Mitchell continued, turning to her. "I'd like to remind you that you signed a three-year contract, which is not quite half over. You're a good doctor, and I hate to lose you."

She and Gershom exchanged thoughtful glances. "A contract is a contract. But I don't dare stay in anyplace too long," Shona said.

"I was going to say that, under the circumstances, it would be appropriate for me to offer you a quit fee to vacate the remainder of the contract." He smiled. "Once you can resume your normal life, I'd like to talk to you about a new one."

"Sorry." She smiled sweetly. "After that, I'll be permanently attached to the Taylor Traveling Medicine Show and Trading Company. But we'll be happy to take on individual short assignments."

"You may count on that," Mitchell assured her.

The government man was still discontented. "I'd be happier if I could keep you here to testify when we need you. Are you sure you won't stay on Mars?"

"Absolutely not," Shona said, smiling but firm. "I'm no longer a resident of Mars. I'd like that on the record." She stood up and offered her hand to the government man. It was too soon for her new pregnancy to show, but a quick test aboard the *Sibyl* three months ago had verified it. No one knew yet but Gershom. Her system had regenerated enough to allow an embryo to adhere to her uterus wall. Having so dearly won a second chance, Shona was going to take the greatest care. That included not allowing this baby to be imprisoned on one repressive planet all its life. The galaxy was far too interesting a place. She wanted her new child to see it all.